Praise for *The Bodyguard*

"Ms. French stays true to her style with this gritty action-romance. Her characters are deftly drawn and appealing, the story lines provocative. *The Bodyguard* is a fun read, complete with sometimes frightening action, sizzling romance, and very human characters."
—Laurel Johnson, author of *The Grass Dance* and *The Alley of Wishes*

"*The Bodyguard* is a witty, intriguing mystery while being a study in human relationships at the same time. The young and beautiful character, Natasha, discovers many truisms about people and life while maintaining a hefty sense of humor mixed discretely with a robust dose of confidence and independence."
—Sherry Russell, author of *Conquering the Mysteries and Lies of Grief*

"Christy Tillery French is the master of shocking, captivating thrillers that propel the reader into a page-turning race, chasing actions full of twists and turns. Her books capture you on the first page and they don't let you go until the last. A must-read author and strongly recommended."
—Capt. David E. Meadows, author of *The Sixth Fleet* and the *Joint Task Force* series

"Christy Tillery French has a talent for concise and action oriented writing. Her multidimensional characters ring with authenticity and her story line binds readers from page one through to her inspiring conclusion."
—Beverly J. Scott author of *Righteous Revenge* and *Ruth Fever*

"French demonstrates her talent for balancing well written detail with believable dialogue. The contrast between the bad and the good zeroes in on her other gift to engage the reader in highs and lows emotionally, resulting in a satisfying reading experience."
—Lynn Barry, author of *Puddles* and *Bjoyfl*

"Anyone that knows me knows what a huge Christy French fan I have become. As a writer, she is second to none and as a person she is terrific."
—Victoria Taylor Murray, author of The Lambert Series (*Thief of Hearts, Forbidden, Friendly Enemies,* and *Le Fin*)

THE BODYGUARD

Other Books by Christy Tillery French:
Chasing Horses
Wayne's Dead
Chasing Demons

THE BODYGUARD

Christy Tillery French

Mystery and Suspense Press
New York Lincoln Shanghai

The Bodyguard

Mystery and Suspense Press
an imprint of iUniverse, Inc.

For information address:
iUniverse, Inc.
2021 Pine Lake Road, Suite 100
Lincoln, NE 68512
www.iuniverse.com

ISBN: 0-595-30893-7

Printed in the United States of America

For Jon and Meghann, my two miracles from God.

"And think not you can direct the course of love, for love, if it finds you worthy, directs your course."

—Kahlil Gibran

Acknowledgments

I would like to offer my profound thanks to Mike Altman and the folks at Mystery and Suspense Press, who have made this publishing experience so smooth and easy, as well as fun. I could not have asked for a better person to work with than Mike.

I have been blessed with friends in the writing community who generously offer professional advice, provide continual encouragement, and make my life as an author so much more pleasurable. Thanks to Victoria Taylor Murray, Sherry Russell, Laurel Johnson, Evelyn Horan, Kathy Bosworth, Lynn Barry, Beverly Scott, and David Hunter. I encourage everyone to read these extremely talented authors' books.

As always, my thanks with love to my husband, Steve; son, Jon; sister, Cyndi Hodges; mother, Margie Clark; and dad, John Tillery. No one could ask for better support.

Last but not least, thanks and love to my beautiful daughter, Meghann, who served as the physical model for my protagonist, Natasha. Well, okay, Meghann also has the propensity to be a little wacky at times and is one heck of a soccer player, but that's as far as the resemblance goes. Honest.

CHAPTER 1

▼

Her mother always warned her, be careful what you wish for because you just might get it. She should have listened to her mother.

Natasha's day at work began like any other, same-old rote duties she performed day in and day out as office manager for Investigative Services, Inc., never suspecting her career was about to end when her office door opened. A faint squeaking of hinges drew her attention, and she glanced up from her computer to send a distracted smile toward the person framed in the doorway. She watched Scott Thomas, the managing partner, turn to a nerdy looking guy standing behind him and grew curious at the unspoken signal that seemed to flash between the two men.

"Natasha Chamberlain, I'd like you to meet Roger Valentine," Scott said, ushering Roger into the room.

Natasha held out her hand, wondering if Roger had just been hired for something or other. Roger stepped forward, gave her one quick, somewhat limp handshake, then retreated back behind Scott.

Scott gave Natasha a forced smile. "Roger's hired us to, well, guard his body."

"Okay," Natasha said, unsure where this was going.

"And Roger here is asking us to provide him with a female protection specialist, as well."

Natasha frowned. Female bodyguard? They didn't have any female bodyguards. Then she got it. "Oh, no."

Scott turned to Roger. "I'd like to speak with Ms. Chamberlain in private, Roger, if you don't mind. Why don't you go back to my office and wait for me?"

After the door was closed, before Scott could even turn back to her, Natasha said, "You're out of your ever-loving mind, you think I'm going to guard that guy."

"Well, now, let me see. As I recall, aren't you the employee who keeps bugging me to let you be more active in this firm?"

"Well, yeah, Scotty, but that's for the investigative part. I don't have any desire to place my body in front of someone else's in order to, you know, stop a bullet or something."

Scott sat down in the chair in front of her desk and gave her a bland stare.

"Come on, Scotty. You know I want to be an investigator. I've taken courses in criminal justice, plus all the self-defense classes you've recommended, gotten a gun permit and learned how to use one properly. I don't know why you and Striker can't just once give me the chance to show my skills." Striker was the founding partner, the one who made Natasha's knees weak and her mouth drool.

"You're getting your chance. This is it; take it, show us what you can do."

"As a bodyguard, and I don't want to be a bodyguard."

"Start off as bodyguard, we'll move you up to investigator if you do this well."

"If I don't get killed is what you mean."

"Whatever."

Natasha gave him an exasperated look.

"Striker's the one who wants you in on this," Scott said, dangling the proverbial carrot.

Natasha brightened at this bit of news. "Striker does? Um, where is he, by the way? I haven't seen him in a few days."

Scott shrugged. "Down in Florida doing whatever Striker does down there."

Natasha wondered, as she always did, why Striker was such a mystery man. Other than the fact that he was wealthier than all get-out, no one in the office knew much about his private life, including Scott. There was constant discussion about Striker and was he married or had he been married, and did he have any kids. And the favorite subject: what did he do in his other life?

As office manager, Natasha was privy to the personnel files, but there wasn't one for Striker. She was curious about his first name, which seemed to be another well-kept secret, but as far as she could detect, there was no paperwork trail divulging that information. Not even the payroll roster since the income he withdrew from the firm was direct-deposited into a charitable trust. And if Scott knew what it was, he wasn't telling.

Natasha had had a crush on Striker since she joined the firm three years before. His Cherokee lineage obvious by raven-black hair, coal-dark eyes, and pale-bronze skin tone, his tall, muscular frame seemed to ooze testosterone from every pore. Known for his expertise with firearms and the martial arts, there was gossip that Striker had been a mercenary at one point; others swore he was with the CIA. Every summer, he disappeared for a month, and it was rumored he would travel into the Smoky Mountains, strip naked, and live among the wild animals, fasting and waiting for a vision to appear. He scared the crap out of Natasha every time he looked at her.

Natasha tried to act like she wasn't really interested. "So, is Striker going to be overseeing this or what?"

Scott gave her a knowing grin. "Yep. He's coming back this afternoon, said he'll handle this baby."

"Okay, I'll do it."

"I knew you would." Scott stood and headed for the door.

"Wait a minute."

Scott paused with his hand on the doorknob and turned back to her.

"Why does this Roger want a woman bodyguard anyway?"

"He wants you to pose as his girlfriend."

Natasha's mouth dropped open and her eyes widened, but Scott was gone by the time she could formulate any words of protest.

Natasha sat at her desk steaming, for a brief moment flirted with scheming, then began worrying. Wanted her to pose as his girlfriend. What exactly would that entail? Surely Striker and Scotty wouldn't expect her to, eeeoooouuu, go to bed with the guy. She shook her head. No way. That definitely would not be considered part of her job duties.

She stood and opened her door, intending to confront Scott about this, but he was busy talking to Roger. When Scott glanced her way, an amused look on his face, she resisted the urge to flip him the bird.

Natasha sat back down at her desk, chewing on her bottom lip, thinking about the offer. She was ready and waiting the next visit Scott paid her.

"Okay, here's the deal. I don't sleep with the guy. I'll be his girlfriend but only in the surrogate sense. You got that?"

Scott took the time to settle into a chair.

"Well?"

"Okay, here's the deal. You're his girlfriend in the surrogate sense, that's fine. I wouldn't expect you to do anything else in that department." He gave her a look. "That is, unless you want to."

Natasha rolled her eyes.

"But you have to play the part of the girlfriend." Scott raised his hands at her look. "Don't worry. Pit and Bigun are going to be there, too."

Natasha considered this while gazing at Scott, who was looking at everything but her. She could sense something was going on. "How long?"

Scott adjusted the crease in his trousers. "As long as it takes."

"You mean as long as he needs bodyguards?"

"As long as your services are required."

Something wasn't quite right about that, but Natasha decided to drop it for now. She would worry about that later. "Who is this guy anyway?"

Scott was relieved she didn't push him on the time span; they needed her tonight. "Don't you recognize the name?" He waited for the appreciation to come into her eyes and nodded when it did.

"He's not the Roger Valentine?"

"The one and only."

"Omigosh. The billionaire computer guy, the one who designs software for those game thingies."

"Among other things."

"But why does he need a girlfriend? As rich as that guy is, women are probably crawling all over him."

Scott gave her a look.

"What?"

"Did you happen to get a gander at this guy?"

Natasha shook her head. "I only glanced at him. Looked kind of nerdy to me, to tell you the truth."

"Let's just say he's not very good in the social skills department."

"Oh, well, who is?"

"You'll see." Scott rose and strode toward the door, then turned back. "Clear up what you need to here, then head on over to Roger's." He picked up one of Natasha's business cards, wrote on the back of one, and handed it to her. "Here's the address."

"Wait," Natasha said, delaying his exit.

Scott stuck his head back in her office.

"Why does he need a bodyguard anyway?"

Scott gave her his most engaging smile. "He says someone wants to kill him."

"He what!"

Scott managed to get the door closed before Natasha's planner collided with it.

CHAPTER 2

▼

Natasha slowly drove up the meandering drive, gazing with astonishment at the expansive grounds and dwelling before her. Shoot, this was it, this was the life. This might not be so bad after all. A mansion, albeit rather small, but a real one nonetheless. She'd never stepped inside a mansion before, not even the Biltmore House.

Natasha parked her dark-blue Jeep Wrangler in front of the house, grabbed her purse, and climbed out. She rang the bell, then turned around to check out a three-tiered fountain nestled in the curve of the circular drive, admiring the miniature rainbows created from the spraying mist. After a lengthy wait, an older, Hispanic woman opened the door and scowled at her.

Natasha's smile withered at the look the woman was giving her. "Uh, I'm the girlfriend, I guess."

The woman opened the door wider and with a sweep of her hand indicated for Natasha to come on in.

Natasha stepped into an expansive foyer and glanced around at the cool, pale marble floor and walls, wondering which mansion on which television show this décor resembled. Her eyes followed a winding stairway to the level above and *The Beverly Hillbillies* popped into her mind. Or was it one of those prime-time soap operas where everyone was rich and evil abounded? Eyeing the crystal chandelier over her head, which looked like it must weigh a ton, she stepped out of its path of descent. Just in case. Natasha turned to ask the woman where Roger was, but she had disappeared.

"Hello," Natasha called. When no one responded, she went in search of a body.

Roger was in what looked to be his office, sitting behind a desk, working at a computer. The other two bodyguards were seated on opposite ends of a black, leather couch with uncomfortable expressions on their faces.

"Hey, guys," Natasha said to her colleagues. Both were of Samoan descent and the biggest men Natasha had ever met, although a little lacking in the cognitive department, but she didn't hold that against them. In their past lives, they had been bouncers for one of the rowdiest nightspots in Memphis but had moved to Knoxville at Striker's behest to work for him in his bodyguard service, where they were much in demand. Their size intimidated all who crossed their paths, along with the fierce looks they wore on their faces and their shaved heads, which most people mistook for the supremacist thing.

Pit and Bigun rose and smiled at Natasha. After giving each one a hug and exchanging pleasantries, she glanced toward Roger, who was staring at her.

She offered him a perfunctory smile. "Hello, Roger."

Roger nodded, then returned his attention to his computer.

"Hey, dudette, where are your things?" Bigun asked.

She turned to him. "What things?"

"We're supposed to live here, man," Pit said. "Stay here 24–7."

Natasha wondered why Scott hadn't let her in on that little secret while replaying what he had said to her. Growing suspicious, she darted a glance at Roger.

"Where am I supposed to stay?"

Roger looked confused. "Anywhere. I don't care." He focused on his computer once more.

Natasha turned back to the two bodyguards. "Have you guys settled in yet?"

Both shook their heads.

"Why don't you go stow your stuff away while I get some information from Roger, then I'll find a place for me?"

After Pit and Bigun left, Natasha pulled out a chair across from Roger's desk, sat down in it, and waited for him to notice her again. When he did, he seemed to startle, as if he had forgotten all about someone else being in the room.

"I'm trying to work here," he said, giving her an irritated look.

"So am I."

He sighed with resignation. "Okay, what do you need?"

"Just some general information, then I won't bug you anymore."

Roger sat back.

"As to why specifically you need bodyguards."

"What do you think? To keep someone from killing me, that's why."

"Who's trying to kill you?"

"How the heck do I know? That's what your investigative department is supposed to be trying to find out."

Doh! She should have insisted Scotty let her do that part. "Well, have any threats been made against you? Anyone, you know, shot at you or something to cause you to think your life's in danger?"

"Okay, here it is in a nutshell. I got this call from this guy who said he had been hired to kill me, but if I'd give him a million dollars, he'd just go away, and he's given me a week to get the money together."

"And you didn't think maybe this guy was trying to get money out of you any way he could, as in extortion?"

"No. He knew too much about me, about my habits. He definitely has plans to kill me."

"Did you call the police?"

"What do you think? They said they couldn't do anything since no attempt had actually been made."

"Go figure."

Roger nodded. "Yeah, right. So, I know Striker from college and—"

"You knew Striker in college? Omigosh! Tell me what he was like." Natasha hesitated at Roger's expression. "Sorry. Um, you were saying?"

"I talked to Striker last night, he said to come to the office today, he'd handle it."

Natasha figured there must be a real threat if Striker was getting involved. "Why did you want a female bodyguard to pose as your girlfriend?"

Roger's face grew red. "Oh, well, there's this banquet thing tonight, and I kind of needed a date, so, you know."

Natasha's eyes narrowed. Now she knew what Scott had tried to pull. "Oh, so I'm just a one-night stand, per se, huh? Just someone to use and abuse, then step over? Like maybe an escort or hooker?"

Roger's jaw dropped. "You're a hooker?"

Natasha rolled her eyes, then leaned toward him. "I'll be your girlfriend, buster, in the surrogate sense, of course. But if you want me to be your girlfriend tonight, you have to accept me as your girlfriend the rest of this gig, or I'm not going to go anywhere with you." She straightened up and crossed her arms, sending him an angry look.

"Uh, sure, whatever. You want to stay, that's fine."

Natasha frowned. "Not good enough."

"What? What do you want?"

"I want you to write down on a piece of paper that we have an agreement that I'm to stay on as your bodyguard slash girlfriend until this case is solved. This is my chance to move into the investigative field, and I'm not going to get schnookered into playing your sweetie for one night, then get kicked back to the office. You got that?"

Roger gave her an uneasy look.

Natasha glared. "In a nutshell, you don't write it down, I walk out that door, and good luck finding someone for tonight this late in the day."

Roger pulled over a piece of computer paper and wrote as she dictated. When he had properly signed and dated it, Natasha grabbed it up.

"Thank you." She folded it, intending to place it in her purse for future reference.

"Sure thing," Roger said, flustered.

Natasha leaned toward him once more. "One more thing."

Roger scooted back, intimidated. "Whatever you want."

"Where exactly are we going tonight and what kind of dress is required?"

"Oh. It's a banquet given in my honor. Black-tie affair."

"Black-tie affair? Shoot, Roger, I don't have any fancy clothes for crap like that. I'm a middle-income woman living a middle-class life. What the heck do you expect me to wear to a thing like that?"

Roger looked like he didn't give a fig.

Natasha considered her dilemma. Well, there was the gown she wore as a bridesmaid at her cousin's wedding, the one that she thought looked kind of slutty for a wedding but still was pretty much dressy: long, silky, sapphire-colored material, spaghetti straps crisscrossing all the way down the low back, slit up the side. The one that caused that problem with her boyfriend...

She headed for the door. "I've got to go home and get a dress for tonight. I'll be back in an hour."

In the foyer, Natasha yelled for Bigun and Pit, who stepped out of the kitchen with sandwiches in hand. She told them to watch their guy, she'd be back, and left.

Natasha drove home, which was a cottage her father had built for her on acreage adjoining her parents' mini-farm. Although couched as a graduation present, she knew it was her dad's way of keeping her close. Even so, she loved her little domicile.

Natasha decided to stop at her parents' place first to tell them she wouldn't be home for awhile and the reason why. When she pulled into the drive, she noticed her dad sitting in the garage, smoking a cigarette. Uh-oh. When her dad smoked, there was trouble in paradise.

Natasha braked to a stop and watched him a moment before climbing out.

Her father gave her a weak smile when she stepped into the cool dimness of the garage.

Natasha pulled over a lawn chair to sit beside him. "Okay, what's wrong?"

Her father shrugged. "You tell me. I got home, went inside, gave your mom a hello kiss, asked what was for dinner, and that was all she wrote."

"Well, it's not her birthday or your anniversary or anything like that. You sure you didn't do or say anything else?"

Her dad shook his head, staring out at the driveway.

Natasha patted his shoulder. "I'll go see what's wrong."

Natasha stood in the kitchen doorway, watching her mom sweep up a broken dish. "Mom, what happened?" She drew back from her mother's bright-red face and glaring eyes.

"For twenty-five years, every night, he comes home, gives me a peck on the lips, asks what's for dinner. Twenty-five years, Natasha." She stood and threw the detritus in the garbage can. "That's all I mean to him, someone to fix his damn dinner every night."

Natasha's mouth dropped open; her mom never swore. "Come on, Mom, you know that's not what Dad thinks."

Her mother turned on her. "I am sick and tired of being mommy and taking care of everybody. When's it going to be my turn? When does someone take care of me?" Before Natasha could even phrase an answer, she stormed out of the room.

Natasha flinched when she heard her parents' bedroom door slam shut. Oh, boy.

In the garage, she knelt by her dad. "I think she's just, you know, tired, Dad. She said something about always taking care of everyone else. Maybe you should offer to take her out to dinner or something. Or make dinner. Yeah, that'd be good. I'd stay and do that but I have to go to this thing tonight. Oh, by the way, I'm going to be gone for a few days. Tell Mom I'll call her tomorrow and let her know what's going on." She kissed him on the cheek and left before he could talk her into staying and doing something as horribly domestic as cooking.

CHAPTER 3

▼

Natasha donned her slinky evening dress, then added dangling sapphire earrings to her ears and a faux sapphire-and-diamond choker to her neck. She piled her long, blond hair on top of her head in as fancy a do as she could manage on such short notice, thankful her mother had been a hairdresser before she married her dad and kept up on all the new styles. She made sure her long lashes were dark and separated, her lips pouty and red, put on the spiked heels which added another two inches to her already tall, 5'8" frame, and went in search of her pretend boyfriend.

Natasha gaped when she saw him. Roger was dressed in a black tuxedo with white socks and tennis shoes. His bow-tie was askew and his long, shaggy hair stuck out at odd angles. She noticed for the first time that his black-rimmed glasses were held together in the middle with black electric tape. She stared at his feet.

"Roger, are you actually wearing sneakers to this thing?"

"I can't wear any other kind of shoe," Roger said, acting not in the least concerned, "they hurt my feet."

"Who did your hair?"

"My hair? Nobody. I just combed it."

Natasha sighed.

Bigun and Pit joined them, dressed in their tuxes, looking like two huge penguins. Each gave Natasha whistles of approval and she smiled and whistled back. Then they noticed Roger and grinned.

Bigun gave Roger the thumbs-up. "Nice, dude."

Roger looked like he didn't know how to take that.

Natasha sent Bigun the evil eye.

"The dude looks cool!" he said.

She rolled her eyes.

Natasha couldn't believe it. Here this guy was a billionaire, maybe even a zillionaire, and he drove a Dodge Caravan, computer equipment everywhere.

"Roger, guy, you need a sports car," Natasha said, climbing in the front, having to throw a mouse and cable off the seat before she could sit down.

"What would I do with a sports car?" Roger said, starting the van and stomping on the accelerator.

Pit and Bigun, trying to clear seats for themselves, went crashing toward the back of the vehicle. Roger didn't even notice.

Natasha did the eye-rolling thing again.

Striker was waiting on them at the valet drop-off with five other men. He opened the door, helped Natasha out, and stepped back. Up until this point, the only times Striker had come in contact with Natasha had been at the office, where she wore glasses and dressed in ultraconservative business suits. He noticed, for the first time, how dark her green eyes were, how slender her body was, how well put together everything seemed to be.

"Wow!"

"Wow back," Natasha said, appreciating the dark tuxedo on his powerful frame, liking the small, silver, hoop-earring in his ear, which gave him a rakish look.

Roger joined them, and this was the first time Natasha witnessed any friendly emotion from him. He and Striker shook hands, grinning at one another like brothers, then Striker motioned for everyone to step inside with him.

"Okay, here's what's doing," Striker said. "We're going to be distributed throughout the room with all entrances and exits guarded. You know what to look for. You see anything suspicious, alert me with your cell using the privacy mode, I'll check to see who it is, send someone your way."

Striker nodded at them and everyone scattered.

Striker placed his hand around Natasha's forearm. "I need to talk to you for a minute."

Natasha's skin tingled where his fingers had been. She glanced down, expecting to see redness there, but nothing. She looked up at Striker, who again was staring at her. Even with the high heels, he towered over her. She admired his size and the powerful presence he seemed to carry, thought he had such panache in that tuxedo. All of a sudden, she had this wild urge to climb him like a tree.

Striker studied the woman before him, liking the way her hairstyle accentuated her almond-shaped eyes and high cheekbones, noticing for the first time the barely discernible bump in her nose and how her lips turned up prettily. Recalling a vision his grandmother had told him about involving a woman with blond hair and dark-green eyes, his brow furrowed.

"What's wrong?" Natasha looked down at her gown to make sure everything was in place and nothing showing.

Striker blinked back to reality. "Damn, woman, you clean up good."

She resisted the urge to cross her legs and coo. "So do you."

"Listen, Natasha, don't even think of doing anything heroic," Striker said, getting down to business. "Just alert me if you see something that doesn't look right. Stay by Roger's side, play the girlfriend part, but be wary. That's all I need you to do."

"You mean I can't shoot nobody?" she teased.

Striker flashed her a grin, looked up, and motioned Roger over. "Okay, Rog, I'm going to go make sure everyone's where they need to be. Stay with Natasha. She knows what she's doing, she'll take care of things."

Roger and Natasha walked to the dais and found their seats. During dinner, Roger appeared to be lost in his own world and seemed content to ignore those around him. Natasha wasn't sure how to act, so smiled at everyone she made eye contact with while vigilantly watching the people milling about. She tried to make small talk with Roger, leaning toward him as if to appear intimate, but was having a hard time of it.

During the awards ceremony, the host gave a short speech about Roger's accomplishments. Natasha was shocked. She had written him off as a computer nerd, but this guy was one heck of a genius, it seemed, regarding the software end of the industry.

Looking somewhat embarrassed, Roger rose and approached the podium, stumbling in the process.

Natasha felt sorry for him and tried not to wince.

As Roger was accepting the award, Natasha's eyes swept the people below them, all sitting at tables sharing drinks and dessert. A silvery glint caught her attention, so she checked again. She saw nothing, moved on, then back. Dang, where was that? Her eyes once more caught the glint: something long and cylindrical, pointing toward the podium. What the heck? Could that be a gun? Omigosh, a gun!

"Gun!" Natasha scrambled up from her seat, intending to run away but tripping herself instead. She fell into Roger, who was standing at the podium turned toward her, and sent him reeling backwards. Both went down, her on top.

Startled at another body landing on his, assuming he had been shot, Roger began screaming. He clutched Natasha and thrashed around on the floor like a man in the throes of a seizure.

"Let me go," Natasha kept saying, fighting with him, trying to get away from him.

Roger hung on for dear life, that shrill scream emitting from his mouth.

"Get off me!" Natasha raised up on arms, only to be pulled back down onto his chest.

She gasped when she realized Roger's hands were now cupping her bottom. "You pervert," she screamed, thrashing her arms and kicking her legs, "you sick, perverted scumbag, let go of me," feeling herself suddenly freed when she was yanked into the air by Striker.

Natasha landed on her feet and went after Roger. Striker put an arm around her waist and pulled her back against his side.

She began struggling, trying to get out of his grasp, saying, "Let me at him, let me at him!"

"Calm down." Striker gritted his teeth, dodging her arms and legs. "Pit! Help Roger up." He set Natasha on her feet again but this time kept a firm grip on both her arms to keep her away from Roger.

After Roger was standing, Natasha managed to squirm out of Striker's grasp and pounded at Roger's chest with her fists. "Pervert!"

Striker pulled Natasha away and handed her off to Pit, then stepped between her and Roger.

"You think you can take me? Come on, bitch, you think you can take me?" Roger was saying, putting his fists in front of his face.

Natasha was furious. "Let me at him! Let me go! I'm gonna kill that son of a bitch, putting his hands on me like that!"

"Calm down!" Striker roared, startling Natasha into silence for a moment.

But only a moment.

She pointed at Roger. "He had his hands on my butt. Cupping my butt with his scummy hands, squeezing my butt, and I'm gonna kill you, you son of a bitch."

Striker gave her a frustrated look. "I said calm down, Natasha. Just hush for a minute."

"I'll show you calm, you let me get my hands on him!" Natasha almost managed to get away from Pit before he grabbed her back at the last moment.

Striker had placed one hand on Roger's chest to keep him back and was relieved his friend wasn't giving him much resistance. Natasha, on the other hand, was proving to be the problem-child. Glaring at her, he raised his voice to a forceful tone. "Shut your mouth, Natasha."

"I will not shut my mouth!" Natasha struggled with Pit, giving Striker an insolent look.

"I mean it, shut up!"

"Hell, no, I won't shut up!"

Striker scowled at her; he wasn't used to such insolence, especially from a subordinate. Forgetting Roger now, he turned to face her. "Natasha, shut your mouth," he said, emphasizing these words. "I'm not going to say it again."

No man told her what to do! Natasha drew herself up and sent Striker a challenging look. Affecting an attitude, she forgot all about him being her employer and she the employee. "You want me to shut up, why don't you just try and make me," she said, in a cocky voice.

Striker blinked in surprise, not sure what to do here. If she were a guy, he could punch her in the mouth, that'd shut her up all right. After a long moment of indecision, he stormed toward her, stood looming over her.

Intimidated by the dangerous glint in Striker's eyes, Natasha stepped back and bumped into Pit.

Striker leaned close and put his face inches from hers. "You really want that? You want me to make you shut up?"

Natasha studied him, trying to gauge if he were serious or not. Surely he wouldn't. But the look he was sending her, she wasn't so sure. She opened her mouth, more in surprise than to say anything.

"One more word, that's all I need," Striker said, in a threatening tone.

Natasha clamped her mouth shut. She glanced at Pit, who gave her a solemn nod. Shit!

Striker turned to Roger and spoke in a tense voice. "Did you mean to put your hands on her butt?"

Roger looked mortified. "I didn't even know I was doing that."

Striker gave Natasha an intense stare. "Think about it. Don't make an accusation unless you're absolutely sure he was doing what you're saying he was."

Natasha was silent, seeming to study Roger while replaying what had actually happened. Shifting from one foot to the other, she gave Striker an embarrassed glance. "I could have been wrong. I probably overreacted."

She turned to Roger, whose face was bright red. "I'm sorry, Roger. You probably didn't mean to put your hands there, you probably weren't even aware you were putting your hands there. I don't know what got into me. It's just this thing I have about being touched like that, something from the past."

Realizing everyone was staring at her, Natasha became self-conscious. She looked at Striker, tears glistening in her eyes. "He didn't mean to. I'm afraid I overreacted."

"Pit, you and Bigun take Roger home. I'll see you there after I deal with a few things here." Striker turned and pointed at Natasha. "Including you, so don't go anywhere."

Yikes! Natasha noticed how quiet it was, turned and looked around the room. Tables were overturned, chairs on their sides. There was food everywhere. She mentally cursed herself. Of course, it must have been pandemonium when she yelled that stupid word, "gun." Everyone must have been in a panic to exit the building.

Pit walked over to her and said, "Take it like a man."

"What does that mean?"

He shook his head in a sad way.

Bigun patted her on the shoulder as he walked past. "Oh, dudette, you're really in for it."

"What do you mean by that? You're not saying he's going to do anything, are you?"

The two bodyguards sandwiched Roger between them and escorted him out. She couldn't see the smiles they wore on their faces since their backs were to her.

Striker returned with the waiter and manager in tow. The manager looked angry. Striker looked vexed. The waiter looked amused.

The waiter held up an extended lighter and pointed it at Natasha as if it were a gun.

"Is this what you saw?" Striker said.

Natasha studied the lighter. Shoot! "I'm not sure, but it could be," she mumbled.

After the grinning waiter left, the manager and Striker entered into an intense discussion about the damage done to the banquet room and who was going to pay the bill.

Natasha tried to sidle away, toward the door. Striker caught sight of her in his peripheral vision, snapped his fingers to get her attention, and pointed, all without looking at her. She got the message and stopped.

After they came to some sort of understanding, Striker walked toward Natasha and motioned for her to follow him. She trailed along to his vehicle, a black, Lexus SUV. Striker held the door for her, waited for her to climb inside, then walked around and got in on the driver's side.

"I don't appreciate you threatening me the way you did," Natasha said, after he was seated.

Striker looked at her.

"When you said you'd, you know, make me shut up. I don't appreciate that at all."

Striker keyed the ignition and pulled out of the parking lot. "You act like a child, you're going to be treated as one, Natasha."

She was quiet a moment, then gave him an anxious look. "You didn't mean that, right? You were just saying that to get me to shut up, right?"

Striker shrugged. "Don't know. You never pushed it, so I didn't have to follow through with anything."

Natasha frowned.

"Of course I didn't mean it. I was trying to get your attention so you'd quit acting so out of control."

"Well, it was all just a gross misunderstanding anyway."

Striker glanced at her, a look of amazement on his face. "Gross misunderstanding? Let's see, first you think a lighter's a gun and cause a riot in there, it's a wonder people didn't trample each other to death trying to get out of that room, then you accuse Roger of trying to cop a feel when he wasn't, he was just panicked. Gross misunderstanding? My dear Natasha, that goes way beyond gross misunderstanding."

"I swear, Striker, it looked like a gun. The barrel was silver and round and fat, fatter than that lighter the waiter was holding."

"You're sure it was a gun? Think, Natasha. This is important."

She weighed it out in her mind, chewing on her bottom lip, then sighed. "I can only say I thought it was a gun. It didn't look like a lighter, Striker, I swear. But I can't tell you it wasn't a lighter."

Striker shook his head in frustration.

Natasha began to panic. "I'll pay for the damages. You can take it out of my paycheck each week until it's all paid back. I don't mind."

"That's not the point."

"And I apologized to Roger. I'm sure he didn't mean to do that. I'll make it up to him for accusing him of that, honest, I swear."

"That issue's moot anyway since you're off the case."

"Off the case!" Natasha shrieked, causing Striker to startle and the SUV to swerve. "I make one fricking mistake—oh, wait, excuse me, maybe two; one for sure, maybe another one, although I won't attest to that ever—and I'm off the case. Not even on the dang case for eight hours yet and you're booting me off. Well, listen up, bucko, 'cause for your information, I am not off the case."

Striker pulled into a parking lot and cut the engine, then turned to her. "If I say you're off, you're off."

She shook her head. "Roger and I came to an agreement that as long as the investigation is going forward, I'm to remain his bodyguard a/k/a girlfriend. You want to fire me, go ahead, I'll just work for Roger."

They glared at one another.

"I'm not going back to that office job, Striker. You dangled the bait and I took it, not knowing you and Scotty had cooked up this little scheme to get me to play girlfriend for one night, trying to entice me with what I want, to be an investigator for the firm, then thinking you can just boot me back down to the office manager position when you're through using me. Well, I won't have it."

"What the hell are you talking about?"

Natasha shook a finger at him. "I know about your little scheme. So I came to an agreement with Roger on my own, thank you very much, that I'm to be part of this bodyguard thingy as long as you-all are investigating who's trying to kill the guy."

"Yeah?"

"Yeah. And I have to say this, Striker, I thought you had more class than to try to set me up the way you and Scotty thought you were. I never would have thought you'd stoop that low, just to get some bimbo to play girlfriend." Wait a minute. Did she just call herself bimbo? *Shut!* she mentally yelled at herself.

"Bimbo," Striker said, a grin playing around his mouth.

"Yeah, I was a bimbo for about five minutes, till I figured out what y'all were doing, you jerks."

Striker sat back and studied her. "Natasha, I have no idea what the hell you're talking about with setting you up. The deal was Roger needed an escort for this evening. I suggested we put you in position to act as his bodyguard, and that's all that was ever discussed between Scott and Roger and me."

Natasha stared out the window. "Yeah, right."

Striker started the car. "You got a real problem with that temper of yours."

"Yeah? Well, if you ask me, I'm not the only one in this car that has a temper."

"I didn't ask you."

She ignored that.

They rode in silence for a moment, then Natasha had to say it. "You are going to Roger's? I mean it, Striker, don't take me anywhere else."

Striker threw her a dark look. "Yes, dear, I'm going to Roger's, so we can get this mess straightened out," sounding like an irate husband.

"Fine."

"Fine."

She reached down and turned on the radio. He turned it off.

She glared. He ignored her. She mentally stuck her tongue out at him.

Striker stopped the SUV in Roger's circular drive, then reached out and put his hand on Natasha's arm to delay her from exiting the vehicle. "One question."

She watched him.

"What you said to Roger back there, about not liking being touched like that because of something that happened, what's that about?"

An uncomfortable expression crossed her face and tears sprang to her eyes.

"Hey, I'm sorry. I didn't mean to say anything that might upset you." Striker reached out with one powerful hand and used his thumb to gently wipe the tears.

Natasha pulled away. "I know."

Roger, Pit, and Bigun were once more ensconced in Roger's office, Roger at his computer, the two bodyguards sitting on the couch playing hand-held electronic games.

Natasha stopped outside the door to wipe her eyes, her back to Striker. She moved away when she felt his presence and entered the room.

The three men, seeing her tear-streaked face, gave her commiserating looks.

"Nothing happened," Natasha said, misreading their expressions. She glared at Pit and Bigun. "And I don't appreciate you two making me think something was going to happen." She pointed at Striker. "And by the way, just so you know, if he had tried anything, he'd be missing a major body part at this point in time."

Striker grinned at her cockiness. "Natasha, you are one bad woman."

Natasha plopped down on the couch between the other two bodyguards and tried to act bored.

Bigun and Pit went back to their games with grins on their faces; they liked Natasha's feistiness.

Striker sat down in a chair across from Roger's desk and addressed his friend. "Okay, what's the deal between you and Natasha?"

Roger had been watching all this, looking a little bewildered. When Striker spoke, he glanced at Natasha, who was sending him a challenging stare.

"I want her to stay on. Play my girlfriend, bodyguard, whatever, but be part of this."

Striker turned to Natasha, who stuck her tongue out at him. "Keep it up," he said.

"Besides," Roger went on, "whether that was a gun or not, she tried to save my life, Striker. She put her body in front of mine, she risked her life for me."

Pit and Bigun looked at Natasha with new respect. She didn't bother telling them she had only tripped and fell into Roger trying to get out of harm's way.

"I appreciate that. No one's ever done that for me. And she doesn't even know me." Roger seemed a little amazed at that fact.

Natasha gave Roger a sweet smile.

Striker nodded, then stood. "Okay, she stays. I guess I'll see you-all tomorrow."

At the door, he turned back. "Natasha, I need to talk to you for a minute," he said, in a professional tone.

Natasha rose, gave Roger another smile, then followed Striker to the front door.

He studied her for a moment, making her feel as if under a predator's gaze. She reached up, felt her hair had come partially undone, knew she must look a mess. She felt miserable, looking back at her boss.

"He has a point," Striker said. "You did risk your life for him, if that was actually a gun you saw." He raised his eyebrows.

"What was I supposed to do, Striker, wait until they fired the darn thing, killed Roger, then yell gun?"

Striker ignored that. "You're part of this, I guess, until it's finished. Just do me one favor, try to control that temper of yours. You can get in a lot of trouble that way. And next time, alert someone, don't go yelling gun and running. You saw what can happen when you do things like that."

Natasha nodded, brushing hair away from her face, then noticed Striker was watching her again. Oops!

"Striker?"

"Yeah?"

"I'm sorry for the way I reacted when you told me to shut up. I never should have challenged you like that. You were right. It was childish."

He remained silent.

"It's just, I have this thing about being told what to do."

"I figured that out on my own."

Natasha felt her face redden at his intense scrutiny and looked away.

Striker leaned toward her, cupped her chin with his hand, and brought her eyes to his. "Whoever hurt you, whatever they did, I hope you made them pay for it," he said, then left.

CHAPTER 4

▼

Scott wasn't expecting to find Striker sprawled in the chair across from his desk the next morning. Grinning at his partner, he raised the newspaper he held in his hand. "Now this is what I call doing a good job." He handed the paper to Striker, who glanced at it, then threw it on his desk.

Striker watched Scott settle into his chair. "Why the hell didn't you warn me about her?"

"Warn you about her? What are you talking about?"

"Let's see, how about irreverent, impulsive, ready to go off at half-cock."

Scott grinned. "Yeah, that's our Nattie. She's a real pistol."

Striker scowled.

"You'd know that if you stayed in the office more, attended some of the firm's functions."

"Somebody's got to oversee the field work. You want to do that, go ahead, I'll stay in-house."

Scott definitely did not want to do that, so chose not to respond.

Striker ran his hand over his face.

"Hey, you're the one that recommended her for this job, you know," Scott said.

"No, actually Pit and Bigun recommended her. I just wish somebody had warned me what the hell we were getting ourselves into letting Natasha on the loose like that."

Scott laughed.

"Who is this woman anyway? Here in the office, any dealings I've ever had with her, she's always treated me with respect, acted like a professional, but last night…" Striker shook his head. "That was not the same woman I've interacted with here in the office."

"Well, that's because you don't know the real Nattie."

"And I take it you do?"

"Sure. Nattie's a good friend of mine."

Striker raised his eyebrows. "I thought our office policy was no consorting among the employees."

"Who said I was sleeping with her?"

"As I recall, the philosophy you're so fond of expressing is that women are good for one thing and one thing only. What was it you told me? Oh, yeah. There is no way a man and a woman can actually be friends, it's just not normal, not the way God meant things to be."

Scott shrugged. "Since I started hanging out with Nattie, I've changed my mind on that."

"Hanging out, huh?"

"Yeah. She plays sweeper for our soccer team; she's one of the best players we've got. Which reminds me, why don't you ever come watch us play, show some support for our firm's team?"

"You're the coach, you show support enough for the both of us."

"Anyway, I got to know her that way; we'd hang out after the games or practice. She's a great gal."

"And you're just friends?"

"Sure."

"She's awful good-looking and I keep going back to all that philosophizing you used to do about women and—"

Scott held up his hands to stop him. "Okay, okay. I've changed my mind on that score. My philosophy now is there are three types of women: those you ball, those you like hanging out with you consider your friends, and those you stay away from." He got a worried look. "But don't tell Nattie I said that. She gets mad at me when I talk like that."

"Yeah?"

"Calls me a sexist Suidae on the verge of being a peripheral misogynist when I talk like that."

Striker grinned. "Suidae?"

"Pig."

Striker laughed.

"You ever want to party, Nattie's the one you want to party with," Scott said.

"I don't party."

"She's a great dancer."

"Dancing's for sissies." Striker's eyes narrowed; he knew his friend too well. "So, there's nothing there?"

Scott sighed. "Okay, maybe I tried a couple of times, maybe I got shot down, all right? You happy?"

"Shot down, huh?"

"Yeah, shot down. She told me last time I brought up the subject that if I didn't stop, she was going to buy me one of those inflatable dolls, seeing I was so obviously hard up."

Striker grinned.

Scott glanced over Striker's broad shoulder toward Natasha's office. "Where is she anyway? I want to show her this paper."

"She's at Roger's."

That got Scott's attention.

"Your plan backfired. And by the way, thanks for putting me in the middle of that one. You mind telling me what exactly you promised instead of offering her what we had agreed on?"

"Listen, I know her, okay? I knew she wouldn't agree to just a one-night thing here, she'd be offended we even asked her to do that, probably think we were looking at her as a professional escort or something. So I might not have been as clear about the details of what we actually wanted her to do, I might have made it sound like there was more to it than there was."

Striker stood. "Well, there is now."

"What do you mean?"

"She's talked Roger into letting her stay on through the investigation. In fact, he's insisting on it."

"Damn! What the hell are we going to do now, Striker? She keeps this office running smoothly, she knows where everything is, what's going on, who's where. What the hell are we going to do?"

Striker walked toward the door. "Hey, you made the offer that backfired, you deal with it."

CHAPTER 5

▼

Pit and Bigun were searching through cabinets when Natasha entered the kitchen. "Morning, guys."

Both men grunted her way.

"What's for breakfast?"

Bigun pointed to a fancy machine sitting on the counter. "Hey, dudette, you know how to make coffee?"

"I can try." Natasha wandered over to take a look at the strange-looking coffee maker, then began searching for coffee grounds. "Where's Roger?"

Pit had his head stuck in the refrigerator. "In his office working."

Natasha found coffee beans and a grinder; measured them out and turned it on. Glancing around, she noticed one of those pancake makers she'd seen advertised on TV she thought was so neat. "Pancakes."

Pit and Bigun looked at her.

"If you can find the mix, I'll make us some pancakes."

They didn't waste any time searching.

After the coffee was brewed and the pancakes made, the three bodyguards sat down around the kitchen table.

Natasha picked up her fork, then hesitated. "Maybe we ought to see if Roger wants anything," she said, feeling guilty about eating the guy's food and not sharing it with him.

Her two cohorts made mangled noises around the food in their mouths.

Roger was sitting behind his desk, his laptop open, fingers flying. He still had on his tuxedo from the night before.

"Roger, haven't you been to bed yet?"

He gave Natasha a blurry look, then refocused on the computer screen. "I'm working on something."

She stood in front of him and waited for him to bring his eyes back to hers. "I made pancakes for breakfast. Why don't you come eat with us?"

Roger looked confused. "It's morning?"

She nodded.

He ran his hand through his hair, seeming surprised at this.

Natasha reached over and shut the laptop. "Come on, Roger, you need to eat something."

Roger stood, gave a reluctant glance toward the computer, then followed along behind.

Natasha served Roger pancakes after he was seated, poured coffee for him, and fetched orange juice for everyone. She paused with the juice carton in hand, frowning. What the hell was wrong with this picture? Oh, well, at least she was being paid for it, she consoled herself, sitting down and picking up her fork.

Natasha watched Roger while she ate, wondering how much she could get him to tell her about her boss. "Hey, Roger, didn't you say you knew Striker in college?"

Roger glanced up, nodded, and resumed eating.

"What's his first name?"

"Jonce."

"Jonce. I like that, sounds old-fashioned."

No one commented.

"Is he married?"

"Hey, dudette, the dude's business is the dude's business. What Striker wants you to know, he'll tell you," Bigun said.

Pit nodded in agreement. "Yeah, man."

Natasha grew defensive. "I was just curious. What's wrong with that?"

No one answered her.

"How'd he get so rich, I wonder," Natasha said, trying to act as if she didn't really give a hoot.

Roger helped himself to more pancakes. "He's partnered with me on some of my software."

"Omigosh, you're kidding me." Seeing their bland expressions, Natasha decided she better not push the Striker information interrogation too far, but she just had to know one more thing.

"How old are you, Roger?"

Roger looked like he didn't know how to take that.

Oops. "I'm just wondering if you're my age," Natasha said, for lack of any other explanation.

"How old are you?"

"Almost twenty-five."

"I'm older."

Dangit. Natasha glanced around the kitchen at the dirty floor and countertops that looked like they hadn't been cleaned in awhile.

"Where's your housekeeper, Roger? I saw her yesterday."

Roger shrugged. "I don't know. She's in and out, I guess."

"She's not live-in or daily?"

"Daily, I think. I never really noticed."

Daily? No way. The bathroom off Natasha's bedroom had been downright nasty and she had had to clean it herself the night before.

"How much are you paying her?"

"I think my accountant pays her five hundred a week."

"Five hundred a week!" Natasha shrieked.

Roger startled and dropped his fork.

"Shoot, guy, she's not even keeping this place clean. For five hundred a week, I'd have it spotless."

"Okay."

Wait a minute. Did she just get hired to do housework here? Yikes! Still, she hated staying in a dirty place. And no one could clean as well as she: one of the joys of being a Libra right on the cusp of Virgo. Plus, five hundred a week, she could save up for that new Jeep Liberty she wanted.

"Okay," Natasha said, then remembered this was a mansion they were talking about. "How big is this place?"

"I don't know, maybe 7500 square feet, something like that."

Natasha's face blanched. That was a lot of cleaning. "How come you live in a place this big if you don't utilize live-in help?"

Roger was becoming irritated. "It was my mom's idea. She thinks I should live in a more pretentious style than what I prefer, if you want to know the truth."

No way was she gonna clean that much for five hundred a week. "Do you utilize all that space?"

Roger shook his head. "Most of it's closed off. I just use the downstairs and my bedroom upstairs."

Oh, well, that wasn't so bad. She could handle that.

After breakfast, Natasha shooed Roger off to bed, Pit and Bigun to check the grounds outside. She cleared the table, stacked the dishwasher, and got busy cleaning the kitchen first. She scrubbed countertops and straightened cabinets, above and below. In the cabinet beneath the sink, she came across something that puzzled her, so set it aside to show to Striker.

Natasha was cleaning the baseboard when she remembered she hadn't called her mom to let her know where she was and what she was doing.

Her mother answered on the first ring. "Hey, Mom." Natasha had the phone tucked into her shoulder and was on her knees, busily scrubbing.

Foregoing any amenities, her mom said, "Is that you having sex on the front page of the newspaper?"

Natasha raised up. "Having sex on the front page? Mom, what the heck are you talking about?"

"Have you seen the paper today?"

Natasha looked around for one. "No, not yet."

"Some woman is on top of some man, and he's got his hands on her bottom, and if I didn't know better, I'd say that bottom belongs to my daughter," her mother said, voice rising.

Natasha sat on her heels. "Oh, no."

"So it is you."

"Well, maybe, probably, but we're not having sex."

"It sure looks like it."

"Mom, Roger and I were not having sex."

"But you are having sex."

Natasha resumed scrubbing, head down, butt in the air. She didn't notice Striker standing in the doorway behind her, a grin on his face, admiring the view.

"Okay, Mom. I have had sex, all right? But I'm not having sex now and definitely not with Roger. I'm, you know, not a virgin. Geez, Mom, I'm almost twenty-five."

Natasha concentrated on cleaning, trying to ignore her mother's tireless and oft-spoken lecture rooted in that old, classic adage having to do with a cow and free milk. One Natasha had heard too many times to count.

"Wait, let's back up a minute," Natasha said, interrupting. "You know, Mom, I could still be a virgin in the technical sense. I mean, it's been awhile since I've had sex, a very, very good while, and don't certain organs of the body regenerate? Well, shoot, I bet my hymen's grown back twice over, so that would make me a virgin, right?" Knowing she was pushing buttons, she grinned. "But then, again, would a vibrator make that whole virgin point moot? Well, maybe not a vibrator, but what about a dildo?"

Cringing at her mother's prudish response, Natasha lay back with her legs tucked under her and glimpsed an upside down, smiling Striker. She dropped the phone in surprise, then righted herself and picked it up. "Mom, Striker's here, call you later, love you," she said, over her mom's raised voice. Clicking off, she stood and put the phone on the counter.

Striker was holding a newspaper in his hand.

"How long have you been here?"

He flashed white teeth.

"Shoot!"

"Technically, I think once intercourse occurs, in the physical sense, a woman is no longer considered a virgin. In the physical sense, that is."

Natasha gave him a look. "Well, gee, thanks for clearing that up."

She noticed the newspaper in his hand and grabbed at it, but he wouldn't let it go.

"Is it that bad?"

Striker grinned, flipped it open, and showed it to her. "Good job, Natasha. No one's going to question whether you're actually Roger's girlfriend or not after seeing this."

Natasha stomped around the kitchen. "Can't I do anything right?" she muttered to herself.

Striker watched her, still smiling. "That remains to be seen."

Natasha's eyes shot daggers his way, although she chose to remain silent.

Striker glanced toward the baseboard. "Are you cleaning?"

Her eyes brightened. "I'm not sure, but I think Roger's hired me to clean this place, and he's paying me five hundred a week. Can you believe it?"

Striker studied her. "If you needed a raise, all you had to do was ask."

"No, no, it's not that. I mean, what else have I got to do around here but sit and watch Roger work? This will keep me busy plus I'm making extra money to boot."

Striker shook his head.

"It's a Virgo thing, okay? I cannot live in clutter or filth. My milieu has to be sanitary and organized."

Striker nodded as if he understood. "Okay, since you've managed to wangle your way into this deal, let's sit down and go over some rules."

Natasha bristled at the word wangled but decided to let it go for now. She followed Striker to the kitchen table and sat down across from him.

"This is how it works. You, Pit, and Bigun will be living here with Roger." Striker waited to see if she had a problem with that.

"That's fine."

"I don't normally do it that way. We usually work three shifts, eight hours each, but Roger doesn't want a lot of people in and out of here, so we're just sticking with you three inside the house."

"I don't mind, really."

"I'll have three teams patrolling outside, two guys on each eight-hour shift."

"So we just worry about the inside."

Striker gave her an intent look. "You just worry about Roger."

"Okay."

"I understand there will be times when you'll need to take a break from all this, get away, you might have a doctor's appointment, want to go on a date, something like that. I don't expect you to guard him the entire twenty-four hours out of a single day." Striker waited for Natasha to nod her understanding.

"But if you do need to leave, alert Pit, Bigun, and me. Don't just go off somewhere without telling anyone."

"No problem. Can I ask one thing?"

"Sure."

"Do I have to stick by his side all day? You know, go where he goes, do what he does, things like that. Pit and Bigun said no, not in the house, but I figured I'd confirm that with you."

"If you're inside the house or on the grounds, stay in the general vicinity of Roger. As for going outside the grounds, yeah, you need to stick right by him."

Natasha smiled. "I can do that."

"You've got your gun?"

"I'm wearing a .22 strapped to my ankle."

"Not much power in a .22."

"I carry a Glock .40 in my purse."

"Okay. Where's your phone?"

Natasha glanced around. Yikes! What'd she do with her phone?

"Wear it clipped to your belt, keep it with you at all times. You need to make sure you've got me, Pit, Bigun, and Scotty programmed on the two-way alert."

"I already do."

"You have any questions as to procedure, get with Bigun and Pit; they can't help you, call Scotty or me."

"Okay."

"Any questions?"

She so wanted to ask him if he was married but didn't dare. "Just one. Is it all right if I go home this afternoon to pick up some more of my things?"

"Sure, but be sure to let Pit and Bigun know when you're leaving. Anything else?"

"No. I understand everything. It's relatively simple."

"Okay." Striker stood.

Natasha remembered what she wanted to show him. "I have something I think you should see." She walked over to the counter and picked up the bottle, which she had placed into a cellophane freezer bag.

Striker looked at it, then her.

"Thallium. You know what that is?"

"I know it's a highly poisonous substance used for extermination purposes."

"As in rat poison. But it's been banned since the '70's, hasn't it?"

"That long?"

"Yeah. So what's it doing here? You think someone like maybe that weird housekeeper who's never here has been trying to poison Roger?"

Striker gave her a look. "That's too easy."

"Still…"

"I guess we need to have Roger tested, see if any of this stuff's in his system."

Natasha nodded. "What about fingerprints?"

"I'll have the lab see if they can lift any," Striker said, making sure the seal on the bag was secure, "but that won't even come into play unless Roger's being poisoned."

"Have you done security checks on the people Roger has working for him? You know, his gardener, housekeeper, pool cleaner, people like that?"

Striker studied the bottle through the bag. "We started that yesterday."

"You know that stuff can be inhaled."

"Yeah, I know. You were smart to put it in that baggy."

She gave him a bright smile. "See, I can do something right."

After Striker left, Natasha finished cleaning the baseboard, then decided to run home to pack up the toiletries and clothes she would need for her remaining stay as bodyguard. Stepping out of the kitchen, she heard noisy chatter coming from the great room and headed in that direction. Pit and Bigun were watching *Jerry Springer* on the big-screen TV.

"Where's Roger?"

"In his office, dudette," Bigun said, without taking his eyes off the set.

"I'm going to go home for about an hour to get the rest of my things," Natasha told them.

Pit was staring at two women bitch slapping one another. "Sure, man, go ahead."

Natasha hesitated in the doorway to Roger's office, unsure whether she should interrupt or not. An older woman, dressed in expensive clothing with salon-styled hair and professional-looking makeup, was sitting across from Roger. It was obvious from the words being expressed, she, like Natasha's mom, was upset over the picture in the paper.

Roger glanced up and gave Natasha a weary smile. The older woman noticed this, stopped talking, and looked around. Her eyes traveled Natasha up and down, as if assessing her. Natasha grew uncomfortable at her inspection.

Roger motioned toward Natasha. "Mother, this is Natasha Chamberlain, one of my, um, bodyguards. Natasha, my mother, Cassandra Valentine."

Natasha stepped into the room and extended her hand.

Cassandra barely touched her fingers while giving Natasha a distasteful look, then sat back. "You have to be the woman in the picture."

Natasha could feel herself blushing. "Yes, ma'am, I'm afraid so."

Natasha didn't like the way Cassandra was staring at her, so focused on Roger. "I'm going to be gone for about an hour. I've already alerted Striker, Pit, and Bigun. You need anything while I'm out?"

Seeming to pick up on the tension between the two women, Roger gave his mother an anxious glance. "No, thanks. I'm fine."

Natasha smiled at him, then turned to Cassandra. "It was very nice meeting you, Ms. Valentine."

Cassandra nodded and turned back to Roger, dismissing Natasha.

Thinking she had left her keys in the foyer, Natasha walked that way. While she searched, she could hear snatches of the conversation between mother and son. Cassandra was making it obvious she didn't like the idea of Roger having bodyguards around, especially a woman. Huh! Natasha filed that away.

Natasha couldn't find the keys, so climbed the stairs to her bedroom and looked there, to no avail, then went back downstairs to the kitchen.

Cassandra was standing near the sink, looking around.

"Can I help you?"

Cassandra regarded Natasha with disdain. "Whomever cleaned this kitchen?"

"I did." Natasha's eyes scanned the room to make sure everything was in place, all nice and clean and shiny, just the way she liked it.

"This is more along the lines of what you've been trained for, I'm sure," Cassandra said.

Natasha was offended but decided to ignore her comment. "Can I help you find anything?"

Cassandra shook her head. "I think I can manage to get my son a cup of coffee, thank you." She gave Natasha the once-over again, sniffing with disgust.

Natasha spied her keys on the counter, grabbed them, and left. She decided not to say goodbye to Cassandra, who had turned her back and was ignoring her.

Natasha drove to her parents' home first, but no one was there. Assuming her mom was out running errands, she scribbled a note, giving Roger's phone number and telling her she'd call later and explain what was going on.

CHAPTER 6

▼

Pit, Bigun, and Roger were gathered in Roger's office with glum looks on their faces. Striker wondered about that before he heard a loud cacophony from the general vicinity of the kitchen.

"What the hell?"

"The dudette's mad, dude," Bigun said.

"Yeah, man, she's throwing one hell of a temper-tantrum," Pit said.

Roger cringed as another clamor resounded from the kitchen. "We thought it might be safer in here."

Striker scowled at them. "Okay, what happened?"

Bigun gave him a defensive look. "Hey, dude, it's not us. The dudette's mom found out she's a bodyguard now, and I don't think she likes it too much."

Pit shook his head. "Man, I thought Nattie had a temper."

"Yeah, dude, her mom's really mad." Bigun paused to listen to more noises.

Striker looked that way, then back at them. "Well, I guess Natasha comes by it honest then."

Striker stood in the entryway to the kitchen, watching Natasha attack the refrigerator with a dishtowel. She had the phone up to her ear and was making strangling noises in the back of her throat. She finally stopped and leaned against the refrigerator with exasperation.

Natasha looked toward the ceiling and raised a hand as if for benediction, then said into the phone, "Mom, would you please just listen for a minute?"

"Mom, stop, okay? I'm well past the age of emancipation, and I think I should be the one to decide what I do with my life."

"Mom. Mom, wait. If I want to be a bodyguard, that's my choice, okay?" She held the phone away from her ear and shook her head, then pulled it back once the screeching from the other end died down.

"Why all of a sudden have you decided it's okay to yell at me? You never yelled before. I mean, okay, maybe you raised your voice a time or two, but dang, Mom, you're hurting my ears here. And besides, so what I've got a college degree? What does that mean in this day and age?" She cringed at her mother's answer.

"Well, maybe I'm actually doing some good here," Natasha said.

She sighed. "Yes, I know I have this propensity to get myself into trouble, you remind me of that enough, but, Mom, I'll be careful, I swear."

Natasha slid down to the floor and sat with her back against the refrigerator. She still hadn't noticed Striker watching her with a grin on his face.

"But I don't want to get married, Mom."

"No, I don't want to have kids, either. Besides, why would I have to get married to have a kid? It's not kosher these days to do that." She winced at her mom's response.

"Well, why would I even want to have a kid, the horror stories you tell about me when I was little? I mean, my God, what if I end up with one just like me?"

Striker rubbed his mouth at that.

"The clock's ticking? Of course I know the clock's ticking, Mom. Clocks are ticking all over the world. What does that have to do with any—"

"Oh, the metaphorical biological clock. Mom, I'm not even twenty-five yet. I've got years to start to worry about that."

Natasha stood. "Because this is what I want to do, all right? Mom? I'm an adult now, you can't tell me what to do, okay? I am a free woman, on my own, independent."

Natasha rolled her eyes at the ceiling. "I don't want to be an office manager anymore, Mom. This is my chance to move into the field I want to be in, which happens to be investigation, not to mention the fact that I finally get to tote a gun."

Striker stiffened, hearing that.

"Well maybe this is all your fault anyway," Natasha said. "Remember when I was a kid and wanted a toy gun but you never would let me have one so I had to make my own out of sticks? Huh? Well, maybe, Mother, dear, if you had just gotten me that toy gun instead of all those sissy dolls you kept cramming down my throat, I wouldn't now be playing with real guns. You want to know what I used to do with all those crappy dolls, by the way? I'd line them up and shoot them with my toy guns, that's what!"

Striker leaned against the doorjamb, playing this image in his mind. Yeah, he could see that.

"No, I won't watch my mouth," Natasha was saying. "I'll say anything I want."

She listened again. "Well, fu-uh…" hesitating, as if the word were stuck in her throat "…uck it. There, I said it. This is what I want to do and I'm going to do it."

She heaved an audible sigh. "Mom, I'm way too old for that and you know it. Besides, you and Daddy don't even believe in doing that anyway. And why is it everybody all of a sudden thinks it's okay to threaten me?"

Natasha startled at the sound of laughter from the doorway. Glancing that way, her eyes widened.

"I've got to go, Mom, talk to you later, love you." She gave Striker an embarrassed look after clicking off.

"Nice to know your mother and I agree on two things," Striker said.

"Very funny." Natasha reached down and plucked the dishtowel off the floor. She walked to the table, straightened the chairs, then placed the barstools in order at the breakfast bar.

She noticed Striker watching her. "You need anything?"

"I made an appointment for Roger to go to the lab, get some blood drawn," Striker said, getting down to business.

Natasha nodded. "Are you going to tell him why?"

"Only that you found the bottle, it's a toxic substance, and since he's been living here, he should be tested in case there's been exposure."

"That's good. We don't want him to, you know, think someone actually…"

"Right. No point in alarming him unless we have to."

Natasha was silent a moment before giving him a wary look. "How much of that conversation did you hear anyway?"

Striker grinned. "Enough to know your age, that you don't want to get married or have kids, and love toting a gun."

"Shoot."

"She's just worried about you, you know."

"Yeah, I know, but like everything else she has to deal with concerning me, she'll get used to the idea." Natasha gave him a quick smile and left.

Striker watched her walk away, thinking this was definitely not the same woman he knew from the office. He was beginning to worry Natasha might be a little bit dangerous.

CHAPTER 7

▼

Ten days later, everyone was gathered in Roger's office waiting for Natasha to get off the phone so they could have a meeting regarding procedure. The men tried making small talk but gave up after awhile to listen to Natasha's one-sided conversation while trying to appear as if they weren't.

Natasha was upside down on the couch with her legs over the back and her head to the floor, much like the posture of the quintessential teenager on the phone. She seemed oblivious to the other five men in the room while she conversed. The khaki shorts she wore revealed long, tanned legs. Her black tank top had slipped enough to expose a belly-button ring. A thin, silver ankle bracelet rested above one shapely foot. Her toenails were painted candy red and a toe ring rested on the second toe on her right foot.

Striker studied this woman, trying to pair her with the other one he had known for over three years, the professional one. He shook his head.

Natasha was doing a lot of squealing and I can't believe that and you go, girl. The men were wondering what the heck was going on.

Natasha finally keyed off and stretched.

Glancing away, Striker noticed Roger staring at Natasha with a funny look on his face. *This could be trouble*, he thought to himself, seeing that.

Natasha placed her hands on the floor, flipped over, and came up bounding, causing Striker to wonder if she had taken gymnastics.

She noticed they were all watching her and gave a smile. "That was my mom. You are not going to believe what she did."

"What, dudette?" Bigun asked.

"Joined a gym. I've been trying to get her to join one for years, and now all of a sudden she went and did it. But what's really great is she has this trainer, and I think she's kind of fallen for him. She says he's tall, blond-haired, blue-eyed, real muscular, very Swedish looking." Natasha hesitated, as if envisioning this guy.

Striker's brow creased.

"I mean, not that she'd ever do anything. She's my mom, for Pete's sake, and she's been married to my dad for, well, forever. But it might do her some good to, you know, become interested in someone, might make her feel better about herself. That plus working out, getting her body in shape, maybe she'll focus on herself for once and stop picking on me so much, stop wanting to know what's going on with my life all the time." She rolled her eyes. "Like yeah!"

Striker, remembering the office Natasha as being very quiet and unassuming, always acting professional, raised his eyebrows at Scott.

Scott grinned as if he knew what Striker was thinking.

Natasha sat down on the couch and addressed Striker. "So, what's the meeting about?"

He turned his attention to Roger. "It's been over a week now, there's been no contact from the extortionist, and I think we need to talk about where we go from here."

Roger looked embarrassed. "Striker, I didn't make this up, I swear. The guy did call me and threaten my life."

Scott, who had Roger pegged as a paranoid, spoke up. "You didn't misunderstand what he said when he called? You're very sure what he was saying to you?"

Roger gave Scott a defensive look. "Of course I didn't misunderstand him."

"You know what I think," Natasha said, drawing attention from the others. "I think since this guy seemed to know so much about Roger and his life and habits and so forth, we have to assume he's been staking him out. It could be that he's aware of the situation now, you know, with the security in place, and he's just biding his time, waiting for his chance to contact Roger again."

Scott wanted the decision to be made today to end this job so he could get Natasha back in the office. "Or maybe we scared him off."

Striker looked at Pit and Bigun.

"I think the dudette's right," Bigun said.

"Yeah, man, that's what I'd do," Pit said.

Natasha turned to Striker. "We can't expect this guy to just walk away from a million dollars, right?"

"So, you don't think my life is in danger so much anymore, that now it's more along the lines of extortion," Roger said, staring at Striker.

"Money's a pretty powerful motive," Striker said. "I don't think he would have brought it up unless that's exactly what he wants."

Natasha settled back on the couch. "Yeah, but who hired the guy to kill Roger? Don't you think that's something we need to find out?"

"Sure, but we can't do that until we catch the extortionist," Striker said.

Scott didn't like the way this was going. "Since you haven't heard anything else, I think the guy's lost interest. I don't see that there's a clear danger here anymore. Besides, he could have been making up the part about someone hiring him to kill Roger."

"My gut feeling is that this guy is still out there, waiting," Natasha said. "I don't think he's just gone away, Scotty, not for a million dollars."

Scott grew angry. "You're just saying that because you don't want to come back to the office."

"Whoever said I was coming back to the office after this?"

Scott and Striker exchanged looks.

Natasha surged to her feet, pointing at them. "I saw that!" She turned to Striker. "Scott promised me that if I did good in this job, I get to move up into the investigative department. So now you're all of a sudden going to renege, demote me back down to office manager? I do not think so."

Striker focused on Scott. "Is that what you promised?"

Scott looked caught. "I might have alluded to it."

Natasha had hands on hips and was giving Striker a challenging glare.

"If that's what Scott promised, then that's the deal."

Natasha sat back down. "Okay."

Striker grinned at her. "The key words, though, are if you do good."

"Oh, and you're saying you don't think I can?"

"I'm saying I think that temper of yours is going to get in the way in that regard."

Natasha's face reddened with the effort to refrain from retaliating. Deciding to ignore Striker, she spoke in Roger's direction. "I think that this should be Roger's decision, not ours. It's his money."

Roger gave Natasha a thankful look.

Striker didn't like the way she had taken control, but there was nothing he could do about it. He addressed Roger. "Okay, what do you want to do?"

"Well, since you think it's the money issue, I don't see that we need to keep the perimeter guards here any longer. But I want Nattie, Pit, and Bigun to stay." Roger smiled at Natasha, who was smiling at him.

"Of course you do," Scott said, rising and stalking out of the room.

Striker stood. "Okay, for now, everything remains status quo with the exception of the perimeter guards."

"Yippee, yahooee!" Natasha exchanged high fives with Bigun and Pit, then hugged Roger behind the desk, ignoring his reddening face.

Striker left to Natasha dancing around Pit and Bigun, Roger watching her, grinning like an idiot.

Striker gave Scott a look after he climbed into his vehicle.

"What?"

"What the hell did you think you were doing offering that to her?"

Scott shrugged. "I was working her, okay, trying to get her to accept the job."

"Yeah, and look what happens, it keeps backfiring. Now we're going to have to find another office manager."

They rode in silence for awhile, then Scott said, "Did Roger look different to you?"

That thought had crossed Striker's mind, but he couldn't place exactly what had changed about Roger.

"I can see a problem coming," Scott said.

Striker glanced at him.

"Roger's falling for Nattie."

"I was afraid of that," Striker said, in a dark mood now.

A few minutes later, Scott said, "You need to go to Atlanta."

Striker looked at him.

"That missing teenage case we've got going on down there, it's stopped dead in its tracks and I need you to go jump-start it again."

"I can do that by phone."

"No, you need to go down there. You get things done when you're actually there in person."

Striker gave him a skeptical glance. "What's the deal?"

"You've for some reason I cannot understand totally gotten yourself immersed in this thing with Roger when we both know it's nothing, he's just being paranoid. We've got more important cases going on, Striker, cases that need your attention that aren't getting your attention."

"Or you just want me out of the way so you can strong-arm Natasha into coming back to the office."

Scott bristled. "Now who's paranoid?"

Striker was silent a moment. "Okay, I'll go. I'll leave this afternoon."

Striker's two-way bleeped. He picked it up and glanced at the readout: Natasha.

"Striker," he said into the phone.

"It just occurred to me that if this guy has been watching Roger, where the heck is he watching him from? I mean, I haven't seen any repair vans or the like across the street from the estate."

Striker thought. "This is a gated community, I doubt if he could get by the guard."

"Unless he walks on."

Striker glanced at Scott. Why hadn't they thought about that? Probably because they really hadn't considered this thing to be as serious as Roger and Natasha seemed to think it was.

"Tell Roger to pull out the blueprints from the security system we installed last year. I've got to go out of town but I'll be back late tomorrow afternoon and I'll go over them then, see if there's anything else we could be doing."

"Sure thing, dude," Natasha said.

Striker grinned, put down the phone, then heard it bleep. "Yeah?"

"Be careful out there, big guy, it's an awfully cruel world."

Striker looked at Scott. "Why didn't you tell me that girl was wacky?"

Scott couldn't help but smile at that.

CHAPTER 8

▼

Striker arrived at Roger's the next afternoon tired and scruffy-looking. He'd had one long night, without much sleep, and after attending to business, had driven straight back from Atlanta. He found the boys in the great room, Pit and Bigun watching the big-screen, Roger sitting at the game table working on his laptop.

Striker glanced around. "Where's Natasha?"

"She went to her mom's, dude," Bigun said.

After waiting for an explanation why she had gone to her mother's, which no one seemed to want to offer, he shrugged. "You find those blueprints, Roger?"

"Huh?" Roger looked up and his eyes widened at Striker standing there. "When'd you come in?"

Striker mentally sighed. "Did you find the blueprints?"

"Yeah, they're right here." Roger closed the laptop and pulled rolled-up parchment sheets from under the table.

Striker watched Roger place the papers on the table, wondering what was different, then it hit him. "Where are your glasses?"

Roger gave him an embarrassed smile. "Nattie likes me better in contacts."

"Yeah, the dudette thinks Roger's got the most beautiful blue eyes she's ever seen on a man," Bigun teased.

Roger blushed.

Striker began unrolling the papers in order to study them. He heard the front door open and close and glanced up to see Natasha standing in the doorway.

"Oh my God," she said in a dramatic way.

"What, dudette?" Bigun said.

"My mom. You're never going to believe what she did."

"What'd she do, man?" Pit said.

Natasha's mouth tipped into a wide smile. "She cut off all her hair. Yeah, all off. It's maybe an inch long at the most. Then, and you're not going to believe this, she bleached it platinum blond and now she's wearing it spiked on top. Oh, man, she looks so totally cool that way."

Striker tried to picture this but couldn't.

Natasha walked over to the table to study the blueprints. "I think I might do that."

"No, dudette, don't cut your hair," Bigun said.

"You think?"

"You've got pretty hair, Nattie," Roger said. "Why would you want to do something like that?"

Natasha shrugged. "I don't know. I guess 'cause it'd be fun."

"Yeah, man, till you tried to grow it out," Pit said. "Take it from me, that's not easy."

Natasha stared at his bald head. "Gee, I hadn't thought about that."

Striker was listening to all this, feeling like he had stepped into a weird version of some family sitcom.

Natasha smiled at Striker, then walked toward the TV. She leaned over the back of the couch to watch with Pit and Bigun.

Striker's and Roger's eyes were on Natasha.

"What's on?" Natasha asked over the orgasmic utterances of a shampoo commercial.

"Oprah's coming on in a minute," Pit said.

The woman herself appeared with a teaser for what was coming up and Natasha grew quiet, listening. When Roger shifted, Striker glanced at him, then remembered the blueprints and went back to those.

Natasha straightened up. "Did you hear that?"

"What, man?" Pit said.

She walked around, settled on the couch between the two bodyguards. "What they're talking about on Oprah."

"Something about older women," Bigun said.

"Perimenopause. They have just been describing my mom to a tee. Now I know what's wrong with her. You know, how she's always so moody anymore? How she doesn't want to be a mom anymore? How she keeps yelling at me? Why she's all of a sudden going to a gym and cutting her hair and—oh, my gosh, my mom is perimenopausal. Shhh. It's coming back on."

Roger scooted his chair back from the table and joined the three bodyguards to watch the program. Striker didn't even want to think about the subject being discussed, so tried to study the blueprints, but his thoughts were constantly interrupted by Natasha or Pit or Bigun and occasionally Roger pointing out that yeah, that's exactly what their mom did or said.

Striker finally gave up and headed toward the kitchen for something to drink, wondering what in the hell was developing here. There seemed to be some sort of weird bonding between his bodyguards and client, and he didn't think that was such a good idea but didn't know what he could do about it.

When Striker returned to the great room, Natasha was reclining on the couch, talking on the phone. Her head was on a pillow in Bigun's lap and her feet were resting on Pit's muscular thighs while he gave her a foot massage.

As usual, Roger, Pit, and Bigun were listening to her conversation.

Natasha was advancing her opinion that her mother was suffering perimenopause to that very person. Who didn't seem to like it.

"Well, I was just suggesting you might want to think about it," Natasha said. "I mean, Mom, you do have all—a lot of the symptoms, you know, the moodiness, the rages, the crying over—"

She listened to her mother's interruption.

"Well, maybe I do have some of those symptoms, but, dangit, Mom, I'm not old enough for—"

She paused, then sat up. "I am not stuck in perpetual puberty!"

Striker laughed outright. Natasha took the time to turn and glare at him. He grinned back.

Natasha went back to defending herself. "Okay, maybe I do cry a lot, Mom, but I've always cried a lot. I happen to be a very sensitive person. And I've always had a temper, okay, I'll admit that, but, hey, I'm not the one who's beginning to turn into a termagant here, you know." She put her head back on the pillow.

Growing tired of whatever her mother was saying, Natasha held the phone in the air and closed her eyes. "Oh, Pit, that feels so good," she moaned, bringing the phone down and resting it on her shoulder. "To the left." She sighed, then made that moaning sound again. "There, right there," then, "Oh, God."

Striker was thinking if he didn't know for sure the only thing happening on the couch was Natasha getting a foot massage, he'd wonder about those sounds.

Natasha put the phone to her ear. "What? Yeah, right, Mom, I'm having sex with Pit, can't you tell? Oh, yes, Pit, right there! Oh, please, don't stop!" She made some heavy breathing sounds. "Mom, I've got to go, see ya, love ya." She disconnected and dropped the phone on the floor.

"I think I want to marry you, Pit," she said.

Pit laughed.

"You are one naughty daughter, dudette," Bigun said.

Natasha sat up and hit him with her pillow, so, of course, Bigun had to hit her with one back, then Pit was in on it, and before Striker could say boo the three of them were having one heck of a pillow fight. Roger got up and joined the fray when Natasha threw a pillow at him.

Striker shook his head, wondering when exactly these four adults had turned into children.

CHAPTER 9

▼

At the office, helping Scott interview office manager applicants, Striker received an alert from Pit on his two-way. "Yeah?" he said into his cell phone, standing and walking to the far bank of windows, leaving Scott to ask the questions.

"Hey, man, Nattie and Roger are heading out in her jeep and we're following."

"Where to?"

"Nattie's talked Roger into looking at that new sporty Mercedes-Benz they just came out with."

"Mercedes-Benz? What the hell does Roger want with a sports car?"

"Who knows, man, but they're going looking."

Striker sighed. "Okay, stay with them. Keep me up on what's going on."

"Sure thing, man."

A short time later, Pit alerted Striker that they were at the dealership.

Thirty minutes later, he told Striker that Roger and Nattie were going to take a test drive.

"Follow them," Striker instructed.

Roger was cruising down the street, trying out the Benz, when Natasha put her hand on his arm. "Stop!" she screamed.

Roger startled, his foot immediately stomped down on the brake pedal, and the car came to a squealing stop. Both of them were slung toward the dashboard, saved from crashing into it at the last moment by their seat belts.

Natasha unfastened hers and was out of the car before Roger had finished saying, "What the heck!"

Grunting in confusion, Roger looked after her retreating form, ignoring the symphony of angry horns behind him. He watched Natasha begin arguing with a woman on the sidewalk, throwing her arms around, her face growing red.

"What the heck," Roger repeated, unfastening his seat belt. Stepping out of the car, he didn't even hear the cacophony of horns this time.

By the time he got to the two women, Natasha had her arms crossed and was listening to the other woman with a belligerent scowl on her face. She noticed Roger when he stepped up next to her and gave her a questioning look.

"It's her!" Natasha said, interrupting the woman, slinging a hand in her direction.

Roger looked at the other woman, then back to Natasha, wondering why she was so dog-gone angry. "Her who?"

"The perimenopausal woman, a/k/a my mom, the woman who is twenty years older than me and who used to look like a mom but who now looks like a hooker!" Natasha turned and glared at her mother.

Roger studied the other woman. Her hair was cut short, spiked on top, and dyed platinum blond. She had lined her chocolate-colored eyes in a matching color, which Roger thought looked exotic. She wore a sleeveless summer sweater and short skirt with high heels revealing long, well-defined legs. One manicured, very feminine hand daintily held a cigarette between the index and third fingers.

"Wow," Roger said.

The woman smiled his way.

Natasha hit him. "You shit!"

"Ow!" Roger said, rubbing his arm.

Natasha's mom placed the cigarette in her left hand and held out her right. "I'm Stevie."

"Wow."

"Shut up!" Natasha hit him again.

Roger gave Natasha a hurt look and stepped out of her reach.

Natasha turned her attention back to her mother. "Stevie? Where the heck does Stevie come from, Mother, dear?"

Her mom gave her a bright smile. "Short for Stephanie, of course. Don't you like it?"

Natasha decided not to answer that, mainly because she did. "So, you into hooking now?" she said, changing the subject.

Stevie turned to Roger and gave him a wide-eyed, innocent look. "Does this look like a hooker's outfit to you?"

Roger wanted to say "Wow" again but didn't dare. His attention drawn toward the street, where the angry blares continued to resonate, joined now by raised voices, he remembered the car. Yeah, that was a good out. "The car's blocking the street, I've got to go move it." He sprinted away.

Natasha didn't even hear him, too busy glaring at her mother. "What the hell are you doing out here dressed like that? Shoot, Mother, you fit right in with all these other prostitutes standing around."

"You think?"

Natasha resisted the urge to roll her eyes.

Stevie preened, her hands going to her almost-not-there hair. "I was just trying out a new look. What do you think?"

"I think you look like a hooker is what I think," Natasha said, her voice rising.

"Well, that's not so bad. At least I don't look matronly, right?"

Natasha rolled her eyes for real this time.

Stevie looked around for Roger. "Well, your friend liked it."

"Mom, Roger's a man. He likes anything that doesn't have a dick hanging between its legs."

Stevie gave Natasha a shocked look. "Your mouth!"

Natasha tried to collect herself. "What's this all about, Mom? Why the heck are you out on the street dressed like this?"

Stevie seemed to remember the cigarette in her hand, put it in her mouth, took a drag, and had a coughing fit.

"And smoking, too. Shoot, Mom, what the heck is wrong with you?"

Stevie took the time to throw the cigarette down, grind it out with one spiked heel, put a finger to her tongue and daintily remove a piece of tobacco. She began to study her fingernails, which were painted silver.

Natasha got the message. "Okay, okay. I realize it's this perimenopausal thing, Mom, but for Pete's sake, to dress like this, start smoking, hanging out on street corners. What the heck do you think you're doing? I mean, you're going to attract the wrong kind of people out here." An idea occurred. "People are going to start talking."

Natasha waited for a shocked expression to come into her mom's eyes, knowing this was her weakness. Well, one of them.

Stevie shrugged her shoulders. "Let them talk."

Natasha's mouth dropped open in surprise.

"Trying to catch flies, sweetie?"

Natasha clamped her mouth shut and looked around. "Where's your car?"

"I had Sherry drop me off."

"Aunt Sherry saw you like this?"

"Well, of course, baby. She picked me up."

"And what did she say?"

"Nothing," her mother said in a defensive manner. "Not a thing."

"Come on, let me take you home." Natasha stepped toward Stevie, who stepped back.

"No thank you."

"Okay, Mom, I'm sorry I yelled at you," Natasha said. Geez, now she was the adult and her mom the kid, when did that happen? "Just let Roger and me take you home, okay? We'll talk about this there."

Stevie gave her daughter a defiant look. "I said, no, thank you."

Natasha glanced at Roger who had joined them once more. "Okay, why don't you want us to give you a ride?"

"I'm waiting on your father. He's picking me up."

Natasha's eyes widened with alarm. "We can't let Dad see you like this, Mom. What's he going to think? What's he going to say?"

"I guess that's for me to know and you to find out."

Natasha drew back at her mother's tone of voice. Okay, let her dad handle it; she didn't know what to do with this woman she used to know. "Fine. That's fine. We'll go."

She noticed Roger giving her mom an appreciative look and jabbed him with her elbow. "Come on, Roger, we're leaving."

Roger extended his hand. "It was very nice meeting you, Stevie. And might I add, you look very beautiful in that outfit."

Natasha elbowed him again.

"Ow!" He turned to her. "You jab me one more time, I'm gonna jab you back." Rubbing his arm, Roger walked toward the car.

"Well, Mom, I guess I'll see you later," Natasha said, backing away.

Stevie opened her purse and pulled out another cigarette. "I'll talk to you soon, honey."

Natasha turned and caught up with Roger. "Where's the car?"

He gave her a look. "I don't know if I want you riding with me. You like to hit too much."

"Okay, I'm sorry I hit you. But she's my mom, Roger, you don't need to be looking at her like that."

"Just because she's your mom doesn't mean she can't look good."

Natasha snorted. "That's not what I call good." She stopped short.

Roger walked on a few steps before he missed her presence. He turned and watched her, then came back.

"What?"

"What if she isn't waiting for my dad? What if she has a boyfriend or something? I mean, isn't that what happens with men during the mid-life crisis, they get themselves a girlfriend, start working out, get toupees, their teeth bleached, all that crap? Well, maybe it's the same with women. Maybe she's found someone else. Omigosh! What if it's that Swedish trainer?"

Natasha turned around to look. Her mother was still standing in the same place, smoking, getting eyed by all the men passing her. She grabbed Roger by the arm and hustled him around the side of the nearest corner building.

"What the heck are you doing, Nattie? The car's over there, not—"

"Shhh. We're going to watch her, see what happens, make sure some pervert doesn't pick her up."

"Yeah, right. You're just afraid she actually does have a boyfriend."

Natasha glared at him, then peeked around the corner.

Roger stopped rubbing his arm and peeked with her.

They watched for a few minutes until a man in a Dodge dually pulled to the curb and braked to a stop in front of Natasha's mom. At first, he didn't notice Stevie, who was watching him, then seemed to startle and hurried out of the truck.

"Who's that?" Roger said.

"My dad," Natasha whispered.

"Does he know it's her?"

Natasha shook her hand at him. "Shhh!"

"Like you can hear anything they say from here."

She glared at him.

"All right, already."

Natasha grew shocked when her dad took her mom in his arms, a big grin planted on his face, and kissed her right there on the street. Her hand went to her mouth. "I can't believe he's kissing her like that, in public, for anyone to see."

Roger gave her a look. "Wait a minute. Who's the mother here, you or her? I mean, you're acting like an old fuddy-duddy, and I know you're not a fuddy-duddy."

"When it comes to my mom, I'll be any way I want to be." Natasha stomped off.

"The car's over here." Roger waited for her to turn back and follow him.

They trooped into the kitchen at Roger's, followed a few minutes later by Pit and Bigun, who cast irritated looks at both of them.

"What's with stopping the car in the middle of the road like that?" Pit said. "Damnit, man, we got caught up in that traffic jam you created, couldn't see anything, couldn't move, didn't know what the heck had happened, till Bigun got out and ran up there and saw you two talking to some hot-looking chick."

Roger gave Natasha a smug look. "Told you."

Natasha pulled the refrigerator door open and studied the contents, ignoring these idiots.

Bigun rummaged around in a cabinet, grabbed a bag of chips, opened them, and crammed some in his mouth. "Dude, who was that woman?"

Roger smiled. "That was Stevie, Nattie's mom."

This was met with silence. Unable to stand it any longer, Natasha glanced around at them. She didn't like the lecherous looks on their faces. "Hey, she's married, okay? She's off limits to you adolescentally hormonal nincompoops."

Deciding to ignore that comment, Roger glanced at Bigun, walked over to the cabinet, and got his own bag of chips.

Pit gave Natasha an offended look, then followed Roger and pulled out a box of Cracker Jacks.

"Hey, that's my stash," Natasha said.

"There's more in there," Pit said, his mouth full of crud.

Natasha glared at him. "Didn't your mom ever teach you any manners?" She yanked the cabinet door open and grabbed her own box.

Pit looked at Roger. "What's with her, man?"

Roger grinned. "She doesn't like it that her mom's a hottie."

Natasha's face grew red. "My mother is not a hottie and don't you call her that."

"Well, she's a hottie to me." Roger threw chips in the air, aiming for his mouth, but missed.

"Hey, you're cleaning that mess up," Natasha said. "I'm not cleaning that crap up."

Roger acted like he didn't hear her.

Natasha couldn't let it go. "And you better not be thinking about calling her or anything, Roger, because she's not that type of woman."

"I'll call her if I want to."

Natasha's eyes narrowed. "You wouldn't dare."

Pit and Bigun backed away.

"I mean, a woman looks like that, sends me the message she's on the market," Roger said.

Natasha shook the box of Cracker Jacks in Roger's direction, and peanuts and caramel popcorn landed all over him.

"Hey!" Roger looked down and brushed himself off.

Natasha slung more food his way. "You keep away from her."

Roger reached into the chip bag, grabbed a handful of chips, and slung them at Natasha.

Pit and Bigun retired to the breakfast bar to watch and eat. This was better than popcorn and a movie.

Natasha shook chips out of her hair. "That stuff's riddled with grease," she shrieked. "Look at what you did to my hair, you jerk."

Roger gave her a smug look. "You want my opinion, a little grease wouldn't hurt your hair any."

Natasha made a noise in the back of her throat, stomped to the refrigerator, withdrew a bag of baby carrots, and began slinging them at Roger.

"Hey!" Roger put his hands up and batted them away.

One landed on the breakfast bar. Bigun picked it up and ate it.

Roger began collecting carrots and chips and Cracker Jacks and flinging them at Natasha, who kept throwing the carrots at him.

Movement in the doorway caught Roger's attention. He glanced that way and stopped throwing food, his hand in mid-air.

Bigun and Pit quietly got up and left the room.

Natasha wondered what the heck Roger was looking at and turned around. Her eyes grew wide.

Striker was leaning against the doorjamb with his arms crossed and a scowl on his face. When he unfolded his arms and stood straight, Natasha backed away, bumping into Roger.

"I want to see you," Striker said to Natasha, then turned on his heels and left.

Natasha glanced at Roger, who gave her a concerned look.

She brushed herself off, shaking her head to dislodge any clinging food particles, then followed her boss.

Striker stood in the doorway of the library, waiting.

Natasha felt like a kid called to the principal's office as she walked past him into the room. After Striker closed the door, she turned and looked at him.

Striker raised his eyebrows.

Natasha gave him an uneasy smile. "I guess you're wondering what the heck was going on in there."

"Nope."

She thought. "Oh, I guess you heard about the car thing."

"Yep."

"You're wondering why we all of a sudden stopped."

"Yep."

"In the middle of the road like that."

Striker nodded.

"Well, it was my mom, see, she was standing on that street corner looking like a—well, let's just say a heck of a lot different than she normally does. And I—well, I kind of freaked out, seeing her like that."

"And in the process forgot your official duty and left the man you were supposed to be guarding," Striker reminded her.

Natasha grimaced. "Oh, yeah, I guess I did do that." She glanced down at the carpet and noticed food debris scattered all around her feet.

Natasha looked back at Striker, who was watching her. "I'm sorry. I wasn't thinking. I let my emotions get the best of me and forgot all about what I was supposed to be doing."

Striker continued to regard her.

Natasha desperately did not want to be demoted back to the office. "I won't do it again. Really, Striker, I won't, I swear. I'll remember next time."

He shook his head in frustration.

Roger stuck his head in the door and offered Striker an uncertain smile. Hey."

"We're in the middle of something here," Striker growled.

Roger stepped into the room. "Uh, what happened, Striker, it's not all Nattie's fault, you know. I was the one who stopped the car, I—"

"Roger, you don't have to say that," Natasha interrupted. "I'm the one to blame. I take full responsibility, even if it does mean I might get fired." Tears were now welling and her voice was beginning to crack.

A horrified look crossed Roger's face. He backed out and closed the door.

Striker waited for Natasha to calm herself. After she had gained control and had stopped sniffing and wiping at her eyes, he put his fingers under her chin and lifted her face, forcing her to make eye contact.

"This is an official reprimand, Natasha. This goes on your record."

She nodded.

"You're green, I realize that, but you can't endanger the man you're supposed to be guarding."

"I know," she said in a small voice.

"I'm not going to fire you, this time."

She looked relieved. "Oh, thank you. Thank you, Striker. Thank you."
"Go back to your food fight."

There was a Chuck Norris marathon on cable and the boys decided they were going to stay up all night eating and watching on the big-screen TV. Natasha stayed with them for awhile, feeling blue, till they got carried away with the excessive gas expulsions, then left, thinking men were nothing but pigs.

In her room, she closed and locked the door, opened the window, then called her mom. The phone rang ten times before Stevie picked it up. Her "Hello," was breathless.

Natasha became alarmed. "Mom?"

"Oh, hi, honey, how are you, everything's fine, I'll call you tomorrow," Stevie said in a rush.

Natasha could have sworn she heard her mom giggle before putting down the receiver. An image came to mind of what her mom might actually be engaged in, followed by *eeeoooouuu*.

Natasha lay on her bed, all alone and lonely, thinking it had been so long since—Her cell phone rang, startling her. She reached over and picked it up. Striker was on the other end.

"Hey," Natasha said, sitting up.

"You feeling better?"

"Uh, yeah. I guess I—well, no," she said, her voice wavering.

"Okay, what's wrong?"

Natasha found herself spilling her guts to him. She told him about seeing her mother and the way she looked, how she had felt when she saw her dressed like that. Then tonight, feeling lonely and blue, calling her mom to talk but her mom couldn't talk because she was, well, obviously, she was too busy making love. Her voice rose to a wail at this last part.

"That bothers you?" Striker said, trying to keep the amusement out of his voice.

Natasha was beginning to feel foolish. "Well, no. It's just, I wanted someone to talk to."

"You got three guys there. Why aren't you talking to them?"

"They're too busy having a fart-fest."

Striker chuckled.

"I had to come in the bedroom, close the door, open the window." Natasha grinned when he laughed longer, liking that sound.

"I do not understand the male species ritual of bonding with each other by trying to see who can expel the most gas the loudest and the longest, from whichever end," she said, drawing more laughter from Striker. The sound was infectious and she joined him.

After he sobered, Striker said, "Not all guys are like that, you know."

"God, I hope not!"

"Feel better now?"

As a matter of fact, she did. "Yes."

"Good."

Natasha didn't want him to terminate the call. "Hey, Striker, tell me what you do when you go to the mountains."

"I will only tell that to the woman I choose as my life-mate."

Natasha was disappointed at first, but then grew delighted. He had said choose, not chose. He wasn't married! She remembered he was still on the phone.

"How about a story, then? Scotty says you know all kinds of Cherokee lore. Tell me about one of your ancestors."

Striker remained silent.

"Please."

"Okay, I'll tell you about my grandmother who listened to the wind."

Natasha snuggled under the covers. "Oh, yeah."

CHAPTER 10

▼

The call they had been waiting for finally came after three weeks of guarding Roger. Natasha was disappointed. She was having way too much fun and didn't want this gig to end.

After taking the call, Roger waved his hand in a frantic motion toward Natasha, indicating he wanted her to listen in. She picked up the cordless and clicked it on, glancing at the display to make sure the caller ID had a number recorded. She cursed to herself when she read "Unknown Caller" instead of a name or number. At the same time, she alerted Striker on her cell phone and keyed in the code to let him know about the call so he could start the trace.

Natasha listened to Roger do what Striker had instructed him to, tell the man he would only meet him in a public place with a lot of people around, then heard the man instructing Roger to meet him at the Dog's Breath Saloon the next evening.

Roger glanced at Natasha. "Dog's Breath?"

She hurried over to his desk and wrote on a sheet of paper, "Sports bar."

"Sports bar?" Seeing Natasha's look, Roger said into the phone, "The sports bar?"

The man told Roger to bring the money in a sports bag, stand there at the bar, the bag at his feet, and he better not see any of his bodyguards hanging around.

Natasha scratched a message, then held the paper out to Roger.

"Can I bring my girlfriend?"

They listened to the negative response.

Natasha moved the paper so Roger could see what she was writing.

"I need someone to help me watch the money," Roger read.

Natasha nodded.

"You can't expect me to stand there by myself, a million dollars at my feet, without someone to help me," Roger embellished.

Natasha gave him the okay signal and smiled.

Roger watched Natasha write. "We'll be there together, the bag between us."

The man finally agreed to their terms. After he hung up, Striker called from his car. "The call came from a pay phone at a mall near Chattanooga. Of course, by the time our guys get there, he'll be long gone. Did you remember to record what he said?"

Natasha rolled her eyes at Roger. "Well, of course."

"Okay, I'll be there in ten minutes."

Striker, Roger, and the bodyguards listened to the conversation. Striker didn't like the way it had gone.

He gave Roger an incredulous look. "Why the hell did you suggest bringing your girlfriend?"

Roger glanced at Natasha.

"I should have known," Striker said.

"Surely you weren't going to send him in there alone," Natasha said. "He's my man, I'm supposed to guard him, so I'll guard him."

"I'll have four other guys in there, I don't need you guarding him."

"Too late now."

Striker shook his head. "You can't go anyway."

"Why not?"

"Well, he knows about the bodyguards, so chances are he knows about you."

"I'll just look different."

Striker looked like he wasn't buying that.

She grinned. "Don't worry. He'll never know it's me. Trust me."

Striker left to pay a visit to the bar to try to talk the manager into allowing him to put in place some sort of surveillance system for the next evening. On the way out, he noticed things didn't look the same. He paused at the front door, his eyes scanning the foyer, up the stairs, and into the library. He walked back to Roger's office, where he found Roger and Natasha studying the computer screen together.

"Why the change?"

They both looked up.

"I don't know what you mean," Natasha said.

"This place. It's different, not as dark as it used to be."

Roger smiled. "Nattie's helping me redecorate. She thinks I need to live in a place that reflects my image, so we're getting rid of all that dark furniture my mom put in here, buying new stuff, making it more contemporary."

"Roger wants to put in a gym, too, you know, a workout room with weights and exercise equipment." Natasha looked at Roger. "We got to do something. Pit and Bigun are starting to get fat."

They grinned at one another in a conspiratorial way.

"I don't think it's a good idea to have workers in and out of here," Striker said to Natasha. "That's too risky."

"No need to worry about that. We're ordering most of this stuff on-line. And what do we need workers for when we have Pit and Bigun here? Shoot, they can move anything."

Striker thought about that, taking note Roger looked a hell of a lot different than he had just three weeks before. Usually, he appeared to be in disarray, his hair uncombed, shirt untucked, always wearing the same scruffy pair of tennis shoes, kind of reminding Striker of an absentminded scientist. Now, Roger was dressed in pressed jeans and a tucked-in polo shirt, with new running shoes. His sandy-colored hair had been cut shorter and was combed into place. The glasses were gone. Striker noticed, for the first time, that Roger was a good-looking guy. He watched Natasha smiling at Roger, wondering in the back of his mind if she was grooming him. But for what or, rather, whom? He didn't like that; he didn't like that at all. And what was that about Roger's image?

"Your image?" he said, voicing this.

"Roger's a very cool dude," Natasha said.

Striker glanced at Roger, who was beaming.

"And a very cool dude should live in a very cool home. Right, Roger?" Natasha said.

"Natasha, I need to talk to you." Striker watched the smile drop from her face upon seeing his expression. "Outside," he added and left.

Natasha glanced at Roger and shrugged, then followed Striker.

They stood beside his car.

"What's going on?" Striker said.

Natasha gave him a confused look. "Going on?"

"With Roger."

She thought a moment. "I'm not sure what you're talking about."

"All these changes, the way he looks, the way he dresses, now remodeling his home. Those things never seemed to bother Roger before, so I'm just wondering what's going on here."

Natasha remained silent.

"One of the most important policies we have in this firm is that we don't allow ourselves to become emotionally involved with the man we're guarding. I'm beginning to think that's not the case here."

"You're right, it's not."

Striker drew back, surprised; he had been expecting a denial from her.

Natasha gave him a stubborn look. "Roger's my friend, if you want to consider that emotionally involved. And if you do, then you're just as guilty as I am, because he's also your friend."

"So that's all it is, friendship."

"Striker, I'm not stupid. I know better than to fall in love with my man."

Striker leaned toward her. "But how, I wonder, does Roger feel about you?"

Natasha shrugged. "Well, I guess the same way I do about him."

Striker felt she had dodged the question but wasn't sure how to corner her. "I'll see you later." He wondered as he left how in the hell in three short weeks Natasha had gotten Roger to buy a sports car and redecorate his house, not to mention, change his appearance. He didn't like that; he didn't like that at all.

The next day, Striker did a double take when he first saw Natasha. She wore a black leather mini-skirt, long, black leather boots, and black leather vest with no shirt or bra on underneath. She had done something to her hair to change it to a copper color and wore it piled on top of her head in a spiky way. Her eyes were lined heavily and appeared dark and sultry. She wore bright-red lipstick, which made her lips seem fuller, poutier. If he didn't know better, Striker would have pegged her as an eighteen-year-old.

Bigun gave Natasha an admiring look. "Dudette!"

Natasha grinned. "What do you think?"

"Man, you're slamming," Pit said.

"Let's go," Striker growled.

They rode in the surveillance van to the bar. Striker talked to Roger and Natasha, explaining that they had placed a hidden camera above the mirror facing the bar, telling them where he wanted them to stand so the camera would catch them and anyone that came within their space.

"I've got four other guys in there, you'll never know who they are," he said, "so don't even try to find them. Everyone will be watching you. Just wait there until our guy approaches, then you," now looking at Natasha, "give the alert."

"How?"

He pulled out a tiny microphone hooked to a small battery pack. "Lift up your vest."

Natasha raised the material to just below her breasts.

Striker placed the almost-flat battery pack below her left breast and began taping it in place.

Natasha drew herself up when his hands touched her skin. "I'm a little ticklish," she said, when he glanced at her.

Striker left the cord dangling. "I'll let you pull it up."

Natasha turned her back on everyone and reached down inside the vest. She pulled the cord between her breasts and left the microphone dangling outside, then turned back around.

"Where do you want it?"

Striker studied her upper attire. "It'd help if I had more area to work with," he said, almost to himself.

"Well thanks a lot."

Striker grinned. "I'm talking about that vest not offering much of a hiding area."

Natasha looked away. "Oh."

Striker reached forward and pulled the material away to expose the swell of a breast. "Okay, we'll put it there. The vest kind of clings there."

While he taped it in place, Natasha's face reddened at his hands touching her. He noticed and grinned a little.

"I've done this a hundred times or more."

The look she gave him was unreadable. "Yeah, but not to me."

After he was finished, Striker smoothed the vest back in place. "Twist around a little," he said. Natasha complied, and he watched to make sure no wires were exposed. "Lean over," he instructed, and she did as he requested. "Okay, I think that'll work."

After Pit parked the van across the street from the bar, Striker turned to Natasha and Roger. "We'll be watching from here. Just do what I told you, stay in place, wait for him to approach you, then give me the signal."

"You never said what signal," Natasha said.

"We need a code word, something you wouldn't say in a normal conversation."

"You're talking about Nattie, man," Pit said. "She doesn't have normal conversations."

Natasha didn't seem offended by his observation. "I know. When he comes up, I'll introduce myself as Roger's girlfriend. If he grabs the bag and takes off without saying anything, I'll yell he's got it or something like that."

Striker glanced at her skirt. "Where's your cell?"

Natasha reached down into the side of her boot and plucked it out.

"What about your gun?"

She pointed to her left, inner-thigh region.

Striker studied the slight protrusion. It looked awfully uncomfortable resting the way she had it, but he liked how she had hidden the bulge. He gave her a respectful look. "That's good."

Striker glanced around. "Any questions?"

No one responded.

"Okay, let's roll."

Inside the bar, Natasha and Roger made a place for themselves within camera range. Pit, Bigun, and Striker remained in the van to watch the video, listening to Natasha and Roger discuss whether they should buy a drink or not. Natasha suggested they order something like iced tea, which would look like an alcoholic beverage, to appear as if they were there drinking and not be so conspicuous by just standing at a bar.

"Good point, man," Pit said.

Striker studied the people moving in and out of their space. Natasha appeared right at home, blending in with the partying crowd, but Roger stuck out like a sore thumb.

An average-looking, dark-haired man gave Natasha the once-over while sidling in between her and Roger.

"Here we go," Striker said.

The man smiled at Natasha. "Hey, baby."

She ignored him.

"That's one fine vest you got on there." He reached out as if to pull the material away so he could see her breasts.

Natasha smacked his hand away without even looking at him.

"Ooh, scrappy lady. I like that," he said.

Natasha wasn't sure if this was their guy or not. "There something you need?"

"Baby, you got all kinds of thing I need."

Pickup! Natasha glanced at Roger, who was watching her, and shook her head. He placed his foot on the sports bag at his feet.

The man made it a point to step back and look Natasha over from that angle, then turned back to the bar.

She was growing tired of this. "Do you mind?"

"Yeah, I mind real good."

He reached out and cupped one hip. Before he even had a chance to squeeze, Natasha had her hand in his crotch, in a vice-grip.

The man made a mewling sound in his throat.

Roger opened his mouth, surprised.

"Oh, dude!" Pit said, sounding happy.

Striker leaned closer to the monitor and swore.

"Next time, you might want to think before you put your hands on a woman," Natasha said in a low voice, stepping right up against him and twisting a little.

The man issued a high-shrilled scream.

The bar grew quiet as everyone turned to see who was making that god-awful noise.

Natasha got in his face. "'Cause next time, I just might have the inclination to yank that nasty old thing off, put an end to your misery." She twisted again and the man went down on one knee.

Natasha put her foot on his chest and pushed him away. She watched him topple over, his hands to his crotch. "Glad you understand." She turned her back on him.

"You go, girl!" Pit and Bigun said together, high-fiving each other.

Striker looked heavenward.

A short time later, Natasha noticed an older man next to her, giving her the eye. She cast him a dark look to send the message, get out of here.

He came closer, leaned over the bar, and looked back at her.

She ignored him.

"You got some nice legs on you," he said.

Natasha rolled her eyes at Roger.

"Nice butt, too."

She tried to act bored.

"Nice all over, I'd say."

She turned her back on him.

"I do like long-legged redheads," the man said.

Natasha glared over her shoulder, giving attitude. "Yeah, but the question of the day is, do long-legged redheads like you back?"

"You want to find out?"

She looked away.

"So, I was just wondering if, you know, the collar and cuffs match."

Natasha turned one hand his way, held the index, middle, and ring fingers up. "Read between the lines, ass-hole."

Striker shook his head at the monitor, trying to ignore Pit and Bigun's laughter.

The man didn't seem put off by her gesture. "So it's like that, huh? Well, I'm flexible. What's your price?"

Natasha glanced away from Roger's shocked face. "Price?"

"Yeah. Say I want you to blow me, what's it gonna cost me?"

Natasha turned and gave him her full attention.

"Here we go, dude," Bigun said.

Natasha was offended. "You want me to blow you?"

He gave her a lecherous look. "You got what it takes, I got what you need."

Natasha reached out, grabbed his shirt, pulled him closer. "Come here."

"Damnit!" Striker raved.

"I got something I want to show you," she said to the man, who was grinning lecherously. "You want to know whether the collar and cuffs match? Well, look here."

Pit and Bigun elbowed each other, their eyes on the monitor.

Natasha began to raise her skirt in a slow, sensual manner.

Roger couldn't resist watching with a fascinated look on his face.

She pulled up the material to reveal a swatch of white satin beneath, a small gun holstered at her left upper thigh.

Striker lunged to his feet in frustration.

Natasha's hand caressed the weapon resting there. "You want me to blow you?"

The man's eyes widened in terror.

"Sure, I'll blow you. I'll blow your frigging head off if you don't get out of my sight." She pushed him backward.

He fell into the man behind him, who shoved him out of the way. After giving Natasha an insolent look, he left.

"Oh, yeah, man, she's the one!" Pit said.

Striker rubbed his face. He should have known better than to set Natasha loose in a bar.

Natasha was growing restless when a tall guy wearing a cowboy hat stepped up beside her. She turned and caught him looking at her. He smiled and tipped his hat. She smiled back, appreciating his good looks.

"How-do," he said.

Natasha wondered who said how-do this day and age. "How-do yourself."

"I hope you don't take offense at my saying so, ma'am, but you sure do have a nice size on you."

Natasha glanced at Roger, then back to the man. "Right back at you, cowboy."

Striker leaned closer to the monitor. "Is she flirting with him?"

Pit and Bigun ignored him, waiting for what was coming next.

The man leaned an arm on the bar. "You from around these parts?"

Natasha nodded, liking his accent. "Let me see, South Georgia, right?"

He grinned.

"I do love men with deep Southern accents."

"She is flirting!" Striker said.

"Shhh, dude," Bigun said.

Natasha was smiling at the cowboy. "So what brings you into this neck of the woods?"

"Just passing through. I'm with the rodeo that's in town, you know, down at the Thompson Boling Arena."

"Rodeo rider, huh?"

The cowboy grinned.

Natasha leaned back and affected her own cowboy stance. "Yeah, well, I've ridden a bull or two in my time," she said in a slow drawl.

The man laughed.

"What the hell is she flirting with him for?" Striker said.

"Hell, man, she ain't flirtin', she's just settin' him up," Pit said.

"Yeah, dude, bringing him in for the kill," Bigun added.

Natasha placed her hand on Roger's arm. "This is my boyfriend, Roger."

The man nodded in Roger's direction.

"Wait, is that the signal?" Striker said.

Pit was growing irritated Striker wasn't keeping his mouth shut. "No, man. She said she'd say she was Roger's girlfriend."

The cowboy was leaning in toward Natasha and Roger, telling them he was looking for a little action, maybe they could help him out with that.

"What kind of action are you looking for?" Roger said.

Natasha tapped him with her foot, sending him a look, trying to convey the message, don't even go there.

Roger didn't get it.

"Well, now, I don't rightly know. I was thinking about something along the lines of maybe a ménage à trois," the cowboy said, sounding French.

Striker threw his hands in the air. "Where the hell are these nuts coming from?"

"Hell, man, Nattie's in there. She attracts guys like that all the time," Pit said.

Striker glanced at him, then back to the screen.

Natasha was standing straight and facing the man.

"Oh, shit," Striker said.

Natasha leaned toward the cowboy. "As in the three of us?"

"Yes, ma'am."

"Ménage à trois doing what?"

"You, me, your boyfriend, you know, getting it on."

Natasha played innocent. "Getting what on?"

He flashed her a rakish grin. "In a sexual way."

Natasha thought for a moment. "How exactly would that work? I've never done that before."

Roger kicked her this time.

The man stared at Natasha for a long moment, unsure if she was serious or not. "Well, you know, him at one end, me at the other, or him in front, me in back. However you want to work it."

Natasha tried to look unconvinced.

"I can promise you a real good time."

She glanced at Roger and flashed him a grin, then turned back to the cowboy. "Well, let's see what you got."

Pit and Bigun hooted.

The man stepped back.

"You're promising me a good time, so pull that thing on out of there," Natasha said, her voice rising. "Let me see what you're offering here, put it on the table, so to speak."

"What the hell is she doing?" Striker said.

Pit and Bigun ignored him.

The area around Natasha and Roger grew quiet, everyone watching to see what was going to develop.

The man waved his hand toward his crotch area, his face growing red. "You're asking me to show you my…"

"Well, you made a promise I don't know if you can keep. Of course, I'm asking you to show me what you're claiming is going to give me a good time."

"I think maybe I made a mistake," the cowboy said, skulking away.

"Yeah, you're a mistake, all right! One hell of a big, bad mistake, you faker!"

Seeing nothing was going to transpire, the bar grew noisy again.

Natasha turned to Roger. "What the hell did you kick me for?"

A few minutes later, Natasha was carrying on a conversation with Roger, who was wondering if maybe they ought to just give it up, it looked like their man wasn't going to show, when she felt movement to her side. She glanced in that direction and was staring at a stocky, scruffy-looking guy wearing a leather vest and blue-jeans. His long, strawberry-blond hair, beard, and mustache were scraggly and uncombed. His most outstanding feature was his huge, protuberant potbelly. Natasha groaned to herself. Biker!

He smiled at her, revealing nicotine-stained teeth. "Hey, Red, let me buy you a beer."

Sending him a tight smile, Natasha put her hand in Roger's. "I'm with my boyfriend. Get lost."

The man leaned around Natasha to stare at Roger, then emitted a short, barking laugh. "A girl like you with a weasel like that? Nah, I don't think so."

Natasha straightened.

Pit and Bigun nudged one another.

"Here we go," Striker said, with resignation.

Natasha was staring at the man's gut. "Nice tool shed you got going there."

He grinned as if proud. "I got some pretty heavy equipment, gotta keep it covered."

"Heavy equipment, is it?"

"Yes, ma'am."

"You know how to use that equipment?"

He leaned toward her. "Bet I can handle my equipment better than that weasel you're with."

Natasha glanced at Roger and gave him a smile, angry at the hurt look in his eyes. "This guy has his own—what was the word you used? Oh, yes, weasel."

Pit and Bigun guffawed.

"And let me tell you something, fatso, he knows how to use his weasel to the extreme, you got that? He is, without a doubt, the best. In fact, every time he pulls that weasel of his out, I swoon with anticipation. I mean, dude, he's so good, every time I think about that weasel of his, I start to come." She paused. "Oh, no," she gasped, "now you've got me thinking about it. Oh, shoot." She held on to the bar, threw her head back and closed her eyes. "Oh, God," she said in an ecstatic way.

The biker stepped back, creating space between the two of them.

Roger glanced around with an uncomfortable expression on his face.

Natasha shuddered, leaned her head down into the bar and stomped her right foot three times. She looked back up at the biker. "Oh, man, that was so good," she said. "Was it good for you?" followed by, "You got a cigarette?"

Pit and Bigun's laughter followed Striker into the bar. He stood beside Natasha, who was back to discussing with Roger whether they should leave or not; it was now over an hour past the meeting time.

Natasha caught sight of Striker in her peripheral vision and glanced at him, then away. "You're not supposed to be in here, remember? He'll probably recognize you."

Striker leaned on the bar. "I'm calling quits on this anyway."

Natasha gave him her full attention. "Why?"

"You've manhandled two men now not to mention the dare and faked orgasm. You're starting to draw some attention."

Natasha looked around the bar. More than a few people were watching her and Striker, some grinning, waiting to see what was going to happen with this dude.

"Well, what the heck was I supposed to do? Let those guys cop their stupid feels, play nice-nice with scum like that?"

"I thought she handled herself pretty well," Roger said.

Natasha smiled at him. "I love you, Roger."

Striker didn't like the way Roger was looking at her. "Okay, we're leaving. It's been over an hour, he hasn't shown, or if he did, he got scared off by Natasha beating up on everybody, so there's no point in staying any longer."

Natasha gave Striker a pouty look. "And just when I was starting to have fun."

Striker stepped back and waited.

"Come on, Roger," Natasha said. "Daddy thinks we've been out too late."

Smiling, Roger reached down and retrieved the bag, then followed Natasha, with Striker bringing up the rear.

The bar erupted in cheers when they left.

Pit and Bigun grinned at Natasha when she climbed in the van.

"Hey, dudette, that was some orgasm," Bigun said.

Natasha dropped into a swivel seat. "Well, it made me mad what he said about Roger. Roger's a great lover, that guy had no reason to poke fun at him."

The van grew silent.

Striker's brow developed deep furrows. This was a violation of company policy if she had slept with her man. He turned and glanced at Roger, whose face was bright red.

"You know this for a fact?"

Natasha began pulling off her boots. "What?"

Sitting down across from her, Striker gave her an intent look, trying to control his anger. "That Roger's a great lover. There something we need to talk about here?"

"Well, I don't know that for a fact, but I know that."

The four men watched her, prompting her explanation.

"Most women can tell from the get-go whether or not a guy's going to be a good lover," Natasha said. "I mean, okay, take Roger, he's a very sensitive, caring guy. He's the type of man that it would be important to him for his woman to have a good time. You know, his agenda would be to please her. And Pit and Bigun here, they're fun dudes, they know how to have a good time, so it's a given that they're great lovers, too, although in a different vein than Roger is."

Pit and Bigun nodded at one another.

"And you," Natasha said, staring at Striker, "you're into this power thing, and a lot of women get off on that, you know." She paused for a moment. Oh, shoot, was that what attracted her to him? Please, God, don't let that be it. She noticed they were all waiting expectantly, so continued. "Plus you've got a temper which shows you're a pretty passionate guy, and you just have that look that tells any and all you've had a lot of practice, so I'd say you're probably excellemente in that department."

Striker didn't know how to take that.

"And the deciding factor for any man is generally that those guys who go around bragging about their accomplishments in the bedroom usually don't have any, that's why they talk about it so much. The ones who keep what goes on sexually to themselves are usually the ones who would have something to brag about but don't need to. And all of you guys are like that, you keep the sex bragging to yourselves."

"I know one thing, dudette," Bigun said, from the front. "If temper has anything to do with it, you got us all beat."

Pit snorted.

Natasha was busy untaping the battery pack and, without thinking, said, "Yeah, well, I don't do that anymore."

Each man watched her, wondering about her statement.

Natasha noticed this and blushed.

"Oh, dudette, you're not telling us you've gone butch, are you?" Bigun sounded forlorn.

Natasha gave him a small smile. "No, I'm not that way. I like men, I like men a lot. I just choose to, you know, not have that sort of a relationship."

Aware Striker was regarding her, Natasha kept her eyes on the tape adhering the microphone to her skin as she slowly peeled it away. *Say something!* her mind screamed. "Gosh, I'm hungry, you think we can get a hamburger?"

CHAPTER 11

▼

Striker was driving to Roger's to check in for the day when Scott alerted him on his two-way. "Yeah?" he said into his phone.

"I'm on my way to Roger's. You going to be there this morning?"

"I'm headed that way now."

"Good. There's something we need to talk about," Scott said, and was gone.

Striker found everyone gathered in Roger's office. Natasha was sitting in a chair in front of Roger's desk with the cordless phone in her hands, staring out the window. The other men were scattered around the room, looking uncomfortable.

"What's going on?"

No one answered.

"What's wrong?" Striker said, wondering why Scott had wanted the meeting.

Roger, Pit, and Bigun glanced toward Natasha.

Striker stood beside Natasha to draw her attention, but she ignored him. He settled in the chair next to her and touched her shoulder.

"You all right?"

Natasha startled, then glanced his way. Shrugging, she gave him a quick smile.

Striker turned and glowered at Scotty.

Scott gave him a perplexed look. "I didn't do anything. I just got here myself."

Striker shifted toward Natasha. "Is there anything we need to talk about?"

She straightened in the chair and looked around. "Not that I know of."

"Everything's fine? No problems?"

"Yeah, everything's fine here."

"What'd your mom say, dudette?" Bigun said.

Now Striker got it.

Natasha leaned back in the chair, looking upset. "I don't think she wants to be my mom anymore. She says she's spent the last twenty-five years taking care of other people, been a wife and mother that long, and somewhere along the way she's lost sense of who she is and what she wants from life."

She glanced at Striker, then away. "As if I'm nothing to her. As if raising me and taking care of me all that time was just a waste of her time."

"Hey, Nattie, that's not what she meant," Roger said.

"She's just going through a mid-life crisis," Scott said. "My mom did the same thing. She'll get through it and everything will be okay. She's just got to figure out what she wants to do from this point on. I mean, you're emancipated, you don't really need her anymore, she's probably looking around, wondering what happened."

Natasha sighed and put the phone on the desk, then seemed to realize the others were there. "What's going on?"

Striker turned to Scott, who sat down behind Roger's desk.

Scott's eyes traveled to Natasha, then on to Pit and Bigun. "Preseason tournaments start next weekend."

"What tournaments?" Striker said.

"Soccer." Natasha's attention was focused on Scott. "You are going to let us play, aren't you?"

"That's why I'm here." Scott addressed Striker. "They're all three starters for our firm's team and we'll lose for sure if they're not in the game."

"So what's the problem?"

"We'll be pulling them away from Roger for most of the day, and I didn't know how you wanted to handle that."

"I'd like to go watch them play," Roger said. "They've been letting me practice with them, and I've kind of developed an interest for the game."

Natasha smiled at him.

"I guess Roger will be there, then," Striker said. "I'll go with him. Don't worry about it, I'll take care of things."

Natasha's eyes remained on Scott. "Who are we scheduled to play first?"

Scott grimaced. "The team from Maryville."

Natasha grinned at her two teammates. "Oh, dudes, we are so going to beat the crap out of that team."

"Yeah, well, you're gonna get the crap beat out of you, you know that," Scott said, staring at Natasha.

She shrugged like she didn't really care about that.

The day of tournaments, Striker drove to the soccer fields with Roger, wondering why he had never taken the time to watch any of these games. He had been surprised when Scott told him Natasha was a player. At the office, he had her pegged as one of those dainty, fragile women who cried if they broke a fingernail but was beginning to find out that wasn't the real Natasha.

When they arrived, the team members were gathered on the field, some stretching, some kicking at balls, some standing around talking. Scott was on the sidelines going over the other team's roster with his assistant coach. Striker and Roger walked over to join them, looking around.

Natasha was kicking balls at the net, trying to get them past the goalie. When he stepped out of the box and signaled, she sauntered over to him. Striker recognized the man: Mark Benton, a young, good-looking, somewhat cocky guy who worked as one of their investigators. Striker wondered about their relationship when the goalie rested his arms over Natasha's shoulders, drew his face close to hers, and grinned like an idiot.

Scott looked up, searched the field, and yelled for Natasha to come to the sidelines.

Striker watched Natasha jog toward them, wearing a sports bra and soccer shorts, long socks over her shin guards. Admiring her athletic build, he noticed she had a nice, subtle six-pack going on her abdomen.

Natasha smiled at Roger, then directed her attention to Striker. "So the big man has finally decided to grace us with his presence. I'm so honored." She gave an irreverent bow.

The slight flare in Striker's eyes told her he didn't appreciate her humor.

Ignoring him, she turned to Scott, who handed her a banana. "Come on, Scotty, I eat that thing, I'll throw it up."

"You don't eat it, you'll run out of energy ten minutes into this game, and I need you in there as long as I can keep you in."

Natasha sighed, then began to peel the banana, listening to her coach.

"Okay, now, you know they're going to come after you, you know they're going to make you pay for what you did last time we played against them."

She gave Scott a look.

"What?"

"You're the one who told me to take that forward out, you know."

"Yeah, well, he was killing us."

She shrugged.

"It's going to be pay-back time. They're out for blood, if what I'm hearing is right."

Natasha munched on the banana. "Well, how was I to know that guy was going to be such a weenie and leave the game over a busted lip? Shoot, if he'd fallen the way I tripped him to, all he'd have gotten was a sore tailbone."

"You forgot about the broken nose."

Natasha grimaced. "Oh, yeah. Well, fair's fair, I guess." She didn't seem concerned to any great extent.

"I already talked to Pit and Bigun. They'll try to keep them off you as much as they can, but some will get past, so you'll be doing a lot of dodging out there today."

Natasha handed the banana peel to Scott, bent over, placed her hands on the ground, and stretched out.

"Just play your position. Keep the aggression down, don't pay back."

She straightened up. "What?"

"Shrug it off. They're mad at you, they're gonna take pokes, try to provoke you, try to get you to give them permission to really hurt you. Don't let them do that. I need you to stay in the game."

Natasha walked toward the coolers while considering this. She pulled a water bottle from the crushed ice, twisted off the top, and drank. When she rejoined them, she said, "You're the coach; if that's what you want me to do, I can handle it."

Striker drew back, surprised.

The referees stepped onto the field and blew their whistles.

Natasha handed her water to Roger, then grinned at everyone while pulling her hair back into a ponytail. "Wish me luck," she said, and trotted onto the field to join the goalie talking to the refs.

Scott noticed Striker's expression. "What?"

"What kind of game are you playing here? Taking players out, letting them hurt her?"

Scott shrugged. "Hey, Nattie's played soccer all her life, she knows that's part of the game."

"She put herself through college on a soccer scholarship, you know," Roger said.

Striker didn't know.

Scott nodded. "She's the best sweeper I've ever seen. She's quick, by far the fastest runner we got out there. She knows how to play the field, knows what needs to be done to win."

"But let them hurt her?"

"It's a co-ed team and those guys can get mean. Well, so can Nattie." Scott grinned. "You'll see," he said, then couldn't help adding, "If you had shown a little support and come to some of our games, you'd know what I'm talking about."

Natasha and the goalie jogged back to the sidelines. Natasha grabbed her jersey and pulled it on, then joined the team in a huddle to say a prayer together.

Striker counted bodies. There were three other women besides Natasha playing for their side. He studied the other team, noting there were only two women included in that group. The men over there looked huge. Striker didn't like the looks they kept casting his team's way.

After the prayer, there was a lot of high-fiving, grunting, psyching each other up, and slapping of butts as the team headed for their zones. Natasha took her position in front of the goalie, grinning when Pit walked over to her, grabbed her by the neck, and gave out a war cry.

Bigun yelled, "Number 13!" She looked at him. "You!" he boomed, pointing at her. Natasha nodded, as if she understood.

From the outset, it was clear to everyone that the other team's goal was to get to Natasha. Pit and Bigun hovered close, trying to protect her as much as they could, but they weren't having much luck. Striker watched in awe as time after time the offensive player headed straight for Natasha, waiting on her to go after the ball, only to get kicked, elbowed, pushed, and tripped by other opposing players closing in. Fouls were being called right and left. But she took it and got up each time, acting unconcerned, staying in position, protecting her goal.

Twenty minutes into the game, Striker was mad. "Get her out of there," he told Scott, who was yelling at their offenders to get off their lazy butts and move that ball downfield.

Scott glanced at him. "What?"

"Get her out. She's getting the crap beat out of her. Pull her off the field."

"Nattie's tough. She can take it."

"She's a woman, for Pete's sake, getting beat up by men twice her size. Pull her out, Scott!"

"If Nattie needs to come out, she'll let me know." Scott turned his back on Striker to watch the game.

Ten minutes later, two opposing players managed to sandwich Natasha between them. One of them tripped her, then pushed her forward, causing her to land face-forward. The other player cleated her in the hamstring, trying to make it appear as if he had tripped. The referees' whistles shrilling in the air signaled they saw through his ruse.

Natasha curled up on the ground, holding her leg to her chest.

Striker stepped onto the field, but Scott reached out and pulled him back.

Scott's eyes were on Pit, who was kneeling by Natasha. "If it's bad, Pit will let us know."

Pit glanced toward Scott and waved his hand.

"Damn!" Scott threw down his clipboard and headed toward Natasha.

Striker joined him.

Natasha was sitting up, holding her leg against her chest, saying, "Shit, shit, shit." Tears were falling down her face. There were grass stains all over her clothes. Her chin was bleeding where she had collided with the ground, scratches covered her arms and legs, and blood was running from her knee into her sock.

Scott leaned over her. "How bad is it?"

"Damnit to friggin' hell, he cleated my hamstring," Natasha said, between gritted teeth. She rested her forehead against her knee.

"Can you walk?"

"I don't know. Let me rest a second. It's burning like fire."

Striker knelt beside her and put his hand on her ankle.

Natasha jerked and gave him a startled look.

"Let me see." He ran his hand up her leg, extending it.

Natasha lay back on the ground with her arms over her face.

Striker fought the urge to go beat up the guy that did this to her. Using his large hands, he massaged the back of her thigh, ignoring Natasha's protests. She finally stopped and let him do what he needed to, raising up on elbows to watch.

"You got some spasming going on here," Striker said. "You might have torn it."

Natasha flashed him a stubborn look. "No, no, I did not tear it."

One of the refs walked over. "You need assistance?"

Natasha shook her head. "No, I'm fine. I was just getting up." She sat up, then struggled to her feet with Scott and Striker supporting her on either side. As soon as they released her, she collapsed on the injured leg.

Striker scooped her up in his arms.

Before he could take a step, Natasha said, "Stop!"

He looked at her.

"Put me down, Striker," she said, in a low voice.

"What?"

"Don't carry me off the field. Don't do that. I have to walk off."

He raised his eyebrows.

"If I don't walk off, they'll think I'm weak. Just put me down, okay, but what-ever you do, don't let go. Let me lean against you a little till I work out this cramp."

"I don't think it's a cramp, Natasha."

She stared at him.

He set her on her feet.

Natasha leaned against him, holding her foot in the air, then wrapped her arms around his waist. "Help me off."

Natasha hobbled off the field with Striker's assistance. A cheer went up the moment she began to move.

The game resumed as soon as they reached the sidelines. After Striker helped Natasha ease to the ground, Scott motioned over their trainer, who had an icebag in hand. He knelt down and bound it to her leg with tape. Natasha fished in her sports bag, came up with a bottle of Ibuprofen, and downed four. She gave Roger a thankful smile when he handed her a water bottle. After drinking, she lay back and put her hands over her eyes.

Striker knelt beside her. "You need to go to the hospital."

Natasha took her hands away. "What?"

"You need to have that looked at, make sure it's not torn."

She sat up. "Hell no!" Using Roger, who was on her other side, as leverage to help her stand, she put weight on her foot, glaring at Striker. She walked around, stiffly at first but limbering up after awhile. Natasha did that for a few minutes, all the while darting looks at Striker, who was closely watching the way she limped on her leg. She began to argue with Scott about putting her back in the game, pointing out to him that the other team had scored a point since she had been on the sidelines.

Half-time was called. Natasha remained standing the entire time, walking around to work out the stiffness. When the referees signaled they were ready to start second half, she tore off the tape around the icepack and, without saying a word to anyone, trotted onto the field.

Striker watched her go, shaking his head. "She's crazy."

Scott was observing her in an appreciative way. "Yeah, that's Nattie, all right."

Striker's attention now was on Natasha, not the game. He watched her on the field, admiring the skill she displayed, her stubborn refusal to give into an injury. It took her awhile to limber up enough to where she was showing speed again. The other team left her alone until she started interfering with their efforts to score, then went after her. Striker wondered when in hell she was ever going to get enough.

Halfway through the second half, an opposing player tried to make it look as though he was kicking at the ball and missed but instead kicked Natasha in the stomach. She dropped to her knees, doubled over.

"Shit!" Striker said.

Pit once more knelt beside her, then signaled Scott.

Striker walked onto the field.

Natasha was on her side, trying to catch her breath.

"Stretch out," Striker said. "Don't panic."

Blood was running from her lip, and Striker reached out to wipe it away, fearful she was bleeding from her stomach. He was relieved to see she wasn't.

They waited for Natasha to catch her breath. She sat up, wheezing, and glanced at Scott, wiping her mouth.

"Damnation! I think I bit my lip. This payback's pure hell, Scotty."

Striker was angry at the abuse she had been taking. "Don't you think you've had enough? Don't you think you need to quit this shit?"

"I'm just paying my dues, Striker. They'll stop eventually."

"Hell, the game's almost over. What makes you think they're going to quit?"

Natasha turned to Scott. "When's it my turn?"

Scott shrugged. "You gave them the chance, but they're wanting more than what we're willing to give, I guess. It's up to you."

Natasha grinned. "Oh, yeah!"

"Just try not to get taken out," Scott warned.

Natasha stood and held her fists in the air. "We got us a war here!"

Her teammates hooted and hollered at this, then gathered around Natasha to do their psyching ritual once more.

Striker walked off the field, shaking his head. "What is this, guerrilla soccer?"

"You ain't seen nothing yet," Scott said. "Nattie's just declared war. All hell's gonna break loose now."

For the next ten minutes, Striker watched Natasha give back what she got. The refs let her get away with it at first, figuring she deserved a little payback, until she took a player out. The opposing team had a breakaway, and Natasha streaked after the man heading away from her. She didn't try to catch up with him as Striker thought she would, instead angled off toward the sidelines. Striker watched her run, appreciating the pure beauty she displayed, her body's fluid movements. When she saw the player getting ready to set up his shot, she cut back in his direction, a little ahead of him. Placing herself between the man and the goal, she went down several feet from him, extending her legs, trying for the ball. She kicked it away, then slid beneath him. The man tripped, somehow flipped into the air, and landed on his ankle. The scream he gave was piercing, pure agony.

Natasha ran over and knelt beside him, then stood and waved for his coach. She leaned over the man, talked to him for a minute, then came to the sidelines.

"I'm dead," she said, approaching Scott. "His ankle's broken. He landed right on it when I tripped him."

Scott nodded.

They watched the injured player being carried off the field. His teammates hovered together, glowering at Natasha.

Natasha noticed Striker watching her. "I didn't mean to do that. We just got tangled."

"Yeah, I saw."

Scott stepped up to her. "We've only got ten minutes left. You need to stay out."

"No. We're tied, Scott, and now they get a penalty kick. I'm not going to give this up."

"They think that was deliberate. They won't play nice now. You know that."

"He's right," Striker said. "You need to stay put."

Natasha gave him a flustered look. "You're not my coach, so just keep out of this."

Striker's jaw muscles clenched. "I might not be your coach, but I'm your employer, and I think you need to stay off that field."

She gave him a challenging look. "Make me."

Scott stepped between them. "Hey, hey, hey. Let's not get into a fight on the sidelines here." He turned to Natasha. "You're going to get hurt if you go back out there, Nattie. You know that."

Ignoring him, Natasha stepped onto the field.

"She's dead," Scott said, sounding weary.

Striker got in his face. "Get her back here. You're her coach, she has to do what you tell her to, pull her off the damn field!"

Scott was surprised by his outburst. "Since when did you get so all-fired protective?"

Striker watched the game resume, silently praying the time would pass and Natasha would make it through.

It only took the opposing team five minutes and looked innocent enough, but everyone knew it wasn't. The team's best kicker waited until Natasha was a few feet away from him, advancing on the ball, then kicked it, aiming straight for her face. Natasha turned at the last second, but the ball whacked her on the side of the head and she crumpled to the ground like an empty sack.

Knowing this could be bad, Striker didn't wait for the signal. When he reached Natasha, sprawled on the ground with her eyes closed, he shook her shoulder. "Natasha."

She made a small moaning sound.

He opened her eyes one at a time and was relieved to see the pupils dilate. He looked at the side of her head, then checked her ear for blood.

Scott joined him and lightly slapped her on the face.

Natasha opened her eyes. "What?"

"You all right?" Scott said.

Striker leaned toward her, holding out four fingers. "How many fingers do you see?"

Natasha frowned. "Y'all sound funny." She sat up and leaned her head into her knees. "Uh-oh."

"What's wrong?" Scott said.

She put her hand over her ear and closed her eyes. "I feel a little woozy, Scotty. Oh, shoot, I think I'm going to be sick." She leaned over and threw up the banana.

Striker moved to pick her up.

She put her hand against his chest. "No, just give me a minute."

One of the refs joined them. "She all right?"

Natasha wiped her face and mouth with her jersey, and Striker grew angry at the red welts on her abdomen. Raising her jersey, he saw her back sported them as well. He touched her arm.

"Come on, I'll help you stand."

Natasha stood, swaying. "Dang, Striker, quit moving on me."

"Close your eyes, it'll help. I've got you. Just lean against me, I'll take you off."

Natasha let Striker guide her to the sidelines and tried to sit down.

"I don't think so. This time you're going to the hospital whether you want to or not," Striker said, keeping her upright.

Scott was watching Natasha with a worried look. "Which one are you going to?"

Striker told him.

"I'll be there as soon as the game's over."

Striker noticed Roger looking with concern at Natasha. "Stay with Scotty," he told him. "He'll bring you when he comes."

Striker started to move toward the parking lot, but Natasha was having a hard time of it, so he picked her up and carried her to his car.

She didn't say a word of protest this time.

Striker was sitting in the waiting room of the emergency room when Roger and Scott entered, followed by Pit and Bigun and the rest of their team.

Scott settled into the seat next to him. "How's Nattie?"

Striker shrugged. "I'm still waiting for them to let me go back there. They kicked me out."

He didn't tell them about the hissy fit he pulled when he first brought Natasha in, demanding she be seen at once, giving the nurses hell over what was taking so long.

Scott cast a worried look toward the examining rooms. "How bad is she?"

"You want my opinion, I'd say a perforated eardrum, maybe a concussion. But I'm not a doctor. Let's hope that's all."

Scott nodded.

"Who won?"

Scott grinned. "We did. We got a penalty kick off that foul and scored."

A few minutes later, a nurse informed Striker he could go to the examining room. Glancing at the others, he left to find his willful employee.

Natasha was sitting on the examining table, watching a nurse apply antiseptic to the cuts on her legs. She had a band-aid over her chin and a gauze pad over one knee. Striker noticed the beginning hues of a bruise on the side of her cheek. When he took her hand, she gave him a smile so radiant he thought his heart might have stopped for just a second. He raised his eyebrows at her.

"Perforated eardrum," she said.

"And slight concussion," the nurse added.

"Nothing they can do for the eardrum, just have to give it time to heal," Natasha said.

The nurse told her to roll over onto her stomach, then began applying antiseptic to the backs of her legs.

Striker placed a hand over the huge contusion that was already developing over her hamstring. Her skin felt hot. "That's got to hurt."

"I can take it," Natasha said into the pillow.

He smiled at her spunk.

She raised her head up. "Who won?"

"We did, off the penalty kick when that guy fouled you."

"All right!" Ignoring the nurse's look of consternation, Natasha rose to her knees, threw herself into Striker's arms, and hugged him. She quickly seemed to realize what she was doing and pulled away, giving him an uncomfortable look.

Striker ignored that. "The team's out there waiting on you."

Natasha turned to the nurse. "I can go, right? There's nothing else you need to do to me, right?"

The nurse smiled at her.

Natasha grinned. "I mean, no more prodding, poking, sticking needles in me? You're through having fun, right?"

The nurse shook her head and gathered up instruction sheets. "I'll go see if the doctor's ready to dismiss you." She handed papers to Striker on her way to the door. "Make sure your wife follows these directions."

Striker looked at Natasha.

She shrugged. "Don't ask me where that came from." She felt woozy and lay back down, then noticed Striker watching her. "What?"

Striker leaned against a table and crossed his arms. "I don't get you."

Natasha cocked her head at him, unsure what he meant.

"Did you enjoy that, what those guys were doing out there, all that rough-housing? I mean, what do you get out of that?"

Natasha made a face. "Oh, that. Actually, I hate that part of it, but I love the game. Besides, Striker, it looks worse than it actually is, you know."

"I doubt that. Look at all the bruises you got to show for it."

"Well, okay, but it's generally not that bad. Guys are usually pretty decent and respect they're dealing with a female. They hold back some, don't put as much power behind their moves as they could. And to be honest, I'd rather have some guy get aggressive with me than a woman soccer player. They can be mean and they know exactly what to do to cause the most pain."

Striker grinned at this revelation.

"I'm not kidding."

"I don't doubt it."

The nurse stuck her head in the door and directed her attention to Striker. "Your wife can go, but be sure she makes that appointment to see her ENT first thing Monday."

"I'll take care of it," Striker said.

"And read and follow carefully the instructions about dealing with a concussion," the nurse reminded Natasha.

Natasha smiled at her. "Sure thing."

Striker helped Natasha off the bed.

"Oh, boy," she said, swaying a little once she was standing.

"Here, kid, I'll help you out." Striker let her lean against him until the dizziness passed, wondering who in the hell this jock was they had working for them.

CHAPTER 12

▼

Striker was enjoying a leisurely lunch with a woman he saw from time to time, thinking he just might like to spend a couple of hours that afternoon with her, seeing as how nothing else was going on, when his phone bleeped. He opened the casing and keyed it to the phone mode. "Striker," he said into the mouthpiece.

Pit said, "Nattie and Roger are gonna go look for a dog."

"Look for what dog?"

"Nattie thinks Roger needs a dog around here, you know, a barker to alert him when someone's on the grounds that shouldn't be. So they're going to that pet adoption place in West Knoxville, see what's there."

Striker frowned. Didn't he suggest that very thing to Roger last year and hadn't Roger told him he was allergic to dogs?

"Where's Roger?"

"He's with Nattie in her jeep. They're leaving now."

"Follow them." Striker wondered about that until the woman placed her hand on his arm, directing his attention back to her.

Natasha and Roger climbed out of the jeep at the pet place and glanced around. Pit and Bigun pulled up beside them but chose to remain in their SUV, in the air-conditioning, until they went inside the store.

Natasha walked over to a grown Weimaraner tied to the back of a truck and began to pet the dog, cooing to him. She smiled at Roger, who had joined her.

"I had one of these when I was a kid. Called him Bradley."

"Pretty dog."

"Yeah, but they're hyper as hell. Between that dog and me, we managed to drive my mom totally nuts."

Roger grinned.

"Gosh, how I miss him." Natasha sounded sad.

Roger reached out to stroke the animal.

"You want a good watchdog, Roger, you might think about a Weimaraner. They're natural barkers, territorial and protective, not to mention intelligent and loyal to the max."

"He's a beaut, isn't he?"

A stocky man in black jeans and a dirty white t-shirt molded over his protuberant potbelly stepped out of the building. He paused when he saw Natasha and Roger at his truck, then walked over to them.

"You want to buy that dog?"

Natasha stood. "How much are you asking for him?"

"Five hundred."

The man untied the animal and held him close. The Weimaraner began whimpering and moving around.

Natasha knelt beside the dog to soothe him, running her hands over his back, chest, and legs. "He bark a lot?"

"Nah, he don't bark. He knows better."

Natasha's eyes narrowed. "He hyper any?" She rubbed the Weimaraner behind the ears, staring into his strange eyes.

"Hell, no. I beat that out of him a long time ago."

Natasha gave the man a chilling glare. "How old is he?"

"A little over a year."

"How long you had him?"

"I reckon I got him about six months ago."

"From here?"

"Nah, from that pet store in the mall."

Natasha rose and faced the man. "You the original owner?"

He glanced away.

"Who owned him before you?"

"Some little old lady lived in an apartment. She couldn't take care of him."

Natasha thought a minute. "You got papers?"

"Yep, in the truck here."

"Why'd you buy him?"

"Thought I'd breed the son of a bitch."

"And?"

Not liking all these questions, he gave her a defensive look. "Not having much success."

"Well, he's just a pup."

"Oh, he's old enough, all right."

The dog grew fidgety, and the man jerked on the collar, causing the Weimaraner to cough.

Natasha resisted the urge to put her hands around the man's throat and choke him just to show him what it felt like. "You don't have to be so rough with him, you know."

"I wasn't being rough." He pulled the dog closer. The canine tried moving away but was jerked back and made a hacking sound.

Natasha was having a hard time trying to ignore the rough treatment. "He been trained?"

"Not by me, but I think the first owner took him to obedience school."

"Let me take him for a minute." Natasha reached out and grabbed the restraining device. She talked to the Weimaraner while tugging on the leash, trying to get him to follow her. She walked around, giving commands, seeing what he could do. The dog, acting like he didn't know what in the world she wanted, danced around her, wagging his shortened tail and giving her happy looks.

Natasha was in love. Next thing she knew, a strap landed against the Weimaraner's hindquarters. The dog yelped and tried to get away from Natasha, who barely managed to control him. She glanced around and saw the dog's owner holding a wide, leather belt in his hand.

"Just hit him a few times, he'll do what you want," he said, doubling the belt.

Natasha tried moving closer to the Weimaraner, but he shied away. It upset her that the dog might be thinking she was the one who hit him.

"Roger," she called.

Roger walked toward Natasha, giving the man his own chilling glare.

"Take him for a minute, why don't you? See if you like him." Natasha handed the leash to her friend.

Natasha looked toward Pit and Bigun, who had their eyes closed, dozing with the air-conditioning on high and the radio blaring, unaware what was about to transpire.

"Give me the belt," Natasha said to the man in a mild voice.

He handed it over. "Like I told you, give him a few swats, he'll mind real good."

"Yeah?" Natasha swung the leather strap as if testing it, then brought it around and hit the dog's owner on the legs with it.

"Shit!" He danced backward out of reach.

She gathered it back. "How's that feel to you, ass-hole?"

"What the hell!" He gave her a menacing look.

"Yeah, come on, you jerk. Try to take this thing away from me, why don't you? Let's see who starts yelping now."

Roger glanced at the SUV and wished Pit and Bigun would do something here, but they were still oblivious to any goings-on other than what was inside their somewhat dense heads.

The man stalked toward Natasha, and as soon as he was within range, she struck him with the belt.

He did another dance. "Shit-fire!"

"Stings, huh? Well, how do you think it feels to a dog like that, hardly any fat covering their body, you lard-butt."

He gave her a mean look. "I'm gonna hurt you bad for that."

"Yeah? You think you can?"

Heaving a sigh, Roger walked over to the SUV.

"Give me that belt," the man said, advancing toward her.

Natasha backed away. "You want your belt? You want your belt? I'll give you your freakin' belt." She hit him with it once more.

He caught it and jerked it out of her hands.

Roger banged on Bigun's window, waking up both of the bodyguards, then pointed into the parking lot.

"Oh, man," Pit whined, opening the car door.

Watching the man double the belt, Natasha reached down and unstrapped her gun, then pulled it out and pointed it at him. "Go on, hit me with it. Go on, I dare you, you creep."

Bigun snatched up his cell and alerted Striker, who at that moment was rather inconvenienced.

At the second alert, he picked up his phone from the nightstand. "Striker," he said in a raspy voice.

"Oh, dude, Nattie's gone nuts." Bigun sounded worried.

Striker lay back on the bed and forgot all about the woman with him. He closed his eyes, wondering when exactly he had been appointed baby-sitter for Natasha.

"What's she doing?"

"Some dude's trying to hit her with his belt and she's got her gun pulled. Oh, dude! That fuck just hit her."

Striker sat up. "Where are you?"

"That pet place in West Knoxville."

"I'm on my way. Get over there and get her out of that situation." Striker lunged off the bed and began pulling on clothes.

The man had hit Natasha on her arm, the one that ended with the hand holding the gun. Her fingers went numb, and she dropped her .22, which skittered across the lot. Pit barreled toward the man, but Natasha stopped him by holding her left hand up and giving him an angry look. "This is my fight. Stay out of it."

Natasha's arm felt like it was on fire and she couldn't feel her fingers, although she tried not to reveal her discomfort to her adversary. "Okay, if that's the way you want to play it, that's fine with me. Come on, fatty, try that again."

Neither one noticed several faces inside the store pressed up against the window glass, watching them with looks of horrid fascination on their faces.

The man began to circle around her, twirling the belt in the air above his head. Natasha backed away, taunting him.

Bigun stepped between them.

Natasha stopped moving. "Get out of there."

"Striker told me to—"

The air went out of her balloon, hearing that. "Why the hell did you have to go and call Striker for?"

"We got us a situation here, dudette," Bigun said.

Natasha gave him a deadly glare. "One that I intend to remedy. And now, thanks to you, here comes another reprimand, maybe even a firing. Why the hell did you have to go and call Striker for?"

The man had stopped circling and was looking at them like they were nuts. "Who's Striker?"

"You don't want to know," Natasha said.

She glanced around. "Roger, you got five hundred bucks I can borrow?"

"Not borrow, but I'll give it to you."

Natasha took the time to smile a thank-you at him. "Put the dog in my jeep, then let me have it, please."

She looked at Pit and Bigun. "He knocked my gun out of my hand. I'd so appreciate it if you'd find it for me, and for the love of God quit calling Striker and telling on me!"

After giving her disgruntled looks, the two bodyguards began to search for her gun.

"Hold on a minute," Natasha said to her opponent, who was watching her with a wary look.

Natasha waited until Roger came back with his wallet and handed her five, one-hundred-dollar bills. She took them from him with her left hand and stuffed them into her right, then gave him a bright smile.

"Thanks, Roger. You're the best, you know that?"

Roger beamed at this.

Natasha looked over at the Weimaraner in the back seat of her jeep. She smiled at him and received a doggy smile back.

Natasha showed the man the palm containing the money. "You said you got the papers?"

"Yeah, in my truck there."

"Can Roger get them for me?"

He glanced from her to Roger, then back to her, seeming indecisive.

Natasha was growing impatient. "Well?"

"They're on the front seat there, in a manila envelope."

They watched Roger walk to the man's truck, open the door, and fish around on the front seat. He turned and held up a large mailing envelope. "This it?"

The man nodded.

"Make sure," Natasha said. "Open it up and make sure it says for a male Weimaraner. Check the date of birth, a little over a year ago."

They waited for Roger to pull out papers and glance through them.

After a few minutes, he looked back up. "Looks legit to me."

Natasha faced her nemesis. "What's his name?"

"Smitty."

She rolled her eyes. "What the hell are you doing naming a dog, especially one as special as a Weimaraner, Smitty?"

Her adversary looked like he didn't know how to answer that.

She turned and studied the dog. "His name's Brutus. What do you think, boy, you like that name?"

The Weimaraner responded with happy barks.

"He likes Brutus," she told the dog's owner.

"You think I give a fuck?"

Natasha watched him for a moment, then showed him the hand with the money. "You want it, fatso, come get it."

Roger rolled his eyes.

Tucking Natasha's gun in the waistband at the back of his pants, Pit joined Bigun to watch the show.

Natasha noticed her colleagues standing near. "Just a minute," she said to her opponent.

"Okay," she said to the bodyguards, "I'm calling this one. It's mine, stay out of it. He thinks he can take me, although I don't think so, but let's see if he can."

"Ten bucks says she takes him," Pit said in a low voice.

Bigun nodded.

The man was glaring at Natasha, who was giving tit for tat.

Natasha's voice was calm when she spoke. "Come on, bubble-gut, try to hit me with that damn, freaking belt again, let's see where it gets you."

Striker pulled into the parking lot and came to a screeching halt. No one noticed.

The man began walking toward Natasha, twirling the belt in the air. She watched his advance with a patience she did not feel.

Striker jumped out of the car and hurried toward them, cursing under his breath.

The man came closer to Natasha, who remained stationary, waiting on him.

"What the hell are you doing?" Striker yelled.

Everyone ignored him.

The man got within striking distance, brought the belt around, and swung it at her. He would have hit her if Natasha had not turned away at the last second. Then she was right at him, her leg behind his, and kicked his feet out from under him. He landed on his back with a whumping sound and lay on the ground wheezing, the breath knocked out of him.

Striker stood watching, admiring the speed at which she had moved away and then back into the man.

Natasha placed one foot on the man's arm, the one holding the belt, then looked toward the jeep. "Hey, Brutus."

The dog woofed once as if to say, "Yeah?"

"What do you think about this piece of crap?"

Brutus barked furiously.

"I agree. Well, boy, it's your decision, does he live or does he die?"

Striker shook his head.

The dog stared at Natasha, as if thinking.

"Take your time, Brutus, no hurry here."

Striker turned around so she couldn't see his smile.

"One bark he lives, two barks he dies," Natasha said.

The man squirmed, so she stepped down harder on his arm. He groaned in a wheezy sort of way.

Brutus barked once.

"You're such a good boy," Natasha said, in a loving tone.

She leaned down into the prone man's face. "You like to hit animals can't fight back, but you don't do so well with those of us that can. You got a major problem, ass-hole." She grabbed the belt with her left hand. "I'll take that."

She stood up and released him, then turned and began to saunter back to the jeep. Halfway there, she stopped, wheeled around, and returned. The man, still lying there, trying to catch his breath, gave her a baleful look. She opened her palm and watched the money drift over his body. "Thanks for the dog." Giving him a bright smile, she turned and walked away.

Striker was now standing at her jeep with arms crossed and a hard look in his eyes.

Natasha hesitated a fraction of a second in her movement toward her vehicle, then continued on, forcing her mouth to form a smile. "Hey, Striker."

She showed Brutus the belt. "You see this?"

The dog looked at it, then her.

"This will no longer be a part of your life, big boy. You've got me now." She took the belt to the outside garbage bin and threw it inside.

"You okay with that?" she said to the dog when she returned.

Brutus panted at her and wagged his tail.

Striker looked heavenward.

Roger grinned.

Natasha turned to Striker. "You come to help us pick out a dog?"

"You want to tell me what's going on here?"

"Just stopped a guy from beating on a dog." Natasha tried to act unconcerned.

"By pulling your gun."

She didn't answer.

"In a public place."

Natasha glanced away, rubbing her arm and working her fingers to get the feeling back.

Striker noticed. His jaw clenched at the huge welt, which was bright red and raised, with bruising already starting to show.

When Natasha looked back at him, she saw this.

"That why you pulled your gun?"

Natasha deemed it in her best interests to remain silent and not tell Striker that not only had she hit the man first, but she had actually pulled her gun before she got hit.

Striker mistook this for a yes. His eyes flashed with fury. "He hit you anywhere else?"

Natasha shook her head, then watched Striker stomp off toward her rival. "Oh, shit," she said under her breath.

Striker knelt by the man, picked him up by his t-shirt, and had a conversation with him in a low tone of voice. The man immediately began to look terrified. When Striker was through, he hauled him up, pushed him toward Natasha, and shoved him into the jeep.

"Apologize!"

"I'm sorry," her nemesis said, his eyes bulging from anger as well as fright. "I shouldn't have hit you with that belt. But you—"

"It's okay," Natasha interrupted before he could tell on her. "It's all right. Let's just forget the whole thing. You got your money, I got the dog, everything's fine."

The man glanced at Striker, then walked away and quickly gathered up the money on the pavement. Ignoring everyone, he lumbered to his truck, climbed in, and took off, peeling rubber.

Pit and Bigun had been standing to the side, arguing as to whether an actual bet had been placed or not. Hearing the truck leave, they ambled over.

Striker was waiting on them. When they got to him, he addressed Bigun. "I thought I told you to get her out of this situation."

Bigun glanced at Natasha, then back to Striker. "I tried, dude."

"Tried? It didn't look to me like you were trying to do anything. When I got here, the two of you were standing around doing nothing, watching that idiot go after Natasha."

"They were only doing what I asked them to," Natasha said.

Striker turned to her.

She shrugged, embarrassed. "I told them to stay out of it. It was my fight, there wasn't any point in them getting involved."

Bigun gave Striker a defensive look. "Yeah, dude, she called it. She said she could take him, so we let her do what she wanted."

"Shit!" Striker walked away, shaking his head.

They silently stood around watching him. Even the dog was quiet.

Striker turned back to Natasha. "I think I asked you a question."

She thought a moment. "I must have forgot what it was."

He waved his arms around, angry again. "What the hell happened here?"

"We bought a dog, that's what," Natasha said with a grin.

She climbed in her jeep and had to use her left hand to start it and put it in gear. After Roger was seated in the passenger seat, she said, "Let's go home,

dudes," to Pit and Bigun. She smiled at Striker and left before he could say anything else.

Striker watched her jeep exit the parking lot. Shaking his head, he got in his
Porsche and sat there debating whether to go back and finish what got started or
go to Roger's. He finally picked Roger's, figuring he better check Natasha's arm
to make sure she didn't need medical attention. He was also curious about the
dog and grinned once more at Natasha offering Brutus a choice regarding the
man's life as he started the car.

CHAPTER 13

▼

Striker had made it routine to drop in on Roger and the gang each morning, usually catching them during or after breakfast, to drink a cup of coffee with them and shoot the breeze, never realizing how much he was beginning to enjoy this part of his day. He was also more than a little intrigued with what had begun to happen between these four people, who now had cohered into some sort of weird family unit. He would usually find Pit and Bigun sitting around the table, wearing t-shirts and boxers, their guns tucked into shoulder holsters, which Striker thought looked pretty bizarre. Natasha would be dressed in what he assumed to be her sleep wear, a tank top and sleep pants, her gun strapped to her ankle. Roger was the only one who seemed to feel the need to dress for breakfast and, of course, he didn't carry a gun. Brutus, after greeting Striker, would settle down on the rug in front of the dishwasher, the place he now claimed as his, watching and listening to his adoptive family.

Somehow Natasha had become the nexus of this little group; the three men seemed to take their cues from her. Well, so did the dog, for that matter. If she was upset, they were upset; if she was happy, they were happy. Striker couldn't figure out what the hell that was about. He had to admit to himself, he found her a little fascinating, the way she managed the three men, getting them to do what she wanted, at the same time, fussing over them like a mother hen, appearing domestic, a feature he never would have applied to her. Well, maybe to the office Natasha, but not the real Natasha.

What puzzled him most, however, was the transformation that had taken place with his friend. For as long as he had known Roger, Striker had always considered him to be the self-isolating type; Roger just seemed to function better alone, in his own world. Now it seemed Natasha, Pit, and Bigun had embraced Roger, brought him into their fold, and made him a part of their group. Roger now looked and acted happy, an emotion Striker had never seen his friend display.

When Striker entered the mansion, he became alarmed at a dog barking, men yelling, and Natasha screaming. He ran toward the sound with his gun drawn. In the great room, Natasha, Pit, Bigun, and Roger were shouting at one another. Brutus was weaving in and out among the four of them, barking and growling with a fierceness he had not shown before. Striker watched Natasha push Bigun, who pushed her right back, which caused her to lose her balance and fall onto the couch. He holstered his gun.

"Hey, hey, hey!" Striker waded in among them, inserting himself between Roger and Pit, who were in each other's faces having a shouting match. He hurried toward Natasha, who was standing on the couch, telling Bigun to bring it on, but didn't make it before the huge bodyguard grabbed her up, threw her over his shoulder, and began swinging her around. Natasha screamed for all she was worth, pounding him on the back.

Striker got in Bigun's face. "Put her down!"

They grew silent, seeing Striker in their midst, then burst out laughing.

Striker watched Bigun throw Natasha on the couch. She began rolling around, clutching her stomach, tears falling, she was laughing so hard.

"What the hell is going on here?" Striker said.

After everyone had calmed down, Pit gave Striker a big grin while wiping sweat off his brow. "Hey, dude. We were just play fighting."

"Play fighting? What is this, kindergarten?"

"No, man. We were watching *Jerry Springer* and Nattie thought it'd be fun if we took sides, had our own bitch fight," Pit said.

Striker scowled at Natasha who was sprawled upside down on the couch, her head almost touching the floor, wiping tears from her eyes. "I should have known this would be your idea."

She flipped over and came up bounding. "You want to play? It's a lot of fun. Helps work off some of that ole testosterone level that's floating around here all the time." She smiled at Roger. "Not to mention, it's great for PMS," she added, grinning at Striker.

Striker looked heavenward with exasperation.

"I guess he doesn't want to play," Natasha said.

Striker turned to his friend. "Roger, there's something we need to discuss." His eyes darted to the others, then back to Roger. "In your office."

Roger's grin faded. "Sure." He glanced at Natasha, then left the room, followed by Striker.

"What do you think that's about?" Natasha looked toward Pit and Bigun, whose attention was on the *Springer* show, watching more bitch slapping among more people. Neither seemed to have heard her.

She shrugged and left to find Striker and Roger.

Roger was behind his desk, Striker sitting in front, when Natasha breezed in. "What's going on?" Her smile faltering at the look on Roger's face, she hurried toward him. "Roger, are you all right?"

Roger's face was pale and sweat was beaded on his upper lip. He nodded at her, then focused his attention on Striker.

"We got the blood test back," Striker said. "You were right. They found traces of Thallium in Roger's blood."

Natasha's mouth flew open. "He's not showing any symptoms, so it's reversible, right?"

"Thank God," Striker said.

"You saved my life," Roger said to Natasha. He turned to Striker. "She saved my life, Striker." Roger began to look upset. "I know for a fact I never even saw that stuff before, so someone must have been trying to poison me."

Natasha sat down in the chair across from Striker and thought about this. "What was the trace?"

"Minute."

She nodded with relief. "Well he could have inhaled that, right? Or maybe even touched the bottle and gotten exposed that way, right?"

"Right."

She turned to Roger. "See? It was just an accidental exposure. You were probably looking for something and touched it, not knowing what it was. So no one was actually trying to kill you, guy. I mean, my God, who would do that? It could only be someone with access to this house, so it has to be you were exposed to it. That's the only logical answer."

Roger turned to Striker for confirmation.

"She's right," Striker said. "You could have picked that up by being exposed to the stuff."

Roger looked relieved.

Natasha followed Striker outside when he left, calling for him to wait.

"What do you think about all that?" she said, catching up to him at his car.

"I don't know, to be honest. When I first talked to Roger about it, he seemed surprised it was even in there, so I doubt if he's ever even touched it."

"Was the lab able to lift any fingerprints?"

"Got a good set but no one to match it to in the system."

"Have our investigators come up with anything at all?"

Striker shook his head. "The mall in Chattanooga had a security camera aimed at the mezzanine close to where the pay phone was, and we've watched the video at least a dozen times but can't connect anyone to Roger. Of course, it would have helped if the bank of phones had been directly in view of the camera. But whoever this is, I don't think Roger knows him personally."

"Which makes it even scarier."

They both considered that for a moment.

"What about that housekeeper that just disappeared?"

"Illegal alien. She probably figured she'd better get before we sicced INS on her."

"Or she was poisoning Roger."

Striker shook his head. "Like I said, that's too easy."

"You're probably right. It's too weird having two wannabe killers after Roger."

"So you think the extortionist guy's telling the truth?"

"I hope not, Striker."

"You don't think maybe Roger's being a little paranoid? I mean, I've known him since college, and he does have that propensity."

Natasha thought a moment, looking away. When she turned back to Striker, he noticed her eyes were a deep green, as dark as a forest without sun…

"No, I don't think so. I think he's really worried about all this. I think that guy scared him."

Striker opened his car door. "Well, let's just hope he actually is after the money, not Roger's life."

"Don't worry, I've got his back," she said cockily.

Striker grinned. "That, Natasha, is what worries me."

She gave him a hurt look. "That's really low."

Feeling like a bully, Striker reached out and touched her chin with one finger. "Hey, I was only teasing you."

Natasha gave him an impish smile. "Gotcha."

Striker watched her walk away from him, appreciating her female form and the way she moved, snapping back to the real world only after the door closed behind her.

CHAPTER 14

▼

"Yeah?" Striker said over the two-way in response to an alert from Pit.

"They're heading out, man."

"Where to this time?"

"Nattie's gonna take Roger to her mom's. She's gonna put tints in his hair or something, man. Don't ask me, I don't even have hair."

Striker leaned back in his chair, his brow creased. Tints? What the hell was Roger doing, having tints put in his hair? "Stay with them, alert me when you get there."

Natasha and Roger were in her jeep with Pit and Bigun following behind in the company SUV. There was a yellow light up ahead, and Natasha, feeling naughty, accelerated through it, knowing her two friends would have to stop. She stuck her arm out the window and waved, continuing on.

"Oh, man," Pit said.

Bigun sighed and picked up his phone.

"Striker," he heard over the two-way.

"Hey, dude, you know where Nattie's mom lives?"

"Why? What's happened?"

"I think the dudette might have pulled one over on us. She's getting away while we're stuck at a traffic light."

"I'll see if I can get her on her phone. In the meantime, try to catch up to her."

"You got it, dude."

Striker alerted Natasha, but she ignored him until he started yelling over the two-way.

"Yeah?" she said, holding the phone to her mouth.

"Where the hell are you and what the fuck do you think you're doing?" Striker bellowed. He caught a glimpse of his secretary's astonished face through his open office door and gave her a thin smile before closing it.

"I was just teasing. I'm over to the side of the road now, waiting on them."

"You better wait on them. I hear you didn't, you'll wish you did!"

Natasha was silent for a moment, then said, "Yes, Daddy," in a small voice.

Striker hurled his phone at the sofa across the room.

Natasha looked over her shoulder. "Where are they, Roger? That light couldn't be that long." She noticed a dark-green BMW pulled over to the curb behind them, the two men inside looking her way. Omigosh. She turned around and stared in the rear-view mirror while she waited for Pit and Bigun, watching the men in the Beamer watch her.

Natasha sighed with relief when the SUV came into view and slowed down to allow her room to pull out ahead of it.

Natasha merged into traffic, then drove below the speed limit, watching to see what the Beamer did. After two cars passed by, it pulled into traffic and followed them.

Natasha grew alarmed. Wasn't that what the bad guys did on TV when following someone, stayed three cars back? Deciding to test them, she increased her speed and watched as Pit increased his. Three cars back, so did the BMW, which slipped into the middle lane but hung back.

Natasha wondered how she could actually tell if they were following her or not, then remembered something she had seen in a movie. She looked up ahead, spotted it, waited until she was right on it, then took a quick right. The jeep tires squealed in protest at this sudden move, the ones on the left barely hanging onto the pavement.

Pit and Bigun, surprised and unable to make the turn, passed by.

Roger gave her a frantic look. "What the heck are you doing?"

Natasha didn't answer, glancing in the rear-view mirror at the Beamer, which veered back into the inside lane and hung a right. There were no cars between the jeep and it now.

Her phone bleeped, but Natasha ignored it, too busy concentrating on the winding road she was traversing, trying to keep her speed up while watching the BMW slowly catch up to her.

Striker's phone twirped and he picked it up, glancing at the display: Bigun. "Now what?"

"Hey, dude, we just lost the dudette again."

"What happened?"

"She hung a right at the last minute and we were going too fast to follow, so we're gonna go up to the next street, turn right, see if we can catch up to her."

"She playing games again?" Striker said with frustration.

"I don't know, dude, but it sure looks like it."

"I'm gonna fuckin' kill her."

He heard Bigun say, "Get in line, man."

In a panic, Natasha glanced at Roger. "Get Striker on the two-way."

"What's wrong? Why are you acting so weird? Why the heck don't you slow down?"

"Get Striker on the two-way!"

Roger picked up the cell phone and alerted Striker, then held it toward Natasha's mouth.

"Striker!" boomed from the phone.

"Striker, it's me. We got a green BMW on our tail. I can't shake him, although I've been trying to for the last five minutes."

"Natasha, if you're playing games—"

"I swear I'm not. I tried to lose them, but I can't, and now I've lost Pit and Bigun."

"Where are you?"

"I don't know. Roger, look for a street sign. Oh, God," she said, her voice close to a scream, "they're right on us!"

Natasha swerved over to the curb and braked the jeep, slinging them forward. The BMW pulled in behind them and stopped inches from their rear bumper. Natasha reached down, unstrapped her .22, and shot out of the vehicle.

Roger was yelling into the phone, "She's got her gun! She's got her gun!"

"Out of the car!" Natasha said, trying to keep her voice at an audible level. "Just get out of the friggin' car." She had her weapon trained on the two men, who sat frozen in their seats with their mouths open, hands up.

"Roger!"

"Hold on, Striker, she's yelling at me," Roger said. He stuck his head out the window. "What?"

"Take the jeep and get out of here."

Roger leaned out further and his eyes bugged. Natasha was at the driver's side door of the BMW with her gun aimed inside the car.

"Move! Go find Pit and Bigun!"

"Shit!" Ignoring Striker's shouts coming out of the phone, Roger climbed over into the driver's seat and took off.

Heaving a sigh of relief, Natasha waved her gun at the two men. "Okay, out of the car. Real slow like. First you," she said, indicating the driver, "then you," indicating the passenger.

The men stepped out with great caution. Natasha was surprised to see they were of Japanese descent.

Natasha motioned for them to raise their hands in the air, then trained the gun on first one and then the other, unsure what to do now. Dang, where was everybody?

One of the men tried to say something to her, but he was speaking Japanese and she couldn't understand him. She shook her head, wondering who in heck would hire a killer that couldn't speak English.

Roger drove from road to road, trying to find Pit and Bigun. Realizing Striker was still shouting at him, he reached over and picked up the phone. "It's me."

"Where the hell is she and what's going on?" Striker was in his own vehicle, trying to get an idea which way to go.

"She's got those two guys in the Beamer stopped and she's holding them with her gun."

"Oh, sweet Jesus. Where the hell are you?"

Roger looked around. "Hold on, I'm coming to a street sign." He slowed down. "Cedar Bluff—I'm at Cedar Bluff, just exiting one of the side roads."

"What's the damn, friggin' name of the side road?"

"Oh yeah. Sunflower—Sunflower Road."

"Okay, I know where that is, I'm not five minutes from there. In the meantime, pull over and stop. I'll send Bigun and Pit your way."

"But Natasha told me to go."

"I'm telling you to friggin' stop that damn, fuckin' jeep and wait!"

Wincing at Striker's roaring voice, Roger pulled over to the curb and stopped.

Natasha glanced around, then back at the two men, who gave her timid smiles. They looked frightened. Would a killer be afraid of her? She cocked her head at them. "You speaka the English?" she asked, sounding Italian.

One man started to step forward, but she motioned him back. "Little," he said, "little."

"Who are you? What are you doing here? Why were you following us?"

The two men looked at one another and shrugged.

Natasha waved her hand in the general direction of the jeep. "The jeep. Why were you following the jeep?"

"Jeep," they said in unison and nodded.

What the hell? "Something about the jeep?"

They nodded. "Jeep," they repeated.

Natasha lowered the gun and studied them.

The younger man stepped toward her, and she raised her weapon. "Get back!"

Natasha heard a car pull up behind her, darted a look, and mentally groaned at Striker's dark SUV. She was beginning to suspect she may have overreacted here and wasn't so glad to see her boss now.

Striker stepped out and stood watching them for a second, then walked toward her. "What's going on?" He tried to keep his voice passive, but she could hear the anger.

"They were following us, and when I pulled over and stopped, they pulled over and stopped, so I got out and sent Roger on," Natasha said, her gun traveling from one man to the other.

Both men were watching Striker with looks of pure terror on their faces.

"Put the gun down, Natasha," Striker said.

"But they could be killers, they could have—"

Striker turned to her and, his voice low, said, "Put your damn, fuckin' gun down, Natasha. This is a neighborhood, for Christ's sake, there are kids around, witnesses to your little show of heroics here."

"Show of heroics!" She waved her arms around, forgetting about the two men.

Striker reached out and yanked the .22 out of her hand.

"Hey!"

She quieted at his look.

He tucked her gun in the waistband at the back of his jeans and approached the two men, who began jabbering away. Striker held up his hands and began speaking slowly in what Natasha thought could have been Japanese.

Before long, Striker and the men were bowing at one another, smiling and getting along grandly.

Natasha walked over to a tree and kicked it.

The men got in their car and left, waving bye to Natasha, who waved bye back.

Striker turned and looked at her, his dark eyes hardening, his mouth tightening.

Natasha resisted the urge to bolt.

"You're a danger to human society, you know that?" he said when he got to her.

"Striker, I thought they were following us. They stayed right on our tail. Even when I hung that right back there and lost Pit and Bigun, they stayed with us, so I knew they were following us."

Striker leaned toward her. "And do you know why they were following you? Did you bother to find that out in a more passive way than holding a gun to their damn heads!"

Natasha flinched at his angry tone.

Striker glanced around. "Get in the car." Taking her arm, he pulled her along, deposited her inside, and slammed the door with force.

Pit and Bigun's SUV, followed by Natasha's jeep, pulled up behind them, and Striker walked over to hold a conversation with the two male bodyguards.

Natasha watched Pit exit the SUV and climb in her jeep, then both vehicles left. Oh, no, he was gonna make her ride back with him!

Striker climbed in his SUV, turned, and faced her.

"So they weren't following me, I take it, intending to murder Roger?"

"Yes, dear, they were following the jeep," Striker said, in a condescending tone. "But they mistook your jeep for the jeep of a realtor they were supposed to meet who was going to show them some property for sale. Which I'm sure they won't buy now. Hell, they'll probably never come back to this city, seeing as how we got banditos like you crawling around all over, waving guns at everyone."

"Well, maybe I was a bit overzealous."

Striker swore under his breath, stepped out of the SUV, stalked to the tree Natasha had kicked, and kicked it himself. Several times.

When he got back in his vehicle, Natasha looked at him. "That helps, doesn't it?"

"What would have helped more, Natasha, dear one, is if that tree had been your body!" Striker keyed the ignition and headed home.

Natasha was wondering how mad he was at her. Well, he had kicked the tree; that was pretty mad. Plus he had called her dear twice. She knew him well enough by now that when he used that particular term of endearment, it was not meant as such but as his cue to her that he was pissed with her. She tried to remain quiet but couldn't.

"Striker?"

His black eyes flashed at her.

"Was that Japanese you were speaking back there?"

He shrugged. "Pretty broken, but yeah, that was Japanese."

She smiled. "I didn't know you were multilingual."

He cast her an ominous look.

She sobered. "When'd you learn to speak Japanese?"

"In one of my former lives," he said curtly.

Natasha sat in silence a moment, then uttered a small "Oh!" She picked up her phone and keyed in her mom.

"Hey, Mom. Just wanted to let you know that Roger and I probably won't be coming over today. There's been a—well, there's been an incident."

She listened for a moment, then sighed. "Yes, Mom, you could say I was the incident."

"If that ain't the truth," Striker grumbled.

She made a face at him.

"I saw that."

Yikes! She remembered her mom was speaking. "No, Mom, I'm not hurt." She rolled her eyes. "No, Mom, I didn't hurt anyone."

Striker grinned.

She ignored him this time.

After Striker braked to a stop in front of the mansion, Natasha hesitated before exiting the vehicle. "I really screwed up, didn't I?"

Striker regarded her for a moment, then cocked his head at her. "What do you think?"

She stared at her hands. "Yeah," she said, in a small voice.

"You have any idea how badly you screwed up?"

She thought about it. "Well, first thing I did wrong was when I went through that yellow light, knowing Pit and Bigun would get caught when it turned red."

She glanced at Striker, who raised his eyebrows. "I was teasing them when I should have been doing my job."

He nodded.

"Second, when I saw that BMW following me, I should have alerted you and the boys instead of panicking and trying to outmaneuver him."

She turned to face him. "Third, when I hauled my dumb ass out of that jeep, leaving Roger there, vulnerable to anyone who wanted at him. Fourth, when I pulled my gun. Fifth, when I approached their car, waving the gun around like a stupid idiot. Sixth, when I made them get out of the car. Seventh, when I told Roger to leave. Eighth, when I held them there at bay. Ninth, for waving my gun around in a public arena. Wait, wait, go back, I forget the sequential number, but when I approached that car, out in the open, where I could have gotten taken out myself. But more than anything for acting impulsively and not taking the time to think this thing through." She gave him a flustered look. "Damn, I can't believe I was that stupid."

Striker remained silent, watching her.

She blinked at the tears in her eyes. "What'd I forget?"

"I think you pretty well covered it."

Natasha sighed and looked out the window. "I guess I get an official reprimand for this one."

"Yep."

"I guess this is going to go on my record, too, right?"

"Yep."

Natasha sighed once more, then gave him an anxious look. "Striker, what the hell are you going to do with me?"

He grinned. "That, Natasha, I've yet to figure out."

She nodded. "Can I go now?" She sounded like a kid. "I think I might want to, like, go to my room and, you know, hang myself or something."

"I hope you're teasing."

"Like yeah," Natasha said, rolling her eyes at him and reaching for the door handle.

"Wait."

She turned back to him.

"What's this thing you got going with Roger?"

Natasha frowned a little. "I think you need to explain that in more detail."

"Tints in his hair, contacts, you've got him looking halfway decent. I'm just wondering what motivated you to do that and the reason for it."

She leaned against the door, quiet for a moment. "Roger is, or rather, was, me in high school."

"Yeah?"

"I mean I was a lot like he was when I first met him, when I was in high school."

Striker couldn't envision that. "I don't understand."

"Well, I was tall at that point, taller than most of the guys, skinny as a rail, wore braces. I didn't fit in anywhere, had no friends really. I—well, as I'm sure you know by now, I kind of have an attitude thing going on."

Striker gave her a wicked grin. "Really?"

She frowned at him. "Do you mind?"

"Go ahead. I was just teasing."

"I was a loner, mainly because I didn't want to call attention to myself. It wasn't until I got into college and met this guy who in a weird sort of way taught me a few things about myself that I stopped being so insular."

"Such as?"

Natasha gave him her own wicked grin. "Like I'd tell you." She opened the door and climbed out, waving as she entered the house.

Striker was surprised to find himself disappointed she wouldn't share that with him.

CHAPTER 15

▼

The second call came the next day. Natasha answered and heard, "Let me speak to Roger." She handed the phone over and waited for him to let her know if this was friend or foe. Seeing his look, she snatched up the cordless, then picked up her cell to alert Striker, who at that moment was walking in the front door.

Natasha was disappointed to see Striker come running into the office. Shoot, now she couldn't manipulate this one.

Roger put the phone on speaker so Striker could hear.

The man wanted to know who that redhead was that kept beating up on everybody.

"That's my girlfriend," Roger said.

Natasha could feel Striker staring at her but decided to ignore him.

"Well, I don't want her around next time," the guy said. "She's too danger-ous."

Natasha noticed Striker's grin and resisted the urge to stick her tongue out at him. He gave her a warning look, as if he knew what she was thinking.

They listened to the man tell Roger to meet him the next day at noon at the Wal-Mart in Powell.

"Where?"

"They got a red riding horse out front. Stand right there at that corner, I'll find you."

Roger glanced at Striker. "Okay."

"I better not see that redhead," the guy said.

Striker smiled again.

Natasha rolled her eyes.

"And if I see any of your bodyguards hanging around, anything suspicious, I'm gone and that's the end of it. No more chances. I'll kill you next time." He clicked off.

Striker called the office. "Damn. Same pay phone as last time."

"I'm going, Striker," Natasha said.

He shook his head. "He doesn't want you there. If he sees you—"

"I'll stay in the van but I'm going."

Striker considered that. "Okay, but you better not set one foot out of the van until I tell you that you can."

"Fine," she said, "whatever you say," followed by, "Can Brutus go, too?"

Striker's scowl was answer enough.

The next day, parked in the Wal-Mart lot, Striker reminded Natasha to stay put in the van.

"How many times are you going to tell me that? Dang, Striker, I only need to be told once."

They watched Roger standing beside the red horse with sports bag in hand, anxiously looking around.

Natasha heard a child wailing at the top of its lungs and glanced out the window, praying no one had run over a kid. She spied a short, rotund woman stalking toward the van, pulling along a small child who looked to be three or so. The woman had on thin, tight, white pants that showed every bulge on her portly frame. Natasha gasped at the way she yanked the little boy and pulled him to her, thinking she could dislocate his shoulder that way. She watched the woman get in the child's face and wag her finger at him. The poor little boy was crying in a loud voice, his face red, his nose running.

They had reached the van and were walking past. "Just wait till I get you to the car," the woman was saying to her child. "Just wait till I get my paddle, that'll shut you up."

"Paddle," Natasha said out loud.

Striker, whose attention had been focused on Roger, glanced at her.

"Did you hear what she said?"

He looked past her, out the window. "Who?"

"That fat lady who just walked by. She's going to go to her car and hit her kid with a paddle."

Striker frowned. "Well, there's not much you can do about that. It's her kid."

Natasha peered outside. The woman had now reached her car and unlocked the door. Sure enough, she had paddle in hand and was pulling the little boy to her.

"Ain't gonna happen!" Natasha clambered over Striker, opened the side door, and ran outside.

The woman was holding the little boy up in the air, whacking at his bottom with the paddle, saying, "I'll teach you to cry like that." The little kid was screaming for all he was worth.

"Quit that!" Natasha said when she reached them.

The woman stopped and gave her a belligerent look.

Striker hurried out of the van, thinking, *Why me, God.*

"Quit hitting that child." Natasha said. "Who the hell do you think you are?"

This was answered with an indignant, "I'm his mother, that's who I am."

"Real mothers don't beat their kids," Natasha said. "I ought to report you to the Department of Children's Services."

Joining them, Striker gave Natasha a warning look. "Natasha, this is none of your business."

The woman pointed the paddle at Natasha. "That's right. I have the right to discipline my child as I see fit."

Natasha glanced at the little boy, who had his fists wadded into his eyes and was sniffling. "That's not disciplining a child, that's beating a child." She moved away from Striker and pointed her finger in the woman's direction. "And I see you hit that kid one more time with that paddle, I'm gonna take it away from you and start hitting you with it."

The woman looked from Natasha to Striker, who was giving her his most menacing glare, to Pit and Bigun, who had joined the fracas, looking huge standing behind Natasha. She shoved her little boy toward the car.

"Get in the car."

"What is the matter with you?" Natasha screamed, startling Striker, who thought this whole mess was over with. "First I see you yanking that kid around, it's a wonder you didn't dislocate his shoulder, then I see you beating the crap out of him, now you're pushing him around. Lady, you do not deserve to be called a mother!"

"Get in the car." The woman herded her son in front of her, looking at Natasha as if she were crazy. She hurried around to the driver's side, opened the door, lifted the little boy inside, then threw the paddle in back.

Natasha followed her and stood outside the car door, glaring at her through the window. "I'm gonna take down your license plate number, lady, and I'm gonna be watching you, and I swear, I see you hit that kid again, I'm gonna come down on you like an elephant on a termite!"

Pit and Bigun nodded their heads at one another over that one.

Striker took hold of Natasha's arm. "Come on."

The woman started the car, black smoke belching out the muffler, and began to back out of the parking space at an accelerated speed. Striker pulled Natasha out of the way before she could get struck.

Natasha tried to go after the vehicle, but Striker restrained her.

"And another thing," Natasha yelled at the departing car, "lose some weight, why don't you, or wear something that won't show all that fat hanging off your body!"

Pit and Bigun lost it at that and began laughing.

Striker let go of Natasha. "What the hell is wrong with you? Can't you keep that mouth of yours shut?"

Natasha put her hands on hips and glared at him. "Oh, and you would have just stood by and let her beat her kid like that and not said a word."

"She's his mother, for Pete's sake. I can't tell her what to do."

"Boy, Striker, I sure hope you don't have kids. You'd probably let your wife beat up on your kids and not say a word, right? Just tell everybody, she's their mother, I can't tell her what to do."

At Striker's look, Pit and Bigun retreated to the van.

"For your information, as their father, I would never let anyone hit my kid. But I can't interfere with another parent's method of discipline."

Natasha stomped away from him. "Yeah, and that's what's wrong with the world today."

Striker stood there a moment, then went after her, catching up to her outside the van. "What's that supposed to mean?"

"Just stand by, let a woman beat her kid, let some man rape a woman, let another man kill his neighbor, and say, I can't interfere, for whatever reason."

"It's not the same and you know it."

Natasha jabbed her finger at him. "No, it's the very same and you know it."

Striker slammed his fist into the van.

Pit stepped out of the van with a glum look. "Roger's gone."

"What!" Natasha said.

"We can't find Roger. He's not by the horse anymore."

"Oh, no."

They raced to the storefront, where the bodyguards stood looking around, searching for Roger, while Striker yelled into his cell phone.

Relieved to see her friend walk out of the store with one of their men, Natasha ran over and hugged him. "Oh, Roger, I was so scared. I thought he took you."

The bodyguard was talking to Striker. "We heard a commotion in the parking lot, so I thought I ought to get him inside where he'd be safer."

Striker turned and glared at Natasha. "You see what you did?"

"What? What'd I do?"

"Probably scared the guy off again. How many times did I tell you to stay in the van?"

"I'm sorry, Striker, but it made me mad, that woman hitting her kid like that. I can't just stand by and watch somebody beat up on a small child and do nothing, unlike some people I know." She sent him a dark look.

"Go to the van," Striker said, pointing in that direction.

Natasha remained where she was with a defiant look on her face.

Striker leaned toward her. "Go to the van, Natasha!"

"Fine, I'll go to the van. But I'll tell you something, Striker, if you're even thinking about giving me one of your official reprimands over this one, then think again, because you'll have to give yourself one, too."

"What the hell are you talking about?"

"Okay, I got out of the van, I admit that. But you got out of the van, too, and you took your eyes off your man, too. So you're just as much at fault as I am."

The look on Striker's face decided Natasha that it would be in her best interests to go to the van.

Striker, Pit, Bigun, and Roger watched her walk away.

"She's right, man," Pit said.

Striker glared at him.

"You did get out of the van."

"Yeah? Well didn't I see you and Bigun standing there right alongside us?"

Pit didn't answer that.

"Let's go," Striker said.

Pit and Bigun reached the van first and, after giving Natasha smiles of commiseration, climbed inside. She elected to stay outside, her own little act of rebelliousness.

Striker drew himself up when he saw Natasha standing beside the van giving him an insolent look. He opened the side door.

"Get in the van, Natasha."

"No."

"Get in the van, Natasha," he said, raising his voice.

"Maybe I don't want to get in the—"

Striker leaned down into her face. "Get in the van, Natasha!"

"Okay, I'll get in the van."

Striker stayed outside and kicked a tire, then climbed inside and sat down, facing forward. Natasha stared sullenly out the window and ignored him.

During the ride home, no one said anything.

After the van stopped in the drive, Striker slung the side door open and exited. He stalked to his SUV, climbed inside, and took off.

Natasha ran upstairs to her bedroom and slammed the door shut.

"Man, you'd think they were married or something the way they act," Pit said.

Roger turned and looked at him.

It had become habit for Striker to call Natasha on her cell phone at eleven each evening to make sure everyone was in for the night. Eleven came and went, and he hadn't phoned. Natasha kept checking her cell, making sure the battery was up, wondering why he didn't call her. She had begun to enjoy their late-night conversations, their ease with one another on a more personal note, not to mention the stories Striker told her about his ancestors when she could talk him into it.

At eleven-thirty, she began pacing, willing the phone to ring.

At eleven-forty-five, she picked it up and keyed in his number.

"Striker," he said, gruff, as usual.

"It's me."

"Anything wrong?" He was instantly alert. "Is everything all right over there?"

"Everything's fine. It's just, well, you didn't call, so I was kind of worried about you."

He was silent in response.

"I know you're probably still mad at me over that incident this afternoon, and I don't blame you. I—well, I guess I acted a bit impulsively."

"That's a good way to put it, although I'd use a stronger word than bit."

Natasha decided not to respond to that. "I wanted to apologize to you, Striker. I didn't want to go to bed knowing you were mad at me. And if you think I should be reprimanded, then go ahead if that will make you feel better."

"No, you were right. If I reprimand you, I have to reprimand Pit, Bigun, and myself. We were all in the wrong there."

She was quiet a moment. "Striker?"

"Yeah?"

"Can I ask you a personal question?"

"Go ahead."

"Do you have kids?"

He wondered why she asked. "No."

"So that didn't bother you today, that woman hitting her little boy like that?"

"You know it did, Natasha. But I'll tell you something I learned a long time ago, you alone cannot save the world, much as you might want to."

"Yeah? Well, I'll tell you what, I might not be able to save the world, but I can sure save a small corner of it," Natasha said in an angry voice.

Striker laughed. "You're so bad, you scare me sometimes."

She knew from his tone that everything was all right again. "Do you think this guy is going to do what he threatened?"

"You mean about Roger?"

"Yeah. Striker, I pray to God I'm not the one who scared him away, because he said he'd kill him next time."

"No, I think he wants the money too much. Besides, we don't know why he didn't show. I'll bring Scott over tomorrow, we'll have another meeting, decide which way to go now."

Natasha heard a feminine voice in the background and grew embarrassed. "Well, I just wanted to touch base," she said, something he always said to her when he called.

"Anything else you want to talk about?"

"No, that's okay. You sound busy. I'll talk to you tomorrow." She hung up the phone, feeling like the world's oldest teenager, frustrated she couldn't get over the crush she had developed for the man.

After disconnecting, Striker studied the woman standing in front of him, thinking of Natasha. Without realizing it, he began to compare the two. The woman with him was very beautiful, albeit in a calculated way as attested to by her large, perfectly shaped breasts, swollen lips, artificial fingernails, masterfully tinted hair. He also suspected the passion she displayed with him could be calculated, as well. Natasha's beauty, on the other hand, he found refreshing. With or without makeup, she glowed with vitality. Her tall, slim body reeked of good health and much energy. Then there was that fire within her, the fire he feared could consume him if he ever got close enough.

He frowned, shocked at the realization that it was Natasha he would have preferred to be here with him at this moment, waiting for him to come to her.

The woman gave him an uneasy look. "Striker?"

He flashed her a quick smile. "If you saw a woman hitting her kid with a paddle in a parking lot, what would you do?"

"I'm not sure what you mean."

"I was just wondering, would you feel like you should stop her, ignore her, what?"

She shrugged. "I'd probably ignore her. It's none of my business what she does to her child."

Wrong answer. Striker stood. "I'm afraid something's come up and I'm going to have to leave. I'll drop you off on my way out." He was more than aware that this was the first time in his life he had turned down sex with a beautiful woman in lieu of something he knew he could not have. But somehow he felt right in doing this, although he chose not to think about that.

CHAPTER 16

▼

"Where's Nattie?" Scott glanced around at Roger and the two male bodyguards watching television in the great room. Brutus was on the couch between Pit and Bigun, doing what he usually did: having a good snooze.

Bigun grinned. "The dudette took her mom to a tattoo parlor."

"Tattoo parlor?" Striker said.

"Yeah, man. Nattie's getting her mom one for her birthday," Pit said.

Striker shook his head. "A middle-aged woman getting a tattoo."

"Hey, man, you seen her mom? I don't call that middle-aged."

"Yeah, the dudette's mom's a real hottie, dude," Bigun said.

"So, is Natasha getting one, too?" Striker asked, trying not to let his interest show.

Roger smiled. "She said she isn't but I think she will."

The front door opened and closed, and after a few moments, Natasha entered the room, walking in a careful sort of way. She stopped when she noticed they were watching her and smiled at everyone but Striker.

"Hey, guys."

Roger raised his eyebrows at her. "Well?"

"You would not believe the tattoo she got." Natasha dropped her purse and didn't seem to want to move very much. "It is so totally cool. It's a tiny little butterfly right here." She twisted her torso and pointed to her tailbone area. "Beautiful! My dad is going to freak when he sees that."

"Okay, let's get the meeting started," Scott said, losing interest.

Everyone moved to the table, Natasha taking the longest to get there.

"Why are you walking funny?" Roger grinned. "Oh, my gosh! Nattie got a tattoo."

Her brow furrowed. "No, I didn't."

"You sure are walking weird, dudette," Bigun said.

Natasha's face turned pink. "I just, you know, pulled something in my back."

"Oh, man, I just lost five bucks," Pit said.

"I told you she'd get one," Roger said.

Natasha was growing angry. "I did not get a tattoo."

"Okay, that's enough, guys, let's get started," Striker said, in an effort to end the tattoo discussion and Natasha's obvious embarrassment.

Everyone sat but Natasha.

They looked at her.

"I'd prefer to stand if you don't mind. I think I've hurt my back." She wouldn't meet anyone's gaze.

The men glanced at one another.

"She got it on her butt," Pit said.

"I didn't get a tattoo!"

"That's why she doesn't want to sit down," Roger said, sounding smug.

"Yeah, dude, those things hurt at first," Bigun said.

Everyone looked at him.

"Let's just have our meeting, okay?" Natasha said.

"You gonna let us see it, dudette?" Bigun asked.

Natasha gritted her teeth. "I do not have a tattoo on my butt, so get off the subject."

Roger was enjoying this. "Then why don't you sit down?"

"Okay, if it will make you happy." Natasha descended toward the chair but hesitated with her derriere inches from the seat, then rose as soon as she touched it.

"Oh, yeah," Roger said.

"It's not what you think."

Pit gave her a challenging look. "Okay, man, you say you don't have a tattoo on your butt, prove it."

Natasha stared at him. "You want me to show you my butt?"

"I got five bucks riding on this, man. Before I give up five bucks, I want to make sure I actually lost it."

Natasha sighed. "Okay. I got a tattoo, all right?"

"Let's see it," Roger said.

"No."

Roger glanced at Pit. "If I'm going to win five bucks, I want to make sure I actually won it."

Natasha looked everywhere but at the men gathered around the table. "Well, you can't, you know, actually see it."

They thought about that.

Natasha grew fascinated with studying a fingernail. "It's not visibly discernible, if you get my gist."

They were silent, each having his own thought about exactly where—

"I mean, you can see it, but only if I were to actually, you know, show it to you. And believe me, guys, I have no intention of showing any of you my tattoo." Natasha boldly looked at each man except Striker.

"You wear those thong panties," Pit said. "You could show it to us that way, right?"

Striker wondered how Pit knew she wore thong underwear.

Natasha gave Pit a frustrated look. "I'm not wearing thongs today. And even if I had those on, I wouldn't show it to you."

The men perked up at that, each wondering where that darn thing was, Striker then moving on to what it was.

"What'd your mom say, dudette?" Bigun said.

An alarmed look crossed Natasha's face. "She doesn't know and you guys have got to swear to me you won't tell her."

"Why not?" Roger wanted to know.

"Because she would absolutely have one hell of a hissy fit if she found out what I did, so you cannot tell her."

Striker was just as caught up now in Natasha and what went on with her mom as the other men were. "She got one, so why would that bother her?"

Natasha addressed Roger. "Well, not so much the tattoo as where I actually had it, you know, placed. She'll think I'm a pervert or something. Besides, I didn't mean to get one. Shoot, I don't even like tattoos, but I started talking to the lady there about her specialty, intimate tattoos, which I never knew even existed, and next thing I knew, I was in one of the rooms with my..." She paused. "Let's just have our meeting, okay?"

"She's right, we need to get started," Striker said, to save her further discomfort.

"First, I'd like to say something," Natasha said, and apologized to Roger for her impulsive act the day before.

Giving up on the tattoo, Roger told her he was glad she had stopped that lady from hitting her kid.

Striker wasn't surprised to hear Roger say that.

The other men looked to Striker for comment. Natasha remained standing, studying her hands, picking at a nail.

"Okay, I'm sure this guy's going to call back," Striker said. "We just have to wait for that to happen. In the meantime, I think it might not be a bad idea if you all curtailed your activities outside these grounds a little." He glanced at Natasha, who still wouldn't look at him. "Try to stay in-house more, just in case."

Roger shook his head. "I don't think he was serious about the death threat, Striker. He's offered to meet me twice now, so I don't see that we need to curtail anything. Besides, I like doing things with these guys." He waved in the general direction of Pit, Bigun, and Natasha, but looked at Natasha.

Striker, Roger, and Scott debated this issue while the other three listened, waiting for their instructions.

Roger asked Natasha what she thought. While she talked, she kept her eyes averted from Striker and never addressed him, as she was wont to do. This bothered him. He wondered what in the hell was wrong with her. He was surprised that she sided with him, though, then decided it was probably guilt that led her to that decision.

The discussion seemed to go round and round, without resolution. Roger, for some reason, was being stubborn about having their activities curtailed.

Striker could see they were getting nowhere. "Listen, I can't tell you what to do, Roger, I can only suggest. I've offered my opinion on the matter, so it's up to you."

Roger nodded.

Striker stared at Natasha, who still wouldn't look at him. "Anything else we need to discuss?"

Everyone remained silent.

"Natasha?"

Natasha glanced at the others and once more didn't even look in Striker's direction, instead focusing her attention on Roger. "I was thinking, if he calls back, Roger, you might want to act a little irritated with him and ask him why he didn't show. You know, preempt any suspicion he might have by distancing yourself from us, in case we're actually what scared him off."

"That's good," Striker said, watching Natasha, who still would not meet his eyes. "Anything else?"

No one said anything.

"Natasha?"

She glanced around at the others, then shook her head.

"There is one thing we should talk about," Scott said, and turned to Roger. "Since it's pretty obvious that this is a case of extortion, I think having three protection specialists guarding you twenty-four hours a day is no longer practical, Roger, it's just not cost feasible. Are you sure you want to expend that kind of money when you don't actually need them here?"

"It's my money," Roger said, in a defensive manner.

"The phone's being monitored and, of course, we'll have bodyguards around you when you deliver the money to the extortionist, but other than that, do you really think it necessary to have three bodyguards here around the clock?"

When Roger glanced at her, Natasha tried not to show the alarm she was feeling.

"It's my call, isn't it?" Roger said.

"Well, of course. We do what you hire us to."

"You haven't found this guy yet, you don't know for sure whether he actually plans to carry through with his threat to kill me, right?"

"Well, no, but—"

Roger looked at Striker. "What do you think?"

Striker shrugged. "Like you said, it's your call."

"Then they stay," Roger said.

Scott tried not to let his irritation show. "How about we leave one here and pull the other two off? I don't see that you need three bodyguards here day in and day out."

"It's my decision, and I want all three," Roger said. "I'm paying for it, so what's the problem?"

"All right, whatever you want."

Natasha tried not to let her relief show.

"Okay then, that's that." Striker rose, ending the meeting.

Striker stood outside the great room, listening to Natasha's halting footsteps on the stairs, wondering if she was angry with him. But she hadn't sounded upset last night when she called. In fact, she had said she didn't want to go to bed knowing he was mad at her. A thought nudged at his mind but didn't catch. He stood there, frowning, until Scott asked him if he was ready to leave.

"Let's go." Striker walked to the front door, darting a look toward the stairs.

After they were in the car, Scott said, "How long are you going to let this farce go on?"

Striker's mind had been on Natasha, so he wasn't sure he heard him right. "What?"

"This thing with Roger. We've had two bodyguards and one office manager tied up with him for almost two months now with nothing going nowhere. Hell, Striker, you know we don't need bodyguards around him until he actually delivers the money to the extortionist. We don't need to be guarding him twenty-four hours a day."

"Roger's being billed, isn't he?"

"Well, sure."

"He's paying, isn't he?"

"Far as I know."

"We don't have a shortage of bodyguards at the moment, at least not that I'm aware of, so what's the problem?"

"Come on, you don't seriously think this guy intends to kill Roger."

"Probably not, but he has made the threat."

"Yeah, and that's all it is, a threat. You know that as well as I do."

"It's Roger's decision, Scott. Maybe he feels safer having the bodyguards around."

"Maybe, but he strikes me as a lonely kind of guy. It's obvious he's got a thing for Nattie and, like he said, he likes hanging out with Pit, Bigun, and her. I think that's his real agenda here."

Striker shrugged. "Whatever his agenda, it's his call, Scotty." He glanced at him and grinned. "Looks like you're just going to have to learn to put up with our new office manager."

Scott glared at him.

"I mean, that's your agenda, isn't it? Getting Natasha back in-house?"

"Hey, things went a lot smoother when she was running the office, Striker. You know that. I'm just wondering how long you're going to let this go on before we get her back where she needs to be."

"As long as it needs to go on, I guess. And even then, you're not assured she'll be back as office manager. You did make that promise, you know."

Striker ignored Scott's epithetic tantrum.

Striker closed the door to his office behind him, then sat in his chair, thinking. After a few moments, he picked up the phone and dialed Natasha's cell. When he was about to hang up, she answered.

"You all right?"

"I'm fine. Please, don't ask me where the freakin' thing is, Striker, please don't."

He grinned to himself. "I think I've got that part figured out. I was just wondering what kind of tattoo you got."

She was silent.

"You won't tell me?"

"I will only tell that to the man I choose as my life-mate."

He thought about that. Well, he deserved it, he guessed. "So, everything's all right between us?" He was surprised at himself for bringing it up.

She hesitated, then said, "Sure, everything's fine."

But Striker didn't want to let it go that easily. "Then why wouldn't you look at me today? I thought we made up last night."

"I guess I'm just feeling a little embarrassed. It was obvious I interrupted something, and I didn't mean to."

"Natasha," Striker said in a low, gravely voice.

Natasha's stomach clenched for an instant, then a shooting sensation went clear to the tips of her toes. She resisted the urge to moan, thinking how much she loved the way he said her name.

"You can interrupt me any time you want. Don't worry about that, all right? It was nothing."

"Striker?"

"Yeah?"

"I'm glad I know you." She terminated the call, leaving him to wonder what she meant by that.

CHAPTER 17

▼

Natasha and the boys were sitting on the floor in the great room, a game of Monopoly between them, at times glancing at the big-screen if something of interest caught their attention. Brutus was on the couch, on his back, paws in the air, sleeping.

A commercial for a national store specializing in women's lingerie flashed on the TV screen. As if on cue, all three men stopped playing and stared at the set with open mouths, fascinated.

Rolling her eyes, Natasha stood, picked up the remote, and turned off the TV in the middle of one of the buxom models giving the camera a full-lipped, pouty look.

"Hey, dudette, we were watching that," Bigun said.

Natasha stomped back to the game and sat down. "Soft porn is what you were watching."

The men glared at her.

"Don't you guys get it? They are subliminally sending you the message that if a woman doesn't look like one of those models, she isn't worthy of your attention. What's the matter with you?"

"Well, you could look like that if you wore one of those bra things," Pit said.

"Have you ever worn one of those things? Dang, dudes, they're painful. They have these underwire thingies that cut into your skin, they don't move when you do. And by the way, just so you'll know, guess who actually designed a bra? A man, that's who. Just another way you men try to control us women, by making us wear crap like that."

Three pairs of eyes stared at her, trying to decide whether that was a cut or not.

Natasha looked down at her breasts, which she rarely encased in a bra, then back up to Pit. "Besides, Pit, dear, it has always been my philosophy, if you don't have a dick, what the heck do you need a jock strap for."

It took them a minute, but they finally got it, and the three men had a good laugh.

After they had quieted down, Roger gave her a shy glance. "I think you're perfect just the way you are, Nattie."

Natasha smiled at him.

"Yeah, dudette," Bigun said. "The Rogster's right. You're all right."

"Yeah, girl. You don't want to go fixing what don't need fixing," Pit chimed in.

Natasha threw her hands toward them. "I love you guys! All my life I've wanted a big brother, and look at what I've got now, three big, beautiful brothers." She bounced up, went around the board game, got to Roger first, planted a kiss on his forehead, then on to Pit and Bigun.

All were grinning when she finished.

Natasha flounced back to where she had been sitting and plopped down. She threw her hands toward the ceiling and looked that way. "You hear that, Big Guy? My three big, beautiful brothers think I'm perfect just the way I am. What do you have to say about that?"

"I think they're absolutely right," Natasha heard from behind her. She turned and was startled to see Striker standing in the doorway with an amused look on his face. She lost her balance and toppled over onto the game board, sending game pieces, cards, and money flying.

Roger surged to his feet, an angry look on his face. "I knew it. I was winning, and I knew you'd do something to make me lose." He stomped out of the room.

"I'll fix it," Natasha called after him, but he ignored her.

Pit and Bigun rose.

"As long as you're here, man, we might as well go check around outside," Pit said to his boss.

The two bodyguards hurried out, fearful that Roger and Natasha would get into an argument, leaving Striker to deal with the aftereffects.

Natasha gave Striker a flustered look. He grinned at her, then knelt down and began gathering play money and game pieces and placing them in the box. She helped him, quiet for once, wondering if he meant what he had said, then remembered what she had said. Oh, shoot, did he think she was talking to him instead of the actual Big Guy?

When they finished, Striker held out his hand and helped Natasha stand. His eyes still had that glimmer which told her he found this amusing.

"You didn't, um, you know, think I was talking to you when I was actually talking to, well, you know." Natasha pointed toward the ceiling.

Striker laughed.

She waited him out. "Well?"

"No, I knew who you were talking to."

Striker was dressed like a businessman in an expensive-looking suit with a white shirt and conservative silk tie. Natasha thought he looked so handsome, dressed this way, but decided she liked him better in jeans. Well, any kind of clothing that showed off his powerful body. Resisting the urge to throw herself into his arms and molest him, she said, "And?"

"And what?"

Her face reddened. "Did you mean what you said?"

Striker leaned toward her and gazed intensely into her eyes. "I don't say anything I don't mean, Natasha."

She stared back, her body atingle. Was this the look she read about, the one she wondered was actually true or not...but no, not Striker, not her, no way.

Natasha looked away, breaking eye contact. "There's something I want you to see." She pivoted and walked toward the game table.

When Striker stepped up behind her, she moved away from him, then leaned over the table to pick up a sheet of paper.

"Roger's been letting me go through all his paperwork. I've kind of been organizing things for him." She glanced up and caught Striker giving her a puzzled look. "It's the Virgo thing."

He nodded as if he understood.

"Anyway, I came across this letter." She handed it to him. "Read the area I've got highlighted."

Striker did as she asked, then looked back to her.

"According to Roger, he and this guy designed virtually the same software program. It's that preschool one that teaches kids how to read. Anyway, Roger got the patent first and this guy sued, but Roger proved his idea was his in origin, so he got to keep the patent."

Striker was studying the letter. "Yeah, I remember when that happened, but Roger never told me about this."

"Roger didn't take it seriously. He thought the guy was just mad because he beat him out of the patent. But," Natasha paused, Striker's attention now on her, "I did some checking. He has two felonious assault charges against him plus a woman filed a stalking complaint against him last year."

Striker's eyebrows shot up.

"So this computer nerd isn't your actual run-of-the-mill, well, nerd. He's got a problem with aggressiveness. And if he's been beating up on other people, what's to stop him from trying to kill Roger if he's mad enough at him? And I got to tell you, Striker, the money Roger's made off this one patent would pay off the debt of the entire third world."

Striker reread the letter, thinking about that. He finally looked back at her, flashed white teeth. "You did good."

Natasha reddened at the flattery.

"You mind if I take this, turn it over to an investigator, see what he can find out?"

Natasha's face fell.

"I mean, go ahead with what you're doing, keep investigating this if you want. But let me put someone on it, someone who might have more ins than you do at this point, who has time to do more digging."

Natasha gave him a forced smile. "Sure."

Striker stepped closer and opened his mouth to speak but was interrupted by a voice of the female persuasion saying his name. He turned toward his realtor.

Natasha looked around him at a woman standing in the doorway, dressed in a tailored pantsuit. She was drop-dead gorgeous, with chestnut-colored hair and cobalt-blue eyes framed by thick, black lashes. She had a short, petite build, and Natasha imagined Striker must seem like a giant standing next to her.

"We're going to be late if we don't leave now," the woman said, giving Striker a slight smile.

"I'll just be one more minute."

After nodding to Natasha, she turned and left.

Natasha felt awful. Here she was, dressed in low-cut jeans with the knees torn out, wearing a crop top showing her navel, her hair in a ponytail, looking like the world's oldest teenager.

Striker turned back to her, reached out, and squeezed her arm in a buddy-like way. "Thanks, kid. I mean it. You did good. Let me know what you find out."

Natasha looked away. "Sure." She moved to the desk and began rearranging files, turning away from him in a dismissive gesture. "I'll keep you apprised."

Natasha felt movement behind her and knew Striker was still there, but ignored him. After she heard his footsteps going away, she waited until the front door closed, then dashed out of the great room. She sprinted down the corridor and into the foyer. Her intention was to stop at one of the front windows so she could peek out to see if he kissed the woman when he got in the car, but she slid on the marble floor in her sock feet. Unable to stop at the window, she grabbed at the curtain, taking it with her when she sailed by. The drapery pulled at the heavy rod, and the rod and curtain came crashing down on top of her. Natasha fell under its weight.

"Shit, shit, shit!" she railed, her voice muffled by the massive material. She kicked her feet and pummeled her arms, having a tantrum.

She heard footsteps coming from the direction of the kitchen, then the front door open, and now Brutus was standing right on top of her, digging at the curtain, trying to get to her.

Natasha raised up, still covered by the heavy drapery, and pushed at Brutus. She began fighting the cumbersome cloth, cursing and yelling for all she was worth, managing to get herself more tangled than she had been.

"Be still!" she heard Striker yelling at her. "You're just making it worse."

Natasha lay back and closed her eyes. When she could see light through her eyelids, she knew they had managed to uncover her face.

"I so wish I were dead right now," she said, opening her eyes to see Striker's smiling face looming over her.

"Shoot, woman, I don't. You're always good for a laugh."

"Yeah, and eff you too." She frowned at Striker's amused grin.

After they had gotten her untangled, Striker helped her up. "How the hell did you manage to do that?" He glanced out the window, noticed his Porsche in full view outside, and looked back at her.

Natasha was trying not to let her embarrassment show. "I was sliding on the floor—I like to do that in my sock feet—and I tripped myself and went into the curtain, so I grabbed it, trying to stop, but it came down on top of me."

Striker nodded. "Maybe you shouldn't do that anymore." He gently chucked her under the chin. "You could get hurt, you know."

Natasha gave him a grumpy look. "Don't you have somewhere you need to be?"

Striker gave her a friendly wave and left, grinning.

Roger had been standing in the foyer watching all this. When Natasha glanced at him, he made it a point to look out the window at Striker's departing car, then back to Natasha.

"Roger, you have got to do something about these heavy curtains," she said, kicking her way out of the one at her feet. "They just don't go with this house and your new image." She escaped to her bedroom and threw herself down on the bed, feeling miserable.

CHAPTER 18

▼

Natasha reached over and shut Roger's laptop.

"Hey!"

"Roger, you need to loosen up, have some fun."

Roger sent her an angry look. "I was working."

"You've worked all day. I'm bored with sitting here watching you work."

Pit and Bigun pushed back from the kitchen table so they could get out of the way if an argument developed.

"Let's do something fun," Natasha said. "Something different."

Everyone watched her with expectation.

She shrugged her shoulders. "I don't know. Something zany, you know, out-of-this world wacko."

The two male bodyguards scooted their chairs closer to the table, their interest overriding their sense of caution.

"Hey, dudette, WWE's on tonight. We got to watch that," Bigun said.

Natasha thought a minute, then gave them a wide smile. "Know what I've always wanted to do but never had the nerve to?"

The three men shook their heads.

"Skinny dip." Natasha watched her two cohorts' eyes glow with intrigue while Roger's developed a frightened cast.

"You mean, swim naked?" Roger said.

Natasha nodded. Seeing his frown begin to form, she said, "I'm not talking about with the lights on so we can all see each other's equipment. I mean, I love you guys, I love you dearly, but I'd rather keep what I've got to myself."

Pit nodded in a solemn manner.

"So, what I was thinking is, let's go out to the pool, each pick a side, turn off all the lights, even the ones inside the pool, take off all our clothes, get in the water and have some fun. I know, let's play Marco Polo."

"Dudette, that's a grand idea," Bigun said.

"I don't know about that," Roger said.

"Come on, Roger, do something different for a change, something a little risqué, something a little naughty," Natasha said enticingly.

Roger still didn't look like he was so sure he wanted to engage in her suggestion.

"And no one, I mean no one, can turn the lights back on until we're all out of the pool and completely dressed," Natasha said. "We have to have that agreement, you have to give me your word. We're like brothers and sister here, and brothers and sister don't go around in front of each other naked, right?"

"The dudette's right, we're brothers and sister, and we have to respect that," Bigun said.

"Right." Natasha turned to Pit. "You in, Pit?"

Pit leaned back in his chair. "Hey, man, I'll try anything."

They looked at Roger, whose face was flushed. He finally nodded his acquiescence.

Natasha placed her hand on the table. "Your word, gentlemen, the lights stay out."

Each man piled his hand on top.

They were in the pool, having a great time playing Marco Polo, laughing and shouting. Pit would at times let go with his Arabian yell, sounding like a blood-curdling demon from hell, scaring Natasha and Roger. Brutus, too much of a chicken to go into the water, was running around the pool barking like mad at all the noise they were making.

All of a sudden the pool area was flooded with lights. Natasha, in the deep end, dropped below the surface, wondering who in the heck did that.

Popping her head above water, she saw Striker at the opposite end of the pool, his eyes shooting daggers. Dangnation! She surreptitiously sunk beneath the surface, swam underwater to the far end, and curled herself into a corner with her head the only part above water.

Roger, Pit, and Bigun were gathered at the side of the pool with their backs turned outward, protecting their nudity as much as possible.

For once, Striker seemed at a loss for words.

"You need anything?" Natasha called to him.

That did it! He headed her way.

"Don't come down here, I don't have any clothes on," she shrieked.

"As if I didn't notice that when I turned on the lights," Striker said, advancing on her.

"You saw me naked?" Natasha looked at the other three. "You guys didn't look, did you? You didn't break the rule, did you?"

"Hey, dudette, I didn't know there was a rule we couldn't look if somebody else turned the lights on," Bigun said.

"Shit, shit, shit!" Natasha said.

Striker knelt above her. She glanced down to make sure her legs were drawn up to her chest and her breasts were covered.

Striker was glowering at her. "Let me guess. This was your idea, right? Only you, Natasha, could dream up something this crazy."

Natasha became defensive. "We were just playing a game."

"Yeah? Where are your guns? Where are your damn phones?" Striker yelled, turning to Pit and Bigun.

Natasha gave herself a mental slap on the forehead.

"I've been calling over an hour, getting no answer, pull up to the house, all the lights are out, it's pitch-black inside. Then I hear all this yelling back here, and I immediately think there's a massacre going on, all the noise you idiots were making. Come out of the house, and here's what I find, four adults playing naked in the pool like little two-year-olds."

"Hey, I resent that," Natasha said.

Striker pointed at her. "You keep your mouth closed. I don't want to hear anything out of you. You're the worst of the bunch."

"Hey!"

"Natasha, do not push me this time."

She decided, as angry as he was, maybe she should just keep her mouth shut.

Striker turned to the other men. "You guys get out of the pool first. Natasha, cover your eyes till they're inside, then you can get out."

Turning her head away, Natasha placed one hand over her face. Unable to resist, she took a quick peek, wished she hadn't.

After a few minutes, Striker said, "Okay, they're inside. You can get out of the pool now."

Natasha glared at him. "Not everyone has gone inside."

Striker gave her an icy smile. "I've just seen you naked, dear girl, so what does it matter if I remain outside or not?"

"It matters to me," Natasha said, embarrassed.

Striker snatched a towel from the table, walked to the ladder closest to Natasha, and held the towel away from his body, turning his head.

Natasha got out of the pool with caution, watching Striker to make sure he didn't try to steal a quick glance. She grabbed the towel and hastily wrapped it around her.

Striker turned to her and folded his arms. Natasha performed a mental genuflection against the fury radiating off his body, firing from his eyes. Although she wasn't Catholic, she figured it couldn't hurt.

"I guess you're wanting some sort of an explanation."

"No, I think I can probably guess. Natasha was bored and came up with this crazy, idiotic scheme to have some fun." Striker raised his eyebrows at her.

"Well, it was fun. In fact, till you turned the lights on, we were having a great time."

"And what if I hadn't been the one who turned on the lights? What if I were the actual killer standing there, fully dressed by the way, a gun or two in my hands, watching four naked adults in the water staring back at me, no guns, no way to call for help? In a matter of seconds, I could have killed the whole lot of you. What then, dear girl?"

Tears sprang to Natasha's eyes. "Quit calling me dear girl!"

A mean look fell across Striker's face. "How about idiot? You want me to call you idiot?"

Natasha felt like a kid being bullied. "That's unfair."

Striker watched her angrily wipe her eyes. "Get dressed and go to your room. I'll talk to you after I deal with Bigun and Pit."

Wait a minute. If they were gonna get reamed out, so was she, she was part of this. "Wait a minute. If you're gonna ream out Bigun and Pit, you're gonna ream me out too," she shouted after his departing back, then could have slapped herself for saying something so stupid.

Striker ignored her.

Natasha ran to the side of the pool where she had deposited her clothes and dressed with haste. She leaned over, used the towel to do a quick fluff and dry of her hair, then followed Striker inside.

Striker was closeted in the library with Pit and Bigun, giving them hell. He pointed at Natasha when she crossed the threshold. "I told you to go to your room."

Natasha came closer. "It was my idea, and I'm part of this group, you know. So if you're going to bawl Pit and Bigun out, then you ought to bawl me out too."

Striker gave her a menacing grin. "I'm not through with you, Natasha, dear. You can count on that."

Yikes! Standing next to Pit, Natasha didn't look so sure now. "Well, I should be part of this."

Striker pointed at the male bodyguards. "These two have been bodyguards much longer than you, Natasha. They know the rules of the game. They know not to ever go anywhere and leave their weapons somewhere else, or their phones, or even their damn, fucking clothes, for that matter!"

Natasha started for the door. "Maybe I'll just go to my room."

Bigun gave her a glowering look. "Thanks, dudette."

"Sure thing."

Natasha ran up the stairs, wondering if she locked her door, would Striker break it down? Did she even want to find that out?

Passing Roger's open bedroom door, she noticed him sitting at his desk, staring at the wall, idly stroking Brutus, who was groaning in ecstasy.

Natasha paused in the doorway. "You okay?"

Roger glanced at her and nodded.

Natasha stepped into the room and knelt beside him to pet Brutus. "I'm sorry about this, Roger. I put you at peril without even realizing I was doing it, and I am so sorry."

Roger grinned. "I had a lot of fun. And I didn't consider the danger, either, so I guess we all have a part to play in this blame thing."

She smiled at him.

Roger's eyes darted toward the doorway, then returned to her. "You have feelings for him, don't you?"

Although Natasha knew what he meant, she gave him an innocent look. "Who?"

Roger's eyes again traveled to the door and back to her. "Striker. There's something going on, isn't there?"

Natasha tried to laugh but it sounded like a hiccup instead. "Striker? Come on, Roger, he's my boss. It would be stupid on my part to fall for him. Besides, I doubt I'm beautiful enough or sophisticated enough, and probably way too redneck, so why would he even look at me, you know?"

"Nattie," Roger said in a scolding way. "I would never categorize you as a redneck. And you're more beautiful and sophisticated than any woman I know, plus smart as hell and a lot of fun and, well, a little on the crazy side but in a good way."

Natasha reached up and kissed him on the cheek. "I love you, Roger, you know that?"

"I love you too, Nattie."

Uh-oh. She didn't like the way it sounded when he said it.

"But what you said earlier, us being like brother and sister, I don't love you that way. I love you more the, you know, other way."

Natasha became alarmed. "You just think you do."

Roger's reddened face wore a hurt expression. "So you're saying you don't love me like that."

Natasha heard movement at the open door and glanced that way. Striker was standing in the corridor outside. His eyes bore into hers.

"I want to talk to you," he said.

"Could you give me a minute?"

Striker disappeared.

Natasha turned to Roger, who was back to studying the wall again. She touched his arm and, when he looked at her, smiled. "Roger, I got to tell you, there have been times when I've been watching you, and I know, I know it would be so easy to let myself love you like that, but I can't. I don't want to be hurt and I know that's what would happen in this situation."

Roger gave her a strange look. "Oh. You're afraid I'm going to get killed."

"No. Oh, no, not that. No. It's just, well, look at you, Roger. You're drop-dead gorgeous, the smartest man I've ever known. You're getting all buff from working out with Pit and Bigun. You're a lot of fun, caring and sensitive, the best friend I've ever had, a really great man. And right now, I have you all to myself, and I got to tell you, guy, I'm loving it. But after this is over, after you go back out into the real world, once those women out there get a gander at you, you'll probably have to hire Pit and Bigun back just to keep them off of you."

A reluctant smile slid across Roger's lips.

"Five years. I've given you five years, because you need to experience that, you know. You need to meet a lot of different women, get to know them, love some, let some love you, before you'll actually get to the place where you'll realize exactly what it is you're seeking from a woman, what you need from her."

Natasha picked up his hand and held it between her own. "Now, say I decide to let myself fall for you, look at what I'm depriving you of, look at what you'll maybe one day wonder you've missed. I can't do that, to you or to me. So five years, guy, and if you're still out there searching and I'm still out there searching, then, shoot, let's go for it."

Roger smiled at her.

Natasha stood, leaned down, and kissed his cheek once more. She whispered as she began to back toward the door, "And one other thing, Roger. I peeked when y'all were getting out of the pool, sorry, I couldn't help it. And darlin', I envy those women out there that are coming your way. I envy them greatly."

Turning and exiting, she didn't see the flaming redness on Roger's face along with the happy grin.

Striker was outside the door, leaning against the wall.

Natasha gave him a haughty look, then turned and hurried to her bedroom at the far end of the hall. She decided the mood he was in, he would definitely kick the door in, so left it open.

Natasha plopped down in the rocker by the window and tried to act bored. She resisted the urge to meet Striker's gaze when he sat down in the window seat across from her.

"What you were saying to Roger," he said, surprising her, "you meant that?"

"Maybe." Natasha drew her legs up and concentrated on picking at a finger-nail.

"Whether you did or not, it was a good thing to say to him. He isn't very secure with who he is and he probably needed to hear that. In fact, I know it did him good to hear you say that."

Natasha nodded, and, unable to resist, glanced at him. "I meant what I said. He does need to get out there, meet different people and experience life a little before he decides he's met the woman he wants to be with."

Striker leaned back and crossed his arms. "And five years from now, you think you'll still be looking around?"

Natasha rested her head against the back of the rocker. "Shoot, the way my life is going, five years from now, I'll probably still be a virgin."

Striker's eyebrows shot up.

She grimaced. "Well, not virgin, virgin. More like love virgin. Roger, he doesn't know it, but he isn't going to have any trouble at all finding someone."

"Neither should you."

Natasha remained silent.

Striker leaned toward her. "What happened?"

She looked at him.

"What happened that you don't want to talk about, that still hurts you?"

She felt the tears come again and cupped her palms over her eyes, wondering if she would ever get past this.

Striker reached out, pulled her hands away, and gently held them while searching her eyes.

Tears were falling. "Striker, I'm too vulnerable concerning that, so, please, don't ask me."

"What happened?"

Natasha tried to pull away, but he held her firm.

"It's none of your business, Striker."

"I care about you, about what's going on with you, that makes it my business."

She was unable to read the message in his eyes.

"Have you ever talked to anyone? Ever shared it with anyone?"

She shook her head.

"Natasha, I'm your friend. You can tell me anything, I want you to know that."

She looked away from him.

He released her. "Is that where all this anger you carry around comes from?"

Natasha sat woodenly for a few moments, having a battle within herself. Unable to stand it, she put her face into her hands and began crying.

Striker watched her for a moment, unsure what to do, then knelt down, gathered her into his arms and held her. He didn't seem to mind that his shirt quickly grew soaking wet at the neck.

After Natasha had gotten some control, she drew back from him. "I'm sorry. I didn't mean to do that."

Striker tucked a strand of hair behind her ear, his hand lingering on the side of her neck, and gave her a gentle smile. "You've just ruined my favorite shirt, so now you have to tell me."

Natasha tried to return his smile but couldn't manage it.

He stood and walked into the bathroom, then returned with a box of tissues and held it out to her.

She took one and wiped her eyes, took another one and blew her nose.

Striker placed the box on the floor beside her, then returned to the window seat.

Natasha leaned back against the rocker, trying not to meet his gaze.

He waited for her to tell him.

"I was raped," she said.

Striker stiffened.

"The actual term would be date rape," she went on, in a trembling voice. "Every time I would hear those two words, I always thought, well, there are two sides to every story. Maybe he thought she said yes or didn't hear her when she said no because he was too involved with what was going on. Or I'd hear about some girl being in the guy's apartment and I'd think, well, she shouldn't have been there to start with. A hundred different little reasons to tell myself maybe she deserved it."

She hesitated, fighting to control herself. "Till it happened to me." She swiped at her eyes.

"What happened?"

Natasha glanced at him, then away, and finally brought her eyes back to his. "Striker, please, you don't want to hear this."

He stared at her.

She sighed and looked down at her lap. "I was dating this guy and he was a little possessive. Or that's what I kept telling myself. We had been to this wedding reception, and this other man kept hitting on me. I don't understand you guys, another man pays your woman some attention, you blame your girlfriend for it like it's all her fault when actually it's not." She glanced at him.

Striker nodded as if he understood, encouraging her to continue.

"After the reception, he wanted me to go home with him, and I knew in my gut I shouldn't go with him the way he was acting. But I thought, okay, I'll make it better, he's just feeling a little jealous. So I went, knowing I shouldn't."

Natasha was plucking at her jeans, working her lips, trying not to cry. "And once he got me inside, he—well, he raped me." She wiped her eyes again.

Striker nodded. "That's why when Roger—"

"He pinned me down using his chest and shoulders to keep me under him. He had his hands on my butt the whole time, clutching my butt, pulling me into him." Her voice was ragged, her breathing raspy.

Striker noticed she was trembling. He leaned forward, stroked her arm, and spoke in a calming voice. "It's okay."

"That thing with Roger, it just kind of triggered that memory," Natasha said, after she got herself under control.

"I owe you an apology, Natasha. I didn't know that or I wouldn't have been so rough on you."

"I deserved that and more. I knew better than to accuse Roger. I just couldn't seem to control myself."

Their eyes met, held.

"And after?" Striker said.

She looked away. "He went into the bathroom, like it was just nothing. I got up, went to his closet, got his baseball bat—he was a ballplayer for an amateur club—went down to the parking lot and smashed all the windows in on his vintage Mustang."

Striker grinned.

That grin made her feel better.

"And?"

"I went back upstairs, walked in on him in the shower, showed him the bat, told him he might want to look out the window, then told him if he ever came near me again I'd do to him what I'd done to his car, and left."

"Good for you."

Natasha gave Striker a defiant look. "Yeah, well, I just wish I could have transferred that terrible pain, hurt, rage he left me with to that shitty car of his."

Striker leaned toward her. "Why didn't you report it?"

"You know why. I would have been the one put on trial. I didn't want that."

She read the question in his eyes. "Three years ago."

"You were working for us?"

She nodded.

"Yet you kept that to yourself, all this time?"

Yes again.

"Why didn't you tell me? I would have done something about it."

"I'm just your employee, Striker. You're not there to fight my battles for me."

He reached out and stroked her cheek with one finger. "You're more than that and you know it."

Natasha wasn't sure what he meant.

"You want me to go kill him for you?"

She didn't know if he was serious or not. She finally decided he was trying for levity, so gave him a shy smile and was awarded with a smile back.

Striker leaned toward her again, staring intently at her.

"What?"

"You've been carrying that around all this time, Natasha. I don't understand your reasoning."

"It's my problem, I'll deal with it."

"And how are you dealing with it?"

"I don't date anymore," she said, "I don't…" hesitating "…do that anymore."

"Don't you think there's a better way?"

"Maybe. I don't know. But it works for me." She looked away from him.

"You so sure about that?"

Natasha shrugged her shoulders, then brought her eyes back to his. "You think I'll ever get this bodyguard thing right?"

"Just like that?"

"Please, Striker. I don't want to talk about it anymore."

He gave her a quizzical look.

"Please."

He nodded. "Okay. As for being a bodyguard, you're pretty green, way too impulsive, but—"

She stood. "Okay, I get it. I'll walk you out."

"I said but."

Natasha nodded.

"You don't want to hear the rest?"

She shook her head. "Maybe later."

At his car, Striker opened the door, then regarded her. "I'm curious about something."

Natasha gave him a pained look. "Please, don't ask me anymore about it."

"No, I'm respecting that. I was wondering if you meant everything you said to Roger."

Natasha frowned as if she didn't understand.

"You insinuated you had thought about letting yourself fall in love with him."

"I don't lie, Striker."

He drew back, shocked.

"I could probably be happy with him. He's a great guy, very sweet and sensitive, a lot of fun, plus smart as hell. You'd never know he's a rich man as unpretentious as he is, and I really respect that in him."

Striker wondered if she considered him pretentious. He hoped not.

Natasha smiled a little. "To be honest, I could get real used to living this kind of lifestyle. I think I'd be, well, very comfortable with Roger." She gave him a look he couldn't read.

"But?"

"But right now, I don't think I'm ready for comfortable. Not yet."

Striker nodded, glad to hear that.

Natasha looked away from him. "So, how much did you see?" she said in a low voice.

"See?"

"You know, when you turned on the lights." She looked back at him and seemed embarrassed. "You didn't really see me naked, right? I mean, I was under the water, in the deep end, pretty far away."

Striker resisted the urge to smile, thinking he had gotten a good enough glimpse to know he liked what he saw.

"Water distorts things, you know. Makes some things look larger than they actually are, others smaller."

He grinned at her. "Yeah?"

Natasha gave him an exasperated look.

"I didn't see anything," he lied.

The relief was evident on her face. She reached out and touched his arm. "Thanks, Striker. Thanks for listening. I think you've managed to help me in some way."

Striker brought her hand up to his mouth and grazed her fingers with his lips. "Take care of yourself, Natasha. You scare me sometimes with your reckless ways."

She nodded.

He climbed in his vehicle, but before he shut the door, said, "Oh, by the way, tomorrow you get the reprimand you missed tonight."

"Shoot!" She caught his grin when she looked back at him.

Striker motioned for her to go inside. She turned and waved at the door.

Natasha walked into the house with a beaming smile on her face, studying her fingers, which were still tingling from where Striker's lips had kissed them. She heard voices from the kitchen and remembered Pit and Bigun were mad at her because she had gotten them in trouble. She sniffed her running nose, knew her eyes were all red and swollen. Okay, she knew how to get them to feel better toward her.

Entering the kitchen, she looked at them long enough so they would see her tear-streaked, puffy face. She used a paper towel to wipe at her nose, then approached the table, where they were sitting, eating, of course.

"I'm sorry, guys. That was all my fault, and I'm so sorry I got you in trouble with Striker," Natasha said, acting as if she were on the verge of crying.

Bigun looked concerned. "Dudette, what'd he do to you?"

"Just gave me a good talking-to." She dabbed at her eyes with the paper towel.

Pit and Bigun glanced at one another.

Pit pulled out a chair, giving her a sympathetic look. "You hungry? Why don't you sit down and have something to eat?"

She squeezed her eyes shut, as if fighting tears, and tried to make her voice sound upset. "No, thanks. I don't think I want to sit down right now. I just think I'll go on to bed."

Natasha kissed each on the cheek, then walked upstairs with a grin on her face, thinking they were so easy. She didn't see the identical frowns on their faces, but knew they were there.

C H A P T E R 19

▼

Striker was meeting with his financial adviser when he got an alert from Pit. "Striker," he said into his phone.

"Hey, man. Nattie and Roger are gonna go pick up that SUV he ordered."

"SUV? What the hell did he order an SUV for?"

"Nattie thinks his van doesn't fit his image, and he likes the one you drive, so he ordered one just like it." Pit sounded amused.

Striker shook his head. "Okay, alert me if you need me."

An hour later, he got the alert. "Striker," he said, praying to God that Pit would be telling him they were on their way home and nothing else.

"We got a situation here," Pit said.

Striker mentally sighed. "What'd she do now?"

"She's got her gun trained on a policeman and we can't get her to let him go. Hell, man, she won't even let us near her or the guy, threatens to shoot him if we get within five feet of them. If anybody calls the cops, she's gonna get her head blown off."

Striker took a moment. This was the first time he had ever heard Pit anywhere near a panic. Ignoring the questioning look from his adviser, he stood and was out the door at a run. "Where are you?"

Striker ran red lights and wove in and out of traffic, all the while keeping Pit on the phone, who tried to get Natasha to take a call from Striker, which she refused.

Thankful his adviser's office was within minutes of Natasha and her latest fracas, Striker arrived to find a policeman belly down over the hood of Roger's new SUV with his arms splayed in front of him and Natasha holding her gun against his temple.

Striker braked his Hummer to a screeching halt behind the company SUV. The male bodyguards, warily watching Natasha, didn't even look his way. He glanced inside their vehicle when he passed by and saw a pale Roger reclining on the back seat.

"I think he's gonna be okay," Pit said, answering Striker's look.

Sirens screaming toward them, Striker jogged over to Natasha and stepped into her field of vision. She glanced at him, then to the policeman, then back.

Striker tried to keep his voice mild. "I hope there's a good explanation for this." He darted a look toward Pit and Bigun, who continued to guard Roger inside the SUV.

"Check him out, Striker," Natasha said, her voice shaking. "Check him out, make sure he's who he says he is. He refused to show us his badge."

Striker's eyebrows climbed his forehead. "Where's his gun?"

"I don't know. I didn't frisk him, I didn't want to take my hands away."

"You got two guys here could have done that."

"They need to stay with Roger. We don't know if there's just this one guy or others."

Striker patted the man down, removing a gun from his hip holster and another one strapped to his ankle. He tucked both into the waistband of his jeans.

"Okay, Natasha, he's clean. You can take your gun away."

She shook her head. "He manhandled Roger, Striker. I don't like that."

The sirens were right at them. Striker touched her shoulder. "Put your gun away, Natasha, or you're going to be some SWAT guy's prime target in about thirty seconds."

Natasha glanced around, then back at Striker.

"It's okay, just step away."

She did so with reluctance and, when the policeman turned around, kneed him in the crotch. He collapsed on the ground, holding himself and gagging.

Natasha leaned down into his face. "You think you can manhandle anyone any old way, huh? Not this time, you piece of shit!" She kicked him in the stomach.

Striker pulled her off. "Will you calm down?" He looked behind him at three police cars converging on the scene.

Four cops climbed out of their cruisers and ambled toward them, their eyes scanning the scene. They looked from the squirming policeman on the ground to Striker, who had placed Natasha behind him in an effort at protection.

Turning her back to them, Natasha knelt down so they wouldn't see her restrap her gun to her ankle.

The oldest of the group, the one with the sergeant stripes, glanced at the heaving policeman on the ground, then turned to Striker. "Striker," he said in an amiable voice.

"How's it going, Mac?"

"Pretty good till I got this call. What's going on here?" His eyes darted toward Pit and Bigun.

Natasha began waving her arms around and yelling about the cop manhandling Roger.

Striker turned and glared at her.

She quieted.

"Why don't you let me handle this?" he said, as nicely as he could. Man, he couldn't wait until he got her to himself.

"But he hit Roger."

Striker's eyes flared.

Natasha grew silent.

Striker turned back to the older policeman and handed over the guns he had confiscated. "Looks like you got a rookie cop here who either doesn't have a badge or doesn't want to show his badge and likes to assault innocent citizens, Mac."

The sergeant regarded the young officer. "That true?"

"Hell, no, it's not true," the policeman grunted.

"You lying piece of shit!" Natasha yelled in Striker's ear.

He turned and gave her another look.

"Sorry."

"Okay, let's take this one at a time." The sergeant turned to Natasha. "Since you seem to like to talk so much, young lady, and he doesn't look like he can at the moment, why don't you tell us your version?"

Natasha stepped from behind Striker to stand next to him. "Okay, we were just riding along—"

"Who's we?"

"Roger and me. The guy in the back of that SUV over there." Natasha pointed. "The one holding his stomach, probably very badly hurt, because this sick scumbag couldn't control himself."

She moved toward the injured policeman and Striker hauled her back.

After Natasha was safely out of kicking distance, the sergeant said, "Think you can tell us your story without going off on a tirade or do we need to go to the station and have a nice sit-down and do it there?"

Natasha glanced at Striker, who gave her a warning look. "Okay, I'll just tell it. We were stopped by this guy." She didn't allow herself to look at the policeman but pointed in his general direction. "And he comes swaggering up to the SUV and asks to see Roger's license and registration. Well, Roger just bought the car, so he doesn't have the registration, only the papers." She pointed again. "So this guy acts like he thinks maybe we've stolen the SUV when Roger tells him that and tells him to get out of the car. I tell Roger he doesn't have to, we haven't done anything wrong, and ask the guy to see his badge. He tells me he doesn't have to show me his badge and for Roger to get out of the vehicle. I told Roger to stay where he was till I called my boss to see what we needed to do. While I'm calling Striker," now waving toward him, "this guy," motioning toward the policeman on the ground, "jerks the door open, pulls out Roger, and hits him in the stomach."

The sergeant looked from Striker to the rookie to Natasha. "And?"

"Well, that made me mad, so I stopped him from assaulting Roger any further."

"You stopped him."

"Yes, I stopped him."

"And how did you stop him?"

"I put my gun to his head," she said with a proud look.

Shit, Striker thought.

Everyone was silent for a moment, considering this.

"You carry a gun?" the sergeant said.

"Well sure. Don't you?"

Someone snorted a laugh; Striker thought it might be Pit.

"You got a permit?"

"Of course I've got a permit. What do you think I am, a criminal or something?"

"May I see it, please?"

"Sure." Natasha didn't sound so sure of herself now.

Striker silently prayed she had it with her.

"It's, um, in the SUV. Can I go get it?"

The sergeant nodded his assent, then turned to the cop on the ground. "What's your story?"

Natasha wheeled around and came back. "No, huh-uh, no way. I want to hear what he says in case he lies so I can tell you he's lying."

Striker turned to her. "Just go get the permit, Natasha. They don't need any input from you at this point. You've already given them your statement."

She thought a moment. "Well, okay, but I'll be right back. You'll tell me what I missed, right? I want to know what bullshit he's feeding you guys, 'cause take it from me, if this guy is actually a policeman, you got yourself a problem child on your hands."

Striker tilted his head at her.

She shrugged, then walked away.

Mac gave Striker a sympathetic look.

"Yeah, I know, there goes my problem child," Striker said.

"Tell us what happened," the sergeant said to the young officer.

He sat up, wincing and holding his stomach, playing this for all he could get. "I pulled them over because they didn't come to a complete stop at that stop sign back there, asked to see the license and registration, and when he didn't have the registration, I asked him to step out of the vehicle while I called it in."

They waited. Apparently, he didn't have more to say, so the sergeant nudged him a little. "Did they ask to see your badge?"

The cop cast his eyes away. "I don't know. I don't remember."

The sergeant leaned toward him. "Did you refuse to show them your badge?"

"I think she might have hit my head. I don't remember."

Natasha joined them. "Oh, for Pete's sake. Go ahead, feel for a lump. You know what? You won't find one, because I didn't hit that idiot in the head. I kicked him in the cojones." She turned to the policeman on the ground. "That is if you actually have any, you pusillanimous—"

"Natasha!" Striker said forcefully, interrupting her tirade.

The sergeant gave the rookie a hard stare. "Did you assault the man over there like this young lady says you did?"

The cop shifted position, grimacing. "I might have pushed him, but I sure didn't assault him. He pushed me first, though."

Natasha pointed toward Pit and Bigun. "Ask those guys over there. They saw the whole thing. They can tell you what happened."

The sergeant looked their way, then motioned for the other policemen to go talk to the two bodyguards and Roger. He focused on Natasha. "You have that gun permit?"

Natasha gave Striker a smug smile before producing it for the sergeant. "Bet you thought I didn't have it with me."

Striker ignored her.

"Anything else you want to tell us?" the sergeant said to the cop on the ground.

"Yeah, Sarge. I want to file a complaint against her. She assaulted me!"

"Yeah, and I want to file a complaint against him for assaulting my friend and acting like the proverbial power-hungry, megalomaniac douche bag you guys are so proud of putting out there on the streets to protect innocent people like—"

Striker clamped his hand over her mouth.

"Hey," she said, in a muffled voice.

The sergeant looked up from the gun permit and noticed this. His eyes darted toward Striker. "Thank you,"

"Anytime." Striker flashed a shark's grin at Natasha.

The other policemen returned and the sergeant took them aside to hold a short conference with them.

Natasha removed Striker's hand from her mouth. "Very funny."

"You don't learn to control that temper and that mouth of yours, you're gonna end up in a whole world of trouble one day," Striker said, facing her.

"Oh, boy, here comes another scolding."

"That comes later, dear. I promise you that."

Shoot!

The sergeant motioned for Striker to join them. Striker yelled for Bigun to come watch Natasha, warning him not to let her get near the cop on the ground.

Bigun held Natasha by the arm and gave her a sympathetic look. "Oh, dudette, I hate to think what the Strikester's gonna do to you now."

"I imagine a lot of yelling," Natasha said, trying to sound bored.

"If you're lucky."

Natasha looked at him, wondering what he meant by that.

They watched the five men confer, then Striker gestured for Natasha and Bigun to join him with Roger and Pit.

Striker addressed Roger, who was sitting up with a colorless face. "How bad is it?"

Roger gave him an embarrassed look. "I'm okay now. Couldn't breathe at first, but it's better."

"Lift up your shirt," Striker said.

They watched Roger raise his shirt, then stared at his chest and abdomen, searching for the beginning signs of bruising or any lacerations.

"Don't see anything other than a slight redness," Striker said. "Can you breathe okay now? Feel any sharp pangs when you do, anything like that?"

"I'm fine," Roger said.

"Breathe deep. Make sure he didn't crack a rib or something."

Roger took a deep breath, then exhaled. "It's okay, Striker. He didn't hit me that hard."

Striker glanced at Natasha. "Okay, if we don't press charges, they won't, and we'll just consider this something that, well, didn't happen."

Natasha opened her mouth to protest.

Striker put his hand over it once more and glared at her. "Listen to me, Natasha. They've got more on you than you have on them. The guy can claim Roger fought him and make it stick; you know that. He's a cop and this is a cop's town. You assaulted him with a gun and kicked him twice. The only thing that saved you is he didn't show you his badge because he apparently doesn't have it on him, the idiot."

Her eyes widened.

Striker removed his hand. "Let it go."

Natasha looked at Roger. "What do you think?"

"Listen to Striker. I don't want to have to deal with this anymore."

"Okay," Striker said. "Pit, you drive Roger home. Bigun, you take Roger's SUV and follow them. I'll bring Natasha after I tie up things here."

Natasha moved toward Pit. "I think I'll just go on home with them."

Striker reached out and caught her arm. "Nope, I do not think so."

Bigun sadly shook his head.

Pit gave Natasha a concerned look. "Good luck, man."

"She was taking up for me, you know," Roger told Striker before being driven away.

Striker turned to Natasha and handed over her gun permit. "Go sit in the Hummer. I'll be there in a minute."

Natasha sat in Striker's vehicle, watching her boss and the sergeant step apart from the others and hold their own conversation, both having a good laugh over something.

When Striker climbed in the vehicle, still grinning, she said, "Well?"

"Well what?"

"What were you-all over there laughing about?"

"Nothing. Just guy stuff."

Natasha became paranoid. "You weren't, you know, talking about me, were you?"

Striker gave her an innocent look. "Why would we be doing that?"

She shrugged. "They are going to do something about that cop, aren't they?"

"The deal is, they do something about him, I do something about you."

"What's that mean?"

"You'll find that out when I get you home."

Natasha mentally gulped.

Striker stayed on the phone during the ride to Roger's estate, talking to his secretary about rescheduling appointments he had missed due to Natasha's skirmish, so Natasha didn't get a chance to try to talk her way out of this mess.

By the time they arrived, Natasha was feeling anxious and more than a little guilty. Watching Striker climb out of the Hummer, then pause on the front steps to wait for her to join him, she resisted the urge to jump into the driver's seat and drive away. She took her time opening the door and exiting the vehicle, frantically searching for a good reason she should not be fired for violating one of Striker's favorite and oft-quoted rules: never pull your gun in a public place.

Striker held the door for Natasha, then entered the mansion after her. She stood in the foyer, gazing uncertainly at him.

"Go on up to your room. I'll be there in a minute," he said, dismissing her.

Natasha gave him a stubborn look. "I'm not going up there. You want to talk to me, do it down here."

"Okay. You want Roger, Bigun, and Pit to hear what I have to say to you, fine with me." Striker stopped outside the door to Roger's office and indicated with a sweep of his hand for her to precede him inside.

Natasha remained where she was.

Striker gave her his full attention.

"Why do you always send me to my room like a naughty child?" she said, sounding like one.

Leaning toward her, Striker flashed his evil grin. "Because, my dear, that's exactly what you are."

Natasha was offended.

Striker straightened. "Think about it." He turned away.

"I don't have to think about it."

He looked back at her, eyebrows raised.

"You want to know what I think?"

He faced her once more. "Go ahead."

Natasha poked a finger in his direction while she spoke. "I think there's a part of me that subconsciously plays to a part of you that subconsciously plays to a part of me back, that's what I think. So you think about that."

Striker frowned, watching her walk away from him. Parts? What parts?

Natasha washed her face in her bathroom, then returned to her room to sit on the bed to wait. Feeling restless, she rose, walked over to the window, and stared outside. She sat in the rocker but couldn't get comfortable, so returned to her bed. She was worried what Striker had told the policeman he would do about her, was terrified he was going to fire her.

Tired of waiting, she opened the door before thinking she had really pushed him this time, maybe she ought to just once do what he said, so sat on the bed again.

Recognizing the footsteps coming down the corridor as Striker's, Natasha sat up straighter and made sure her hair wasn't all mussed, then remembered she hadn't put on lip gloss since they left the car lot. She was looking toward the bathroom, wondering if she had enough time, when the door opened. Striker stepped into the room, affecting her the way he did each and every time she first saw him, his powerful presence seeming to smack into her like a hot summer wind. She felt her face flush.

He brought the rocker close to the bed, sat in it, and studied her for a long moment.

Growing uncomfortable at his examination, Natasha smoothed her hair.

Striker's eyes bore into hers. "I don't get you. At the office, you're every bit the professional, a real businesswoman, but get you out of the office and you turn into this wild, free-spirited, out-of-control..." He shook his head, searching for words.

"Zany? I've always liked that word."

"More like nut case," he said, glowering.

Natasha shrugged her shoulders. "Go figure."

Striker leaned toward Natasha and she leaned back. "Which one's the real Natasha, I wonder."

She grimaced. "You probably don't want to hear this, but it's not the business-woman you referred to earlier."

Striker nodded as if he already knew this. "I'm going to talk to you, Natasha, and you're going to listen to me and you're going to sit there and hear me out and not say one damn word, you understand?"

Nodding, she tried not to look anxious.

"We're going to discuss this propensity you seem to have developed to place yourself in situations that go way beyond the norm, as well as this aggressive side of yours I never even knew existed until you took this job, along with your inability to control your mouth or your body, not to mention this liking you have for using other people as punch bags."

Natasha tried not to wince at the angry tone in his voice.

"Then we're going to discuss ways to help you, Natasha, dear, learn how to focus that aggressive energy in a more useful, productive way."

Yikes! "As in?"

Striker glared at her.

"Sorry," she said in a small voice.

There ensued a rather intense discussion on Striker's part, during which he reminded Natasha about what he liked to call the rules of the game, meaning, conduct yourself in a professional manner at all times and for the love of God don't ever pull your firearm in a public place unless absolutely necessary, among others. Rules she had by now heard countless times. He then proceeded to suggest to her that she might want to think of more productive ways to occupy her time that would not involve altercations with other human beings.

"As in?"

He tilted his head at her.

"So you're saying I need to keep myself busy."

"I'm saying, you need to find a way to get rid of that aggressive energy of yours that doesn't involve harming or threatening others," he said in a tight voice.

"As in?"

Striker scowled at her. "Do you really want me to tell you?"

Actually, she didn't. "Okay, I understand what you're saying."

Striker finally got to the part she had been waiting for all along. "I've talked to the boys about this, and they understand what I'm doing here, so don't think you can go crying to them to get you off the hook."

"Like I'd do that."

"Where are your guns?"

Guns? Why was he asking where her guns were? Then she knew the answer. Her face reddened. "You wouldn't!"

Striker waited for the verbal tantrum he knew was coming.

"What is this? You going to treat me like a Barney Fife, let me have a bullet to carry around in my pocket? Come on, Striker, this isn't Mayberry, North Carolina. I'm not some incompetent, high-strung, neurotic deputy ready to go off half-cock, you know."

Her flashing eyes met his and she knew without being told that he would not vacillate.

Natasha looked away and gave a sad sigh, then turned back to Striker. "Please, don't do this."

"You've pulled your gun in a public place three times now, without reasonable cause as far as I can see. You've given me no choice, Natasha. You know that."

She focused her attention on her hands while considering this. "How long?"

"Until you've learned how to keep yourself under some kind of control." Striker watched a lone tear slide down her face. Shit.

"You know what you're doing, don't you? This is the ultimate humiliation, Striker."

He stood. "The ultimate humiliation, Natasha, dear, is if I pull you off the case. Let's hope it doesn't get to that point."

Natasha reached down, unstrapped her .22 from her ankle holster, and held it out to him. She rose from the bed, walked to the dresser, pulled her Glock out of her purse, and handed it over.

"That it?"

She nodded, looking away from him. She was trying hard not to let him see how much this upset her but knew she was losing the battle.

Striker resisted the urge to comfort her. "Just prove to me you've gotten that impulsive side of yours under control, and I'll return the guns."

She didn't acknowledge this.

"It's not the end of the world, you know."

Natasha was studying the carpet at her feet.

"Okay. I've got to get going. I'll talk to you later." Striker left, frustrated with himself for feeling sorry for her.

CHAPTER 20

▼

There was a preternatural stillness to the mansion when Striker entered. Accustomed to noise, usually lots of it, when he visited, he stood in the foyer, ears alert, trying to gauge where everyone could be. He closed the door behind him and walked toward the kitchen, glancing at his watch, thinking they must be eating an early lunch.

The kitchen was as vacant as the rest of the house seemed to be. Okay, they had to be here. The company SUV was out front, along with Natasha's jeep. They could have taken one of Roger's vehicles, but Pit hadn't alerted him, and the fact that the SUV was still there indicated otherwise. Brutus wasn't in his usual place in front of the dishwasher, so he had to be with them. Maybe they were on the grounds somewhere.

A faint oofing sound got Striker's attention. He paused with his hand on the doorknob and glanced behind him. There it went again, followed by muffled laughter. He headed downstairs, in the direction of the gym Roger and Natasha had recently completed.

Striker stepped into the room, which looked like it occupied at least half of the basement, and grinned. Natasha and Bigun were facing each other across mats laid on the floor, engaged in some sort of physical combat. Natasha was taunting the huge bodyguard, telling him to bring it on if he was man enough, as she circled him. Bigun stood glowering, his eyes tracking her moves, reminding Striker of a bull ready to charge; he half-expected to see Bigun plow the floor with his foot and blow smoke out his nose any minute now. He watched Natasha dance up to the bodyguard, lightly kick at his body with her foot, then flit away before he could capture her.

Natasha was dressed in a sports bra and biking shorts rolled to reveal a lovely navel. Her hair was pulled back into a ponytail with dampened strands around her face and neck. Sweat glistened on her body and dark splotches saturated her pale-gray sports bra. Bigun, wearing nothing but a pair of baggy nylon gym shorts, seemed unaware of the perspiration running in rivulets down his torso. Striker noticed several red places on the bodyguard's abdomen where he assumed Natasha's foot had landed.

Striker glanced around, saw Pit sitting on the floor, a bag of crushed ice between his legs—that held Striker's attention for a few seconds—then moved on to Roger, standing against the wall, watching Natasha with a grin on his face. Brutus was lying beside Roger, his head resting on paws, watching the show on the mats.

Striker leaned against the wall and waited to see what was going to happen next.

"Come on, you big weenie," Natasha jeered at her colleague, grazing him with her foot. "You want me on my back, put me on my back if you think you're man enough."

Bigun grunted in response.

"Come on, you chicken. I opened me up a whole can of whoop-ass and it's still full. Give me something here."

Bigun, deciding he'd had enough of this, lumbered toward Natasha with murder in his eyes. He kicked out with one bare foot, which Natasha sidestepped with ease. She caught his foot in her hands, pushed up, and sent the bodyguard toppling onto his back.

"Shit!" he roared.

Natasha danced away. "Oh, yeah, I'm the one."

She ran over to Roger. "Hit me, baby."

Striker watched them high-five one another and shook his head.

"What do you think?" Natasha swept her hand toward the makeshift gym.

Striker took time to study the room in more detail. A punching bag hung from the ceiling, grouped with a weight bench and set of free-weights, a complicated-looking resistance weight machine, and rower. Two treadmills, a stair-climbing machine, and an exercise bike stood in front of a 60-inch plasma television mounted on one wall. Four medicine balls rested near the mats, which occupied the greatest floor space in the room. Striker noticed boxing gloves hung on the wall nearest the mats, along with what looked like fencing swords and masks. His eyebrows rose at that.

He nodded. "Looks good. You-all did it up right down here."

Natasha and Roger beamed at one another.

"Okay, who's next?" Natasha said.

Roger shook his head with a good-natured grin. "Hey, I know when I'm out of my league."

Natasha looked at Pit.

"Hell, no, you already kicked me in the balls once today. You think I'm gonna give you another chance?"

"Hey, I pulled that kick short, you doofus. You're the one that stepped into it."

Natasha turned to Bigun, still on his back on the mats.

"Like I told you, dudette, I don't hit girls."

"Yeah? That's only 'cause you can't catch them."

Striker laughed at Bigun's expression.

She turned to Striker. "What about you, big man? I need a new opponent, somebody I haven't completely throttled, and you look like you'll do just fine."

Grinning at her arrogance, Striker shook his head. "Better not. I might hurt you."

"I doubt it. Come on, Striker, show me some stuff here. Your choice, karate, kick-boxing, wrestling, touch boxing. You pick. And I promise I'll pull my punches."

"I outweigh you by at least eighty pounds. You'd be too easy for me. I need more of a challenge."

That got her back up. "Challenge? You don't think I'm a challenge? Well, come on, then, give me a chance to prove you're wrong, or are you gonna be like Bigun and hide behind the I-don't-hit-girls-'cause-I'm-nothing-but-a-big-old-weenie defense?"

"Hey!" Bigun said.

Striker stepped away from the wall. "I don't think so."

"I knew it," Natasha said. "I knew all that macho posturing was nothing but an act."

Their eyes met.

She smirked at him. "What's the matter, you afraid?"

Striker studied her for a moment, sorely tempted to put her in her place.

"I'll be gentle, I swear," she said, smiling at him.

"I don't doubt."

Her eyes narrowing, she brought her chin up in a defiant way. "You need a handicap? I'll give you one, whatever you need. Want me to tie one hand behind my back? Sure, no problem."

Striker stepped onto the mat. "Name it."

"Since you're a virgin in the I got beat by Natasha club, I'll let you choose your form of torture."

Striker was starting to enjoy this. "Nah. I'll be a gentleman and give you the edge. What's your best event?"

She thought. "How about a combination of kick-boxing and wrestling? Every time you hit the mat, that's a pin. Five pins and I'm the winner."

"Easy enough."

"Take off your shirt."

Striker raised his eyebrows at her.

"I don't want to have to listen to you whine when I beat you 'cause I grabbed clothing and you weren't dressed properly."

Natasha watched Striker unbutton his blue oxford shirt, then pull his shirttail out of his pants. After shrugging out of the shirt, he threw it toward the wall and stood before her, clad in jeans and boots. His well-defined, muscular body looked huge, powerful. She had to force herself not to say "Wow!" out loud.

When she looked into his eyes, she could see he was aware of her admiration. That made her mad.

"Shoes, too."

"Oh, yeah." He gave her his own smirk and sat down to remove his boots, then socks.

They stood face to face.

"This is gonna be so easy." She grinned at him, offering her clenched fists for him to butt with his own.

They faced off on opposite sides of the mat.

"Roger, you call the pins," Natasha said.

The first one was easy. Natasha let Striker come after her, waited for the kick, which would have taken her in the abdomen if she wasn't so quick, grabbed his foot before he could gain his full balance, twisted behind him and shoved, sending him crashing onto his stomach.

"Hooh-wah!" She strutted away from Striker. "I am woman and I am strong!"

"One to Nattie," Roger said, grinning at Natasha's victory dance.

Striker was on his back, raised up on elbows, watching her. "So you want to get serious?" he said, his voice mild, his eyes shooting daggers.

"Oh, the big man thinks he gave me that one. Well, come on, then, get me on the mat, you think you can do it."

Striker rose to his feet, trying not to let her irritate him.

Half an hour later, they were circling each other, sweat glistening on their bodies, eyes locked, warily watching the other one. The score was four for Striker, three for Natasha.

Striker was a little out of sorts; he had thought he'd win this hands down, but she surprised him with her agility, not to mention speed. She kept catching him off guard, sending him reeling. He had been trying to hold back, afraid he'd harm her, but was tired of chasing her around, tired of her circling him like a pesky fly.

Natasha could see the ominous glare in Striker's eyes but didn't let that intimidate her; she was having way too much fun. She had gone into the match knowing he would win but was glad to see that he found her a more formidable opponent than he expected her to be. She knew he was pulling back, knew he was going easy on her, but not as much as he had initially thought he'd have to. She had stopped taunting two pins back, saving her breath for those energetic spurts when she spun away from his well-placed kicks. She knew not to let him get his hands on her; he had proven himself too strong in that regard.

Striker made half-hearted attempts to take her, which she dodged with ease. This didn't concern him; he was waiting for the moment she wouldn't be so on-guard, letting her think he was more winded than he actually was. The whole match had been Striker on the offense, Natasha on the defense. She was smart enough not to go for him, knowing if he got his hands on her, there was no match. He watched her keeping her distance, her eyes tracking his hands and feet, and realized with some surprise that he was having a lot of fun here, even if she did aggravate the hell out of him.

He suddenly stopped and stood still.

She quit moving, watching him with skepticism.

"Come on," he said, sounding out of breath. "Let's get this over with."

She circled him, gauging his look, thinking he should be in better shape than that, *looked* to be in better shape than that. She stepped closer, giving herself enough space to dance out of reach if he came for her, but he surprised her with his quick reflex. Before she knew it, he had her in his arms. She wrapped a leg around his and kicked, trying to make him off-balance. Reciprocating, Striker overbalanced, and both crashed to the mat, Natasha on her back, Striker on top. If Striker hadn't cushioned her fall with his arms, she would have been knocked breathless.

Her legs, of their own volition, spread enough to allow Striker's hips to settle between them. If the two had been nude, one quick, fractional movement would have consummated a deal neither one was ready to forge. They stared into each other's eyes, both breathing heavily, both more than aware of the other's physical configuration in relation to their own.

"Five for Striker," Roger called. "He wins."

Neither one heard this nor Pit and Bigun making a lot of congratulatory sounds toward Striker.

CHAPTER 21

▼

They were sitting around after a quick lunch, drinking iced tea with Striker, when the third call came.

Natasha answered, listened for a moment, then handed the phone to Roger, signaling Striker.

Striker picked up the phone from the wall, checked the caller ID, and swore under his breath at the Unknown Caller display.

Natasha ran into the office and snatched up Roger's other cordless. She clicked in, heading back to the kitchen.

Roger was giving the man his own passive kind of hell for not showing up at Wal-Mart that day.

"Hey, man, I was there, but this dude and his woman got into some kind of argument in the parking lot, drawing all kinds of attention, and I wasn't about to hang around. They got security cops there, you know."

Natasha was relieved that he didn't sound angry over the missed rendezvous. When her eyes met Striker's, her face reddened at his disgruntled look.

The extortionist instructed Roger to meet him at a club in the Old City the next evening at nine.

Roger glanced at Natasha.

She nodded to indicate she knew which one he was talking about.

After Roger hung up the phone, before Natasha could even open her mouth, Striker looked at her and said, "No."

She started to protest.

Striker interrupted her. "You're not going with Roger, don't even ask it. We've had two aborted attempts so far, each of which was your doing."

"But—"

"No, you're not going to go sit in the van," he said, before she even asked it.

"Well why not?"

"Because I can't depend on you to do what you promise me you're going to."

"But Striker, he doesn't know who we are. He said a man and his woman in the parking lot, which means he didn't recognize us. So I can be there, if that's what you're worried about."

Striker gave her a bland look. "No."

Natasha started to argue again, then hesitated. Wait a minute. He said she couldn't go with Roger, that she couldn't go sit in the van, but he didn't say she couldn't actually go. She turned her back on Striker, walked to the sink, and busied herself with the dishes.

Striker watched her, expecting an argument, and grew surprised when he realized she wasn't going to push it.

Roger was staring at Natasha's back. "I want her to go."

Natasha turned around, wanting to waylay any kind of discussion where Striker might get real specific about things. "It's okay, Roger. He's right. It's better if I don't go with you."

"You're sure?"

She smiled at him and tried to act unconcerned.

"Well, okay." Roger sounded disappointed.

Natasha loaded the dishwasher, ignoring the men while they made plans for the next evening, until Roger asked what kind of a club it was.

"Kind of alternative," she said, approaching the table. "They have live bands. Most people go there to dance, but they've got a bar toward the back. That's where he said to meet him, right? It's past the dance floor, almost in the very back of the room."

"I take it you've been there," Striker said.

Natasha shrugged. "You want to go clubbing, that's one of the places to go."

Natasha waited until Striker was leaving, then caught up with him at the front door to walk outside with him. "Since I'm banned from going with Roger or riding in the van, is it all right if I have tomorrow evening off?"

That didn't sound right to Striker, but he couldn't figure out why. "You're not going to pout?"

"What's the point, just wasted energy." She tried to act like she didn't care anymore. "So?"

"Sure. No problem."

Natasha smiled. "Thanks. I think I need to get some family time in, you know, and I don't want to hang around here by myself, just waiting."

Striker climbed in his vehicle with an edgy feeling he didn't trust her.

"So, you gonna give me a rematch?" she said, before he could close the door.

Striker glanced toward the house. "What's going on with that?"

"You told me to find some way to get rid of my aggressive energy, so…"

"So instead of beating up on outsiders, you're choosing to stay in-house."

"Actually, I'm just trying to keep in shape."

Striker nodded like he didn't believe her.

"You gonna give me a rematch or not?"

"Maybe."

"One thing, Striker."

"Yeah?"

"Don't pull your punches next time. I don't need you to go easy on me."

He gave her an innocent look. "Who said I was easy on you?"

"Well, I know I was easy on you, so if that was your best, you're not even worth the effort. I could give you some pointers, though, if you want."

Smiling at his scowl, she gave a wave and went inside.

The next evening, Natasha was gone by the time Striker arrived at Roger's mansion. "What'd Natasha do, go to her mom's?" he asked Pit.

"No, man, I think she had a date."

"I thought Natasha didn't date," Striker couldn't resist saying.

Pit thought, then shrugged. "Whatever she's doing, man, she's dressed fit to kill."

They arrived at the nightclub fifteen minutes early and trooped inside. Striker decided if the extortionist hadn't recognized Natasha and him in the Wal-Mart parking lot, there must have been some other way he found out about the bodyguards than actually seeing them. He wondered about this as he stood at the bar with Roger, watching Pit and Bigun moving around, never staying in one place for long, keeping an eye on Roger and the bag.

Striker's gaze roamed the large room, making sure his other men were in place. His eyes focused on a woman with blond hair dancing to the blaring music. Although she had her back turned toward him, her long legs gave his brain a familiar nudge. He liked the way her body moved so fluidly, so loosely beneath the short, black dress she wore. When she turned around, his eyes narrowed and his jaw muscles clenched.

Roger followed his gaze. "Is that Nattie?"

Both watched her now; Roger's mouth open, Striker's in a thin line. Natasha was engaged in what looked to Striker to be some sort of weird mating dance with a tall, slender man endowed with wide shoulders, narrow hips, and dirty blond hair. A guy who looked like one of those male models Striker always thought were such sissies. The two moved together synchronistically, smiling at one another, and seemed to be having a lot of fun.

Pit joined him at the bar. "Hey, man, Nattie's here."

"I see that," Striker said, between gritted teeth.

Pit watched her with a smile on his face. "Man, nobody can hip-hop like Nattie."

Striker gave him a look, then walked toward the dance floor.

"Uh-oh," Pit said, stepping up beside Roger.

Natasha was having a great time, thinking it had been too long since she had done this as she moved with her partner. She turned away from him, felt someone staring at her, and glanced up. Striker was standing a few feet away, glaring. Her breath caught at the sight of him and she stopped moving at once.

Striker was dressed in black this evening: shirt, leather coat, pants, shoes. He wore a small, silver hoop in his ear and there was black stubble on his face. He looked more powerful and dangerous than anyone she had ever seen, and this only served to deepen her attraction for him.

Striker tried to control his temper, more than cognizant of Natasha's short, clingy dress showing those gorgeous legs of hers and a tease of cleavage, her hair curling around her face, the way her body had been moving. He became aware he was feeling more than a little movement in the nether regions. He didn't like that; he didn't like that at all. He approached her, watching her watch him, her expression that of a deer caught in the headlights just moments before impact. Deciding he liked that, he gave her his grin, the evil one.

Natasha stepped back away from him and bumped into her partner, who had also ceased moving and was watching her, wondering what was going on.

Natasha forced a smile on her face. "Striker! Hey! I'd like you to meet Cameron."

She turned, grabbed her partner's hand, and pulled him toward her. "Cam, this is my boss, Striker."

Striker's eyes never left Natasha's. "I want to talk to you."

Natasha frowned at his rudeness.

Shit, Striker thought.

"Actually, I think you gave me tonight off, so I'm not actually employed by you at this moment. So if it involves anything along the lines of my job and working for you, I'd rather we table this conversation until a later time," Natasha said, in a somewhat snippy tone.

She watched Striker's eyes darken. "Listen," Natasha said, before he started hitting something or someone, maybe her, "you said I couldn't come with Roger and I couldn't sit in the van, but you did not say I could not come with anyone else. You never specifically said that."

Striker visibly bristled.

"Listen, Striker, Roger's my man. I can't just sit at home like a good little girl and wait for y'all to come tell me what happened. I'm not going to interfere with anything. I just thought I'd hang out here, you know, make sure Roger's okay." Natasha looked around Striker toward Roger and waved at him. "That every-thing..." Her eyes grew wide. "He just grabbed the bag!" She dashed away.

Striker wasn't sure what she said, so was a little slow in reacting. He turned and noticed Roger frantically looking around, Pit and Bigun nowhere in sight. Natasha was streaking through the crowd toward the entrance. Striker ran after her.

Natasha kept the man with the bag in view, angling away from him in an effort to get to the door first. Seeing he was going to make it before her if she didn't do something, she moved toward him, sliding down into the side tackle she loved so much in soccer. She kept telling herself, *Don't let your knees hit the floor, don't let your knees hit the floor,* knowing that would slow her down. She slid on her hip, which was protected by her silky dress, mindful of the fact that if her bare legs hit, she'd have one hell of a floor burn.

He was right at the door when she skidded into him. The man tripped and crashed toward her, but Natasha rolled away just in time. He landed on his back with the bag still in his hand.

Natasha scrambled up and planted a spiked heel on his crotch. "You move one inch, they're gonna be calling you choir boy, if you get my gist." She applied enough pressure to show him she was serious. She wished she had strapped her .22 to her leg, then remembered she didn't have a gun anymore.

Beside them in an instant, Striker darted an angry glance toward Natasha before reaching for the man. "Get off him!"

After Striker had the man standing, he pulled his coat open to show him his holstered gun in an effort at intimidation. A customer standing nearby watching this scenario yelled, "He's got a gun!" For the next few minutes, there was nothing but utter chaos in the room as people began scrambling for the door, veering away when they saw an ominous-looking Striker at the front entrance, all running toward the back of the club.

Striker handed his catch off to Pit and Bigun, retrieved the bag, and turned to Natasha. "Go home, now!" he barked, then left to find Roger.

Natasha arrived home around two a.m., cursing to herself when she saw Striker's Porsche in the driveway. She stayed outside for awhile, trying to think of a way to sneak into the mansion and get upstairs without being detected by her boss. She stepped back, eyeing the windows on the second level, wondering if there were any ladders in the gardening shed that would extend high enough to reach. But she had this thing about heights. What if she climbed the ladder and it fell or something and left her dangling off a window ledge? She mentally shivered. Okay, she had done some rock climbing, how hard would it be to negotiate brick? She stepped closer to the house and tried inserting her fingers into the mortar line. Nope, not deep enough. She wouldn't be able to get a good enough purchase with her hands or feet.

She looked up at Roger's windows, which reflected the night sky. What if she got his attention and got him to, like, tie sheets together or something and drop them out the window? She could climb that, as long as she braced her feet against the wall. Yeah, that was good. She searched around, found a small rock, and flung it that way. It bounced off the side of the house, well below the glass panes. She found another rock, slightly larger, and hurled it upward. Instead of angling toward the window, the rock flew straight up and came back down, bonking her on the head.

"Ow!" she yelled, cradling her head with both hands. "You are such a girl," she told herself with disgust. Why in the world hadn't she played softball as a kid? A fat lot of good soccer had done her developing a pitching arm. But wait a minute. Maybe she couldn't throw, but she could sure as heck kick. She eyed another rock, then grimaced when she remembered she was wearing strappy sandals. Open-toed, expensive strappy sandals. She sighed with frustration.

Out of options, she decided she couldn't stay out there forever, might as well face the music. Besides, her head hurt like a bitch.

Striker had placed himself in the library, where he had a bird's-eye view of the front door and intended to stay until Natasha got home, even if it meant he would be there all night. He was curious about Cameron, although he wouldn't admit this to himself, instead rationalizing he needed to talk to her about why she had disobeyed his orders and gone to the club. He had ledger sheets from the office and meant to go over those while he waited but was surprised to find himself thinking about Natasha and feeling a little betrayed at the fact that she was with another man. He analyzed his feelings, finally admitting to himself he was more attracted to her than he wanted to be, but knew he could not take it further than that; after all, she was his employee. He was troubled that, of late, he was no longer interested in pursuing other women, none seeming to measure up to Natasha. His musings were interrupted when the front door squeaked open.

Natasha tiptoed in and closed the door as quietly as she could, wincing at the screeching sound the hinges made. She reached down, slipped out of her shoes and, holding them in her hands, walked toward the stairs. She was almost there, thinking, *Made it*, when she heard, "Natasha!" from the library. She stopped, thinking, *Shoot!*

"In here," Striker said in a low voice that carried in the hushed house.

Natasha hung her head for a moment, then turned and reluctantly walked toward the library.

"Close the door," Striker said.

Natasha glanced at Brutus, on the couch, snoring loudly, oblivious that anyone had come into the house or even the room, for that matter. She shook her head in frustration. "Can I pick a guard dog or what?"

Striker resisted the urge to smile. "Sit."

Natasha sat in the chair beside the desk and reached up to gingerly touch the crown of her head. She withdrew her hand and studied her fingers, then noticed Striker watching her. "You see any blood?" Bending forward, she pointed toward her scalp.

Striker leaned toward her and squinted his eyes. "Maybe." He touched her head and felt a small lump. He looked at his fingers, rubbed them together, then smelled them. "That's dirt, not blood."

Natasha nodded.

"You hit your head?" he asked, when she didn't explain.

"Well, kind of."

"How do you kind of hit your head?"

"It's real easy when you throw like a girl."

"You threw something and hit your head?"

"You could say that."

"What were you throwing?"

"Rocks."

"Where?"

"Outside."

"Because…"

"I was trying to get Roger's attention."

"Because…"

Her face flushed. "I was hoping he could throw down some rope or something so I could climb up the side of the house and get inside without having to talk to you."

Striker nodded. "So you were going to, what, scale up the side of the house, thinking you could get past me and not have to deal with me, right?"

It sounded so foolish when he said it. "Well, yeah, I guess."

"Figuring I'd get tired of waiting on you and leave, right?"

"I was hoping."

"Did you think that I'd walk right by your jeep out there and not realize you were back?"

"Damnit!"

Striker leaned back and shook his head, unable to stop the grin that slid along his lips.

She sighed. "Okay, how much trouble am I in this time?"

"What took you so long getting here?"

She made a face. "I had to wait for Cameron to decide whether I got the honor of taking him home or not."

Striker didn't think he liked that.

"Cameron's my cousin. He's gay."

Liking that, Striker nodded.

"He met this guy and couldn't decide whether to leave with him or go home." Natasha shrugged. "Cam's a slut."

Striker grinned.

"Okay, I took my time. I was hoping you'd be gone by the time I got here."

Striker nodded.

"Well?"

"Well what?"

"Did he tell you who hired him to kill Roger?"

Striker shook his head. "Wasn't our guy."

"But he took the bag."

"Yeah. Our man gave him a twenty, told him to go grab it, bring it to him, he'd give him twenty more."

She thought about that. "And was gone by the time you got this dude to tell you where he was supposed to meet him."

"Yep."

Natasha sat back. "Did I screw this up?"

"I don't know. You stopped the guy. I'd say you probably helped more than hindered."

She gave him a worried look.

"What?"

"He'll be mad now. He probably won't approach us anymore, not if he saw…"

"Yeah, I thought about that. But he keeps coming back for the money, so he'll probably call again, maybe have stricter terms next time."

"As in?"

"Meeting one-on-one, in an isolated area, no one around; something along those lines. He's played it our way three times now, I don't think he will next time."

They thought about that for awhile.

"Striker?"

He looked at her.

"You understand why I was there, right? I mean, I know it made you mad, but I couldn't just do nothing. I had to make sure Roger was okay. And I didn't violate any policy or go against any instructions, maybe just interpreted what you said in a more vague way than how you meant it."

Striker took his time with this, knowing she had a point, but then, again, she knew exactly what he meant when he told her he didn't want her to go with Roger or wait in the van. He noticed her worried look and decided he didn't want to argue with her.

"I guess I'll know next time that when dealing with you, I need to be more specific."

"Yeah, well."

Their eyes met.

Striker felt drawn to Natasha as if she were magnetized. Realizing he might do something he shouldn't if he didn't remove himself from the situation, he stood and began gathering papers together.

"I'll walk you out," Natasha said, sounding disappointed.

They stood by the car with the open door between them, once more gazing at one another.

Natasha wasn't sure she liked the way Striker was looking at her, almost as if considering something. "What?"

"I've been thinking about what you said the other day, about a part of you that plays to a part of me that plays to a part of you back."

"Why do I always have to open my big mouth?" Natasha said, sounding caught.

"You meant that?"

She shrugged.

"Explain to me what you meant specifically by that."

She glanced up at the sky, toward the house, and finally brought her eyes back to his.

He raised his eyebrows.

"Well, I did say it. Okay, this is what I was feeling initially, you know, that maybe the child in me plays to the paternal side of you, which plays back to the child in me."

Striker looked like he didn't appreciate that.

"But then, that's not it. Well, not entirely. That's part of it, but not the whole of it."

He leaned toward her. "And what is the whole of it?"

"It's hard to explain, but you're like this big, powerful, sturdy rock, and I'm like one of those Mexican jumping beans. I mean, here you are, well-grounded, secure in yourself, in what you do, who you are, the space you inhabit. And here I am, bouncing around, not sure about anything, going from one extreme to the other, until I come into your space. And when I do, it's like you kind of catch me, you know, and keep me from bouncing around so much. Well, until I bounce back out of your space."

Striker stiffened.

She sighed. "I know that's rambling, Striker, and way too allegoric, but I swear, I can't think of any other way to put it."

Striker regarded her for a moment, then reached out and put his right hand on the side of her face. "You're a little bit nuts, I think."

Natasha gave him an offended look.

"But very beautiful," he added, in a tender voice.

Natasha put her left hand over his, turned her face into his palm, and grazed it with her lips. "So are you," she said softly, then pulled away.

Striker studied his hand. The palm felt afire where her lips had been. He looked back up, but she was gone.

CHAPTER 22

▼

At breakfast, Natasha told Roger she'd be gone for a couple of hours.

Roger glanced up from his laptop. "Where are you going?"

Natasha left the table to fetch the cereal box, then returned. "I'm taking my mom to the doctor."

"She okay?"

"Other than being half-crazy from a severe hormonal imbalance, yeah, she's great."

"You're taking her to a psychiatrist?"

Natasha gave him a grouchy look. "No, Roger, to her OB-GYN."

"So why do you have to go?" Roger sounded like he might want to complain about this.

Natasha sighed. "I am going, Roger, darlin', so I can speak to her doctor and see if that nincompoop will put her on some sort of HRT regimen so her hormones will go back to normal and I'll get my mom back."

"HRT?"

"Hormone replacement therapy!"

Roger scowled at her. "You ask me, you're the one needs HRT, not your mom."

"Oh, boy," Pit said, rising from the table and moving to the breakfast bar, Bigun right behind him.

The three men watched in fascination Natasha's internal battle to control herself. They had been privy to a lot of these since Striker had taken her guns away, most of which she had been losing.

"You want me to go with you?" Roger said, trying to appease her.

Natasha fanned her face, which was bright red. "I can handle this."

"No, I'll go with you. We all know how crazy your mom makes you. I'll talk to her, keep her occupied. Besides, I don't have anything else to do."

Natasha gave him a look, suspicious Roger had a crush on her mom. "You gonna come talk to the doctor with me, too?"

"Of course not. We'll drop you off, then I'll have Pit and Bigun take me by Circuit City so I can pick up some things I need."

Pit snatched up his phone to alert Striker.

Stevie seemed to be having a hard time trying to decide what to wear and, after making them wait what felt like forever to Natasha, appeared dressed in black from head to toe: long top, ankle-length skirt, and boots. With the blond, spiky hair and darkly lined eyes and lips, Roger thought she looked exotic but refrained from saying anything since Natasha would hear.

Natasha gave her mom her routine skeptical look, then headed for the car.

They climbed into Natasha's jeep, Natasha and her mom in front, Roger in the back seat. Pit and Bigun had been waiting at the curb in their company SUV and fell in behind Natasha's vehicle when she pulled out of the driveway.

The road they had to traverse to get to the interstate was narrow and curvy. Almost at once, they came upon an old man driving a red sports car, creeping along at twenty miles an hour on a forty-mile-an-hour road. Natasha held her temper in check until he started stepping on the brakes every other second, probably trying to get her off his rear.

"We're gonna be late, he doesn't get out of the way," she said. "Dang, Mom, why'd you and Daddy have to pick to live in the boondocks with all these old geezers driving around who don't have anything better to do than aggravate people like us who have some place to go."

Her mother reached over and blew the horn. They watched the man's eyes travel to the rear-view mirror, then his left arm somewhat arthritically extended out the window and one lone finger on his hand went up. The middle one.

Natasha rolled her eyes.

Stevie reached over and began beeping the horn. "Get out of the road, you old pervert!"

The old man repeated the rude gesture, but this time with emphasis, jabbing his finger into the air.

"Get out of the way, you old shit!" Stevie yelled.

Natasha's mouth dropped open; she had never heard her mom say the "S" word before. She glanced at her mother, whose anger seemed to be progressing with each blurt of the horn. Uh-oh!

"Mom, it's okay, we're not that late, just let him act like the idiot he is."

"Yeah," Roger said, from behind them. "It's no big deal, Stevie. He just wants to be an ass-hole."

"Ass-hole? He wants to be an ass-hole? Well how about I give him another ass-hole?" Stevie reached down toward the floorboard and picked up her purse. Plopping it on her lap, she zipped it open and pulled out a shiny object.

Natasha did a double take when the metallic gleam of a gun barrel caught her eyes. The jeep swerved, and they would have gone off the road if Roger hadn't reached forward, grabbed the steering wheel, and set them on course again.

In the vehicle behind them, Pit glanced at Bigun. "Here we go, man."

"Mom! What the hell are you doing?" Natasha said, her voice rising to a shriek.

Ignoring her, Stevie unfastened her seat belt and climbed up on the seat so that her head and arms were above the roll-bar. She pointed the firearm at the old man. "Move over, you ass-hole, or you're gonna get a brand spanking new one!" She waved the gun around.

"Roger, do something," Natasha said.

Roger, watching Stevie with his mouth open, appeared not to have heard her.

"Mom!" Natasha continually glanced from Stevie to the road to her mother again. "Mom, come on, get down. You know you're not going to shoot him. Come on, Mom. Get down off that seat, you could get killed." Natasha reached out with her right hand and tugged at her mom's skirt.

Stevie glanced at her. "Pull up beside him. I don't think I can get a clear enough shot like this."

"Mom!" Oh, geez, what was she going to do?

The old man took off, barreling down the road at a good sixty miles an hour.

Stevie watched him for a second, then glanced at her daughter. "He's getting away. Go after him!"

Natasha was busy searching for a place to pull off the road.

"Didn't you hear me? He's getting away. Catch up to that old fart. I'll teach him to flip me the bird!"

Natasha was frightened of this woman who used to remind her of June Cleaver. "Mom, please, just calm down, get back in the jeep, sit down, put that darn gun away."

"You don't catch up with him, I'm gonna boot you out of this car and go after him myself," Stevie threatened.

Natasha gave her mother a shocked look. Roger had to grab the steering wheel once more, which forced Natasha's eyes back to the road. Spying a church up ahead on the right, she sped up, pulled into the parking lot, and braked to a stop.

Pit and Bigun, right behind them, clambered out of the SUV and ran over to the jeep.

Stevie ignored them, giving her daughter an indignant look. "What the hell did you do that for?"

"Mom, please, just sit down." Natasha looked at her mother in her most pleading way while waving her hand at Pit and Bigun, meaning, back away.

They did, but their eyes remained on Stevie and the gun.

Stevie studied her daughter's face for a moment, gave a slight shrug, then climbed back inside the jeep.

Natasha waited until she was settled. "Mom, I think it'd be a good idea if you give me the gun."

Steve frowned at her. "Why should I give you my gun?"

"Because, Mother, you can't go around threatening to shoot people. You could get arrested for that. Where'd you get that thing anyway?"

Smiling, Stevie caressed the weapon in a loving manner. "I bought it. I've been taking lessons."

Natasha glanced at Roger, who looked just as surprised as she.

"Whatever did you buy a gun for? Mom, you used to hate guns. You were always afraid of guns—"

"Well, that was then and this is now. I'm tired of being afraid of every old thing that comes down the pike." Stevie picked up her pocketbook and placed the gun inside. "I'm taking control of my life, sweetie, getting rid of all those old fears and insecurities."

"Mom, shooting someone won't help you get over anything. It'll only land you in jail, you shoot somebody, don't you know that?"

"Of course, baby, I know that. Now, come on, let's get back on the road. We don't want to be late, do we?"

Natasha glanced at Roger, who did the whirlybird sign on the side of his head to indicate what Natasha already suspected: her mom was loony-tunes. She nodded in agreement, then looked over at Pit and Bigun, who were hovering close by.

"You didn't by any chance call Striker, did you?" she said, silently praying she wouldn't have to explain this to Striker.

Pit cast a wary look toward Stevie. "No, man. He gets too upset over shit like this."

Natasha nodded. "Thanks, guys." She gave them a wan smile and started the jeep.

Striker's SUV was parked in Roger's circular drive when Natasha arrived home. She cursed to herself, thinking Pit and Bigun had told on her after all. Climbing out of the jeep, she wondered with irritation why it was taking so long for the new surveillance system to be installed and why the heck Striker felt the need to oversee it. She stepped into the foyer, hoping he was on the grounds somewhere. She heard voices from the direction of Roger's office, so headed for the stairs instead.

Striker was descending as she was ascending.

He stopped when he got to her. "I was looking for you."

Natasha gave a burdened sigh. "It wasn't as bad as it looked, Striker, I swear it wasn't."

He raised his eyebrows.

"I mean, okay, there was a gun involved. But hey, it never went off, nobody got hurt, so, you know, it was okay. Everything turned out okay."

Striker's brow furrowed.

"You don't know," she said, reading his confusion.

"There something you need to tell me?"

She tried to pass. "I don't think so."

He barred her way past him.

They were close on that one stair, their bodies slightly grazing. Natasha felt her face flush as heat traveled through her body at lightning speed. Striker noticed this and frowned even more, wondering what that was all about.

Natasha looked away from him and cursed under her breath. Striker was thinking whatever she didn't want to tell him must be pretty bad to get her all flustered like that.

Natasha stepped down, away from him. "Okay, if you have to know," she said, and told him about the incident with her mother.

Striker had a good laugh.

Natasha's mouth formed a pout. "It's not funny."

"Did you get the doctor to prescribe medication?"

"Shoot, no. She insists she's fine, that she doesn't need anything, and somehow managed to convince that quack of the very same thing. In fact, to tell you the truth, by the time she got through with him, he was looking at me like I was the one in need of hormone replacement therapy," Natasha raved.

Striker laughed even harder.

The sound was infectious and she couldn't help but smile.

Striker leaned toward her. "Natasha, darlin', maybe you just need to let your mom figure this thing out on her own." He reached out with one finger and tenderly trailed it down her cheek.

Natasha tried to suppress the shiver that shot through her body at his touch. She felt her face redden again, turned away from him, and ran up the stairs, leaving Striker to wonder if he had offended her in some way.

CHAPTER 23

▼

They were standing outside what looked to be the kitchen window at Striker's house, the sill just over the top of Roger's head.

"Can you see anything?" Natasha whispered, watching him stand on tiptoe and crane his neck.

Roger grunted in response.

"Jump up a little. See if you can see anything that way."

He jumped three times, quick, little bunny hops.

Natasha sighed.

"Nope." Roger wiped his brow and looked at her.

"Okay, lift me up. Let me see if I can look in."

Roger's forehead crinkled. "How?"

"Just lace your hands together. I'll put one foot in there, and you can boost me up that way."

Roger leaned over and interlaced his fingers, forming a cup with his palms. Natasha placed her right foot in his hands, then braced herself with her left hand against the brick wall and her right hand on his shoulder. Bouncing with her left foot, she propelled herself upward. Roger yelped and undid his hands, and they both tumbled.

Natasha sat up and glared.

"You're heavier than you look," Roger said, sounding out of breath.

Natasha rose to her feet and brushed off her knees. "Oh, you're such a he-man," she snarled. Seeing Roger was offended and might not be so willing to help, she said, "Why don't you get down on all fours and I'll just stand on your back? Surely you can bear my weight in that position, you big weenie," unable to resist the name-calling.

"Hey!" Roger took the time to shoot her a dark look, then crawled on his knees closer to the wall and got down on all fours.

Natasha put one foot on his back.

"Ow!"

"Shhh."

"You're going to have to take those shoes off, Nattie. The heels are digging into my back."

"Damnit to hell." Natasha sat down on the ground, removed her shoes, and threw them at the wall. "Why do you have to make everything so complicated?"

She put one foot on his back and eased her weight down. "That better?"

"Yeah," he grunted, "that's much better."

"Okay, I'm going to put my other foot on you. I'll just take a quick peek, then be right off, all right?"

"Sure, sure, go ahead."

Natasha placed her other foot on Roger's back and began shifting around, trying to keep her balance.

"Will you just look?"

She raised up on tiptoes and had a brief glimpse of a speckled black-and-white granite countertop before she was in the air. She landed with a whumph.

"Ow!" Roger straightened up and rubbed his back. "What the heck did you eat today?"

Natasha sat up. "You're the biggest wimp I've ever in my life seen." She got to her feet and dusted off her backside. "I swear, Roger, we probably would do better if I got down on all fours and you stood on my back, you big baby."

Roger shrugged. "Okay."

That stopped her tirade. She thought about it. "Okay, let's try that."

Natasha approached the wall, got down on all fours, and glanced at Roger. "Take your shoes off first." She waited for him to do so, then braced herself when he stepped onto her back. She could feel her arms giving. "Oh, dang."

Roger placed one foot on her rear-end. "That better?"

Actually, it was. "What do you see?" she sputtered.

"Not much, the light's not on."

"You see Striker?"

"Yeah, you see Striker?" they heard from behind them.

Roger yelped, lost his balance, and fell off Natasha, landing on his side. He rolled over, scrambled up, then ran away, emitting short, panicky sounds.

Natasha closed her eyes, praying the voice she thought she heard wasn't it. She turned her head and squinted. Striker was standing close, watching Roger weave his way toward the street, still making those weird noises.

She hung her head. "Shoot."

Striker turned his attention to her.

Oh, God, she thought, seeing his look.

"You want to do this out here or go inside?" The mild tone of his voice belied the anger flaring in his eyes.

"Well, actually, I think I'll just go on home," Natasha said, standing and sidling around him.

At the sound of a car door slamming followed by an engine starting, Striker turned toward the street. "Looks like your ride just left."

"Roger! Don't leave me here, Roger, get back here, you big old baby!" Natasha watched with despair the smoke from her departing muffler dissipating in the night air.

Striker pulled out his phone and alerted Pit. "You realize you've got a problem over there?"

"Yeah, man, I was just getting ready to call you."

"You got Roger coming your way, hopefully, in the jeep. Natasha's here. I'll take her home later."

While talking to Pit, Striker stared at Natasha, who got busy putting her shoes back on. After he clipped the phone to his belt, he walked toward her. She backed up until she ran into the side of his house, realizing how truly dangerous he looked, glaring at her like that, looming over her like that.

She tried to make herself as small a target as possible. "I don't suppose you're in the mood for any sort of an explanation." She gave him a sick grin.

Striker put an arm above her head, leaned over her, and gave her his most evil glare. "Go in the house, Natasha, dear. I don't think I want witnesses to what I'm about to do to that nubile body of yours."

Natasha sidled along the side of the house to the door, then darted inside. She stepped into the kitchen, hurried to a large barstool near the cooking island and sat down on it.

Striker made it a point to slam the door closed. He stalked to the refrigerator, pulled out a bottle of water and twisted off the top.

Natasha felt a twinge in her neck and prayed he wasn't about to do the same to her. She tried smiling at Striker, which resulted in his frowning even more.

Striker took drinks from the water bottle while watching her, never saying anything.

Natasha wondered why he didn't just start yelling or something, what the heck he was doing, and finally figured it out when his phone twirped.

Still staring at Natasha, Striker pulled it out of its casing. "Striker," he barked into the two-way.

It was Bigun. "Hey, dude, we just picked up Roger."

"Well, that's just fine," Striker said, his voice low, almost musical, then clicked off.

Natasha literally gulped this time. "Can I talk?"

Striker put the water bottle down, crossed his arms, and waited.

"Well, Pit and Bigun were, you know, watching that WWE thingy on cable tonight, and you know how they get when wrestling's on, that's all they concentrate on. So I bet Roger that we could leave, go out somewhere, then go back, and they'd never even know we'd left."

Striker raised his eyebrows.

"Oh, you're probably wondering why we chose your house to come to."

He didn't respond.

"Well, I was just curious, you know, about where you live. And Roger told me he'd been here before, so I said, why don't you show me, I bet he lives in a great house. And by the way, Striker, this house is beautiful, right on the water, your own boat dock, that gorgeous cruiser out there." She paused, seeing his look.

"Anyway, I talked Roger into bringing me here. And then, once we were here, I thought, oh, man, this place is so beautiful, I wonder what it looks like on the inside. And Roger tried to explain, but he's just a guy, guys don't really pay attention to how another person's house is decorated—at least most guys don't. So, I—well, I talked him into helping me try to peek inside."

Striker remained silent, staring at her.

"Okay, I was looking for you. You happy? I was wondering if you were home, that's why I was looking in the window. Well, actually, Roger was. I tried to look first, but I was too heavy for him, so he was looking for me."

Striker picked up the water bottle and took another drink, his eyes never leaving hers.

"You're probably wondering why I was looking for you. It's just, you've become an enigma to me, Striker, and I'm a naturally curious person. That's why I want to be an investigator, you know. And okay, I admit it, I'm a little infatuated with you, with your mysterious ways. I mean, at the office, everybody's always wondering about you. No one knows anything about you, your personal life, what you do outside the office. By the way, is it true you were with the CIA?" She waited but he didn't answer.

"Okay, you don't have to tell me. I understand. I totally understand. It is so not my business."

He glowered at her.

"I messed up, huh?"

He raised his eyebrows.

She smacked herself on the forehead. "Oh, God, what was I doing. I took Roger from a safe place into an unsafe area, placed him in danger, all because I was bored and wanted to know where you live. Shit, shit, shit, I am so utterly stupid it's not even funny."

Striker nodded in agreement.

Natasha gave him a tentative smile. "Um, Striker, I was just wondering, how many reprimands does this make?" She grimaced. "No, don't answer that. Okay, I know I need to be disciplined for this little…" she hesitated at his expression "…okay, *major* indiscretion, so just tell me what the penalty is and I'll accept it. I know, how about a cut in pay? Yeah, that's good. I'll have a week's pay deducted from my paycheck. Okay, that's fine. I totally understand the need for that, so don't worry about it, I'll be okay. I mean, I'll feel the pinch, but I need to, you know, feel the pinch. I understand the need to take this sort of action."

Striker was looking at her as if she were crazy.

"Okay, that's settled then." Natasha slid off the stool. "I'm ready to go home now."

"Sit down!" Striker roared at her.

Natasha returned to her seat with haste.

"Now it's my turn," he said, advancing on her.

"Oh, shit," she said in a small voice.

"How old are you, Natasha?"

She blinked in surprise.

He cocked his head.

"Almost twenty-five," she said, wondering why he asked that.

"So you're not a child."

She snorted. "Of course not."

"At least in the physical sense."

"Hey!"

"As for mental, that's another case entirely."

"Hey, I resent that!"

"Answer me this. Did you maybe miss out on a part of your childhood that you're now trying to catch up on?"

Natasha thought about it. "Not that I know of."

He stared at her.

"You're saying I'm acting childishly."

"What do you think?"

"Well, maybe, you know, a little."

"A little?" he said with disbelief.

"Okay, a lot. But Striker, you've got to understand, I'm having so much fun living over at Roger's, hanging out with him and Pit and Bigun. We're like a family, you know, they're like big brothers to me, and I've never had siblings before and it's great. And I—well, I guess I tend to forget the seriousness of this situation, I get so involved in being part of a family unit with them."

"Well, maybe you need to feel a little hurt to remind you how serious the situation is next time you get in the mood to play one of your childish pranks."

"Uh-oh," Natasha said out loud.

"You're suspended."

"Suspended?"

"I'm suspending you from the job for one week."

She looked at him with alarm. "What does that mean exactly?"

"You're off the job for one week. Next time you do something this reckless, you're fired."

"So, I'm suspended from performing my job duties. That's what you're saying."

"Which means that you're suspended from Roger's. Come on, I'll take you home."

She was on the verge of tears. "Home Roger's or home home?"

"You're not going to Roger's. You're suspended from there."

"Striker, you can't do this to me," she said, standing and looking at him in a pleading way. "I'll take the suspension, fine, but at Roger's."

"No. You go to Roger's, what's to stop you from doing something even more stupid next time?"

"I won't, I promise. I'll stay in my room the entire time, or the house. I won't do anything, go anywhere, Striker, but you can't suspend me from Roger's."

Striker leaned toward her and spoke in a stern voice. "Don't buck me on this, Natasha. Take what's being offered or the punishment is going to be much more severe than that."

Natasha watched him for a moment, wondering what he meant. Then remembered this would have been her fifth reprimand, two past the official dismissal one. "You're talking about firing me?"

Striker stared back but didn't respond.

She walked past him. "Okay, fine."

"The garage is this way."

Natasha turned and glared at him. "I'd rather not be near you right now, if you don't mind, so I'll just get home on my own."

He stalked toward her. "You live at least ten miles from here, you gonna walk?"

She gave him a petulant look. "I'll go find a convenience store or gas station and call a cab."

"At one in the morning, you're going to go walking the streets." He leaned down in her face. "Will you for once consider the action you're about to take and the subsequent consequences?" He was shouting now.

Natasha drew back. He was right, she knew it, but she didn't want to admit it. "Okay, I'll let you take me home," she said, acting as if she were doing him a big favor.

Striker came real close to booting her on out the door.

Natasha was surprised to find Striker knew where she lived, but she wasn't talking to him so couldn't ask how he had come by that information.

He stopped the car in front of her cottage and studied it in the headlights. "I like the style."

"My dad built it." Natasha loved her house, even though it was tiny.

"Yeah? Well, looks like he did a good job."

"He's a great dad."

Striker turned to her. "Okay, speaking as your employer, Natasha, the suspension stands for one week. During that time, you disengage yourself from your man and your job, you understand? No paying visits, calling, nothing like that. You're out of it for now."

Natasha looked out the window, chewing on her bottom lip.

Striker touched her arm to gain her attention. "Speaking as your friend, accept the suspension as it stands, use it to your advantage."

Natasha didn't know what he meant but decided she'd figure that out later. She climbed out of the car, started to close the door, then leaned her head back in. "Thanks for the ride," she said, her voice cracking, tears falling, leaving Striker feeling like he usually did when dealing with her: the world's biggest bully.

CHAPTER 24

▼

The next day, Natasha spent most of the morning at the family barn, mucking stalls and grooming her horse, then saddled up and went for a ride. Afterwards, she cleaned her small cottage. When she was finished, she walked to her parents' house to have lunch with her mom, telling Stevie she had taken a break from the constant supervision of Roger and would be home for a week or so.

That afternoon, she sat outside on her back deck, smoking cigarettes, ignoring her continually ringing cell and house phones, pondering what Striker had said.

Scott showed up mid afternoon. After knocking and not receiving an answer, knowing she was home since the front door was open but the glass door was locked, he strode around back.

"There you are," he said, stepping onto the deck.

Natasha ignored him.

Scott pulled a chair over next to her and sat down, then took a moment to enjoy the pastoral view. "Nice out here."

Natasha remained quiet.

Scott shifted around to face her. "So, when are you coming back to the office?"

Natasha glanced at him, then away. "I'm not."

He frowned. "You're off the case, so I—"

"I'm suspended from the case for one week, Scotty. I'm not off the case."

"Okay, suspended for one week. During that time, I figured you could come back into the office and help me straighten out the mess that temporary's made of our accounts."

"Thanks, but no thanks."

"Well, why not? You're still in our employ, and as your boss, I'm telling you I need your help in the office this week."

Natasha ground out one cigarette and lit another. "I don't think so."

"Why the hell not?" Scott said in a loud voice.

She glanced his way, then back to the pasture. "Because I am no longer an office manager, Scott. I'm a bodyguard. I don't do that anymore."

"I'm your employer, Natasha, and I am telling you, get your butt back to the office."

"I do not think so."

Scott lunged out of the chair, walked in a circle, then stalked up to her. "Okay, you're not in the office tomorrow morning, nine o'clock sharp, you're fired."

Natasha gave him an insolent look. "I'm fired anyway."

"No, you're suspended!"

She stood and faced him. "Thanks for clearing that up."

She entered her house and closed the door, ignoring his shouts.

Striker showed up later that afternoon, following Pit, who was bringing Natasha's jeep to her.

Natasha was back on the deck, doing what she had been earlier.

Pit climbed out of the jeep, walked around, and handed Natasha her keys. "Hey, man, this sucks."

She gave him a wan smile. "It's okay, don't worry about it."

Pit gave Striker a belligerent look when he stepped onto the deck and said, "I'll wait in the car, man."

"Pit," Natasha said.

He turned and looked at her.

"Y'all be sure and feed Brutus on time. You know how gassy he gets if he doesn't eat on schedule."

"Don't worry about that, man. Roger's taking care of Brutus just fine."

Natasha nodded.

Striker watched the bodyguard walk away, tired from the hell he had had to endure from Pit, Bigun, and Roger, all three acting like kids forced to be without their mommy.

"You all right?" he said, sitting down in the chair formerly occupied by Scott.

Her eyes regarded him for a fleeting moment. "If you came because Scotty sent you, then go away. I'm not coming in."

"Coming in where?"

"To the office, to be office manager again. He said if I'm not there by nine o'clock tomorrow, I'm fired." She cast a quick glance his way, long enough for him to see the emerging tears. "Is that true?"

Striker sat back, thinking now he had to deal with Scott on top of the other three men. "No, that's not true."

"Well, then, thank you."

"I'll deal with Scott, don't worry about it. Your official job title is still body-guard, not office manager."

"Thanks," Natasha said in a small voice.

Striker watched her take a drag from the cigarette. "When'd you start smoking?"

She shrugged, blowing smoke, keeping her eyes on anything and everything but Striker.

Striker's eyes traveled the property, appreciating the view. He nodded in the direction of three horses grazing near the fence. "Those yours?"

Natasha gave the animals a loving look. "My family's. The bay's mine."

"You ride?"

"Since I was a kid," Natasha said, still not looking at him.

Striker's eyes returned to the two Tennessee Walkers and the bay Quarter Horse. "How come you don't ride a gaited horse?"

Natasha turned to him, her eyes alight.

For a flicker of a moment, Striker felt as if someone had reached into his head and rattled his brain a little.

"You ever ridden a Quarter Horse, Striker?"

He nodded.

"Then you know what I'm talking about."

He smiled. "Full gallop, all the way."

She returned his smile. "There's no better feeling in the world than to be on a Quarter Horse that's going full out, is there? It's like sitting in a rocking chair. They got all that power in their butt, faster than shit, smoothest ride you'll ever want." She paused, remembering she was supposed to be mad at him.

Striker was grinning, nodding in agreement, then caught her tenseness again. "You still mad?"

Natasha looked at him. "Maybe embarrassed more than mad."

Their gazes locked, and there it was again, that pull he felt for her, his body responding to it, wanting to reach for her. Instead, he said, "Well, better get back to the crybabies," and left.

Striker dropped Pit off at Roger's, then drove to the office in search of his business partner. He found him in the conference room with papers spread out on the table in front of him.

Scott glanced up. "I'm glad you're here. I need to talk to you about something."

Striker pulled out a seat, sat down, and before Scott could even start, said, "Natasha stays on as bodyguard. Quit pressuring her about coming back in here."

Scott leaned back, surprised at this; he had thought Striker would agree with him.

"And quit threatening to fire her," Striker said, with an angry look. "She works under me now. I'll be the one to decide whether she goes or stays."

Scott glared at Striker, trying to control himself.

Striker waited him out.

Scott straightened in his chair. "Why don't you just fuck her and get it over with?"

Striker's eyes hardened.

"Hell, Striker, we all know there's something weird going on with the two of you, the way she keeps baiting you and the way you bite every time, almost like you're just sitting there waiting for it."

Striker remained silent.

"You've never gotten as involved with a case as this one, and it doesn't even merit your attention, if you want my opinion. But that's all you seem to want to focus on, what's going on with Roger and Nattie, and what's she going to do next. If she were any other bodyguard, you would have fired her after the first reprimand. We both know that. You need to pull out or you need to pull her out, because this can only lead to disaster and you know it."

"You through?"

Scott didn't like the stormy look in Striker's eyes. "Yeah, I think I've said what I wanted to."

"Okay, first off, as a bodyguard, like I said, she's under me, Scott, so step aside and leave her alone. As for my overt interest in this case, Roger's my friend, so this does merit my attention. And as far as Natasha goes, I'm simply trying to uphold the agreement you made with her. Second, there's no kind of baiting and biting going on here, much as you'd like to think there is. We got us one loose cannon out there, thanks to you, and I'm doing everything I can to keep her in line, which means I monitor this case the way I see fit. Third, I can't pull her off, because if I do, Roger's going to immediately hire her back as his own personal bodyguard. Now, think about it, what's the safest way to go here, keep her in as my employee, where I do have some kind of authority over her, or let Roger have her with no one overseeing what she does? That's disaster waiting to happen right there and you know it."

Striker stood, a truculent look on his face. "Anything else you want to talk about?"

"What's the point? You're in her corner now. You won't listen to me."

Striker turned and left.

Scott was back the next day.

Natasha was in the same place, doing the same thing.

He stormed up to her, pointed his finger in her face. "How'd you do it?"

She lit a cigarette. "Do what?"

"Get Striker to agree to keep you as bodyguard and not let me have you as office manager."

"Go figure."

"When are you gonna stop playing with this guy?" Scott yelled.

Natasha frowned. "Playing with whom?"

"Striker. Ever since you got this job, he's like a bull in a china shop. Before this shit started, Striker was where he needs to be, in the field, overseeing what goes on out there. Since this job and you, by the way, he stays in-house, driving me and the whole staff crazy, throwing things around, having his little temper-tantrums when you pull one of your pranks. Yet you somehow manage to convince him to let you stay where you obviously do not need to be."

"I'm not coming back."

Scott sighed. "Nattie, this company is going to the dogs. All Striker can concentrate on anymore is you and what the hell you're up to now, so the fieldwork isn't being monitored like it needs to be. We got an office manager who can't seem to add two and two and has our accounts in all kinds of disarray, not to mention Striker making everybody grumpy with his fuckin' moods, thanks to you. The only way we can get everything back to normal is if you come back where you're supposed to be, where you need to be, as our damn, friggin' office manager."

Natasha gave him a sweet smile, then stood. "Thanks, but no thanks."

She went inside, ignoring Scott's temper-tantrum on her back deck.

That evening, Natasha packed a few things into her jeep and drove to her parents' cabin on Norris Lake, one of the most picturesque bodies of water in East

Tennessee. Before leaving, she told her mother where she would be and left her cell phone behind.

Striker showed up the second day. Natasha had been swimming at the lake and was strolling back to the cabin when he arrived. She startled when she saw him, then modestly wrapped a towel around her, staring at him as she approached. Appreciating the pure masculinity of the man standing there watching her, his powerful frame dressed in jeans and a chambray shirt, with sunglasses covering his eyes, her body broke out in goose bumps.

She stopped when she got close to him and cocked her head, giving him a puzzled look.

"I called your mom and cajoled her into telling me where you were," he said.

Natasha nodded, then silently led the way to the cabin.

Striker followed her inside and looked around. "I like it," he said, nodding with approval.

Natasha smiled at him over her shoulder. "Pretty rustic compared to your place." She didn't bother to close the bedroom door after her and let the towel drop as she walked further into the room.

Striker realized just before she disappeared from view that she had been wearing a thong. He grew frustrated when he caught himself thinking how much he liked the way her butt looked walking away from him.

Natasha joined him a few minutes later, dressed in a short sundress. "Would you like something to drink?"

"Water if you've got any bottled."

She took a bottle from the refrigerator and handed it to him.

"Let's talk," Striker said.

Natasha plopped down on a roomy couch in the living area and drew her legs up to sit Indian style. "Go ahead."

Striker took a seat in an overstuffed chair across from her. "You need to come back," he said, without any preambles.

Natasha looked alarmed. "Oh, gosh, Roger's okay, isn't he? Nothing happened to Roger, did it?"

"No, no, everything's okay." Striker sat back and rubbed his face. "I can't take it anymore," he said in a miserable voice. "They are giving me pure, unmitigated hell and I just can't take it anymore."

Natasha watched him but remained quiet.

"So I'm shortening your suspension. Just come back and take care of that crew. I'm tired of dealing with them."

Natasha leaned back. "Actually, I'm glad this happened. It's given me a chance to do some pretty heavy introspection. I've kind of found out a few things about myself, things I wasn't aware of."

Striker raised his eyebrows.

"You ever take psychology, Striker?"

"Yeah, a few classes."

"You know the reason a child acts out, severely misbehaves?"

"For attention, I think."

"Right. They're trying to get attention, even if it's in the negative form."

"And?"

"Think about it."

"So you're saying that applies to you."

"I think we would both agree I was acting pretty childishly."

"Trying to get attention from?"

"We both know the answer to that one."

He was stunned by her revelation. "You want to talk about this?"

"Nope. Just making an observation."

He was a little shocked she was being so blunt with him. "You're sure? I mean, I'd like to explore this a little."

"No."

Striker watched her. Why had she told him this if she didn't want to talk about it?

Natasha grew uncomfortable at his scrutiny. "I'm not ready to explore the reason why in any real depth, not at this point, okay? Maybe at a later time, maybe when this is over, but not now. I choose not to now."

"Okay. I can respect that."

"I think I needed to grow up. I think I needed to get back in control."

"Are you?"

"I guess we'll find that out," she said, then added, "but I'm not coming back until the suspension's up."

Striker frowned at her insubordination.

"You're sending the wrong message to me and the others if you give in to what we all so obviously want."

Striker drew his head back, dumbfounded.

"You have to stand strong on this one, Striker. You've dealt out the punishment and you can't go taking it back. It makes you look weak. And we all know you're not weak," Natasha went on, seeing that he was growing offended "You're the employer, we're the employees, and you can't back down from a disciplinary action just because no one's happy with it."

Striker rubbed a hand over his face. "I don't get you."

"Join the club."

Their eyes locked, and Striker felt the pull once more.

"Don't make me or the others feel that we can manipulate you or force you to change your mind, not over something like this," she said in a soft voice.

"Damn, Natasha, where the hell did you come from?"

She gave him an impish smile. "My mom swears I was beamed here from another planet."

Striker grinned.

Standing, Natasha gave him a sober look. "Now, if you don't mind, you need to leave."

Striker felt rejected; he didn't like that.

"I'm suspended from my job. That means you, too."

Striker rose to his feet, aware of how much he would like to stay.

Neither one spoke as Natasha walked him to his car.

Striker opened the door, turned, and regarded her once more.

Natasha smiled at him. "Thanks."

"For?"

"For coming, even though you shouldn't have. But it was great seeing you. I've missed you." She stood on tiptoes, leaned forward and pecked him on the cheek, then turned around and sashayed back to the cabin.

Watching her swaying hips, admiring her graceful body, Striker realized he had missed her much more than he ever would have thought possible. He became cognizant of gathering priapic heat and wondered where that came from, the kiss or her body. Probably both, he decided.

He forced himself to get into the car and leave before he said the hell with it and went inside after her, which was what he actually wanted to do.

CHAPTER 25

▼

Natasha and Roger were playing golf with Bigun and Pit trailing behind in their own golf cart. By the time they arrived at the ninth hole, their carts had somehow gotten separated and the other two bodyguards were nowhere to be seen. Natasha wasn't particularly concerned about it, more interested in having a better score sheet than Roger than with what had happened to her colleagues.

Natasha waited for Roger to set his tee in the ground, looking up at the sky, feeling the warm sun on her face, happy to be back with her friends. She smiled and sent a silent prayer upward, thanking God for such a perfect day. Something buzzed by her left ear and she waved at the air around her head, fearful it was a bee come to feed on her. She glanced around but didn't see an insect of any sort.

A few seconds later, she noticed Roger's hands flapping at the air around his head. "Dang fly," he mumbled, positioning himself, shifting his hips, then his shoulders, readjusting his grip on the golf club, doing his little routine which was starting to bug Natasha by now. Not liking the way the ball was sitting, he bent down to place it in a better position.

Natasha saw something glinting in the sun hurtle into the space formerly occupied by Roger's upper torso, then continue on. Huh, a silver bee. She heard a twanging sound when it smacked the golf cart. What the heck kind of bug was that? She looked at the cart, saw the nice round hole in it, opened her mouth and shouted, "Gun!"

Natasha crashed into Roger and both fell to the ground, this time landing apart.

Roger started to sit up, saying, "What the heck is with you and yelling gun, then tackling me," but stopped short when Natasha pulled him back down, seeing the look on her face.

They felt more than heard a whizzing sound over Roger's head, followed by a metallic ping when it hit the side of the golf cart, about six inches to the left of the first one. Roger and Natasha looked at the bullet hole, then at one another.

"Gun!" they yelled, beginning to panic.

Natasha started to rise but thought better of it when another bullet rammed into their cart. Nudging Roger, then motioning with her hand, she began crawling on her belly around the golf cart, trying to get away from the ambush, thankful the cart was close but hating they had to maneuver a slight incline.

On the other side, Natasha sat up and leaned against the front tire and Roger sat up and leaned against the rear tire.

Roger gave her an anxious look. "Where's your gun?"

Shoot! "Striker still has it."

Natasha remembered her cell phone with the two-way. If it was in the cart, she thought she could reach it.

Both instinctively dodged when a bullet slammed into the side of the golf cart.

"Stay down," Natasha hissed at Roger.

Keeping her back against the tire, she put her right arm inside the cart and began fishing around, feeling for the phone. When her fingers only touched an empty floorboard, she began to panic. Had she lost it or left it back at the clubhouse?

"Where's my cell? Didn't I have it in the golf cart?"

Roger shrugged and his eyes seemed to be darting everywhere. "Where's Bigun and Pit? They were right behind us not five minutes ago."

Natasha moved her hand closer to the seat and brushed something plastic. She snatched up her cell phone, keyed it to the two-way mode, saw Striker's number was the one that came up. She pushed the button to alert him.

A bullet dug a furrow in the ground between the two of them.

"Damn!" Natasha molded herself against the tire. She glanced at Roger when she pushed the alert button once more and didn't like the panicked look in his eyes.

"He's got to be in that copse of trees over there. To get to us, he'll have to come out in the open, so as long as we stay behind the tires, we ought to be all right," she said.

Natasha was relieved to hear "Striker" coming over her two-way.

"Striker, we're at the country club playing golf and somebody's shooting at Roger and me. We're hiding behind the golf cart, but I don't know how safe—dang!" Natasha almost screamed this when a bullet tore into the front seat right by her head.

"Where's Pit and Bigun?" Striker said, his voice pressured.

"I don't know. We somehow lost them."

Natasha noticed Roger inching his head up. "Roger, for Pete's sake, keep your head down. You don't want to get it blown off."

They both looked skyward when a bullet buzzed by about six inches from the top of Roger's head.

"Give me the layout," Striker said curtly.

"We're on the ninth hole, hiding behind the golf cart. He's to the—shoot, let's see, the sun rises in the East, so he's—Striker, I don't know. It's noon and I can't tell from which direction he's shooting. But there's a copse of trees across from us, and he's somewhere in there, shooting right at us."

"Stay hidden as well as you can. I'm on my way. I'll see if I can locate Pit and Bigun and get them headed toward that copse."

"Okay," Natasha said in a shaky voice.

"Natasha!" Striker said, after she thought he had gone.

She put the phone up to her mouth and noticed she was trembling so violently, the phone was shaking from side to side. "I'm here," she said, trying not to cry.

"Stay where you are, don't do anything foolish, you hear me? If he hasn't been able to hit you up until now, chances are he can't get a good enough shot, so stay where you are," Striker said, emphasizing these last words.

Natasha looked at Roger, who had his face in his hands and was huddled up, trying to make himself as small a target as possible. "We're not going anywhere."

"I'm heading that way, girl, you better stay safe."

Laying the phone beside her, Natasha took a quick peek around the front of the golf cart and was rewarded with a flying bullet, just inches from her nose. "Shit!" she said, settling back against the tire.

Natasha glanced at Roger, who hadn't moved. "Striker's on his way. He's locating Bigun and Pit. He'll head them this way, so we're going to be okay. Don't worry."

Roger raised his head and gave her a miserable look.

"Hey, guy, would I let anything happen to you? You're my best bud. We're joined at the hip, so to speak."

She was rewarded with a weak smile from Roger.

A few minutes later, they heard a motor in the distance. Both glanced to their right and saw a golf cart heading in their direction.

"I do believe the posse has arrived." Natasha gave Roger a wide smile, then ducked when a bullet hit the top of the cart. "Dang! How many bullets has that dude got?"

When the cart drew closer, they could clearly see Pit and Bigun, their expressions grim, guns held at the ready. Natasha waved her arm back toward the copse of trees and they veered off in that direction.

"Whew!" Natasha leaned against the tire and closed her eyes. She felt movement, glanced over, and saw Roger starting to rise.

"Stay down!"

Roger ducked as a barrage of bullets slammed into the golf cart. Natasha cringed, put her hands over her head, and rolled herself into as tight a ball as she could.

They huddled behind the cart for a good ten minutes, waiting to hear a gunfight in progress, but nothing ever happened. Growing restless, Natasha raised up on her knees and looked over the tire toward the copse. She could see Bigun and Pit in among the trees moving with stealth, searching in silence.

"You see anything?" Roger whispered.

"Just Pit and Bigun looking for him." She turned and scanned behind her, then beyond Roger, then in the opposite direction. Nothing.

"You think he's gone?"

"God, I hope so." She continued to turn and search, wondering if the gunman could have circled around and was now coming up on them from another direction.

Natasha heard another engine, squinted her eyes in that direction, and heaved a sigh of relief to see Striker at the wheel of another golf cart, Scotty sitting beside him. Two more carts followed closely, one occupied by what looked to be security people.

Striker motioned toward the copse of trees and the two carts behind him headed off in that direction while he continued on toward Natasha and Roger.

They had a race to see who would get to Striker first. Natasha wanted to throw herself in his arms but didn't dare; besides, Roger was in the way. Instead, she stood, shifting from foot to foot, wringing her hands, listening to Roger somewhat hysterically tell their story.

Roger finally wound down and turned his attention to Scotty.

Striker took Natasha's arm and led her a short distance away from the other two. His eyes ranged up and down her body. "You okay?"

"Just scared is all," she said, her voice shaking, realizing how close to tears she was.

Striker stepped forward and wrapped his arms around her.

Natasha clung to him and wept, feeling like a baby, but unable to stop herself.

Striker let her cry it out. When she was down to sniffling, he pulled back from her.

Natasha was embarrassed. "I'm sorry. I don't mean to be such a sissy."

Striker smiled. "Darlin', I would never call you a sissy." Giving her an appraising look, he handed her a handkerchief.

Natasha noticed Roger and Scotty watching them.

Following her gaze, Striker turned to Scott. "Why don't you take them back to the clubhouse to pick up their things and then on to Roger's? I'll join up with you later. We need to talk about what happened in more detail." He looked at Natasha a long moment before leaving.

They rode in silence to Roger's mansion. Natasha's thoughts were on what had happened, the fact that she and Roger had come so close to death. By the time they pulled into the drive, she was holding her stomach, which seemed to be having its own gymnastics tumbling event.

She bolted out of the car, ran into the house and upstairs to her bedroom. She barely made it into the bathroom before collapsing in front of the toilet and throwing up.

After the spasm had passed, Natasha flushed the commode, then sat on the floor with her head in her hands, crying. She felt something cool on the back of her neck and glanced up. Roger was standing beside her, a washcloth in hand, giving her a concerned look.

"I'm okay," she said, then leaned over the toilet when her stomach clenched.

Afterwards, she was surprised to find Roger still there, kneeling beside her, patting her back.

"Roger, I love you dearly, but I would appreciate it if you'd just let me throw up in private." Natasha gave him a weak smile. "I'm okay, really," she assured his worried look.

"You'll let me know if you need anything?"

Nodding, Natasha put her hands over her face again.

Roger leaned down and touched her on the shoulder. She looked up. "You're my hero, you know that?"

"Well, guess what, Roger, you're my hero, too." She watched his face brighten, then another convulsion twisted her stomach and Natasha put her face into the toilet bowl. She was relieved to see Roger gone when she finished.

Striker entered the mansion later that afternoon, followed by Pit and Bigun. Roger and Scott were in Roger's office, conversing in low voices. Brutus was lying beside Roger, looking glum.

Striker glanced around the room. "Where's Natasha?"

Roger's eyes traveled toward the ceiling. "She's kind of sick," he said, with a worried look.

"Sick?"

"Yeah. She was throwing up. I tried to stay with her, but she wouldn't let me."

"Probably just nerves," Scott said.

Striker nodded. "I don't doubt." He turned to Roger. "Roger, after what's happened, I think it'd be a good idea to place perimeter guards back on the grounds, like before."

Roger nodded.

"I'll take care of it tonight," Scott said, in response to Striker's look.

"Have you talked to both of them?"

Scott shook his head. "Just Roger. Natasha wouldn't let me in when I went up."

"I'll go talk to her."

"You find anything?" Scott said, delaying his exit.

Striker turned back. "Shell casings, that's all. Not even a damn footprint to cast."

"Striker," Roger said.

"Yeah?"

"She saved my life. She probably won't tell you that, but she pushed me down right before a bullet went by and she got me behind that golf cart, out of danger. She kept me from panicking, doing anything stupid."

Striker nodded, his mouth forming a tight line. "Thanks, Roger."

Natasha was sitting on her bed cross-legged with a damp washcloth over her flushed face.

Striker knocked once, then entered.

She looked up at him and tried to smile but couldn't manage it.

"I heard you were sick," he said, walking toward her.

She shrugged, tried to act nonchalant. "Guess I'm not as ballsy as I thought I was."

Striker reached out and stroked along her jaw line with the back of his index finger. "You all right?"

She nodded, glancing away from him.

Striker pulled over the rocker, sat down, and spoke in a gentle voice. "You feel like talking about what happened out there?"

He let her tell it first, noting she did exactly what Roger said she would, leaving out the part about saving his life. Then Striker led her through it again, asking questions, getting her to reveal facts that she had initially left out.

After they were finished, he stood and began pacing.

Natasha watched him. "Did you find anything?"

He glanced at her, shook his head.

"Can I ask one thing?"

He stopped moving and waited.

"What the hell happened to Pit and Bigun?"

"That's exactly what I asked them. Seems they had trouble with their golf cart, the battery cable or something, and they tried to alert you on your cell phone but you didn't answer." Striker raised his eyebrows.

"I had it with me, but I didn't hear them."

"With you on you or with you in the cart?"

She gave him a dismal look. "I guess you know the answer to that one."

Striker stood, studying her.

Natasha grew uncomfortable. "What?"

"I'm pulling you off this case."

"What!"

"It's too dangerous for you, Natasha. I made the mistake of thinking there was only a perceived threat here, not an actual one. If I had thought there was any real danger, I never would have suggested you be part of this initially. But now we're playing a different game, and I can't put you in harm's way by keeping you on as part of this team."

"Bullshit!" Natasha lunged off the bed and stalked up to him.

Striker's jaw muscles were working. "You could have gotten killed out there today."

Tears sprang to her eyes. "What'd I do wrong? What'd I do wrong other than forget to clip my phone to my pants?"

"You went on without Bigun and Pit, for one."

"But I knew they were right behind us, Striker, and what would they have done differently than me?"

"You're too green for this, Natasha. You're out of it, so don't try to talk me into keeping you on."

"No." She stood on tiptoe and got in his face. "No, I will not leave this. I was hired to protect Roger, and damnit, I did my job today and I will continue to do my job until you find this guy."

They glared at one another.

"You're off," Striker said.

Natasha burst out crying.

"Tears won't work this time, Natasha," he said, in a firm voice.

She pointed her finger at him. "You can't take this away from me. I will not go back to that office job, Striker, not after getting a taste for this. So if I'm off, I'm out, you got that?"

Striker thought a moment. "Okay, I'll move you up to the investigative department. That's what you wanted anyway."

"No," Natasha said, surprising him. "I want to protect my man and I will protect my man, whether you say I can or not."

"I'm the one who makes the decisions here. If I say you're out of it, then you're out of it, and you are out of it, Natasha!" Striker said, his voice rising angrily.

"Then I quit."

Striker stepped back, not expecting this.

"Now, if you will excuse me, I need to talk to Roger."

Striker gave her a suspicious look. "What for?"

Natasha wiped her face with the washcloth. "I'll get him to personally hire me as his bodyguard."

"I won't let him."

She gave him a sardonic smile. "Try," she said in a challenging way.

"He'll listen to me. He loves you, he won't want you exposed to anything dangerous."

Natasha stood close to him and spoke in a whisper. "Yes, he loves me, Striker, and I think he'd give me anything I wanted to keep me in his life, and you know it."

"You'd do that?"

"I want to do this job. I'll do anything to keep it, to see it through. I will not let you kick me out just because you get scared. I am not a quitter, in case you haven't noticed, and I will not quit him."

Striker stepped in front of the door to bar her way and gave her a warning look. "Natasha."

She gave him a stubborn one in return. "One way or the other, Striker, I'm going to stay on as Roger's bodyguard. I do it in your employ, where you have some control over me and the circumstances surrounding me, or I do it on my own, where I am the one doing the controlling."

He leaned down into her face. "You're going to get yourself killed, don't you realize that?"

"What's this all about? Are you actually afraid I'm going to get killed or is this some sexist thing you got going, protect the woman at all cost?"

"That doesn't even warrant an answer," Striker said, his eyes glaring.

"Yeah? Well, guess what, Striker? Even if you take me out of it, Roger's still in it. And he's my best friend and I love him and I will not leave him, not now!" She screamed this last part.

They were not aware of it, but Roger, Scott, Pit, Bigun, and yes, even Brutus, were all gathered at the bottom of the stairs, listening.

Natasha tried to pass, but Striker reached out and grabbed her back. "Don't fight me on this, Natasha. For once do what I'm asking you to."

"Only as your employee, only as one of Roger's bodyguards."

Striker released her with a frustrated look.

Natasha rubbed her arms, which were burning as if they were on fire. She glanced down, but they weren't even red.

Striker began to pace again. Natasha had seen him angry before but never agitated. He would run his hand over his face, pause, look at her, then resume pacing.

After a few minutes, he stopped moving. "You're a wild card, you know that?"

"That's one of the reasons I need you."

He cocked his head.

She brought her chin up in a defiant manner.

"You want to explain that?"

She glanced away. "At the moment, no."

"My reasons for pulling you off aren't just professional, you know," he said in a low voice.

She blinked at that, then asked what he had, "You want to explain that?"

"You won't reconsider, step aside?"

She shook her head.

"All right, you stay on as my employee. That way, like you said, I can still control you somewhat."

"Thank you."

"But things are going to change now, Natasha. No more of this flitting around you and Roger have been doing, no more of this game-playing shit that goes on around here, no more pranks, trying to outwit Pit and Bigun all the time. This is serious business and you cannot afford to screw up."

"I know. After this afternoon, I know how serious this is more than anyone, Striker."

He considered this. "I guess you do," he said, then was gone.

CHAPTER 26

▼

The boys were watching a Braves game on the big-screen, yelling and having a fine time. Brutus was zonked out on the couch between Pit and Bigun, in his favorite sleeping position: on his back, paws in the air. Natasha was bored five minutes into the game, so went to her room, slipped into a bikini, then out to the pool to swim laps.

She swam underwater in a leisurely fashion, coming up when she needed air, her thoughts on Striker. Two days since she had last seen him and she already missed him a great deal. He hadn't called her in the evening to check in as he normally would, and this time, she would not allow herself to call him.

The morning after their argument, she had found both her guns on the kitchen counter. She assumed Striker had placed them there, although there was no note or explanation. She hoped this meant he trusted her to maintain control.

Her mind kept turning to his statement that he wanted to pull her off for other than professional reasons. She desperately wanted to give herself permission to hope he felt for her as she did him, but refused to even go there.

Nearing the end of the shallow water, her eyes caught a shimmering reflection, and she surfaced. Striker was standing on the pool deck, watching her.

Natasha rose and began to wade toward him, returning the smile he was giving her.

Striker was dressed in a flak vest with black fatigues, black boots, and a sleeveless black t-shirt revealing black hair on the backs of his forearms and hands and a lot of muscle. His hair was pulled into a low ponytail beneath a black baseball cap with the bill turned to the back. She couldn't see his eyes for the black shades covering them. There was black stubble on his face. He looked big and mean and powerful.

Her nipples grew hard.

Striker picked up a towel from the table and met her when she stepped out of the pool. "Water must be chilly," he said, giving her a grin she couldn't read.

Natasha wrapped the towel around her, wondering if he was teasing or not. Did he even suspect the powerful effect he had on her? God, she hoped not.

She studied him, trying to gauge his mood. "You still mad at me?"

He gave her a wicked smile. "Natasha, how could I stay mad at you, beautiful as you are?"

She thrilled at the way he said her name. "So, Black Bart, what are you up to today?"

Striker favored her with his sexy grin. "Baby, you don't want to know."

Resisting the urge to squirm, Natasha fought the impulse to drop the towel, step into his arms, and see what happened. "I was starting to worry about you."

"I had to go out of town, take care of an unexpected emergency." Striker chose not to tell her he had cut his trip short, worried about her and Roger.

The way he said it, along with the way he was dressed, Natasha wondered if this was a CIA thing or not, like most everyone at the office suspected. She waited for him to tell her more, but he remained silent.

Giving a mental shrug, she walked toward the table, combing her hair back with her fingers, trying not to look at him. "Would you like something to drink?"

Striker stepped up beside her and touched her elbow. "I'll get it."

She broke out in goose bumps and was glad the towel hid most of her body from him.

"What about you? You need anything?"

"Peach-flavored water, if you don't mind," Natasha said, looking away.

After Striker had gone inside, Natasha sat at the table and gave herself a good talking-to. She was going to quit this shit and quit it now. Okay, so he was good-looking, so she was attracted to him—well, all right, highly attracted to him, more than anyone before him—but this guy was strictly off limits. She knew that. So she had to stop this little fantasy thing she had going for him and—

"Here you go," Striker said, placing her drink on the table.

Natasha startled, then noticed his raised eyebrows. "Sorry. I was kind of thinking about something."

"Yeah? What were you thinking about?" Striker pulled over a chair, placed it in front of her, and sat, way too close for comfort.

"Nothing really, just, you know, thinking." Natasha watched the sparkling pool water and wished one of the boys would come out of the house.

Striker leaned toward her and began to stare at her.

She glanced at him, then away, then back. Damn!

"If this is too uncomfortable for you, all you have to do is tell me."

He knows, she thought, with despair. "It's okay. I can handle it. I'm a big girl."

"Don't feel that you have to hide your feelings from me, Natasha, or try to act like this doesn't bother you when it actually does."

"I'm not hiding anything from you," Natasha said, mentally calling herself a liar.

Striker gave her an intense look. "I still want to pull you out."

He didn't know. Oh, thank goodness, he didn't know, she hadn't given herself away.

Striker was watching her.

"No, Striker, really. I'm still a little shaky over that golfing incident, but I'll get over it. And no, I do not want out, not now, not ever, not until this guy is caught."

He sat back. "Don't think you have to try to be brave here. If you don't want to do this, you don't have to."

Natasha developed a slight, vertical crease between her eyebrows, which Striker knew to be her stubborn look.

He gave up. "I'm afraid I made the mistake of originally thinking Roger was being paranoid, that there was no real threat."

"I just thought he was lonely." She frowned. "Whoever was shooting at us, you think that was the extortionist?"

Striker took his time answering, knowing she was probably feeling guilty about that. "I don't know, Natasha. If it was, then I misread his actual intention here." He removed his sunglasses and his eyes were pitch-dark under his heavy black brows.

Natasha shivered.

He reached forward and touched her knee. "You cold?"

Her leg jerked. "Just a little."

Striker gave her a strange look.

To take her mind off him and what was going on with her body, Natasha brought up something she had been mulling over. "Striker, I think I have another suspect in mind."

He leaned back in his chair and waited for her to tell him.

"Cassandra. I think she could be the one who hired this guy to kill Roger."

Striker didn't say anything, which prompted her explanation.

"I know, you're probably thinking, she has no motive. She lives a rich life, thanks to Roger, has everything anyone could ever want, doesn't have to work, travels all the time, has her country-club lifestyle."

"But," Striker said.

She nodded. "But the first time I met her, when Roger told her I was one of his bodyguards, the look in her eyes, I could tell she didn't like it one bit, and I overheard her expressing this to Roger."

"Maybe she just didn't like Roger having a woman around."

"Well, that's what I initially thought, but one day—this was before the shooting at the golf club—I overheard her talking to him, and she was trying to convince him that he didn't need bodyguards around him, that there wasn't any kind of a threat to him. I didn't say anything at the time because I kind of agreed."

She sat back. Yikes! She sounded like an eavesdropper. "I mean, it's not like I'm skulking around, trying to listen to other people's conversations," she added. "I just happened to overhear these."

Striker rubbed his chin.

Natasha watched his large hands and got involved in this fantasy where his hands were on her body, traveling over her breasts, cupping them, then on to her back, moving down…

"Or could just be a mother concerned for her son," Striker said in a musing tone.

Natasha blinked back to the real world. "Well, sure, could be. But there's something about her I don't trust. Call it woman's intuition, call it what you want, but she just doesn't feel right to me."

Striker tilted his head and seemed to be studying her while considering this.

She stared back, thinking how beautifully shaped his lips were, wondering what they would feel like against her lips, against her skin, against her…

"You could be right."

Natasha resisted the urge to slap herself. "Yeah, but I could be wrong, too."

Striker contemplated, his eyes on the ground.

Natasha began envisioning what it would be like to lie naked beneath him, his powerful body looming over her preparatory to mounting her…

He moved in the chair, bringing her back to the present.

Stop it! she yelled at herself.

Striker brought his eyes back to her.

She could feel her face blushing. "It's just, I caught her looking around the kitchen that day I found the Thallium, and I got the feeling there was something sinister about her reason for being in there. Plus I've been wondering about the extortionist who said he knew about the bodyguards but didn't recognize us, how weird that was, and also, how did he know about Roger's activities if he wasn't watching him."

Striker leaned back in his chair and extended one leg.

Natasha glanced down at his muscular thigh. Her eyes flitting to his crotch, she wondered about what was ensconced in the pants he wore, if he knew how to use it. Well, of course he did, look at all the women who always seemed to be circling around him, like planets around a sun. She began to imagine what it would feel like to have that particular part of his body inside her, friction building, sweat pouring, hearts beating...

"There's nothing we can do at this point. There's actually no evidence pointing to her," Striker said, startling Natasha back to the present.

"Dangit!" She lunged out of the chair and walked away, angry with herself.

Striker watched her, confused. When she turned back to him, he noticed her face was bright red. "You all right?"

Natasha shrugged her shoulders in a noncommittal way. "I'm probably wrong," she said, returning to the subject, walking back to her chair.

"Probably."

Natasha sat back down, gave him a challenging look. "But I don't think so."

Striker shook his head. "Nah. I don't think it's her."

"I bet you it's her." Natasha settled back and the towel fell open to reveal her body. She smiled to herself, watching Striker's eyes travel over her torso to her legs. When he brought them back to hers, she gave him the smile this time.

He ignored it.

She leaned toward him. "The bet's on the table, big man. What are you going to do about it?"

His eyes traveled to her breasts, then abdomen.

Natasha looked down, saw the little pooch there, and straightened up, flattening her stomach.

Striker flashed her a knowing grin.

"I hate you," she said, her voice low.

He laughed, then reached out, put his finger on her belly-button ring, and studied it.

She almost gasped with pleasure.

He lounged back, looking at her, then leaned toward her again. "Okay, I'll take you up on your little challenge. I bet it's not Cassandra. I bet it's that computer nerd jealous because Roger beat him to a patent, although so far we can't connect him to those calls to Roger."

Natasha nodded. "So what's the bet going to be?"

Striker thought a moment.

"Money? Although I don't have near the amount you have, I do have a small savings account."

Striker gave her a wicked grin. "I wouldn't want your money, darlin'. I play for higher stakes than that."

Her eyes widened. "What's the bet?" she said, aware she was moist down there and it wasn't from the wet suit she wore.

He moved closer, rested his forearms on his long thighs, and gave her an intense look. "I win, I get my way with you."

"Your way? What exactly does your way entail, please?"

Striker flashed white teeth at her but didn't answer.

Natasha could feel her face growing red. "It wouldn't involve me bending over and a jar of Vaseline, would it?"

Striker laughed. "And if you win, what's your bet?"

Natasha smiled. "If I win, you have to tell me what you do when you go into the Smokys."

Striker considered this, his eyes on the ground, then looked up at her. "I will only tell that to the woman I choose as my life-mate. You know that."

Natasha stood and handed him the towel. She watched his eyes travel her body again. "We'll work out the details later," she said, walking away from him, smiling.

CHAPTER 27

▼

Natasha had spent a restless night filled with lurid dreams involving Striker, in all of which they were both naked and engaged in various eroticisms with one another. She finally gave up trying to sleep and went downstairs to breakfast earlier than usual.

Cassandra and Roger were in the kitchen, engaged in a heated discussion. Natasha paused outside the door to listen, growing angry over the disrespectful way Roger's mom was addressing him, giving her son hell over having these inept bodyguards around, making it obvious she wanted them fired and sent packing. It seemed she had found her own set of bodyguards to put in place who would do a much better job at protecting Roger.

Natasha usually made herself scarce when Cassandra was in the house but, hearing this, decided to interrupt. She stepped into the kitchen and flashed Roger a wide smile.

"Morning," she said, walking toward the coffeepot.

Cassandra turned toward Natasha, a look of contempt on her face. "My son and I are in the middle of a discussion."

"I'm sorry." Natasha glanced at Roger, who looked flustered. "I didn't mean to interrupt."

"No, it's okay." Roger gave his mother an angry glare. "We were through anyway."

Cassandra stared at Roger as if unable to believe her son was defying her. He returned her look with his own challenging one.

"Fine, it's your life." She snatched up her purse and stomped out the door.

Natasha walked over to Roger. "You all right?"

He smiled, which surprised her. "That's the first time I've actually stood up to her. I think I'm better than I've ever been."

Natasha hugged him. "Good for you." She glanced toward the dishwasher. "Where's Brutus?"

"Sleeping with Bigun."

Natasha gave him a questioning look.

"Yeah, right in the bed with him."

Natasha laughed.

After breakfast, Natasha cleared the dishes, conversing with Roger, Pit, and Bigun, who were sitting around the table drinking coffee. All were waiting for Striker to show up without realizing it. After the dishes were done, Pit and Bigun took Brutus outside with them to check in with the perimeter guards, then test the alarm system, something Natasha knew could take awhile. Roger did what he always did after breakfast, headed to his office to work for a couple of hours.

Natasha put a load of laundry into the washer, picked up her .22 off the counter where she had placed it before breakfast and tucked it into the waistband at the back of her short, denim skirt. She walked toward Roger's office to tell him she was going to swim laps, wondering when the transformation had occurred, how in the world she had gotten so domestic in such a short time.

She opened the door and was startled to see Roger at his desk, his face ashen. A man was sitting on the windowsill behind Roger, holding a sawed-off shotgun to his head.

Natasha froze, uncertain what she should do. She quickly realized she could only go inside, not chance the man pulling the trigger. Glancing behind her, she stepped into the room.

"Shut the door," the man said.

Natasha closed the door, then walked closer to them, studying the man with the gun, memorizing his face. He looked dirty and unkempt. His long, dark hair hung about his shoulders in greasy wads. His eyes were sepia-cast and beady, his face unshaven. She guessed his age anywhere between thirty and forty.

"Stop," he said, when she drew close to the desk. "Take the phone off your belt, throw it this way."

Natasha literally felt her body sag at this instruction, knowing he was taking away their only chance for any kind of help. She unclipped it and threw it toward him. The man caught it with ease.

She became alarmed, fearful that he might have killed someone to gain access to the house. "How'd you get in here?"

He ignored her question.

"What do you want?"

He nudged Roger with the shotgun. "I came for the money he owes me."

So, this was the guy, the extortionist. She glanced at Roger, who looked terrified. "The million dollars."

He poked Roger's temple with the gun. "I'll take that to start with."

"You're not the man who keeps calling?"

"He's the one who sent me that letter," Roger said.

Natasha studied the gunman. "The computer guy."

"None other," he said.

"You don't look like a computer guy," she said, vying for time.

He shifted but kept the gun at Roger's temple. "Just get me the million dollars, bitch."

"We don't have it."

He looked at her like he couldn't believe she had said that. "Well, then, I guess I'll just have to kill you, won't I?"

Natasha tried not to relay the panic she felt. "No. We have it, but not here. It's at Roger's bank."

He poked Roger with the gun. "That true?"

Roger nodded.

"You don't think we'd keep that kind of money here, do you?" Natasha said. "Come on, that's just not safe."

The man glanced from Roger to Natasha. "Go get it."

"I can't."

He cocked the firearm.

Natasha knew she had to get Roger away from this mess. "Roger has to. It's his money. The bank won't give me his money."

The man considered this. "Okay, this is what we're gonna do." Jabbing Roger with the gun, he addressed him. "We're all gonna get in that jeep out there in front of the house. I'll be in the back with a blanket over me, the shotgun on you. You alert any of those outside guards, you're both dead. You're gonna go get the money while I take this bitch with me. After you have it, you bring it to me and I'll exchange her for the million dollars."

Roger shook his head.

The man kicked at him.

Natasha picked that moment to make her move. She pulled her gun and yelled, "Get back!" sidling around the desk, going for the man.

He gave her a scornful smile. "Go ahead. You shoot me, I shoot him. Your gun doesn't have the power to stop me from doing that and you know it."

He was right. Natasha dropped the gun and raised her hands in the air. "Don't hurt him. If you do, you deal with me."

The man barked a harsh laugh. "Listen to this scrappy bitch."

"I'm serious. There's no reason to hurt him."

The man nodded his head in the direction of the door. "Where's the other two?"

"Outside checking the perimeter alarms," Natasha said, with dread in her heart.

"How soon before they come back inside?"

"I don't know. It depends on what they find out there. They could be gone awhile."

"Call them, get them in here."

"What do you want them for? At this point, they're of no threat to you."

"Get them in here! I'm not going to go out there, those two goons hanging around. Soon as they come in and see you two gone, they're gonna send out an alert. I'm not stupid, you know."

Natasha was terrified that he intended to kill her friends. "I'll send them away. I'll get them out of here, that way you won't have to deal with them."

"I said get them in here, bitch!" He pressed the gun against Roger's temple once more.

Natasha tried to sound reasonable. "Listen to me. If you kill them, do anything to them, Striker's going to know within minutes that something's happened."

He gave her a suspicious look. "What's that mean?"

She frantically tried to think of a believable lie. "They each have to alert him every thirty minutes, within a different time span. He doesn't get the alert, he knows something's wrong and calls in all the guys on these grounds plus comes running with help."

He gave her a smug look. "Well, that's simple enough. We'll get their phones and alert him ourselves."

"No, we can't. They use a code. We're each given a code, and I don't know what theirs is. Just listen to me, okay? I can send them away. I'm second in command under Striker. I'll get rid of them, don't worry about it. They'll go where I send them. They'll never know you've even been here."

Natasha heard voices in the foyer. "Let me send them out of here, or this is going to go badly for you."

He gave her a skeptical look. "Hey, I know you're not concerned for me."

"You're the one with the gun on Roger. I'm trying to protect him."

The voices were coming closer.

"Okay," he said, "send them away. But I'll be listening, and I hear you say one wrong word, I'm coming out there, and there's gonna be a blood bath."

Natasha turned and ran to the door, stepping into the hallway just as Pit and Bigun were closing in. "Hey, guys!" She tried to smile at them.

"Everything's clear, dudette," Bigun said.

"That's good. But listen, I just got off the phone with Striker. He's out at that rock quarry in North Knoxville and says he needs your help with something. That's why he's late this morning."

Pit frowned. "Man, he wouldn't pull us away from you and Roger to go help him."

"He said he's got the guys patrolling the perimeter, he's sending two more for in-house, don't worry about it, but he needs y'all for this. He said you can't reach him on his cell because he's down in the quarry and the range doesn't carry."

Pit gave her a wary look. "Hey, man, you're not pulling something here, are you?"

Natasha tried to appear irritated. "Striker made it clear, one more prank and I'm fired, Pit. You don't think I'd chance that, do you? Come on, I'm not that stupid."

Pit and Bigun looked at each other for a long moment.

"Well, man, I guess we're going to the rock quarry," Pit finally said.

Natasha noticed Brutus sniffing at the floor in front of the office door. "Hey, why don't you give Brutus a treat and take him with you? You know how much he loves to ride in a car, and out at the quarry, he can run all over the place."

"Sure thing, man," Pit said.

"You sure you're gonna be all right here, dudette?" Bigun said.

Natasha tried to smile but had a hard time getting her mouth to move. "Just do me one favor."

"Sure thing, dudette."

"Tell Striker I'm sorry."

"Oh, dudette, you and the Strikester been fighting again?"

"Just tell him. He'll know what for."

Natasha watched them walk into the foyer, then turned to go back to Roger's office. She glimpsed his cell phone lying on the foyer table as she passed by and stopped long enough to snatch it up. Tucking it in her skirt pocket, she went to join Roger and the gunman.

They did as he told them to, Natasha driving, Roger sitting in the passenger seat, the gunman in the back with a blanket over him, holding the shotgun muzzle against the back of Roger's seat. Natasha waved at the exit guard when they left the estate. She wished she could give him some sort of signal but didn't dare do anything, fearing for Roger's safety.

On the way to the bank, the gunman instructed Roger where to bring the money after he had it. He warned him not to make any calls or give any indication of alarm, telling him he had people watching him, and the first wrong move he made, Natasha was dead.

Natasha braked the jeep to a stop in front of the bank. Before Roger got out, she reached over and hugged him. "Call Striker," she whispered into his ear, slipping his cell phone into his pocket.

Roger shook his head.

Natasha put her face close to his, her eyes intense, and brought her mouth to his ear again. "He's our only chance, Roger. Promise me you'll find a way to call him."

"What's going on up there?" the gunman said from the back, poking Roger's seat with the gun.

"I was just telling him to be careful," Natasha said.

Roger reached over and kissed her on the cheek, then exited the vehicle.

Called to the office by Scott for an early morning meeting, Striker had been closeted with him for over an hour, trying to make sense out of the mess the new office manager had made of their accounts payable, when his phone bleeped.

"Striker," he said, keeping it in the two-way mode.

"Where are you, man?" Pit said. "I thought you were out here waiting on us."

Striker noticed the alarmed look in his partner's eyes. "What are you talking about?"

"Nattie said you wanted us to meet you out here at the quarry—"

Striker had a sick feeling in the pit of his stomach. "Wait, wait, hold it. Natasha told you to meet me? When?"

"This morning, right after breakfast, she said you called and needed our help out here—"

"Shit!"

"Oh, man." Pit sounded miserable.

"You think this is one of her stunts or was something going on?"

Pit was silent for a moment. "I don't know, man. I asked her if this was a prank, but she said you'd fire her next time and she wasn't that stupid. Oh yeah, she did ask us to tell you she's sorry."

"Damnit to fuckin' hell!" Striker hurled his phone at the wall. "Just wait till I get my hands on her this time!"

Scott was watching him with an angry look. "You're going to have to do something about her."

Striker retrieved his phone, checked to make sure it wasn't damaged, and clipped it to his belt. "Don't worry. After I get through with her, she's not going to want to have anything more to do with this case."

Striker drove toward Roger's estate, cursing Natasha and himself for trusting her good behavior since the suspension. His phone chirped, and he reached down, plucked it out of the clasp. The display showed Roger's cell phone number.

"Roger! Where are you? Where's Natasha? What's going on?" He stopped himself when Roger began talking over him.

"He's got her." Roger sounded on the verge of crying. "He says he'll kill her if I don't do what he wants."

Oh, God, please, no, Striker prayed. "Who?"

"That guy that sued me last year, the one who wrote the letter."

"What's he wanting from you?"

"Money. I'm at the bank, waiting for them to put it together. He's got Natasha, he's got a shotgun on her. Striker, I think he's going to kill her anyway. He looks crazy." Roger's voice broke. "He will if he finds out I've called you, but Nattie made me promise. He says he's got people watching me, but I came into the bathroom and no one's in here, so I took the chance. Striker, if he kills her because I've made this call—"

"Roger, he's probably bluffing you. I doubt if anyone else is involved with this. Let me think a second."

"I've got to go. He might get suspicious since I've been in here so long."

"Roger!" Striker was relieved when Roger answered. "Where are you supposed to meet him?"

Roger gave him the name of a seedy motel near downtown Knoxville.

"What's the room number?"

"108. Striker, I've got to go—"

"Just one more second. Do what he told you to do, all right? Get the money, give him the signal you've got it, whatever, but don't go into that motel room.

Give me a chance to get there ahead of you. I'll be there, ten minutes at the very latest."

Roger clicked off without saying anything.

"Damnit!" Striker hit the steering wheel. He keyed in Pit's alert, and when he answered, said, "How far away are you from downtown Knoxville?"

"I don't know, man. Maybe ten to fifteen minutes if I push it."

Striker told him what was going on and to meet him on the street behind the motel.

The gunman instructed Natasha to get out of the car, and he climbed out, right on her heels. He had covered the shotgun with the blanket and stood behind Natasha while he unlocked the door to the room, then pushed her inside. After the door was closed, he uncovered the firearm and told her to go over to the bed.

"No," she said, wondering why he wanted her there.

He reached out and shoved her, causing Natasha to fall onto her hands and knees. Approaching from behind, he kicked her in the lower back, which sent her sprawling.

Natasha pulled herself up to sit on the floor. She rubbed her lower back, massaging the spasm that had developed in the area of her right kidney, wincing with pain, trying not to cry.

He put the muzzle of the shotgun to her head with his right hand and with his left unbuttoned, then unzipped his jeans. "Let's have some fun," he said in a gleeful voice.

Oh, please, no. Natasha felt nauseous, light-headed.

Pulling out his flaccid penis, he nudged her temple with the gun. "Do me."

Natasha gave him a baleful look.

He jabbed her with the gun. "I said, do me, you bitch."

She drew back. "No."

He reached down, grabbed her hair, and yanked her toward him. The smell was unbearable.

Gagging, Natasha pulled away from him.

He kicked her in the abdomen.

She doubled over, panting, the area he had assaulted burning as if on fire.

He reached down, grabbed her hair, and sat her upright. "Do me!"

She glared at him. "I do you, I swear to you here and now you won't ever be able to threaten anyone with that puny little thing again, much less screw anything, if you can even do that, which I doubt."

He kicked her in the shoulder. Natasha fell back, and before she could right herself, he was on her. He pulled her up by the arm, dragged her to the bed, and lay her over it, using the gun to hold her down.

Oh, please, God, no, she prayed when he pushed her skirt up and began pulling at her panties.

"You want to see if I can fuck, I'll show you fucked," he said, fumbling with her underwear. "Ever been butt-fucked before, bitch? Ever had one stuck up your butt so far you can taste it in your throat?"

Natasha tried for his midstep but missed, so kicked back and caught him in the shin. He brought his knee up, into her hamstring. She immediately collapsed on that leg, but he caught her, got her upright, and bent over the bed again.

Natasha felt cool air against her skin and knew he had gotten her panties down. Screaming with rage, she began fighting him with renewed effort. When she managed to turn herself around, he slapped her face hard with the back of his hand. She felt blood spurt from her lip.

"You think you can fuck me?" she screamed at him. "You think you can do that, you stupid jerk-ass, just try it, 'cause I don't think you got it in you. And even if you could get it up, I probably wouldn't even feel that damn thing, it's nothing but an ugly old worm you got hanging between your legs, you dick-face, stupid—"

This time he punched her in the stomach. Natasha collapsed on the bed, doubled over. Losing all sense of breath, she began to panic. She couldn't move, she couldn't fight, she couldn't do anything but heave, trying to get air into her lungs.

He took the time to zip up while watching her, a maniac's grin on his face. Picking up the shotgun up with one hand, he grabbed her with the other and shook her like a rag doll. "Let's try something kinky." He threw her back onto the bed, reached out and pulled her toward him, then suddenly dropped her.

Natasha heard movement around her and glanced up. Striker had the man by the collar, and she watched as he effortlessly picked him up and flung him across the room. Pit and Bigun descended on the man before he landed.

Natasha began trying to pull up her panties, watching Striker come toward her. She backed away from him, holding her right hand out in front of her to keep him away. "No," she said. Her left arm didn't seem to want to function, so she began to pull at her clothes with her right hand.

Striker waited for Natasha to right herself, then approached her once more. He knelt down beside her and touched her injured face, trying to be as gentle as he could. His eyes traveled her body. "How bad are you hurt?" He ran his hands over her arms, then her legs, checking for blood.

Natasha was trying not to cry. "I can't breathe too good. My face hurts, Striker. I can't move my left arm, I think he might have broken something."

She heard cursing and looked around Striker. Pit and Bigun were kicking at the gunman's body, which was doubled over on the floor.

Striker abruptly stood, got between them, picked the man up, and shoved him into the wall. "You like to beat and rape women, huh?" He kneed him in the crotch and the man bent over, gagging.

Striker dropped him, then kicked him under the chin and watched as he landed on his back, unconscious. He looked at Pit and Bigun. "Make sure by the time you're through with this sick prick that he won't ever be able to even think about raping a woman again."

Striker picked Natasha up in his arms and hurried toward the door with her. Hearing sirens approaching, he turned back to the two male bodyguards, who were bending over the man. "When the cops get here, tell them what happened, then go get Roger. I'm taking Natasha to the hospital."

"Please don't take me there, Striker," Natasha said, her voice weak. "Please, take me home. Don't take me there. Please, Striker, don't take me to the hospital."

Ignoring her, he opened the back door to his SUV and placed her on the seat with great care, then drove to the hospital, thankful it was only a few minutes away.

Striker pulled up to the emergency entrance and hurried out of his vehicle. He yanked open the back door and collected Natasha, who now seemed to be in a daze, then carried her inside, yelling for help.

A resident came running up, took one look at Natasha, and called for a gurney. Striker put her down on it and watched the resident and an orderly whisk her away.

After a few minutes, he couldn't stand it anymore, so went in search of Natasha. He found her in a room, arguing with a nurse who was trying to remove her clothing.

Natasha noticed Striker standing in the doorway. "Striker, help me." Her voice was raspy. "She wants to take my clothes off. Don't let her take my clothes off."

Striker crossed over to Natasha, relieved to see her alert.

The nurse gave him a suspicious look. "Are you family?"

Natasha lay back, exhausted. "Of course he's family."

Striker placed his hand in Natasha's right one and she quieted at once.

Striker tried to speak in a rational tone. "Natasha, honey, let them do what they need to do to help you."

Natasha's body was trembling. "Take me home. Get me out of here, Striker. Don't let them touch me. Please, don't let them near me."

Fear touched him then. He leaned down, put his face close to hers. "They have to examine you, baby, make sure you're all right, collect DNA, do all that. You know the procedure."

Her eyes widened with alarm.

"I'll stay here with you if you want, Natasha. I'll hold your hand—"

"He didn't rape me, he just hurt me," she said, crying, shaking her head.

Striker didn't know what she meant by that. He had seen Natasha on the bed with her panties down, and his first thought was the guy had sexually assaulted her...Oh, God, he used the gun on her.

Striker stroked her hair, feeling miserable. "Just let them do the exam, baby, let them do what they need to do to help you."

It took Striker several minutes to talk Natasha into allowing the doctor to check her body, but she still refused to have the rape kit performed.

The doctor met Striker in the hallway afterward and told him Natasha had suffered a severe beating along with a bruised kidney, ribs and abdomen, a possible hairline fracture of her cheekbone, and that they had had to reset her shoulder. He then explained to him that some women tried to repress the memory of a rape, actually denied it had happened, in order to keep from dealing with the pain.

Striker nodded. It wasn't right; this had happened to her before; it wasn't right. "I'll talk to her," he said.

Natasha was dressed in a hospital gown and had her eyes closed. Her face was already beginning to show the multihued bruising that would cover it in a couple of days.

Striker pulled the doctor's stool over and sat beside her, relieved to see her breathing had returned to normal. He stroked her hair, watching her.

Natasha opened her eyes and turned her face to him.

"Do you trust me?"

She nodded.

"Then let them do the rape kit, Natasha."

"He didn't rape me!"

"Yes, but he may have left some evidence. Let them do the test, Natasha. They seem to think it's necessary."

"Don't you believe me, Striker? You know I don't lie to you. Why won't you believe me? Don't let them do that to me, don't let them violate me in that way."

Striker felt terrible. "I'll stay here with you. I'll be right here, right where I am now, holding your hand."

"If he had raped me, you would be the one person I would tell, don't you know that?" she said, anguish showing on her face.

They stared at one another.

"What about the gun?"

"He didn't get the chance, thanks to you." Her eyes swam with unshed tears. "Striker, I'm not stupid. I would know to give them that evidence, so, please, don't let them put me through that."

Striker nodded, then glanced around for her clothing. "Do you want me to help you get dressed?"

Natasha shook her head. "They cut everything off. I don't have anything."

"I'll ask the nurse to find you some clothes."

"She said she wasn't raped," Striker told the doctor.

"Yes, but she's acting like a typical rape victim and we can only assume that she was. DNA can rule that out for us."

Striker could have hit him. "Why should she have to go through the ordeal when there isn't a reason to? Listen to what she's telling you."

"I'm trying to listen to what she's not telling me," the doctor said, giving Striker a look that said, so should you.

Striker rubbed his face. "What can I do to help her?"

Someone was screaming and Natasha woke to the sound, surprised at first it was her voice she was hearing. Seeing the man walking toward her, she shrieked. She pummeled at him, moved backward, tried to get away. She fell off the bed, rolled over, and scuttled back. The man was saying something she couldn't hear; she didn't want to know. She came up against a wall and huddled there, saying, "No, no, no," holding out her right hand.

Striker swam into vision. Natasha covered her face with her arms.

He reached out to touch her, but she batted his hand away, so he settled beside her and waited for her to calm.

Natasha had her knees drawn up to her chest, her face down, hitching. Sensing movement beside her, she remembered Striker. She raised her head and looked at him.

He didn't say a word, watching her.

She could see the concern on his face. "Striker," she said, in a miserable voice.

He reached for her, gathered her into his arms, and began to rock her, speaking words of comfort to her as he held her.

When Natasha woke the next morning, in bed now, Striker was there, in the rocking chair near the window, watching her, looking tired, like he hadn't slept. She smiled when she saw him, glad to see him, then the pain flaring in her kidney and ribs reminded her why he was there. She felt the hot tears come again.

"Come here, baby," he said.

She went to him, climbed into his lap, let him hold her and rock her while she cried.

CHAPTER 28

▼

Striker stayed at the mansion the next week, converting Roger's library into a makeshift office and conducting business from his cell phone. He helped the boys nurse Natasha during the day and slept in the bedroom next to hers at night so he could tend to her when she would have the recurring nightmare. He insisted she take the pain pills the doctor had prescribed, which helped her to sleep the majority of time the first few days while her body healed. When she started ranting and raving at all the unnecessary attention they were giving her, he knew she was going to be all right.

Striker waited for Natasha to tell him what had happened. He had already interrogated Roger as to his place in the events as they unfolded, and now he wanted to talk to Natasha, but not until she was ready. Although the nightmares told him she might need more time, he was having a hard time keeping the police at bay, who wanted their own statement from her.

Natasha found Striker in his provisional office, once more riffling through computer ledger sheets with a big frown on his face, hating this part of the job.

Striker looked up when he heard the door open, smiled when he saw it was Natasha, and stood like the Southern gentleman he was.

She stood in the doorway, wearing a black tank top and loose-fitting, beige cotton pants with a drawstring waist. Her hair down, her face devoid of makeup, she was the most beautiful woman he had ever seen, even with the facial bruising.

"Can I talk to you?"

"Sure. Come on in." He hurried over to her and took her elbow, intending to help her to a chair.

Natasha gave him a grumpy look. "I'm not an invalid, for Pete's sake."

Striker smiled; he had missed her spunk. He grew concerned, watching her ease into a chair.

"How's the pain?"

When she smiled at him, his heart felt lighter and his mouth turned up in response.

"Better. I haven't had to take a pain pill today." She looked down at her arm. "I took the sling off."

"That's great." Striker got the worried look back. "No blood in your urine?"

"I'm fine, Striker. Quit worrying about me."

"You really should stay in bed, you know, give your body a chance to completely heal."

"Striker, could you do me a favor, please?"

He sat in the chair next to her. "Sure."

"Quit babying me. I don't need it, okay?"

He felt rejected. "If that's what you want."

They gazed at one another.

"I still think you need to let your parents know what happened," he said.

"You ever met my mom?"

He wondered why she asked this. "No."

"If she sees me like this, you know what she'll do?"

"No."

"She'll kick my butt all the way home, and that's just for starters."

Striker grinned.

"I'm not kidding. This will only confirm to her that I shouldn't be doing what I'm doing. So, no thanks, I do not want to hear that from her."

"She still needs to know."

Natasha gave him a stubborn look. "All she needs to know is that I'm alive and breathing at this point."

Striker shrugged. "She's your mom, so I'll leave that up to you."

Natasha studied him, aware that there had been a shift in their relationship, wondering when it actually occurred. She hoped it wasn't because of the computer nerd's attack on her. She feared Striker was feeling sorry for her or, even worse, guilty because he had allowed her to remain in a position that had placed her in harm's way. She had noticed that he would occasionally call her baby, especially during times he would comfort her after the nightmares, and wondered if this was meant as a term of endearment or that he perceived her as helpless. She prayed it wasn't the latter.

Striker stared back, cognizant of his admiration for her. She had backbone, this one, was full of spirit and fire, blunt and forthright—

"I think we need to talk about it," Natasha said, "about what happened."

"If you're ready, but first I want to apologize to you."

She gave him a quizzical look.

"When you told me in the hospital he hadn't raped you, I made the mistake of listening to the doctor instead of you, and I'm sorry, Natasha. I'm sorry I tried to talk you into letting them do the rape kit. I know how traumatic that can be for a woman."

"It's okay. You don't need to apologize. I understand why you were concerned." She glanced away, embarrassed, remembering he had seen her with her panties down.

Striker didn't know what to say to ease her discomfort.

She looked back at him. "Why are you here anyway? Why aren't you at the office?"

"I was worried about you. I wanted to be near in case you need anything."

Natasha leaned toward him and put her hand on his arm. "Striker, go home. You don't need to be here."

He raised his eyebrows.

Her face reddened. "I mean, I like having you here, don't get me wrong, but let me deal with this on my own. Let me wake up from a nightmare and handle it without you there helping me, because sooner or later, I'm going to have to anyway, and I'd rather do it now." She gave him a flustered look. "I'm getting too used to you being here, and that's not good."

Striker remained silent.

Sighing, Natasha looked away from him. "That morning, after breakfast," she began, and told him what had happened. As he expected her to, she left out her part in protecting Roger, Pit, and Bigun. He made a mental note that he was going to have to talk to her about that.

Natasha held her stomach when she got to the part where she was alone with the gunman. Striker squeezed her hand, wondering if she was telling him everything, hoping she was.

After she was finished, she looked at him. "Did I thank you for coming that day? I can't remember if I did, and if not, I apologize."

"Natasha," he scolded.

"You saved me, Striker. I wasn't having much success fighting him and he probably would have raped me with that gun. He probably would have killed me as well." She reached over and hugged him. "Thank you, Striker," she said into his neck.

He stroked her hair, then pulled away from her, resisting the urge to kiss her.

"There's something I've been wondering about," Natasha said.

"What's that?"

"How'd he get in here that morning?"

"Cassandra turned off the inside alarm when she came into the house. As for getting onto the grounds, we still haven't figured that out yet."

Natasha nodded. "Cassandra."

"Yeah. I'm beginning to wonder if there isn't credence to what you suspect. I want to talk to her, but Roger tells me she's in the Caribbean and won't be back for a couple more days."

"I'm just glad he didn't kill anyone trying to get in here."

"Me, too."

Natasha noticed the papers on the desk. "What are you doing?"

"Going over ledger sheets, trying to work out some problems at the office."

"Yeah? What kind of problems?"

"Accounting. It's nothing."

"You want me to help?"

"That isn't your job anymore."

Natasha gave him a small smile. "So you're not going to demote me?"

"Nope. In fact, Scotty and I have decided to promote you into the investigative division."

Natasha frowned.

"What? I thought that's what you wanted was to be an investigator."

Natasha gave him a haughty look. "I like it just fine where I'm at."

Striker moved restlessly. "Oh, shit."

"I want to be a bodyguard. I like this field, it's—well, I think it kind of fits my nature."

"Oh, shit."

"This is what I want to do with my life."

"Shit!" he raved.

"I've found my niche, so to speak."

"You just found a legitimate way to go around beating up on people!"

"Whatever."

"Damnit!"

Natasha rose from the chair. "So, thanks, but no thanks. I think I'll just stay right where I'm at."

Striker couldn't hold it in any longer. "You're out of your ever-lovin' mind you think I'm going to let you stay in this field!"

"Let me? Since when do you let me do or not do anything?"

He stood and faced her, infuriated. "Since I became your employer, that's when!"

"Well, that can be remedied, you know."

He was beyond furious now. "Damnit, Natasha! Didn't you learn anything from all this? Did it not occur in that somewhat dense noggin of yours that this is not the safest job in the world, especially for a woman? What's it going to take next time, actually getting killed, to make you realize just how dangerous this is?"

"Did it not ever occur to you in that dense noggin of yours that this is my decision, what I do with my life, not yours?"

"You don't have sense enough to know what you want to do with your life."

"Yeah? Well I got sense enough to know that you're not going to tell me what to do." Natasha stomped away, then turned back to him. "My employer or not!" She slammed the door behind her.

Pit, Bigun, and Scott were standing in the hallway with grins on their faces.

"What the hell are you smiling at?" she asked when she passed them.

Crashing noises came from the library.

"She's back," Scott sang.

The investigating detective with the Knoxville Police Department showed up early that afternoon. Striker was in the library, sitting behind the desk, staring out the window. Papers and books were strewn everywhere.

McGarrity looked around with amusement. "In-house tornado?"

Striker chose not to respond.

The detective sat in the chair in front of the desk. "She ready yet? We need her statement, Striker. We can't wait any longer."

Striker stood. "I'll go get her."

McGarrity gave him a serious look. "There's something we need to talk about first."

Striker sat back down.

"We may have more than one killer wannabe here."

Striker was stunned. "What?"

McGarrity pulled out his note pad. "Seems our gun-toting computer nerd wasn't the same one at the golf course that day taking pot shots at Natasha and Roger."

Striker wondered how in hell he was going to get Natasha out of this mess.

"Conyers has an alibi for that day," McGarrity went on. "I talked to him yesterday after he woke up from that coma your boys put him in. When he calmed down after he found out his plumbing was messed up…" he gave Striker a questioning look, which Striker ignored "…he told me he was in court that day at that particular time, on an assault charge. It checks out. Dozens of witnesses can attest to that fact."

Striker rubbed his hand over his face. "So it's not over."

"Not by a long shot, it seems."

Striker considered this, then remembered McGarrity, who was watching him. "I guess we'll just continue covering Roger. I'll go get Natasha for you."

After closing the door behind him, Striker paced the hallway for a couple of minutes, worrying the issue. Sighing, he went in search of his willful employee.

He found her in the kitchen, surrounded by Pit, Bigun, and Roger. All were eating homemade chocolate-chip cookies and drinking milk.

Bigun grinned at Striker when he entered. "Hey, dude, try out these cookies the dudette made. They're like totally awesome."

"Dang, Bigun, you need a new vocabulary," Natasha said, mirroring Striker's very thought.

She noticed Striker was staring at her and gave him a questioning look in return.

"The detective's here. He needs to take your statement, if you're up to it."

Natasha put her cookie down with a look of agitation on her face.

"I can tell him to come back."

She gave him a wavering smile. "No. It's okay, I'm fine." She crossed over to him, rubbing her hands on her pants and chewing on her bottom lip.

Walking toward the library together, Natasha reached over and took Striker's hand. She looked terrified. "You'll stay in there with me?"

He squeezed her hand. "Sure. I'm not going anywhere."

Entering the library, Natasha noticed the mess and glanced at Striker.

Striker acted like he didn't see her puzzled look.

Natasha told the same story to the investigator that she had told Striker. McGarrity, unlike Striker, pointed out to her what Roger had told him about the part she played in trying to protect the others.

"I was only doing my job," she said.

"You need to tell me everything," McGarrity said.

Natasha shrugged and wiped at her eyes, but didn't offer anything else.

McGarrity glanced at Striker, who was watching Natasha. "Is there anything else you want to tell me?"

Natasha shook her head.

Striker noticed she was holding her stomach. He reached out and squeezed her arm in a reassuring way.

"I take it you fought back when he was trying to rape you," McGarrity said.

"What do you think?" Natasha gave him an insolent look, then glanced at Striker.

McGarrity was tired of no one knowing anything about the damage done to the perpetrator, although he didn't particularly care, to be honest, but it had to be asked. "I'm just wondering whether it was you or those two huge Samoans who did so much damage to the man."

Natasha stared at him.

"Viagra isn't even going to help him now, if you get what I'm talking about here."

Natasha looked as if she couldn't believe he had the gall to question her about this. "Are you going to arrest me for trying to defend myself?"

McGarrity gave her a slight smile. "Hell no. If you ask me, he deserved more than what he got."

Natasha turned to Striker. "I'm not feeling so well. I need to go lie down."

Striker looked at McGarrity, who nodded. He reached over and grasped Natasha's hand. "I'll take you up."

As soon as they were in the corridor, Natasha doubled over, gasping.

Striker leaned down, worried. "What's wrong?"

"Nothing," Natasha said, in a muffled voice. "It just makes my stomach hurt to think about that whole mess."

Striker stroked her back and waited for her to right herself. When she did, he noticed her face was flushed. "Come on." He took her hand and led her up the stairs to her bedroom.

Outside her door, Natasha stopped.

"What?"

"Thanks."

They both knew for what.

Striker helped her into bed, then pulled the afghan over and tucked it around her.

Natasha gave him a smile.

"What?"

"You're so big and powerful and mean-looking, and I was always so scared of you. I never even thought this side of you existed."

He gave her his wicked grin. "So I don't scare you anymore?" he said, acting like that hurt his feelings.

Natasha turned onto her side and closed her eyes. "You scare the hell out of me every time I look at you."

Striker watched her for a moment, processing this, wondering about it, then left.

The remainder of the afternoon, Striker kept himself closeted in the library, conferring off and on with Scotty, trying to formulate a plan to get Natasha out of this mess, although both knew that she would find her way back in no matter what they did.

"You're going to have to keep her on it, Striker, because if you don't, she's not under your protection," Scott told him. "And like you said, that girl's a loose cannon. No telling what kind of trouble she'll get herself into."

Striker sighed.

He was staring out the window when the door to the library opened. Natasha stood at the threshold, wearing a loose, white, cotton dress that fell to her ankles. The light from the corridor glowed softly behind her, highlighting her long, blond hair and willowy frame. For a brief moment, Striker thought he must be envisioning an angel.

Natasha stepped into the room and gave him an uncertain smile. "I made dinner if you're hungry."

When he got to her, she said, "I hope you like Italian."

Everyone gathered around the kitchen table. Natasha had turned off the lights and lit candles, lending a cozy ambiance to the room. The odor of freshly baked lasagna made Striker's mouth water. Natasha also served a fresh garden salad, garlic bread, and iced tea, and Striker and the boys ate with relish.

The conversation was rambling; they seemed to switch easily from one topic to the next, with a lot of joking. Striker watched the interaction between Natasha and her boys and thought she was right, this was a family. He was glad to see her smile and hear her laugh again.

After dinner, Striker insisted Natasha rest while the men performed the cleanup. When they were finished, he found her in the library, straightening up the mess he made. "Hey! I did that, I'll clean it up."

She gave him an impish smile. "It's nice to know I'm not the only one around here who throws temper-tantrums."

"Yeah, well, I never had temper-tantrums until you came into my life."

Natasha studied his face. "There's something you're wanting to tell me but you don't know how."

Striker was shocked by her perspicacity. "Yeah, you and Roger; well, everyone."

"It's not over," she said, watching him.

He gave her a solemn nod.

Natasha put down the book she had been holding. "Damn."

"I know."

She strode toward the door. "You just lost the bet."

"What?" he asked her retreating form. He thought a moment, then caught up with her. "Oh, no. I actually won the bet. He was the killer—well, a killer."

She stopped and gave him a look. "Or maybe he actually did just want the money." She raised her eyebrows and headed off again.

"Damn!"

Natasha smiled over her shoulder. "I'll go get the others."

They met in the great room, where they could be comfortable. Everyone waited for Striker to say what he needed to say.

"Okay, the situation is this," he said, then told them about Conyers's alibi.

Roger's face grew pale while Striker talked. Natasha noticed this and sat closer to him, holding his hand.

"So, we're still on this case as long as Roger wants us here," Striker concluded.

Everyone looked at Roger, who nodded affirmation.

"Including me," Natasha said, staring at Striker.

"Including you." Striker waited for Natasha's reaction, expecting her to crow at this news. When she didn't offer one, he gave her a puzzled look, then continued. "I'm going to put more security on the outside. I've already called in four more men. We'll have six on each shift who will be patrolling the outside perimeter 24–7." He glanced at Natasha. "As for the inside perimeter, everyone stays put. Nobody goes anywhere until we can get some kind of handle on exactly what's going on here."

Roger was upset. "Why does everyone want to kill me? What have I ever done to anyone?"

"We're going to find that out." Striker walked toward the door. "I'm going to go outside, make sure everyone's where they're supposed to be."

"What about you?" Natasha said.

He turned toward her.

"You said everyone stays put."

"Including me, much as you'd prefer I not."

Pit, Bigun, and Roger turned their gazes to Natasha.

Natasha gave them a defensive look. "I don't know what he means."

"Striker," Roger said.

Striker stopped at the doorway and turned back.

Roger glanced at Natasha, then back to Striker. "I want Nattie off."

"What?" Natasha said.

Striker strode back into the room. He had been wondering when Roger would show his noble side.

Roger kept his eyes on Striker and wouldn't look at Natasha. "It's too dangerous for her. She's almost gotten killed twice now because of me, and I want her off the case. I don't want her as my bodyguard anymore."

"Oh, dude," Bigun said with admonishment.

"This is wrong, man," Pit said.

Natasha glared at Roger, tears shimmering in her eyes. "How could you do this to me? We're best friends, we love each other, how can you just kick me aside now?"

"Hush, Natasha. Roger's only trying to protect you," Striker said.

She turned on him. "You're the reason. You did this. You talked him into it."

Striker chose not to defend himself to her.

Roger gave Natasha a defiant look. "This is my idea. I want you off."

"She stays," Striker said.

Natasha's mouth opened in surprise.

Pit and Bigun smiled at one another.

"But you've wanted her out of this all along," Roger said.

"I still do. But she's safer here, with us." He glanced at Pit and Bigun, who were nodding in agreement.

Roger stood, then moved away from Natasha. "I say who goes and who stays, and she's not staying. That's my decision."

"Roger, let's go to your office," Striker said. "There's something we need to discuss."

Bigun approached Natasha after they left. "I hope he lets you stay, dudette. We're a team here."

"Yeah, man," Pit said.

"Thanks." Natasha was worried; she had just lost her ace in the hole.

Natasha waited for Striker to come back and give her the news, but after thirty minutes grew tired and went upstairs to her bedroom. Praying Striker wouldn't let Roger talk him out of allowing her to stay, she wondered at the flip-flop between the two men.

Striker knocked, then entered, looking weary and depressed. She knew the news was bad.

"You're still on the case." He turned to leave.

"Striker?"

"Yeah?"

"What'd you say to him? Why this change all of a sudden?"

Striker didn't tell her he had told Roger essentially what he and Scotty had been talking about all afternoon: Natasha was safer under their protection, not out there on her own, doing God knows what, because they all knew she wouldn't let this investigation go, not now. She had a vested interest in finding their killer now.

"I just told him the facts, Natasha." He closed the door behind him.

Facts? What facts? she wondered.

CHAPTER 29

▼

The man had her bent over the bed, her panties down, the shotgun touching her skin, forcing its way in…

She woke, screaming and thrashing, then lay there, crying, praying, "Oh, please, make it go away, just make it go away."

Striker was in the next room with an arm over his eyes. He had come awake at the first cries of alarm, something he now subconsciously listened for in his sleep. He had to force himself to remain where he was and not go to her, to do what she wanted him to, let her handle it. When he heard her crying, he sat up, then lay back down, remembering what she had said to him. He heard a toilet flush and water running. Good, she was over the worst part of it.

A few moments later, his door snicked open. He took his arm away to see who was there.

"Striker?" Natasha whispered.

He raised up on elbows. "Yeah?"

"I'm scared."

"You want me to come sit with you till you fall asleep?"

She closed the door, then walked toward the bed. "I was wondering, could I stay in here with you for a few minutes?"

"Sure."

Before Striker could rise up, she had joined him and was lying beside him. He stared at her for a moment, then lay back down.

Natasha turned on her side and molded herself against him, placing an arm over his chest and nestling her head into his neck. She was trembling.

Striker maneuvered his arm so he was holding her against his body.

After a few minutes, she said, "Striker?"

"Yeah?" he growled, stroking her hair.

"Thank you."

"For?"

"Talking Roger into letting me stay."

"It's for your own protection."

"The killer's not after me."

"I meant from yourself."

"Oh. You're probably right about that."

He drew his head back and gazed at her. Her eyes were shut. He rested his head against hers.

She reached up and kissed him near his lips.

He looked at her. "What's that for?"

"That's to thank you, Jonce, for respecting my wishes and not coming to my aid this time."

Jonce. Where'd she learn that? Roger, of course. He put his other arm around her and held her closer against him. "Did it help?"

"No." She sounded on the verge of tears. After a few moments, she said, "I'm so afraid I'm beginning to need you," her voice trailing off as she drifted to sleep.

That kept him awake a good while.

The next morning when Striker awoke, Natasha was still in his bed, under the covers now, snuggled into him with one arm over his chest, one leg between his, her head tucked into his neck. He untangled himself, careful not to wake her, placed covers over her once more, then crept downstairs in the sweat pants in which he had slept.

The boys were sitting around the kitchen table. Brutus was asleep on the floor.

"Where's the dudette?" Bigun asked.

Striker stared at the empty coffeepot. "She's still asleep."

"No, she's not. I just looked in her room and she wasn't there," Roger said.

Striker began searching for the coffee grounds. "She's in my room." Realizing how quiet it was, he glanced around and noticed their expressions.

"It's not what you think," he said.

Roger pushed back from the table and left the room.

"Oh, dude, you just violated one of your own rules," Bigun said.

Striker glanced after Roger's departing back, then looked at the bodyguard. "Do you honestly think I'd be crazy enough to get involved with Natasha?"

"Hell, man, I think you'd be crazy if you didn't," Pit said.

"The dude's right, dude."

Striker left to find his friend.

Roger was in his office, sitting behind his desk. "I don't want to talk to you right now," he said, opening his laptop.

Striker sat in the chair across from him. "Roger, look at me."

Roger gave him a defiant stare.

"Natasha had a nightmare last night. She got scared, came into my room, asked if she could stay there for a little bit till she calmed down, and she fell asleep. It's as simple as that. Nothing else went on in that room."

Roger looked hurt. "Yeah, but she came to you, Striker. You're the one she went to for protection."

Striker wasn't sure how to answer his accusation.

Roger glared at him. "When are you two just going to get it over with and do it?"

Striker's eyes hardened. "She's my employee, Roger. I don't sleep with my employees."

"I see the way she looks at you when she thinks no one's watching. I'd give anything if she looked at me like that, just once." Roger leaned toward Striker and gave him an intense stare. "Do you love her, Striker? Do you love her so much your heart hurts just looking at her? Do you love her so much you'd do anything to get her to look at you, smile at you? Or is this all a cat-and-mouse game you keep playing with her, a way to keep her right where you want her?"

Striker drew back in surprise. "Is that what you think?"

"Yeah, that's what I think. I think you're having fun with her, playing with her, and you're going to hurt her, you don't just leave her alone."

Striker became agitated. "I don't want to leave her alone." He stood, then leaned over the desk. "Hell, man, I doubt if I could leave her alone even if I wanted to." He threw the door open and stormed out of the room.

Natasha was descending the stairs as Striker was climbing. She paused, awed by the beauty of him. His hair was free and flowing around his face, not tied back as he normally wore it; his broad, muscular chest was bare; he wore a fierce scowl on his face. She likened him to an Indian warrior going to battle, as she stood, watching him.

He saw her and stopped.

"You're magnificent," she said breathlessly.

He came to her, still wearing that scowl, reached out, put his hand on the back of her neck, and drew her against him. "Is this a game?"

"What?"

"What's between us, is this a game with you?"

"Oh, God, please, no."

Striker kissed her with fierce abandon. Natasha seemed surprised at first, but her passion quickly caught up to his and beyond. Her soft breasts pressed into him, her pubis gyrated against him in a subtle way, and he knew she felt his desire for her as he felt hers for him in the movement of her body. The slight vibration he had felt as her body leaned into his quickly became a violent tremor. When she withdrew herself, there were tears in her eyes. He cocked his head at her and waited.

Her voice was barely audible. "Not here. Not now, not like this." She turned from him, ran up the stairs to her bedroom, and closed the door.

Striker went to his makeshift office and threw some furniture around.

CHAPTER 30

▼

The rest of the day, Striker remained closeted in the library, ranting and raving at his investigators to get off their asses and find their shooter, driving his secretary and Scott crazy when he wasn't dealing with his men. He would at times find himself staring out the window, thinking about Natasha, the way her body felt against his, the passion she had displayed with him. He wondered what it would be like to have her beneath him, naked, showing her the power she seemed to think he possessed but in a gentler, albeit more pleasurable, way.

Natasha kept to her room, sitting in the rocker in front of the window, replaying that kiss, wondering what it meant. Reliving what it had felt like to be drawn into Striker's powerful embrace and crushed against him, his mouth on hers; shocked at the powerful orgasm that had swept through her body from that one small act of intimacy. Roger, Pit, and Bigun would at times drop by her room to ask if they could do anything for her, but she would distractedly shake her head at them while staring out the window.

When it grew dark, hunger drove Striker out of the office and into the kitchen. Roger, Pit, and Bigun were sitting at the table, putting together sandwiches.

"Where's Natasha?"

Bigun was concentrating on cutting a tomato. "In her room, dude. She's been there all day."

"She eaten yet?"

Pit glanced up. "No, man. I tried to get her to come down, but she said she wasn't hungry."

Striker looked at Roger, who ignored him.

Striker prepared a ham-lettuce-and-tomato sandwich and placed it on a plate. He added some chips and a cut-up pear, then poured a glass of milk, and put everything on a tray. He left to take the dinner to Natasha.

He knocked once, then opened the door. Natasha was sitting in the rocker by the window, staring out. Her legs were pulled up to her chest, her chin resting on her knees.

"I brought you something to eat," Striker said, advancing toward her.

Natasha glanced at him, then away. "Thanks, but I'm not hungry."

"I'll put it over here in case you want it later." Striker placed the tray on her nightstand, watched her for a moment, then left.

After the door closed, Natasha put her face in her hands, allowing her thoughts to turn to the last few years and what she had been doing to herself.

Striker gave up, exhausted from not sleeping well the night before as well as all the stress he had put himself through that day, and ascended the stairs to his room. He took a long, hot shower, then climbed into bed naked. He lay there, thinking he should perhaps get up and put on something in case Natasha had another nightmare, then shook his head, remembering she didn't want him there.

He could hear Natasha in the next room moving about and placed his hand on the wall, thinking about her. He was reminding himself she was his employee, this was not what she wanted, when his door opened.

Striker raised up on elbows and looked toward the door: Natasha. His mind registered the fact that she was wearing a long, silky, black nightgown.

Natasha stepped inside and softly closed the door behind her.

Striker sat up, keeping the sheet around his waist. "Are you all right?"

"No," she said, her voice breaking. "I was hoping you could help me with that."

She came to him and climbed onto the bed, her eyes never leaving his as she sat on her knees beside him.

Striker wanted to speak but was afraid he might say something that would drive her away, so waited.

"Striker?"

"Yeah?"

"I need to ask you something."

"Okay."

"You're not feeling, well, sorry for me, are you, or guilty because of what happened? That's not the reason for the kiss, is it?"

He reached out and traced his thumb along her lips. "That definitely was not the reason for the kiss." He realized she was shaking a little. "Are you cold?"

Natasha shook her head. "I want to resign for tonight," she said, in a quiet voice.

Striker studied her, unsure what she meant. "Resign?"

"For tonight, resign from the firm."

He processed this.

"I have to see this thing through with Roger. I'm not resigning permanently, just temporarily, just for tonight. That is, if you'll accept my temporary resignation."

He stroked her hair. "I don't know, Natasha. I have the feeling that just one night won't take care of this thing."

She smiled, put her hand on his, turned her face into his palm, and kissed it. "Then I'll resign every night for as long as it takes."

They slept little that night. They could not seem to sate their desire for one another, moving from one intimate act into another as fluidly as water through a riverbed, their passion overriding their need to do anything but give and receive physical pleasure.

Toward morning, as they coupled, Natasha beneath Striker, her beautiful body naked, squirming with bliss, making her now-familiar low, guttural pleasure sounds, he above her, much as he had fantasized the day before, watching her, plunging deep within her, kissing her, tasting her, wanting her more than any other woman he had ever wanted, she burst into tears.

Striker stopped his movements, concerned.

Natasha put her hand over her face.

He began to pull away.

"No," she said, touching his chest.

He gave her a questioning look.

"It's not you."

He leaned down to her.

She stroked his face.

He gazed into her eyes. "What?"

"I'm so scared, Jonce."

He fleetingly thought she hadn't called him Striker once since they had begun to make love.

"I came to you with a motive."

"Motive?"

"I wanted you to take away the nightmares, the flashbacks, the anger. After that kiss, I knew the only one who could do that was you. But I didn't know it would be this beautiful." Tears were falling now. "I never imagined it could be this beautiful."

He drew his face close, put his lips on hers, murmured, "Natasha, baby, you scare the living hell out of me." Kissing her, he began to move in her, causing her to gasp.

After the love, still joined, he brought his mouth to hers. "Natasha."

"Yes, Jonce?"

"After this is over, you're fired."

The next morning, Striker disentangled himself from Natasha, trying not to wake her. He leaned down and kissed her when she stirred. "Go back to sleep."

She snuggled into his pillow, smelling his scent, feeling comforted by it. "Where are you going?"

"Downstairs. Go back to sleep."

Natasha squinted at him. "Striker?"

"Yeah?"

"There's something we need to talk about."

He sat down on the bed, watched her sit up and brush hair back from her face. The sheet fell away to reveal her naked breasts and Striker reached out to trace one, then the other.

Natasha's body responded to his touch at once.

His eyes went to hers and he saw the troubled look she was giving him. "What?"

"I might have misled you about last night."

Striker wasn't sure he wanted to hear this. "God, I hope not."

She chewed her bottom lip, a sign he knew meant she was feeling agitated.

"Natasha—"

"I'm not on the pill." She looked embarrassed. "You're the first man I've been with since..." she hesitated. "I didn't ask you to use anything because I—I wanted it to be pure between us, the love. I should have told you because of the chance I could, you know, get pregnant, but God help me, I wanted only you inside me, if you can understand, and I was reckless enough to be willing to take that chance." There were tears in her eyes now. "I apologize for that. It was very selfish on my part, and I take full responsibility for any consequences, if there should be any—"

Striker put his fingers to her lips, then leaned toward her. "What will be, will be, Natasha." He watched the relief come into her eyes. "If you had asked me, I would have used condoms, but I was glad you didn't. Besides, I didn't have any here and would have had to leave to get some, and that might have ruined the moment. So, to be honest, I was actually praying you wouldn't ask me."

She smiled a little at this.

He smoothed her hair back. "I felt much as you did. And if it happens, it happens, and we'll deal with it together."

She hugged him. "I knew you were an honorable man," she said into his neck, then drew away and gave him a solemn look. "Thank you for last night. You gave me a great gift, one I can never repay."

"Just being with you is payment enough, you should know that by now." Using his body, he maneuvered her onto her back, kissing her.

Striker found the boys in the kitchen again. He stood in front of the coffeepot, scratching his head, wondering why Natasha was the only one who could figure that damn thing out.

Roger gave him a sullen glare. "Where's Nattie?"

Striker turned around. "In my room," he said, in a way that challenged any of them to speak a word.

No one did.

Later that morning, the library door opened to reveal Natasha standing in the doorway. Striker stood, noticing she was wearing a long, loose-fitting dress. This brought a pang of guilt, remembering how he had been with her at times during the night in the grip of his passion for her, hoping he hadn't hurt her already bruised body.

Smiling at him, Natasha stepped inside and closed the door behind her, then leaned against it.

He smiled back. "You okay?"

"I'm perfect." She crossed over to him, nudged him back into the chair, climbed in his lap, and straddled him. "I'm taking the afternoon off, so I'm not in your employ at the moment," she said, before kissing him.

After awhile, she drew back and studied him.

"What?"

"This probably sounds dopey to you, Jonce, as much experience as you've had with women, but I never knew what the word sate meant until you." Her face grew red.

He kissed her. "Yeah, well, guess what, baby, neither did I."

Natasha maneuvered herself so she was sitting in his lap.

He stroked her hair, thinking how beautiful she was.

"Striker?"

He knew now it was time for business. "Yeah?"

"About last night."

"Yeah?"

She tilted her head back and looked at him. "What happens now?"

He smiled. "I told you, Natasha, after this thing with Roger is over, you're fired. You will no longer be my employee. We won't have to worry about that."

"What about now, today, and tomorrow and all the tomorrows until we find the man who wants to kill Roger?"

"For now, I choose to violate my own policy. Who's gonna fire me?" He grinned.

Natasha turned around so she was straddling him once more. "You fit me perfectly."

Striker pulled back to give her a lecherous look.

She smiled at that. "Well, there, too, but I was talking about how well your body fits mine when we're joined, or even like this when we're not one, almost like pieces of a puzzle."

He caressed her breasts. "You noticed that too, huh?"

Natasha leaned into him when he moved his hands to her back. "I'm so sore I can hardly walk." She gave him a mischievous look. "I thought I was hiding it, but Bigun asked me if I pulled a muscle or something."

Striker laughed.

She drew back. "After I leave here, I'm going to go talk to Roger, try to explain this to him."

"I don't think Roger's in the mood to hear it."

"We'll see. But in the meantime, Jonce, I was wondering if I could ask a favor of you."

Jonce now. He grinned. "That being?"

"Take me to my room, make wild, passionate love to me, the way you did last night." She gave a contented sigh. "I can't get it out of my mind."

His tumescence was becoming painful. "I thought you were sore."

She was kissing in a more intimate way. "It's a good kind of sore."

"They'll know what we're doing if I take you upstairs. Do you want to do that to Roger?"

She studied him with her deep-green, emerald-like eyes, then gave him an impish grin. "I thought you might say that, so I locked the door when I came in." Her hands traveled to his belt buckle. "And I left my panties upstairs," she whispered in his ear.

"Oh, baby, you are so naughty."

When Natasha left Striker, she climbed the stairs to her bedroom to take another shower; she didn't want to go to Roger with Striker's scent on her. Afterward, she found her friend in his office, working on his laptop. She stepped inside and closed the door behind her.

Roger glanced up at her, then back to the screen.

Natasha walked toward him. "Roger, there's something we need to talk about."

He ignored her.

She sat in the chair in front of his desk and waited for Roger to bring his eyes back to hers. When he did, she felt a stab of guilt at the pain she saw displayed there.

"I made love with Striker last night," she said, watching the anger start to creep into his eyes. "I don't want you to blame Striker for this," she went on in an insistent voice. "I went to him. I wanted to be with him. I chose to give myself to him."

"So you love him after all."

"Yes, with all my heart. I've loved him for a long time, I think."

Roger's look told her he already suspected this.

"Remember when you asked me if there was something going on between the two of us and I dodged the question? I knew then, Roger, but I wouldn't acknowledge to myself it could ever get to the point it has now. But by the same token, I did not lie to you about my feelings for you. We have a karma, you and I, we have a connection. I feel that and I know you do, too. But what I feel for Striker, I've never felt for a man before. I've never actually been in love like this and its—well, it's wonderful. I didn't know it could be this intense, this viable. And I want to experience this as long as he'll let me, explore it, live in it. I hope you can understand that, Roger, and that I can't be with another man, not as long as I feel what I do for Striker."

Roger leaned toward her, his eyes intense. "But does he love you?"

"I don't know. I can't speak for him."

"He'll hurt you. You know that, don't you?"

Tears sprang to her eyes, and Roger regretted saying that.

"Even if he does, I'll always be thankful for what he gave me. And if that happens, I pray to God I still have you as a friend, because I'll need someone, Roger, and I can't think of anyone who would be able to see me through that other than you."

Roger sat back and regarded her. "I hope he doesn't hurt you, Nattie. I don't want to see you hurt. I just want to see you happy."

"And I wish the same for you, you know that." Tears were falling down her face. "Please don't deprive me of your friendship, Roger. It means too much to me. If I lose that, I'll lose a part of myself, I think."

Roger wished she'd stop crying. "You'll always have my friendship. Don't worry about that."

Striker kept an eye on the office door the entire time Natasha was closeted with Roger, wondering what she was saying to him, what he was saying to her.

After Natasha left Roger, she didn't look Striker's way when she passed the library and climbed the stairs. Striker could see she had been crying and that bothered him. He resisted the urge to go punch Roger in the mouth.

He wondered why she didn't tell him what had happened. After thirty minutes of worrying this, he thought, *What the hell,* and went upstairs. He opened the door to her bedroom, but Natasha wasn't there. He went next door to his room, opened the door, and looked in.

Natasha smiled at him from the bed. "What took you so long?"

Locking the door behind him, Striker couldn't join her on the bed fast enough.

After the love, still joined with her, Striker asked, "What did you say to Roger?"

Natasha hesitated before answering. "Promise you won't get scared, okay? Because I understand your feelings probably don't match mine, and I don't expect them to, really, so don't get scared and—"

"Natasha, hush. Just tell me what you said."

"You might want to, um, withdraw, because you might be a little uncomfortable after I tell you."

Striker remained inside.

Natasha gave up. "Okay. I explained to Roger that I love you." She gave him a challenging look. "That my feelings for you were very deep, very intense, and that this is the first time I've ever actually been in love, and I want to explore this, go with it, as long as you'll let me."

He kissed her.

She moaned low.

"What else?"

"That I love him but not the way I love you, and that as long as I have these feelings for you, I can't conceive of loving any other man in this way." She looked with angst at him. "Oh, please, Jonce, don't make me say anymore."

"Then tell me," he said, moving in her.

She arched her back, gasping with pleasure. She was having trouble focusing. "Tell you what?"

"Tell me personally how you feel." Striker put his mouth to her neck. "Tell me you love me, Natasha, because God help me, I love you like I've loved no other woman before you, and I pray to God we explore this relationship the rest of our lives." He paused, looked at her. "Tell me."

She did.

Later, near dusk, she was lying full-length on top of him. Their bodies cooling as the sweat evaporated, they gazed into one another's eyes. Striker was thinking this was the true thing, this had to be. He had never before experienced the intense heat that flared inside his body just looking at her. Never wanted to protect, care for another person as he did her. Never knew that making love was more than just a basic body function or venting of lust but rather a giving and receiving of physical love, an expression of their unification of spirit when they became one.

He kissed her. "You are so beautiful, Natasha." He ran his hands down her body, felt her shiver, and smiled, delighted at this. Natasha had by now confided to him what his touch did to her body.

She smiled back.

He put his hands in her hair. "This is so beautiful."

Tears sprang to her eyes.

"What?"

"You said exactly what I was thinking. Oh, Jonce, I never thought this would happen to me." She looked with intensity at him. "I didn't even know this kind of love existed before you."

He smiled. "I was just thinking that same thought a minute ago." Stroking her body, he grinned once more at her reaction.

"It's not funny, you know."

"No, it's not, but I do love it." He kissed her, then drew his head back. "My grandmother once told me of a vision she had."

Natasha smiled; she loved hearing these stories.

"She told me a woman would come into my life with hair of the sun, eyes of the forest, and a spirit of fire."

"Really?"

He stroked her hair. "She told me her heart would be pure and her love would be true."

Natasha nodded, agreeing. "But?" she said, knowing there was more.

Striker gave her a wicked grin. "She told me," he whispered, "that this woman would create great havoc in my life."

Natasha smiled.

"Would cause me much consternation, bring forth great anger, frequent worry." Striker cupped her face with his hands, drew his mouth close to hers. "She told me that this woman was my destiny."

Delighted, Natasha shivered at this and kissed him with passion.

Much later, Natasha cocked her head and studied him.

"What?"

She smiled. "I have something I want to show you."

His eyes lightened. "The tattoo?" He had been hoping for this.

She nodded.

"Wait," he said, leaning over her. "Let me find it."

"Oh, yes." She sighed with contentment.

He seemed to study it for a long time, and she grew worried, watching him.

He kissed her there, then raised his head and smiled at her, knowing what the Cherokee symbol meant. "You knew even then?"

She gave him a lazy grin back. "I've known since the first time I saw you, you big oaf."

He laughed, but not for long.

And when they were one, he whispered, "I join myself to you, I commit myself to you, I choose you as my life-mate," kissing the tears from her eyes.

CHAPTER 31

▼

They awoke at dawn to find themselves in the preliminary stages of making love, their bodies hungering for one another, seeking the other's touch. Both were a little uneasy at the unrelenting passion that existed between the two of them but in a good sort of way. Afterward, they lay together, whispering love words to one another, stroking, feeling the fire ignite then flame.

When Striker's cell phone bleeped, he glanced toward the phone, reluctant to interrupt loving Natasha. At the second alert, one of the perimeter guards yelled, "Striker!" He reached over and picked it up.

"Yeah?"

"We've got an intruder here."

"Deliberate?"

"It looks deliberate. You better get down here, the guy's packing."

Shit! "On my way."

Natasha moaned.

"I've got to go, baby."

"Just a few minutes. Oh, please, Jonce, just a few more minutes. It's almost unbearable what you do to my body."

He leaned over her and kissed her. "I have to, babe, but I'll be back as soon as I can, I promise."

She smiled. "You better. I think I'm becoming addicted to you."

Striker left, grinning.

Natasha was too stimulated to go back to sleep. Groaning with frustration, she rose and walked into the bathroom to shower, shivering with pleasure, reliving their night together. Striker beeped her while she was drying off.

"Hey, gorgeous, it looks like I'm going to be awhile. We've got KPD here and they've arrested the intruder. God, you wouldn't believe the ammunition this guy has."

"You're okay?" she asked, worried.

"I'm fine. Well, babe, I think we've finally got our extortionist. They want us to go down, give them a statement about what we found, and I'd like to sit in on the interrogation."

"So it's over?"

"I hope so, but for now, I'd like you to stay there, okay? I'll be back later this morning, but stay there till I get back."

"Don't worry, darlin', I'll stay."

Natasha stepped into the kitchen, surprised to find Cassandra sitting at the table with a gun in her right hand and a coffee cup in her left.

Natasha thought, gleefully, for just a second, *I was right, I won the bet*, followed by, *Shoot, what am I going to do?*

"Natasha," Cassandra said in her husky voice, "I was hoping I wouldn't have to deal with you."

Natasha tried to keep the panic out of her voice. "Where's Roger?"

"I imagine he's still abed."

Natasha wondered who said abed, this day and age.

"He'll be down shortly, I'm sure," Cassandra continued. She waved the firearm at her. "Have a seat. Fetch a cup of coffee if you want one."

Natasha moved to the counter, the gun following her. She poured a cup of coffee, laced it with sugar and milk, then turned toward Cassandra.

Cassandra pointed to a chair with the gun. "Sit."

"Where are Bigun and Pit?" Natasha silently prayed, *Oh, please, God, don't let her have killed them, I love them like brothers.*

Cassandra gave her a quick smile. "I sent them off on a wild-goose chase."

"Where's Brutus?"

"They took him with them."

Natasha studied Cassandra, unsure whether she believed her.

Cassandra gave Natasha a frightened look and said, in a shaking voice, "I saw a man in the woods at the back of the property and it looked like he had a gun. Oh, God, everything's all right, isn't it? He didn't get in the house, did he?"

Damn! Natasha noticed Cassandra's attention was now on the doorway, where Roger stood with mussed hair and a confused look on his face.

Roger glanced from the weapon to Cassandra. "Mother? What in the world are you doing with that gun?"

Cassandra gave him a bright smile. "I'm going to kill you with it, of course."

Roger seemed to consider this for a moment. He glanced at Natasha, then his eyes roamed the room.

"She sent them away," Natasha said, answering his unspoken question. "They think they're chasing the killer."

Cassandra waved at a chair with the gun. "Sit. Would you like a cup of coffee? Natasha, be a sweetie and pour Roger a cup of coffee."

Natasha prepared coffee for Roger the way he liked it, all the while wondering what the heck she could do to get them out of this predicament. After she had given Roger the cup, she thought, *Doh!* She had missed two chances now to throw the hot liquid in Cassandra's face.

Natasha eased back into her chair, staring at Cassandra, who gave her an inquisitive look.

"I knew it was you," Natasha said.

Roger grunted in surprise.

"I even told Striker it was you."

Cassandra frowned. "I may have to pay Striker a visit after this."

"He didn't believe me. He said I was nuts for thinking it was you, so what's the point?" Natasha said, trying to keep her voice even and not relay her alarm for Striker.

Cassandra shrugged.

"So you're going to kill us, then what?" Natasha said. "Dump the bodies somewhere, what?"

Cassandra seemed proud. "Of course not. I'll simply tell the police I came by to pay a visit to my son, saw the intruder at the back of the property, alerted his bodyguards, then had coffee with the both of you this morning before leaving." She waved her hand at her cup, then theirs, indicating the evidence. "And oh, my God, why didn't I stay with you? I might have been able to save my wonderful son from his terrible fate." She now wore a look of bereavement on her face.

She was good. Natasha was impressed.

Roger leaned toward Cassandra, wearing a hurt expression on his face. "Why, Mother? What did I ever do to you?"

"You've been a good son," Cassandra said, in a hard voice, "but why should I have to share your wealth with you when I can have it all? There's so much I want to do, Roger, dear, that on my limited income I'm unable to."

Natasha couldn't believe this. "Limited? What's Roger giving you every month, something like thirty-five thousand, and you call that limited? Dang, Cassandra, I don't make much more than that in a year."

Cassandra gave her a sympathetic look. "It must be hell to be poor."

Natasha hated her for that. She sat back, trying to act nonchalant. "Your theory won't work, you know."

Cassandra gave her a bored look. "And why is that?"

"Well, gunshot residue, for one. You shoot us, they'll find it on your hands."

Cassandra was offended. "They won't even think to test me."

"They'll test anyone who was near the scene of the crime within a twenty-four-hour span," Natasha said. She wasn't sure if that was true or not, but it sounded good.

Cassandra glanced at the kitchen sink. "Well, then, I guess I'll just have to wear rubber gloves, won't I?"

Shoot! Natasha then remembered the residue would also be on her clothes.

"What about your clothes?" Roger said.

Natasha lightly kicked him under the table.

He looked at her. "What?"

"Roger, will you just shut?" Natasha rolled her eyes toward his mom. "You do want them to find the person who kills us, don't you?" Well, she was a fatalist if there ever was one.

"Hey, you started the discussion."

"Oh, well, I didn't think about that," Cassandra said, ignoring their spat. "Not to worry. I'll just get one of those garbage bags and put it on over my clothes." She gave them a sweet smile.

Natasha thought if she could keep her talking, she could prolong this thing. "Then what are you going to do with the bag?"

Cassandra considered. "Dispose of it, I suppose."

Roger opened his mouth to say something, but Natasha kicked him again.

Cassandra gave Roger an irritated look. "Hurry up and finish your coffee so we can get this over with."

She noticed Natasha studying her. "What's your problem?"

"How old are you, Cassandra?"

"None of your bees-wax, cornbread and shoe tacks."

"It's just, I was wondering if you're, you know, perimenopausal. Because if you are, you might want to wait a few minutes, see if this urge to kill Roger and me passes."

Cassandra scowled at her. "Whatever are you talking about?"

"Well, you know, older women, women in their forties, fifties, they go through this perimenopause thingy, and it's like you're on an emotional roller coaster, up one minute, down the next; you feel rageful, feel used and abused, stuff like that. And I speak as an expert on the subject because I've been dealing with this very same thing from my own mom. So I'm just suggesting maybe what's going on here is a little hormonal imbalance that will pass in the next little bit. So it might behoove you to wait long enough to see if it does, you know, pass."

Cassandra looked at her as if she were nuts.

"Just a suggestion."

"I'm not old enough for menopause, or that peri whatever you called it."

"Perimenopause. And actually, Cassandra, you are. That is, unless you had Roger when you were a child."

Cassandra glared at her. "I wasn't so sure I wanted to kill you before, but I am now." She pointed the gun at Natasha.

"Oops. I meant to say unless he was adopted."

"Nice try, dear."

Natasha stared at the weapon and everything all of a sudden fell into place. "You're the one who brought the gunman in that morning."

Roger looked at her, surprised.

Natasha turned to Roger. "She was here that morning, remember? That's when she was giving you hell about having us around, trying to talk you into firing us."

Roger's eyes narrowed.

Natasha turned her attention to Cassandra. "What'd you do, hide him in your car, sneak him in when no one was looking?"

Cassandra looked proud of herself. "It was simple, really. I knew from speaking with Roger that everyone was usually up around seven, so I made sure to come earlier than that, while it was still dark. He hid in the trunk of my car to get by the perimeter guards, then I drove around back to the kitchen entrance, and we waltzed right in."

Natasha nodded. "And placed him in Roger's office, knowing that's where Roger usually went right after breakfast."

Cassandra glanced at Roger. "She's smarter than I thought she was."

"He knows who you are," Natasha said. "What's to keep him from talking, especially now that he's in the hospital without the million dollars?"

Cassandra shrugged. "For now, he thinks that I'm willing to pay him to keep his mouth shut. After this is over with," she continued, pointing the gun at Natasha, then Roger, "I suspect he's going to meet with an unfortunate accident in the very near future."

Natasha's eyes narrowed. "So who was at the golf course that day? I know it wasn't you. You're too smart for that."

Cassandra gave a sardonic smile. "It's amazing how easy it is to hire someone to commit murder on your behalf."

Natasha nodded. "The extortionist."

"I simply put forth to him that he might like to contact Roger, threaten him with murder if he didn't pay him a million dollars, then do what he had threatened after he had collected his money." Her eyes hardened. "But you, Natasha, dear, kept interfering with that plan, so I had to up the ante, offer him my own money to murder Roger, which, as it turns out, I now won't need to pay."

Natasha was nodding again. "So we have another killer. That's who the guards found this morning, the one Striker's with now."

Roger's face was ashen.

"All hired by one person," Natasha said.

"Yes, and since no one seemed to be able to get the job done, I thought I'd take care of it myself," Cassandra said, with a smug expression.

"But what if the extortionist tells?" Natasha said.

Cassandra shrugged. "How can he? The only information he has is an email address which as of this morning no longer exists."

"The police can trace that, you know," Natasha said.

"A computer, bought second-hand with cash, an email account set up under a server that doesn't require formal identification." She gave Natasha an evil smile. "Let them try."

Angry with herself for leaving her gun upstairs when she knew better, Natasha tried to think of a way to disarm Roger's mom.

Cassandra glanced at her watch, then waved the gun at them. "Get up, stand over there," she said, pointing with the weapon.

Natasha and Roger stood, giving each other helpless looks.

"Over by the windows," Cassandra said.

They moved in that direction, then stopped and turned around. Natasha stepped in front of Roger, who nudged her aside to stand in front of her. They got into a little pushing match there for a few seconds, seeing who would stand in front of whom, until Cassandra slammed the gun down on the table, gaining their attention. They ended up with Natasha in front of Roger.

"You can't protect him," Cassandra said. "I'll kill you first, then him."

"You won't get away with this, you know," Natasha said. "They'll figure out it's you sooner or later."

Cassandra shrugged. "Maybe. But by then I'll be long gone. I'll have so much money I can disappear forever." She leveled the gun at Natasha.

Natasha extended her hands, palms forward. "Wait, wait!"

Cassandra frowned at her.

"You forgot."

Cassandra thought a minute. "Oh, right, the gloves. If you'll be so kind as to get them for me."

Natasha drew back with an attitude. "You expect me to fetch rubber gloves for you so you won't get gunshot residue all over your freaking hands when you shoot me dead? Forget about it, lady. I'm not your slave."

Cassandra cocked the gun.

"Go ahead, shoot me, get the residue all over yourself, why don't you?"

Cassandra took a moment to send Natasha her most deadly glare, then stalked toward the sink.

Natasha watched her, hoping the B would take her eyes away long enough so she could get to her and try to get that dang gun away.

But Cassandra seemed to have figured that out, constantly glancing at Natasha as she crossed to the sink, opened the door to the cabinet beneath, and took a quick peek inside.

Another memory slammed into Natasha's mind at this. "I knew it!"

Roger startled and forgot about his gun-toting mama for a second. "What?"

Natasha turned to him. "She's the one who was trying to poison you, Roger. The first morning I was here, I found that bottle of Thallium underneath the sink there and took it out to show to Striker. Later, I was trying to find my keys and caught her down here looking around, and she tried to tell me she was getting you a cup of coffee. Like yeah!"

Natasha turned and glared at Cassandra. Well, shoot! Cassandra had found the gloves and she had missed her one and only opportunity to catch Cassandra unawares.

Cassandra was angry. "From day one, you have spoiled each and every attempt I've made to kill Roger, and I do think I'm going to enjoy shooting you more than I will my son."

"I'm so scared," Natasha said, mocking her.

Roger nudged her. "Nattie, will you just shut?"

"I'm trying to buy more time here," Natasha said sotto voce.

"Oh."

"I heard that!" Cassandra said, pointing the gun at them once more.

They watched her struggle to get the gloves on while holding the firearm.

"You need me to hold the gun?" Natasha said.

Cassandra ignored her. She finally donned the gloves and once more pointed the gun, at Natasha first.

"Wait!"

Cassandra rolled her eyes. "What is it this time?"

"Your clothes. You better get one of those garbage bag thingies and cover your clothes, remember?"

Cassandra thought. "I'll just burn these when I get home."

The front door bell rang.

They looked at each other.

"Roger, you better go get that," Natasha said.

Cassandra glanced at her watch. "We don't have time. We've wasted too much time already."

"He doesn't answer it, whoever that was sees you exit the estate after you kill us, they put you here at the time of death," Natasha said.

"Roger, go answer the damn door and bring whomever is out there in here."

"Run, Roger!" Natasha shouted when he left the room.

"You don't come back, I'm killing your girlfriend!" Cassandra yelled after him.

A few moments later, Roger was back, giving Natasha a sorrowful look. "No one was there."

Natasha stared at him, bug-eyed. "Why the hell did you come back? Damnit, Roger, you just signed your own death warrant, coming back in here."

"She said she'd kill you. I can't have that on my conscience."

"Like you're going to have a conscience for all of ten seconds." Natasha's eyes darted toward Cassandra, who had a determined look in her eyes. Uh-oh!

Staring at the barrel of the gun, another memory slammed into her head. "Omigod!"

Roger jumped. "What?"

"That wasn't a lighter I saw at the banquet, was it, Cassandra?" Natasha glared at her. "That was a gun pointed right at Roger."

Cassandra shrugged.

"You. It was you. I knew that was a gun," Natasha said, proud of herself, then grew frightened, seeing Cassandra's expression.

Someone knocked on the kitchen door, startling them all. When Cassandra glanced that way, Natasha backed up, picked up the toaster from the counter, and yanked its cord out of the outlet. She hurled it at Cassandra, hitting her gun arm, moving toward her as the toaster struck. Cassandra's arm jerked, the gun went off when Natasha tackled her, and both went sprawling.

Cassandra still had hold of the weapon and was trying to point it at Natasha, who was struggling with her, trying to get it away. Both noticed at the same time a silver-colored gun barrel placed against Cassandra's temple.

Natasha looked up to see her mother standing over them. "Mom!"

"Let go of the gun, bitch, or I'm gonna blow your brains out," Stevie said to Cassandra.

Cassandra seemed to waver, so Stevie cocked the firearm and pressed it harder against her temple.

Cassandra dropped the gun.

Natasha retrieved the weapon, then stood. She kept it trained on Cassandra while smiling at her mom. "Thanks, Mom! You just saved my life."

Remembering Roger, Natasha glanced behind her and was shocked to see him lying on the floor. "Roger!" She ran over to him and knelt beside him, beginning to cry, thinking he must have been shot.

Stevie wandered over to take a look, keeping her gun pointed at Cassandra. "Quit that bawling, Natasha. He's just fainted. Get some ammonia and hold it under his nose, he'll come around."

Natasha wiped at her eyes. "Yeah, that's good."

After Natasha got Roger awake by managing to spill half a bottle of lemon-scented ammonia on his shirt, she helped him to sit up and lean against the wall.

She threw her arms around her mother. "Mom, I'm so happy to see you!"

Stevie hugged back. "Find me some rope, sweetie. Let's hog-tie this bitch."

After Natasha had bound Cassandra's feet and hands with duct tape, per her mother's instructions, since she couldn't find any rope, she ran upstairs, snatched up her phone, and alerted Striker.

"I'm here, baby," he said into the phone.

A tingle started in the pit of her stomach and traveled all the way to her toes, just hearing his voice. "I think you need to get back over here."

"What happened?" He sounded worried.

"Everything's fine, thanks to Mom. Just come, okay? Like five minutes ago. Oh, and Striker, just so you'll know, I won the bet!"

Striker entered the mansion, yelling for Natasha.

"We're in the kitchen," she called out to him.

Striker paused just inside the room. Roger was sitting on the floor, his face pale as watered milk. Natasha was kneeling beside him, holding a wet cloth to his forehead, smiling up at Striker. A woman with platinum-colored, spiked hair was holding a gun on Roger's mom, who was on the floor, trussed.

Striker drew Natasha up and into him. He hugged her, running his hands over her to assure himself that she was all right. She was trembling, and this concerned him. He thought it was from fear or shock. It wasn't.

Still holding Natasha, Striker asked Roger if he was all right and was relieved to see Roger nod and give him a weak smile.

Striker then turned to Stevie. "You have to be Natasha's mother."

Transferring the gun to her left hand, Stevie stepped forward to shake with Striker.

Striker studied Stevie, comparing mother to daughter, thinking this was how Natasha would look in twenty years, liking what he saw. Natasha began telling him what had happened and, hearing this, Striker now knew from whom Natasha got her spunk.

He looked around the room. "Where's Pit and Bigun?"

"Cassandra sent them away. She told them she saw a gunman in the woods at the edge of the property."

Striker frowned.

"It's not their fault," Natasha said. "Really, Striker, she's good. She almost had me convinced."

Striker didn't look like he was buying that. He gathered Natasha to him once more and said, over her head to her mother, "I'll owe you forever for this."

"There will probably be times when you might want to take that back," Stevie said, watching these two, aware of the looks they were giving one another.

"Mom!"

Striker and Stevie smiled at each other.

Stevie noticed for the first time the bruises, which Natasha had tried to cover with makeup. "What happened to your face?" She reached out and touched her daughter's cheek. "This is the reason I haven't seen you in over a week? Were you trying to hide this from me?"

"Mom, I didn't want to worry you. It's not as bad as it looks."

Stevie's eyes angrily darted to Striker, then back to her daughter. "Who did this to you?"

"A guy who was trying to extort money from Roger," Natasha said.

Stevie regarded her daughter. "Opened your mouth one too many times, did you?"

Striker grinned.

Natasha's response was interrupted by McGarrity and a small police battalion arriving at the front door, followed by Pit and Bigun.

McGarrity kept them there most of the morning, taking statements from each one, while other cops milled around, trying to act important.

Striker listened to Natasha repeat her version to McGarrity, then Roger, scowling widely at Roger's rendition. Afterward, he took Pit and Bigun into the library and did some heavy yelling.

Natasha stayed behind with Roger, holding his hand. She felt sorry for her colleagues but was relieved she wasn't in there with the other two, getting reamed out by Striker for once.

Striker came back, followed by Pit and Bigun, who now wore hangdog expressions, and told Natasha he wanted to see her. He still looked angry.

"Oh, boy," she muttered, wondering what exactly she had done wrong this time.

In the library, Striker pulled her against him and kissed her, his hands freely roaming her body.

Natasha gave back what she got.

When Striker released her, she drew back. "Whew! You scared me. I was afraid I was going to get yelled at."

"You are."

She looked at him, surprised.

"What the hell is wrong with you?"

What the? "What'd I do?"

"For one, stepping in front of Roger and offering yourself as a target for Cassandra."

"Oh, yeah."

"Damnit, Natasha!"

She shrugged. "I was protecting him, Striker. Doing my job, doing what you pay me to do."

Striker made strangling noises in his throat and walked away from her.

Natasha watched, trying to gauge just how mad he was. She hoped he wasn't so angry that they wouldn't be spending some quality time together later, the kind that took place under the sheets. After all, he owed her for this morning.

Striker finally came back to her. "Where, dear Natasha, was your phone during this whole ordeal?"

She closed her eyes.

"Where the hell was your fucking gun?" His voice was close to roaring.

She chose not to answer.

"It's a wonder you're not dead. You do realize that, don't you?"

Natasha sighed. "That thought did cross my mind."

"How many times have I told you, where you go, your phone and your gun go, too? How many, Natasha?"

"Quite a few times, actually."

"And how many times would it take, do you think, before you actually got that through your head?"

"Well, it's partly your fault, you know."

"My fault? And how, my dear, sweet darling, is it my fault?"

"Because of what you were doing to me before you left," Natasha said, looking agitated. "Damnit, I just look at you and I can't focus on anything else. I think of you and my body starts responding like you're in the same room with me, even though you're not. And in case you forgot, you were loving me when you got called away. Do you happen to remember that?"

Not waiting for his response, she continued. "You go away from me, leaving me there in a state of high agitation, frustration, titillation, stimulation." Her voice rising, really getting into this, she didn't notice Striker staring at her, surprised at this outburst. "Expect me to just, I don't know, forget all about what's going on with my body, the way you make my body feel, the things you do to my body. Get up, strap my gun to my ankle, clip my phone to my belt, instead of doing what I was doing, thinking about you and how much I love you and how much I love loving you and how much I love you loving me! Okay?"

"Okay," he said, startling her.

But only for a second.

"I could have finished the job, you know," she said, not letting it go. "But I didn't. I chose not to. And do you know why? Because you have ruined me for any other man or any other thing, so thank you very much for that!"

Striker watched her with a proud look on his face.

"Anything other than you or your mouth or your body would be ersatz, so what would be the point." She was on a roll now. "And while we're on the subject, do you know what kind of hellacious ride this is for me, being in love with you? Damnit, why do you have to be so beautiful? Why do you have to smell so good? Why do you have to be so smart? Why do you have to have that big, masculine body of yours? Why do you have to fit me so well? Why do you have to scare me so much? And worst of all, why the hell do you have to be such a fantastic lover? Can't you at least give me something bad I can focus on when I'm pissed at you, which I am right now, very much, in case you haven't figured that out, bucko!"

Striker grinned.

"And let me get something else off my chest." Natasha went up to him and poked her finger in his direction, really into this now. "I have loved you for over three years now. How long did it take you to even notice me, you big galoot? Huh? Three years to even think of me as another being on this planet, while the whole time I've been in love with you, trying to get you to notice me, pining for you—yes, pining for you, does that make you happy?" She was shouting again.

"God, yes."

That stopped her. Natasha gave Striker a suspicious look.

But wait. Now he was giving her a look she knew well, his furious one.

"You finished? Is there anything else you want to add to that little diatribe you just delivered?"

She chewed her bottom lip. "Well, there's more, but I choose not to disclose that at this time, and I do take offense at the word diatribe."

Striker nodded, angry because she had insinuated she loved him more simply because she had loved him longer. "For the record, you are not the only one on this, let's see, what did you call it, hellacious ride, you seem to think you've been cast on. Like you, my dear, I question why you have to be so beautiful; smell so good; be so smart..." he hesitated "...well, for the most part." He ignored the glitter that came into her eyes at that. "Have such a gorgeous body, not to mention those beautiful eyes of yours or those long, beautiful legs, but let's not discuss that at this time; why you drive me up the fucking wall every other minute of every day, and when you're not driving me up the fucking wall, scaring the shit out of me with your reckless ways or just with the way you look at me sometimes; and last but not least, why you have to fit me so well and be such a fantastic lover." He stepped back from her. "That make you happy?"

She was smiling. "God, yes."

Striker itched to put his hands on her. "We have one serious dilemma here."

"What?" Natasha pouted, afraid he was still mad at her.

"The bets. We both won."

She thought about arguing with him, because Cassandra had been the mastermind behind this whole thing, but then remembered what his bet had been. She felt a thrill run up and down her spine. "Gee, whatever are we going to do about that?"

Striker gave her his wicked grin.

Natasha guessed that was answer enough as goose bumps broke out over her body.

Stevie rapped on the doorjamb and entered the room. "Now that everyone in this house and probably the world knows how you two feel about each other, I think that Mr. McGarrity wants to wind this thing up." She watched Striker pull Natasha to him, give her a quick, albeit passionate, kiss and leave.

Natasha noticed her mother studying her. "You heard everything?"

"Every little word. You might want to think about closing doors when you're alone with him."

"Shoot."

Stevie frowned at her daughter. "You would have to announce to the whole wide world you're sleeping with the man before you're married to him, wouldn't you?"

Natasha's face turned a deep shade of red.

Stevie regarded her. "I do think, Natasha, you have finally found the one person who may well be man enough to take you on."

Natasha smiled.

Stevie kissed her daughter and left, saying she'd had enough excitement for one day.

CHAPTER 32

▼

McGarrity, who seemed to find something amusing, judging from the grin that kept sliding around his mouth, invited Striker to sit in on the interrogation of Cassandra.

"I'll be right behind you," Striker said, glancing at Natasha.

McGarrity got the message and left, smiling again, shaking his head.

Striker spoke with Roger for a few minutes, making sure he was going to be all right, then approached Natasha. "Walk outside with me?"

Natasha glanced at Roger, who looked a little forlorn. "I'll be right back, Roger." She nodded her head at Pit and Bigun, indicating, take care of him.

Striker took Natasha's hand and led her into the foyer. He stopped at the door, drew her against him, and put his lips on hers, his hands moving over her body. Natasha made small, moaning sounds in the back of her throat, thinking if he didn't stop she'd be screaming in another thirty seconds, but she didn't want him to stop.

"It would kill me if I lost you," Striker said, pulling back from her.

"I feel the same about you." Natasha lay her head against his throat. "Oh, how I love you, Jonce." She kissed his neck, began moving to his lips.

They heard movement in the hallway and turned to see a red-faced Roger standing behind them.

"I was just going to my office," he apologized.

"I'm leaving now, Roger. I'll see you later." Striker opened the door and led Natasha outside.

He stopped beside his car, leaned down, and kissed her, with chaste this time. "Oh, by the way, you are now no longer an employee of Investigative Services, Inc."

Natasha grinned. "Oh, gee, and just when I was starting to build my pension plan."

"I'll take care of you. Don't worry about doing anything until you're ready."

Natasha frowned.

Striker didn't like that.

"But I already told you what I want to do."

"No."

"Yes, Striker. I like doing this. I want to continue on in this field. I told you that."

"No!"

"This is what I want to do."

"I won't give you a good recommendation. I won't help you place yourself in harm's way just because you happen to like toting a gun."

Natasha got her stubborn look. "That's not it. Besides, I don't need your help. I've saved some money and I think I'll just try to do this on my own, thank you very much, without your help."

Striker slammed his fist into his car. "Damnit, Natasha!"

"I'll be like Kinsey Milhone, you know, go my own way, work for myself."

"Who the hell is Kinsey Milhone?"

"You know, that private investigator in the Alphabet series by Sue Grafton? That kind of wacky woman—"

"You're not a character in a book, are you not aware of that fact?" he bellowed.

"Well, yeah, but I'm sure there are female bodyguards out there doing this very same thing—"

He roughly drew her against him. "Listen to me, Natasha. Just once shut that beautiful mouth of yours and listen to what I have to say."

She watched him.

"I love you. I can't tell you that enough. I can't express to you the depth of my feelings for you because, God help me, I've never felt this before and I can't put words to the feelings you seem to bring forth from me. But, and listen close, Natasha, I will not love someone who has placed herself on a suicide mission, someone who when I kiss her or hold her I may be holding her or kissing her for the last time. I cannot live like that, I will not live like that."

He released her.

There were tears in her eyes. Natasha stepped up against him and said, her voice barely above a whisper, "And I love you more than anyone I have ever known or ever will, Jonce. I know that, in here." She touched her heart. "I pray I spend the rest of my life with you, but I will not do so if it means I give up my self-concept. It would be so easy to just lose myself in you but I can't allow that to happen, and I won't, because if I do, I lose first myself, then you. And I could not live like that."

Without saying a word, Striker got in his car and left.

Natasha had to force herself not to run after him, stop him, tell him she'd do anything, just please don't leave.

Natasha stood outside for several minutes after Striker left, wiping at her eyes and trying to gain control. She finally gave a hitching sigh and went inside to Roger, who was in his office, staring out the window.

Natasha sat on the corner of his desk and, when Roger turned to her, noticed he had been crying. In her concern for him, she lost all thought about her worries with Striker. She leaned forward and hugged him.

"I'm sorry, Roger. I'm so sorry this happened to you."

"She was willing to murder her own son," he said, sounding dejected.

Natasha rubbed his arm. "Greed will do strange things to people."

Roger leaned back with a sad look. "Now I don't have anyone."

"Well, thanks."

He looked at her.

"You have Pit and Bigun and me. You're the best friend I ever had. You think I'm just going to go away, get out of your life now that this thing is over? I don't think so. I'm not that easy to get rid of."

Roger smiled a little at this.

"I think Pit and Bigun would just as soon stay on here, if you wouldn't mind," Natasha said, echoing something they had voiced to her more than once. "They love it here and they love you, and we're all a family now anyway, right?"

Roger's eyes brightened. "You mean, like, live here?"

"Sure. I mean, guy, have you seen their apartment? It is rank. Plus I think they kind of look at you as their little brother, you know."

"I'll ask them to stay then." Roger looked almost happy. "I guess you're going home, huh, or to Striker's?"

Natasha hadn't thought about that. "Can I ask a big favor?"

"Sure, Nattie, anything."

"Can I keep my room and stay here when I feel like it? I love my house, I really do, but I love being here, too, and hanging out with you guys and Brutus.

And to be honest with you, Roger, I don't think I can give this up, at least not yet."

"You'll have that room as long as you want."

"I think I'll go home tonight, though. I've been neglecting Mom and Dad, and I should spend time with them."

Roger nodded.

"But I'll be back tomorrow. Oh, and is it all right if I leave some of my clothes here so I'll always have something to wear?"

"Sure," Roger said, smiling for real this time.

"Oh, thank you, Roger, thank you, thank you, thank you." Natasha kissed him on the cheek. Pulling back, she noticed his crimson face and thought for the zillionth time that Roger was the sweetest man she'd ever known.

He was giving her a strange look.

"What?"

"What you were saying to Striker while ago when you-all were in the library, is that how it is with you and him? Is that how he makes you feel?"

Natasha nodded, embarrassed that everyone had heard their discussion. She mentally kicked herself for being so stupid and not keeping her mouth shut.

Roger smiled at her. "I'm happy for you, Nattie. I'm happy for Striker, too."

She returned his smile and the memory of Striker loving her slammed into her mind full force, taking her breath away. She couldn't lose him, what was she going to do here?

Natasha stood, averting her face from Roger so he wouldn't see the tears brimming. "I'm going to head home after I say bye to Pit and Bigun. I'll call you tonight, Roger. Love you."

Once home, Natasha noticed how dusty her small domicile had become during her absence and forced herself to get busy scrubbing. While she cleaned the cottage from top to bottom, her mind never strayed far from Striker. She was worried that their relationship had ended before it had even begun and knew she would never again experience a love that intensely passionate. Her ears remained on the alert for the phone to ring, hoping he would call her, not step out of her life, just like that.

Unable to stand it anymore, she threw herself down on her bed and had a good cry. Afterward, she rested there, thinking about him. Recalling their love-making, her body ached for the feel of his body on hers.

Depressed, she rose and opened all her windows to let the cool breeze blow in, realizing she was glad to be home; she had missed her little cottage.

She despondently walked to the bathroom and turned on the water in the tub. After she had adjusted it to the right temperature, she put in the stopper, added scented body beads, and whisked the water around. Waiting for the tub to fill, she stripped down, then lit candles she had placed around the bathroom. She turned out the light and thought, *Ah ambience*, as she settled in the enveloping liquid warmth. Her mind turned once more to Striker and what it would be like to make love to him here, like this. But that wasn't going to happen. She began crying once more.

Natasha lay back, tired now, and placed a very hot washcloth over her swollen eyes. She was close to drowsing when she heard movement outside the bathroom door. She sat up and glanced around, wondering where her dang gun was and why it was never where she needed it to be.

The door to the bathroom opened to reveal Striker standing at the threshold, staring at her. Once more his appearance distracted her from everything else, appreciating his powerful build, rugged good looks, gazing into his dark, unreadable eyes. It took her a moment to realize she was naked in the water and the bubbles weren't covering the places they should. But then, what did it matter, he had seen that and more.

Striker crossed to the tub and sat down on the side. He picked up the body sponge and dipped it in the water, his eyes never leaving hers.

Natasha was so scared, she was trembling. At least, that's what she told herself.

Striker took the sponge out of the water with one hand and with the other reached forward, picked up one leg, extended it, and began to wash it.

Natasha stared into those magnificent eyes of his, tingling from head to foot, thinking if he moved any higher, she was going to climax right then and there.

"About those bets," Striker said.

Printed in the United States
23036LVS00003B/8

0-595-30893-7